C. C. MACDONALD

C. C. MacDonald is a writer and actor based in Margate where he lives with his wife, two children and dog Frankie. *Happy Ever After* is his debut novel.

C. C. MACDONALD

HAPPY EVER AFTER

VINTAGE

1 3 5 7 9 10 8 6 4 2

Vintage
20 Vauxhall Bridge Road,
London SW1V 2SA

Vintage is part of the Penguin Random House group
of companies whose addresses can be found
at global.penguinrandomhouse.com.

 Penguin
Random House
UK

First published by Vintage in 2020
First published in the UK by Harvill Secker in 2020

This novel is a work of fiction. All names and characters are the product
of the author's imagination and any resemblance to actual
persons, living or dead, is entirely coincidental.

Reference on page 323 to 'Novocaine for the Soul' by Eels
(lyrics by Mark Goldenberg and Mark O. Everett)

penguin.co.uk/vintage

A CIP catalogue record for this book is available from the British Library

ISBN 9781529111385 (B format)

Printed and bound in Great Britain by Clays Ltd, Elcograf S.p.A.

Penguin Random House is committed to a sustainable future
for our business, our readers and our planet. This book is
made from Forest Stewardship Council® certified paper.

MIX
Paper from
responsible sources
FSC
www.fsc.org
FSC® C018179

For Joanna

CONCEPTION

ONE

It doesn't start with a kiss. It starts with the touch of bare knuckles under a molehill of cornflakes. That's when he looks at her and something changes.

Naomi still doesn't know his name. Doesn't want to. Knowing if he is a 'David' or a 'Paul' would reduce him somehow. Like all figures of fantasy, he's broad-shouldered. Thick hair. Everything about him is thick. Not fat. Rigid. He always wears a bulky check shirt over a T-shirt so, to her, he is 'The Lumberjack'. She's often wondered whether the nursery nurses use the same name. They're probably too young to know what a lumberjack is. They're too young for him. Maybe his outfit is a conscious choice. Perhaps he knows the power such an archetypal uniform holds.

Naomi feels the heat of a blush so she yanks Prue up out of the 'messy-play' tray and walks to the other side of the room, her struggling toddler dropping cornflakes behind them like breadcrumbs from a labyrinth. Naomi glances back at The Lumberjack, engrossed with his son, who's laughing and squirming as his father throws clumps of cereal into his face. His eyes recapture hers at the exact moment that Prue succeeds in wriggling from her grasp. Naomi throws her arms behind her back and catches her little girl before she crashes head first into the wipe-clean flooring. She flicks The

Lumberjack a sardonic eyebrow – *Kids*. His features are fixed, perhaps his jaw tenses. He doesn't want the complicity of the harried parent. He wants something else.

TWO

Naomi flings milk into a bowl of oats and yoghurt and clatters it on to the highchair tray, putting a stop to Prue's tears. Her raisin face unwrinkles to reveal skin so smooth that the sunlight streaming through the bi-folding doors seems to halo off it. How can anything as perfect as her daughter's skin even exist?

She drinks Prue's plumpness in for as long as she can before pushing herself off the kitchen island and making her way to the living room. She keeps her eyes on the floorboards and their shreds of belligerent underlay as she opens her dressing gown, his dressing gown, flattens herself on to their inherited sofa and arranges herself.

She looks over at her husband's naked back, skin pulled taut over his spine; unrecognisable from the back she thought she knew. Two flat floury baps for an arse.

'Bubble, bubble, bubble … Pop,' Prue sings from the kitchen. Charlie sighs with exasperation, shakes his head.

'It's not going to happen, is it?' She tries to keep her words as matter-of-fact as possible but she can feel the swell of rage brewing inside her. He turns his head towards her but only so she can see his profile, keeping his body hidden from her. He opens his mouth to speak but says nothing. 'How is it so difficult to have sex with your wife?' He turns back to the mantelpiece and lets the word 'fuck' out in a long, whispered breath. A cry comes from the other room.

'Spoon. Spoon. Spoooon.' Prue delivers her message and when no action is taken a desperate wail sirens along the ground floor.

'It has to be today.' She sits up and wraps the dressing gown around her top half, knowing how impossible it is to be commanding with your boobs on show.

'She's crying,' he says, arm extended towards the kitchen. 'I can't just— Do you know how hard this is for me?'

'Are you serious?' She has forced him to do this but she has no compassion. It has to be today. They have to have sex today because he barely managed it last night and the ovulation app on her phone says tonight will be too late. It has to be today. Prue's cries ramp up.

'You can't just click your fingers—'

'What do you want? Foreplay? We're not twenty-five any more, for fuck's sake, Charlie.' She thinks he might cry so she bounces up off the taupe sofa and walks down the hall towards her howling daughter. 'You'll have to come into work.'

'You honestly think we'll be able to do it there?'

'It has to be today. You know it has to be today and you promised me,' she calls along the hall before reaching her daughter. 'Did you drop your spoon, sweetheart?'

'Spooon.' Prue intones the tragedy of the lost implement like a professional mourner. Love bursts through the cloud of Naomi's anger.

'I'll pick you up at lunch, we can come back here and I can give you a lift back to work afterwards,' he says from the living room. She imagines him, lost in the middle distance like a victim of shell shock, bum-cheeks primed at the bay window. She pretends to eat some of Prue's breakfast.

'Naaaaao,' Prue barks, threatening further screeching. Naomi gives her back her spoon and she leans back in her highchair and munches her breakfast like a tiny Henry VIII.

'I'll make it work,' a weak voice from another dimension. She knows she should show him some sign of affection, understanding, something. But she can't. She physically can't.

'OK.'

He emerges from the living room and they stare at each other down the barrel of the hallway, high ceilings and acres between them.

'I'm sorry,' he says.

'Yeah.'

THREE

<u>What is the optimum moment for conception?</u>

What we know?
i)   Sperm fertilises egg.
ii) Following the egg's release there's a <u>24-hour</u> window
     in which point (i) can happen.

What we **don't** know:

- When exactly does ovulation occur? About 2 weeks before
  next period? 28 day cycle = day 14.
- How long can sperm survive in the uterus?
- What factors affect sperm motility AKA 'get-up-and-go'?
  Stress? Low mood? Diet?
- How long between each ejaculation do the sperm need
  to regenerate?
- Is it better to have one big load the day the egg drops or
  lots of little loads in and around it?
- How can we invent smartphones yet have no definitive
  instructions for the most crucial procedure for the on-
  going <u>survival</u> of our <u>species</u>!

They'd been trying for a year and Naomi had spent every evening poring over the Internet for answers. She couldn't find consensus. Various discoveries along the way had made her amend their schedule several times but, in truth, these changes were often inspired more by restlessness than empirical evidence. She tried to involve Charlie in the planning, reading him Californian fertility studies, reports of cutting-edge Scandinavian ovulation prediction. Once, she even shared eighteenth-century advice for barren women in an effort to amuse him into engagement. He would always mumble acknowledgements as if he was listening but she knew that, if tested, he'd have a much better sense of the episode of *Grand Designs* that was on than of her research into how they should go about conceiving their second child.

By now she had settled on their having sex six separate times straddling the day of ovulation. D–Day –3, D–Day –1, D–Day, D–Day (2nd time) and D–Day +1. When she found a medical paper declaring that sperm were mostly incapable after three days in the uterus she'd had to smoke three cigarettes in a row to get over the four months of 'reservoir' loads they'd wasted on D–Day –5.

With Prue, they'd managed it before they even knew there was an optimum moment. It had been straightforward. Every other night, after Naomi got back from the office and Charlie had returned from the unit, they'd have dinner – vegetables and some sort of grain with avocado or Feta on rotation – and then they'd head to bed and have speedy, passionate sex. It was a routine but because it had never been codified nor discussed, it never felt like one.

Before they got married they were making love about twice a month and fucking three, maybe four times. They were both delighted to up their quota in order to create what would become Prue. It gave Charlie a convincing glint in his eyes as he extolled the virtues of being newly married to his less grown-up friends.

The sex, the extra sex, made Naomi optimistic. She'd married the man she loved. He was nice-looking, had a big, technical brain she was proud to be baffled by and he wanted children with her. Three children. Just the same as her.

She *was* thirty. If she was honest with herself and with Charlie – and she had been, telling him early in their relationship that she'd wanted to start having kids in her twenties – it was later than she'd planned. Three babies, one baby every two to two and half years meant that her starting this late gave her no chance of having them all before she was thirty-five. She'd lost count of the number of blogs, articles and research studies she'd read about the increased chances of complications in pregnancy and birth for a woman past thirty-five.

'My mum was thirty-nine when she had me,' Charlie would say whenever she mentioned this to him. Two years into their relationship she found a study from the University of Nebraska that indicated that when a subject was anxious about something, and Naomi can acknowledge that she's a worrier, when that subject was told 'it'll be fine', it was twice as provocative to their anxiety as any other statement. She printed the study out and stuck it to the fridge and every time Charlie's 'glass-half-full' attitude chirped up she'd pat it and give him a pointed look. And it would always make him laugh. The whole act, the research, printing it out, sticking it on the fridge, the voiceless reminding him of his transgression, it was so resolutely the behaviour of the wonderful maniac he fell in love with. They used to laugh all the time; they used to talk about how much more they laughed than all the other couples they knew. They'd always fought like wildcats, but they still used to laugh.

They were trying for a baby and she was optimistic about their future together. Their family together. The family she'd been planning for her whole siblingless childhood. The family she'd conceived of while pushing her toy pram around the New Forest when she wasn't three years old was soon to come to fruition. And then it did. She missed her period. They did the test together. Charlie managed to bodge it somehow but she had a spare and it told them she was expecting a baby. They were so happy. She was happy and a bit scared. Charlie seemed genuinely happy.

FOUR

A ding-dong. Naomi swallows spit. Lisa, the manager of the Bank of Friendship Nursery School, presses the security button and snaps the handle of the front door down. A boy with auburn ringlets busies through the door with his mother trailing behind. Naomi closes Prue's scrapbook and returns it to the front desk. She's been sat in the reception area looking at it since she dropped Prue off a quarter of an hour ago. Too long to be looking at a book with seven pages of photos and finger-painting. Not exactly *War and Peace*.

She wanted to see him. The Lumberjack. After what happened in the living room with her husband earlier, she feels she deserves to. He often wears shorts. She wanted to see the indent above his knee. That shadowy space at the foot of his thigh, a muscle so defined it seems to be a separate entity, tied to the rest of his leg with cable-sinews. She's daydreamed about what he must do to have legs like that. He drives a van, so she's pictured him building houses single-handedly. Squatting down, pushing up entire walls, creating a full-sized doll's-house home in minutes. A child's imaginings.

She needs to go back and brief her builders before going to work. She has to be at the house every morning and today they're meant to be finishing off the stud wall on the first floor. Charlie works from home but she doesn't trust him to deal with them properly because he thinks the builders know what they're doing. But Charlie didn't grow up moving from one 'doer-upper' to the next, he didn't spend his childhood blowing his nose and finding strings of grey cement dust in his tissue like she did. Which is why he sold moving in to a house that requires structural refurbishment on every floor to her as 'an adventure', but after what happened to his business, they didn't have much choice in the sort of house they could buy.

She's meant to be at work in ten minutes, she still has to get home and yet she's hanging around a nursery reception waiting for a man who might, at best, describe her to his mates on site as 'some desperate single mum at my boy's nursery' and, at worst, not describe her at all. She thought his son was in on a Wednesday. Lisa, a woman with the narrow physique and posture of a garden-brush who Naomi has always thought hates her, opens the door for her before she's even moved towards it. She's definitely been there too long.

When she reaches the car park, her already low mood digs a few feet down. Hatchbacks are boxed snugly at front and back of their new Nissan. Charlie insisted they get a 'mini-SUV'. A family car. Perhaps an effort to convince her that he really did want another baby. She finds driving it horribly stressful. She couldn't remember ever feeling comfortable in a car. As a child, if she ever spotted the aftermath of a collision on the hard shoulder from the back seat of her parents' car, it would always fill her up with tangible dread.

These feelings of dread featured occasionally as she grew up but they'd become far more frequent since Prue was born. They presented themselves as momentary visions, disturbingly real. If she saw a lorry approaching on the other side of the road she would often imagine it piling directly into her car, shattering the skeletons of her passengers like crash test dummies. These imaginings went beyond being in the car. Even at home, sometimes she'd stand at the top of the stairs holding Prue and picture herself losing her footing and tumbling down, dashing the baby's head on the spindle of the banister and snapping her own leg in two places on the bottom step. Since moving into their wreck of a house where every creaking beam seems on the verge of collapse, these reveries have become, on occasion, paralysing.

She settles herself into the higher driving position, which Charlie assured her would make her feel much safer, and starts the car. She goes forward, angling the steering wheel as much as she dares. Stops. Into reverse. Wheel full lock the other way. Beep of the parking sensor. She goes forward millimetres, waiting in terror for the crunch of headlight on plastic bumper. In the rear-view mirror she catches the sight of Prue's empty car seat. The pain of her and Charlie's failure this morning, their failure for more than a calendar year, hits her like a bereavement. Her eyes begin to fill; she shakes her head hard, trying to rattle the coming tears away. She cranks the gearstick into reverse and—

A frenzied thumping on the back of the car. Looking through the back window, eyes wide, brow furrowed, it's him. The Lumberjack.

'Do you want me to get her out?' He's leaning into the car, his big Viking head filling the open passenger window. He doesn't sound like she had imagined. For a moment Naomi thinks he's talking about Prue in her car seat but that can't be what he means. 'These two buggers must be trying to ruin your day.'

'What?' It comes out more aggressive than she intends, as if he were giving her directions in a language she can't understand.

'These two blocking you in.' He laughs. Is he joking? Has he got a northern accent? She can't get her mind to decipher what's happening. His wide forearms press down on the black rubber lips at the base of the open car window. She's suddenly worried he's going to break them. She almost presses the button to make the window go up.

'I can drive it out for you if you want. Not to be all ... I mean, you've done the hard bit.' He's nice. That's all that's happening. She beams at him. He grins back and it's wonky. She'd never noticed. The lips angle upwards to the right. She feels warmth flood the pit of her stomach.

'Or I could guide you out?'

'No, you driving it would be great.' He nods and moves round towards her. 'It's my husband's new car and I've no idea how long I am,' she tells him, stepping out.

In spite of all the nods, the swallowed 'Mornings', his 'Ah's in response to Prue obsessively counting the fish in the fish tank, this is the first time they've properly spoken and she's already mentioned Charlie. She could pat herself on the back for her loyalty but the truth is she's just cried 'husband' to surround herself with bear traps because she's scared of how The Lumberjack makes her feel. There's something about him, the man fumbling underneath her car seat, there's something about him.

'Is there ...? To get the seat back?' He's asking for her help. Charlie would always prefer to struggle with something and make a mess of it than ask for his wife's help. She wants to go to him, adjust the seat, show him how capable she is, but she stops herself, wary of putting her body too close to his.

'It's on the left-hand side,' she says instead, 'you pull it out like a drawer.' He finds the handle and his wedged legs push the seat back with thrilling abruptness. He gives her a Roger Moore eyebrow and she huffs a silent giggle.

'I'll bring it round to the entrance,' he says, 'get you past that Audi.' Before she's a few steps away she can hear that he's eased the car out of the impenetrable space and is making his way round. She's not jealous or resentful. She doesn't feel that she's compromised any feminist principles. He's an incredible driver. Of course he is. She's thought of saying something, initiating a conversation with him, many times but she never knew how to begin. He didn't seem like a man who wants to talk about the weather, the traffic, children, what he thinks of the nursery, how long his son has been there, did he like it. The questions she would happily ask another mum never seemed like questions she had a right to ask a father. The embarrassing truth was that she wanted to impress him and, on the nursery run, she never feels very impressive.

She walk-runs over to the entrance, not wanting him to have to wait for her. The nursery car park has a tennis court at one end with a net that sags on to its corroded concrete surface, there's a bank of recycling bins in the corner that spew non-recyclable household rubbish out on to the street through overstuffed apertures. There are so many pockets of desolation in this town they've moved to.

She looks at The Lumberjack, large still in the large car, framed in the windscreen. The blackness of the car's interior makes him twice as blond, the darkness accentuating his fairness and it could be a scene from a film noir. The car pulls up next to her and, as if she were the supplicant gangster's moll, the murdered man's wife who's fallen for the detective, she snaps the passenger-side door open and hops in next to him. She's hit by the smell. Smoky, like he spent the summer barbequing, but with an aftertaste of soil. She stares at his huge hand spread over the gearstick, fine hairs, nails clipped short and shining, no ring. Lots of married men don't wear a ring. She shouldn't even be wondering if he's married. The trapped air in the car vibrates with an energy she's sure he doesn't feel.

'Where are we going, then?' he asks, eyebrows arched. For a moment she thinks about how to answer him before realising what she's done.

'Oh God!' she laughs, nervous. 'Sorry, sorry!' He opens his door with a swallowed chuckle and she watches his broad back eclipse the doorframe as he exits their family car. She follows suit, walking round to the driver's side where he's standing a few paces off, leaving her space to get in.

'Thanks so much for this.'

'No worries.' She clambers behind the wheel and he closes the door for her like she's an old friend who's been staying for the weekend. His scent is still there, she has no idea what sandalwood smells like but, based on the name, it should smell like him. She looks down for the chair lever to see a few bricks of mud his boots have shed on the floor mat. She'll have to hoover it later. He's still there, watching her. She goes to turn the key but it's not there. She looks at him. He can tell something's wrong and seems genuinely concerned. She lowers the window.

'Did you take my keys?' she asks, her voice turning it into a joke. He pats his pockets before producing her car keys like a rabbit from a top hat.

'Thought you wouldn't notice.' He hands them through to her and as she takes them her index and middle fingers feather his palm and her skin fizzes. Just as it did at the nursery coffee morning, buried in the cornflakes, ten days ago.

'Sorry,' he says, a hint of colour in his pale skin. She shakes her head quickly as if it was nothing. It was nothing. But they're both acting like it was something. He steps back. She puts the keys in the ignition, the heat of his touch lingering on her fingers, and the engine hums into life. She looks at him, arms crossed, waiting for her to drive away. They see each other. Two smiles drop.

'I'm Sean.'

'Naomi.'

'Look after yourself, Naomi.' She presses the button on the armrest of the car and her window glides up, putting a colder coloured filter on him. She puts the car into gear, knowing that he'll be watching her as she leaves. Knowing that he cares if she gets away safely. That he wants her to be looked after. She can't think of the last time she felt looked after. She grips the wheel he's just held and puts her foot on the accelerator. She gives him a light wave and he returns a slow, purposeful nod as her heel presses the earth he's been walking on, deeper into the mat.

FIVE

BEHAVIOURAL ACTIONS WORKSHEET

a) List your partner's core values starting with the most important.

b) For each of their values, indicate the key issue with regard to how you feel you're not meeting their expectations. Give both recent and historical examples.

c) We will discuss and agree on a practical *action point* that you can implement to address each key issue.

CORE VALUES: Naomi

1) Honesty:

Issue: Naomi thinks I hide things from her.

Possible reasons:
Recent:
- I forgot to order Prue's food for nursery and told Naomi it was their fault.
- When I was getting rid of an armchair in the new house, I made a hole in the wall and told her I didn't know how

19

it had happened but she knew I was lying. She always knows I'm lying so I don't know why I do???

Historical:
- Last year the business had big problems over a patent. We lost a couple of years' income. I kept it from Naomi for several months.

Suggested action:
A ten-minute 'meeting' every night with an agenda created by Charlie and supplemented by Naomi. Focus on logistical/financial concerns.

Creates: – Routine for transparency.
– Improved communication.
– Shows respect.
– Effort to speak her language.

SIX

She wrestles through Prue's changing-table drawers trying to separate the 12–18 month clothes from the 18–24 month ones. Some of the 12–18s definitely still fit her but there has to be a system and she hasn't been able to find anything efficiently for weeks. She couldn't face going back to work this afternoon. She's so overqualified for her job project managing the Kent Arts Biennale that she isn't concerned about the repercussions of bunking off.

Charlie managed to come inside her after he brought her back at lunchtime. He must have spent all morning psyching himself up because the whole thing was fairly painless. In fact, she enjoyed it more than she has for nearly a year. Although she'd been consciously trying not to think about her earlier encounter with The Lumberjack, the warmth in her stomach still hadn't dissipated by the time she and her husband got to the bedroom.

The death of her and Charlie's sex life wasn't down to any catastrophic breakdown in their relationship. It was a gradual division. When she was pregnant with Prue, Naomi often didn't want to be touched so Charlie eventually stopped trying to initiate things in the bedroom. Then after their daughter was born, sleep became a more precious commodity than intimacy. When they started trying to conceive again in earnest and they hadn't got pregnant within the first couple of months, the pressure grew and the joy diminished. Charlie suggested that they take a break for a few months but it felt like he was trying to avoid the problem rather than overcome it. Naomi had accepted that they'd left it too late for three children but she was convinced that as soon as she became pregnant with a second child, as soon as their family was complete and they were no longer striving for the next thing, their marriage would get back to how it was before. Although Naomi and Charlie would never be the bright, fun things they once were, what they would have, a perfect little family in a perfect home by the seaside, would make their relationship so much richer.

She puts the stack of bodysuits on her breastfeeding chair ready for Charlie to put in the attic for Prue's sibling, if she ever gets one, and looks down into the half-empty top drawer. Now it's manageable. She starts to reorganise the various piles. The flow can be improved. Leggings. One pair of jeggings. They go with the leggings. Long-sleeve shirts. T-shirts. Dresses. Tights. Skirts. Babies don't wear skirts. Prue's a girl. Soon she'll be a woman. She'll never love them as much as she does now. It's horrifying.

Under a small pile of jumpers she sees something that makes her navel flinch. A faded corner of material she's never seen before. She tugs at it and pulls out a baby's sleepsuit. Prue hasn't worn them since she turned one. Hers are all in the attic. Naomi smells it. Not Prue's warm sweetness nor the synthetic flowers of their washing powder. It's white with pink rubber dimples on the feet and a logo on the chest. Three cartoon children with big eyes. Naomi remembers them from when she was at school. *The Powerpuff Girls*. It doesn't belong in here.

She looks around Prue's nursery for some clue as to where it might have come from. Naomi insisted on the room being finished before they moved in. They hammered nails into the floorboards and covered them with a large rug, filled holes in the plaster and repainted everything in gender-neutral pale green. Pink robot stickers now march around the skirting board. It's the one room in the whole house that Naomi feels is safe for their daughter. Her eyes travel over a huge cuddly bear her parents bought Prue, an impractical antique rocking horse from Charlie's, a miniature multi-storey car park, monochrome prints of the four most recognisable animals. Elephant, lion, owl, monkey. Everything is exactly where it's supposed to be. She puts thumb and forefinger of each hand at the suit's waist, snaps it in half and carries it out of her daughter's room, rubbing the inside knuckle of her left thumb over the embroidered cartoon characters.

SEVEN

Naomi is in the kitchen reading a business plan written by one of Charlie's trendiest football mates, Tayo, when the washing machine beeps the end of its cycle. The house is quiet today. The builders clocked off early claiming they had to wait for some frame they'd glued to set. She's enjoying the silence. Her life now is a cacophony of sound. Prue's night-time wailing has ended but it's been replaced by the minor-key screeching of drills, sharp hammering, never-ending chart radio punctuated by bursts of machine-gun male laughter. It's affected Charlie more than it has her. When Prue was born, as the noise, the chaos bloomed into their lives, it was like someone let the gas out of Charlie and he withered.

The business plan is exceptionally well written; the planning and timescales are well thought through and the pitch, a plant-based junk-food café, is very compelling. The branding looks fantastic. But even without doing the research Naomi knows it will struggle to sustain itself here. People who live in London think 'the rest of the country' are just a slightly less cultured version of themselves and if only they can enlighten them with coriander and a sustainable vision of the future then 'the rest of the country' will jump on whatever they're selling with glee. The reality is that 'the rest of the country' has its own tastes and desires and it absolutely loves bacon.

Naomi used to work for one of the top management consultancies in the world. The sort of company that has an office that looks like some fine Italian marble and polished steel had tantric sex and birthed a beautiful interior dressed in priceless artwork. Most of her work involved telling companies how their consumers thought and she'd always found it straightforward. Consumers want more of what they already like but they want it to feel like something they don't already have. Be it a new lifestyle regime, an even smaller food processor or a new route around their supermarket, it should seem like the final piece in their lives that makes them feel complete. People loved her there and she rose through the company quickly. Her obsessive eye for detail, work ethic and plain-speaking approach endeared her to her bosses who were more accustomed to a vague Oxbridge delicacy.

Yanking out a clump of laundry from the machine she sees specks of sodden paper covering the dark wash like it's cut itself shaving. Charlie never checks his pockets. She piles the damp mass on the kitchen island and goes about hanging everything up on the drying rack. Prue's stuff on the bottom. Charlie's on the middle. Hers on the top. She can't shift the sleepsuit out of her mind. It's on the hall table, ready to be taken back to nursery. She's decided it must have got jumbled up with Prue's spare clothes at nursery and when Charlie picked her up, he brought it home and packed it away in her drawers. The only thing she can't make sense of is why there's a piece of clothing made for a 0–1 month old in a nursery with a minimum age of six months? And who's still into *The Powerpuff Girls*? It could be one of the hipsters who live up the hill from town, she thinks, there's a couple of them, bearded and clad in trucker's caps, whose kids go to

Prue's nursery. Those sort of people like ironic retro things. Maybe it fell out of one of their bags. Naomi closes her eyes tight and shakes the train of thought from her head. These are the things she allows herself to get flustered by now that she doesn't have the fast-paced seventy-hour week and the constantly expanding inbox that came with her old job.

She's got to Charlie's black jeans, which seem like they must belong to a giant compared to Prue's cute indigo cords she's just hung up, and she finds the cause of the paper explosion. It's a receipt. The bottom has been munched together by the machine but the top is— It's a cinema ticket. Cineworld. Screen 4. 13:35. The film title is obscured. Charlie's been to the cinema during the day. He's meant to work during the day. She works part time, she does the lion's share of the childcare when Prue isn't at nursery, she handles the renovation of the house and he works a solid nine-to-five in his study on the top floor. That was what they agreed.

Naomi finishes the laundry and picks up Tayo's business plan. She'll take it up to Charlie. She won't confront him about the ticket because she's not meant to call him out about things any more because it makes him feel like she doesn't trust him.

She gets to the top landing and pushes his closed door open. He starts like a rodent. Hand dashes to half-close his laptop. Body snaps his wheelie chair away from her. He looks up at her, brow furrowed over his eyes like a shield. She sees her husband's body clenched into a spiral on his office chair and an image of The Lumberjack's broad frame, shoulders like the top of a wall, springs into her mind. She glances down at Charlie's crotch. Nothing. She's caught him doing something on his computer he doesn't want her to know about but it wasn't that. She scans his office. Of course it's one of the more finished rooms in the house. Even down to his having completed his 'I want all my units, desk and storage on wheels because you can always find a new configuration that works better' project. Charlie designs products. Prototypes for new products. He had aspirations to be an inventor but there's no viable business model for that.

'Yeah?' he says, as if she were a long-standing colleague he's never warmed to.

'I looked at your friend's business plan.'

'Oh, cool.' He keeps his hand on the half-cock laptop. He has a headphone in the ear that faces away from her. He was doing something on his computer that definitely wasn't work and he's hiding it from her like a schoolboy with a dirty magazine. Naomi has the cinema ticket in her back pocket. She wants to lay it on his desk like a poker player revealing a final ace but instead she holds out Tayo's translucent turquoise folder. Charlie stands up, pushing the laptop screen back up to its normal position. What was he doing?

'What were you doing?'

'What?' He laces his hands together in defiance.

'When I came in, what were you doing?'

'Sorting some emails.' He swings the computer towards her. She makes a show of not looking to tell him she trusts him. She doesn't. It proves nothing. He could have done any number of things to cover for himself. He understands technology in a way she never will. She jerks the folder towards him.

'I've made some notes on it.'

'Is it any good?' He takes the business plan, pivoting on the ball of his foot, not wanting to plant himself too close to her.

'He's obviously really bright.'

'He wants to do carbon-free music nights. He's asked me if I can help with making a set-up that powers all the AV equipment with someone riding a bicycle on the side of the stage.' Charlie slaps the folder to congratulate it. Naomi feels the ticket steaming in her pocket but she knows she can't confront him now. He seems up, high on enthusiasm for Tayo's doomed café. She cannot allow herself to be cast, once again, as the arch-villain in the saga of her husband's happiness.

'He's written all that in his business plan.'

'Course.' He hunches back to his workstation and crams the folder into the bag sitting on the floor next to his desk. Naomi studies his workspace again. There's an avocado anglepoise lamp glowing dimly at the end of the desk that she hadn't noticed earlier. Their soft furnishings budget seemingly doesn't apply to items for Charlie's office. He's put his artiest band posters up on the far wall. DJ Shadow. LCD Soundsystem. Gorillaz. Life before Prue. Lightless rooms humming with beer and humanity. Their clammy cheeks pressed together. Heads bobbing infinitesimally. Fingers intertwined. Their ritual as they'd wait for the beat to drop. And when it did they'd push apart like opposite poles of a magnet, launch hands into the air, whoop and smile and smile and smile until the house lights came on or the drugs wore off.

'It'll be a really great space,' she says.

'Whenever I chat to someone like Tayo, makes me feel like we did the right thing moving here.' Perhaps he went to the film with Tayo? Perhaps it was a hipster-creatives' version of a business meeting. She hopes that that's it. She wants him to be spending his days making the business work, making their future work. He's come over to her, closer than he wanted to before.

'You know what I mean?' He rests a hand on her hip. They used to go to the cinema together. He taught her to love films, action schlock as much as award-season fodder. A gig or the cinema, alternating every Thursday night. She made him set up a shared online calendar for it to make sure they always had tickets for something. They learnt everything about each other in darkened rooms. She meets his eyes, eyes that have become frosted glass to her in the last eighteen months, and presents him with a half-smile.

'You know what we haven't done for ages?' she says.

'What?'

'Cinema.' She looks right at him, trying to decipher his reaction like someone playing a memory game. He's nodding, though he's not aware he's doing it.

'We could get a babysitter,' he says, 'date night. Maybe in a month's time if … If it hasn't worked this time.'

'There anything on you want to see?'

'Not really looked for a while.' He chuckles, forehead creasing. He's giving nothing away. But, like anyone who needs everyone to like them, Charlie is an excellent liar.

'Anyway, you're working.' She removes his hand from her hip, keeping hold of his fingers and squashing them together tenderly as she turns from him. What the hell was he doing?

EIGHT

13 September 2017 at 17:22

Buying something expensive
Bad news about the business
Porn
Surprise for us
Affair

'Naomi,' she looks up from writing a note on her phone to see it's him, The Lumberjack, 'how you doing, all right?'

'Oh, hello,' she says, her voice a few notes higher than its normal pitch. She always goes into the park after nursery for as long as the light holds out. A month after they moved into the house Prue put both feet through one of the stairs. She wasn't hurt past a few grazes below the line of her leggings but she howled for five minutes with the shock of it. Naomi was furious with Charlie at the time, she'd asked him to ensure that all the areas of the house Prue would be using were safe before they moved in. He got defensive straight away. Said it didn't make sense. Said he'd checked everything thoroughly and the stairs had been completely solid. He said it looked like the stair she'd fallen through had been damaged in some way, that perhaps it was the builders. When she asked them they said they didn't know anything about it. Naomi wasn't convinced by her husband's explanation. Their idea of 'thorough' has always been continents apart. However it happened, for Naomi, their home's threat level moved from 'Mummy-kiss-it-better' to 'trip to A&E' so she tries to keep Prue out of the house as much as possible.

'This is Greg.' The Lumberjack indicates a pale boy of about two with a dark helmet of hair standing behind him.

Prue runs back from an outcrop of small trees and crashes into Naomi's thigh, pretending to be shy, before slaloming between her legs, swinging on them like she's been watching *Singing in the Rain*. Greg marvels at the dynamo Prue as she repeatedly bashes her head on her mother's pubic bone. Naomi can see that Greg is one of those wan, reflective little boys. Someone doomed to a life of thinking too much. Perhaps how Charlie might have been as a toddler. The air shows itself autumnal, piquant with moisture and goose bumps bloom on Naomi's wrists.

'Prue,' she tells him, ruffling her daughter's fledgling hair.

'Hello, Prue.' The Lumberjack squats down to the little girl's level. Prue stops behind Naomi and glares at the big man.

'You hiding from me?' He talks to her like an adult, it's lovely.

Suddenly, Prue jumps out and roars at Sean, making him stumble back, and then she proceeds to lick her hand ferociously.

'Oh God! She thinks—' Naomi can't get the words out, seized by sudden laughter. 'She thinks you're—' Prue roars again and continues to lick her hand. Greg frowns at his counterpart like a snob at a cheap restaurant while Sean knots his hands in front of him, not getting the joke.

'She thinks you're a bear. There's a book we read where there's a bear eating honey and that's what we do. She thinks you're a bear,' Naomi manages to tell him through her subsiding laughter. He looks uncomfortable still, hurt even.

'It must be your beard.' She leans her head to the side and smiles at him as if getting through to a pouting child. 'The bear's yellow in the book, and with your beard …' His face brightens but now she's seen a chink of vulnerability that makes the fantasy human. 'Thanks, by the way,' she says, cutting off a look between them that was on the verge of lingering. 'I think I said, but thanks for getting me out, in the car park.' She tucks a swathe of hair behind her ear, loosened by laughter.

'I love driving other people's cars. Always have.'

'You like the extra pressure?'

'No, the lack of consequences.' He grins. The aftershock of her earlier laughing fit hums out of her in response. The rain that's been waiting in the air like a cold compress breaks. Thin rain that looks innocuous but within seconds Prue's chestnut hair goes black with it. Naomi magics a hat from her back pocket and screws it on to her daughter's head. Sean ducks down to pull up the hood of Greg's raincoat. Thick fingers fumble to tie the coat's drawstring. The boy pulls away from his father. As the rain deepens Naomi notices the man her daughter thought was a bear getting flustered. She squats down, her face inches from Sean's rain-beaded beard, leans in towards Greg and, with her long, hand-model fingers, spins the boy's raincoat's string into a neat bow.

'So you're meant to *tie* the string,' Sean jokes as they rise up together to adult level. She beams, and, holding the feeling of the upper hand for the first time in their acquaintance, she asks him the most innocent question a parent can ask another parent as they both struggle to draw out the witching hour between teatime and bathtime.

'Do you want to get a coffee?'

NINE

'So I'm there in all me gear, thermal this, thermal that. Camos, balaclava. Might as well've been wearing a ghillie suit. Anyway, four in the morning, I've been there since one, and I hear that noise. You know the noise foxes make? Scratch, scratch, scratch, and I'm thinking there's two of them behind me! I've got a .22 between my legs and there's bloody two foxes behind me, know what I mean?' Charlie smiles though he has no idea what the man means. He and their carpenter, Lenny, are standing on the crazy paving of their front garden looking up at the house. They'd had the exterior painted shortly after moving in. Naomi wanted something big ticked off the list. An easy win. And now, sitting alongside its neighbours, window frames and sills painted an obsidian grey that 'makes the red brick pop', it looks like the child at school who's turned up in his uniform on mufti day; infinitely more robbable than the other houses in the street. A three-floor, early-Georgian town house with a roof that triangles up more acutely than you'd expect, tall and narrow like a witch's hat.

A fluttering of whiteness catches Charlie's eye. The dormer window at the top of the house is open and the net curtain waves out in the wind. He's asked Naomi to keep the window on the top-floor landing closed, the wind blows into his study disarraying the papers on his desk, so it can't have been her. Perhaps the latch on it's faulty. It sometimes feels like this house and all its little niggles will drive him over the edge. Death by a thousand cuts. Maybe the builders opened it, he thinks. They're not up there today but he's sure they'd do it just to annoy him.

They probably think he's an arsehole because he goes to great lengths to avoid them, but he quite likes Lenny, he's different to the others. He sings folk songs as he measures up wood in a sweet tenor voice, vibrato and everything. He doesn't take sugar in his coffee. And he kills things as a side-job.

'I'd do the pest control three hundred sixty-five days a year if I could make it pay,' he had told Charlie. He'd spotted a pigeon infestation under the rafters of the roof and offered to lend Charlie an airgun and teach him how to get rid of them for free. Charlie misinterpreted his kindness for some kind of pity so he made excuses every time Lenny suggested going out. But after Naomi nearly caught him out in his study earlier, the guilt triggered a spiral that ended with him crouched against the ridges of the radiator in his study, moaning tears into the crook of his arm, so when Lenny bellowed up the stairs that there were thirty birds on the roof and that he'd already called the police to let them know he was going to 'cull' them, it felt like an opportunity to shake himself out of his funk.

A pigeon wafts above them, black against the strings of cloud. Lenny points a pistol-shaped hand up and follows it until it lands on the sloping roof yards above Charlie's front door. He fires his finger-gun before giving Charlie a pirate grin of expectation. There's an air rifle broken — that's what it's called when it's open – over Charlie's wrist. He'd almost forgotten it was there. Lenny holds out a small plastic box full of pellets.

'Flattened dome-head. Squashes on impact delivering maximum destruction without messing with the aerodynamics too much.' Charlie takes the pellet, pushes it into the hole and snaps the rifle shut, feeling a bit like someone in an action film.

Lenny's staring at him still so Charlie doesn't really know what else to do than put the gun in the crook of his shoulder and 'adopt the position'. He looks through the sight, the sort of sight you'd expect to see in *The Day of the Jackal* rather than the front garden of a house on the North Kent coast, and lines the bird up in it. The pigeon, huge in the telescopic sight, moves its puffed chest from side to side, a glint of metallic purple in the feathers under its beak. Charlie breathes out just as he's finding his aim, a move he might have picked up from *Robin Hood: Prince of Thieves*, and pulls the trigger. A flit of compressed air, a puff of feathers and a swarm of pigeons and seagulls fly up into the air. He takes his eye away from the sight and watches the pigeon he's shot teeter on the ledge before it falls through the air, two vain flaps of its wings, and thuds down on to the paving stones in front of them.

Charlie looks up at Lenny who watches the bird convulsing on the floor with a face of respectful earnestness. It slams its wings against the ground, thrusting its body into the air as it writhes in pain. Charlie blinks hard several times so his eyelashes entwine. It's as if he's trying to remind himself to feel something as the pigeon's bright acrylic-paint blood smears out on to its feathers.

'There's over a thousand different types of bacteria in their shit and if your little girl ingests some, she could die from it.' Lenny's looking at him, he must be mistaking the numbness in his expression for remorse.

'I've seen it happen,' the carpenter says. The bird lies on the ridiculous paving stones, motionless. Lenny's promised to show him how the nail-gun works next week.

TEN

Naomi closes the door behind her as gently as she can and lowers her tote bag to the floor. It's 6:53 in the evening. Charlie's reading Prue a story. She never usually drinks coffee after lunchtime and she can feel the caffeine flickering behind her eyes like strip-lighting.

She listens to them for a moment as Charlie tells their daughter about how the penguin, the turtle and the bright clownfish swim through the water. She often pauses at the bottom of the stairs and tunes in to her husband and daughter. In the early days it was in a spirit of gratitude but now she does it to find out which version of Charlie she'll get this evening. Will he invest the animals with different voices and, goaded by Prue's delight, make his performance more and more exuberant, or will he sound how he does now? Hard and brittle like the rusted sheet metal at the back of an abandoned washing machine, his words crumbling as he says them. Will he sound frustrated, bored, desperate to be back at his desk designing the product that will change the world?

He loves Prue. He really does. He swings her around in the air and lets her use his body as a climbing frame. He blows raspberries on her honeydew belly, holds her to him and looks at her with the melting fondant eyes that only a father has for a daughter. But he resents the rest of it, resents

38

the mundane and incessant tasks that make up ninety-five per cent of parenting. His father, Anthony, was a dentist who revolutionised the industry with a new technique. Naomi was never sure exactly what it was, something to do with crowns. When they were with his parents, if Charlie took Prue away to change her, Anthony would take great pride in telling everyone that he's never changed a nappy. Charlie once made a joke, they'd had his best mate Felix and his then girlfriend down for lunch, and Charlie said that when it came to parenting, his father's generation 'didn't know how good they had it'. That 'joke' stayed with Naomi.

Anthony had been mostly absent from Charlie's childhood. Working long hours, speaking at international conferences and, Naomi has always assumed, having affairs. Charlie used to talk to her pregnant belly and tell the unborn Prue that above everything else, he'd be around for her, he'd be present. It made Naomi cry. But that was before he realised that being 'present' includes bleaching the nappy bin every week.

A pain buzzes in the front of her head so she goes to the fridge and gets a half-finished bottle of fizzy water out and takes it to the synthetic armchair they've put at the end of the kitchen.

Sean is a carpenter – number two on the *Daily Mail* website's list of the most attractive jobs for a man. She'd guessed that he made things. It wasn't just that he drove a van, it was the way he held his hands in front of him as if they don't know how to behave unless they're at work. And his forearms. Men who sit in front of computers have sapling wrists. Sean's are boughs of a beech tree.

He didn't offer much about himself so she'd had to goad him into talking about his work, worrying that asking about his circumstances, his relationship with Greg's mother, might seem invasive, even flirtatious, but once he opened up about carpentry, he talked with such passion, such humility. When she first got together with Charlie, he said he didn't believe in humility, he thought it was a pose. But Sean's was genuine and it drew you in. A 6'4" siren with a mild Yorkshire accent.

He's from Sheffield and has that gentle lilt that makes a person seem a thousand times nicer than anyone who lives south of Nottingham. He was nicer. Not too nice. He made conspiratorial jokes about some hipster man-children who were laughing too loudly on a table nearby. So they now had in-jokes that either of them would be able to call on in an awkward moment. If they were to meet again.

He'd never been to the café before. It was on the other side of the park. Naomi and Prue sometimes met another mum, Lara, and her daughter here. It was one of the trendy places that had migrated down to the coast to provide Londoners with sanctuary from the incumbent fish and chip shops and greasy-spoon caffs. Judging by how many children were barrelling around down that end, the owners clearly knew their market – yummy mummies. Although she was the only mum sitting at a table with a man she barely knew.

'It's the nearest to a good coffee I've found down here,' Naomi had told Sean, instantly cringing at her pretentiousness. She doesn't think liking coffee is either cool or interesting and she's fairly sure Sean doesn't either as he bought himself a can of ginger beer.

Sean listens. He has grey-green eyes the colour of lichen. There are moments when they look blue, but they're not. As Prue showed a reluctant Greg how to drive using a computer console steering wheel, Naomi told Sean a selection of facts about herself. How she always imagined herself living by the sea after growing up in Dorset. That it was an idyllic childhood playing on the beach every day after school with whichever children were there that day and she wanted the same for Prue. That they chose this town because of its proximity to their old life in London. How she'd really grown to like it but that she was struggling, a little bit, to make friends. Not because she wasn't invited to things, she was. Just, with Prue, she didn't have time to really get out there and get to know people. Sean didn't respond to any of this with more than a nod, a half-smile, a glance round his shoulder to check the kids were OK. After Naomi stopped speaking he still said nothing, just looked at her, looking into her like he was trying to yank her thoughts out by the hypothalamus.

'I'm quite lonely,' she found herself saying. Then Greg cried out. Sean didn't move instantly, he held Naomi's admission tenderly in the air for a moment.

'I think we all are,' he said before heaving himself up to go and see what the commotion at the other end of the café was all about.

ELEVEN

Agenda 13/09/17:

Front spare room furniture

Confirm plan/dates with Lenny

Felix text with dates for a visit. Maybe Feb/March next year?

Prue's nursery lunch – should we make it ourselves?

Any other business

Naomi has other business. They're sat at the breakfast bar. The kitchen was the only thing the previous owners had managed to finish before they lost their bottle when they realised how much doing up the house was going to cost. It's all dark, matte greys, polished granite worktop. Light cascades in through a gaping skylight. It could be the inside of a temple, faintly monolithic. It's being done meant that they spent almost all their time in here. Watching Netflix on an iPad, arms and legs folded, trying to get comfy on a wooden stool is not a relaxing way to unwind. She can't remember the last time she unwound. Ever since they moved down here, to their bright new future together, she'd felt like a violin string being gradually tightened. And his bored silence at this precise moment, after giving her monosyllabic explanations about his day, twists her creaking nerves towards snapping point.

He's been spending weekdays at the cinema and whatever it was he was doing when she interrupted him this afternoon, it definitely wasn't work. He has to have some 'other business' otherwise his 'behavioural activation strategy' or whatever these ridiculous sit-downs are called is nothing more than the sort of meaningless jargon for which she set up a financial punishment jar at her old work.

Charlie's been doing sessions of Cognitive Behavioural Therapy for the past few months with a counsellor called Amy who Naomi has been told nothing about. He says that it's making him feel better. He says that Naomi should do it too, because she shouldn't have to live with the level of worry that she does. Which translates to he, Charlie, shouldn't have to live with Naomi worrying legitimately about the many worrying things that she spends her time worrying about. Like their being unable to conceive another baby, like bringing up their young daughter in a death-trap of a house, like him starting to display the exact behaviour he did when he managed to hamstring the family into this horrible situation in the first place.

In the first year of Prue's life, he pleads sleep deprivation, Charlie neglected some fundamental parts of his business – he didn't secure patents for a virtual-reality headset he'd spent two years working on – and the big payday he was expecting for it never came. He has theories about all sorts of corporate espionage but Naomi figured out that his client, a start-up called Burman VR, got frustrated with him not delivering what he'd promised on time and seeing that he hadn't tied up the copyright, they made their own version. It all would have been avoidable if he'd enlisted her help or advice but the worst thing about the whole disaster was that he didn't tell her anything. Even after it happened. He didn't tell her that he was going to his office and essentially twiddling his thumbs every day for months while she was breastfeeding Prue, dealing with chronic sleep deprivation and twenty nappies a day.

He had hinted that there might be some problems with one of their contracts but she only understood the extent of it when their mortgage adviser, a genial Essex wide-boy called Graham, told them that he wouldn't be able to get them a big enough mortgage to buy the house they'd had an offer accepted on, the house Naomi had set her heart on. More than her heart, she'd poured all of her life up until that moment into that house. She'd worked twelve-hour days since she left university to save up for a deposit to buy her two-bed flat in Tottenham. She'd lived in that undesirable part of London – as it was then – where knifings and gangs were rife because she'd had the foresight to see that it would be a great investment for when she moved away from the city and when she sat in front of an open fire in the front room of that house, that incredible house, she would know that all of that graft and discomfort had been worth it. But that's not where they are and, perhaps she's being paranoid, but, with the way Charlie's acting, it feels like it's happening again. So Naomi thinks it unlikely that Cognitive Behavioural Therapy is going to save them.

'How are you today? You know, how do you feel? Your mood.' She tries to penetrate him with empathy. He always complains that she doesn't believe in depression, doesn't believe that he is depressed.

'Didn't get a lot done,' he looks at her from the side of his eyes, 'after this morning. Couldn't get my head clear.'

'What did you do, then?'

'It was bitty. With picking you up and having to have sex. Then afterwards, I'm just meant to sit down at my desk and be able to throw myself back into it?'

'Throw yourself into what? If you're stuck with something again, maybe I can help.' Charlie scratches the few days of stubble growth. The image of Sean's beard flies into her head. Bright blond bristles that get darker the further they are from his lips, the rain clinging to them like dew on a cobweb.

Charlie grabs his phone off the worktop, snapping Naomi back into the greyness of their kitchen, and goes into some app he knows she won't understand. In retaliation she clicks their chrome kettle on. Their evenings used to be white-wine spritzers, cigarettes and crisps on their polluted balcony overlooking the Victoria Line. Charlie talking her through an album by some crossover world music superstar, her blowing his mind recounting the underlying theory of whichever 'brainy' non-fiction title she'd just devoured. Now they're dictated by agendas and unremarkable acts of passive aggression and still Naomi can't let it go.

'You were working when I came up in the afternoon, weren't you? What were you working on?' He looks up at her through his eyebrows.

'Just don't worry about it.'

'But I am worried. You say you've not done anything all day, not for the first time, and yet I pick Prue up a lot of the time and deal with the builders, do all that stuff, on top of my job, just so you can work, and you're refusing to talk to

45

me about what you're doing up there. I don't think I'm being unreasonable.'

He gets up and picks the iPad up off the counter.

'Maybe if you tell me I can help you?' He's walking away. What can she do? Get in his way? Physically stop him? Ask him, straight up, why he's been wasting his apparently precious time going to the cinema? 'You called this "meeting".' She does air-quotes. 'If you'd ever had a job, a real job that made money, you'd know that if you call a meeting you can't leave while it's still going.' He stops down the hall. She couldn't help herself. Every time he walks away from her she's forced to go straight for his Zeppelin-sized pride. He's silhouetted against the streetlights, glaring through the glass squares of their door. It seems like he's swaying. She's not scared of him, she never has been.

'If you didn't do any work, what were you doing all day?'

He grabs ones of the banister's spindles, his voice wrings with fabricated calm, as if he were telling a bulldog detective where he was on the night of the crime.

'I was emailing Rinalds. Doing some designs for a new smartphone steadicam. Speaking to an adhesive supplier who says I owe him money. I was doing fucking work.' His eyes are watering. It's a strange quirk of when he's angry. He's not forged for confrontation and it's as if rage has to dribble out of him before it bursts. 'I don't have to justify my day to you.'

'You don't think I have the right to ask what you are doing to make money for this family, when I'm living in this death-trap house, permanently terrified that our daughter's going to be crushed to death under a pile of rubble, because I had to bail you out?' He looks beyond her, eyes almost vibrating in their sockets, then he reaches both hands up to the collars of his polo-shirt and rips it down the middle. Naomi laughs involuntarily. He glances at her with disgust, or is it shame, then he turns and storms up the stairs to his office half-naked.

Naomi breathes deeply three times, puts her index fingers together and presses them gently into the corners of her closed eyes. When she opens them she sees the tattered shreds of his navy-blue shirt lying discarded on the floor. This is the most aggressive gesture she's ever seen from her husband. She thinks of Prue snoring lightly on her front, clutching Elvis, her little pink elephant.

TWELVE

http://www.yourrelationship/justacrush/377493

It's just a little crush …
5 Ways to Deal With a Crush When Married
Our bodies are packed with chemicals that respond to other humans … and not always just our spouse. Here's how to deal with the feelings of an extramarital crush.

BY DR FIONA BELFRAGE

1. It will pass. According to psychologists, a crush lasts, on average, five months; if it continues for longer it could be you're 'in love'. But it probably won't.

2. Learn from the crush. Being attracted to someone or even noticing others' attractiveness is what psychologists term 'attention to alternatives'. Research has shown that people who claim greater relationship satisfaction pay significantly less attention to alternative partners.

3. It's time to talk. A crush may reveal you're not having as much fun with your partner as you used to and have fallen into bad habits. It might indicate that there's too much emotional distance between you. If you're feeling lonely, this is the time to discuss it with your husband or wife.

4. It may or may not be OK to keep your crush a secret. Generally, I would say never keep secrets from your spouse, but there are some caveats. You might be able to see it as a harmless folly but your partner could be drastically affected by it. If you're only telling your spouse to relieve your own guilt you're doing the wrong thing.

5. Play it safe. Although you can't control chemistry, you can control your actions. If you are making regular coffee dates with your secret crush because you just want to spend time with them, you've crossed the line between a normal crush to a slippery slope that can lead to emotional or physical infidelity.

THIRTEEN

'Is Charlie picking you up?' Lara, the closest Naomi has to a friend in the area, asks.

'What? No. No. Sorry, miles away.' Naomi's been glancing over at the entrance of 'Ladybird's Landing' too often. 'Not slept so I'm a total space cadet.'

She waves her mug of instant coffee in front of her face.

'Ah, look.' Lara indicates to her daughter Margot and Prue, playing in the under-3s section of the aircraft-hangar-sized soft-play centre. The girls are competing to see who can press their face hardest into the semi-spherical Perspex porthole on the upper floor of the structure.

Naomi keeps looking over at the door because she invited Sean to bring Greg along to the playgroup, 'Sing, Sign and Movement', that she, Lara and the girls have just attended, but he hasn't turned up. She was sure he would and now she's worried. They exchanged numbers after their coffee date but it was only after it was too late, after she'd already texted to invite him, in the early hours as Charlie snored lightly next to her, that she realised she knew nothing about Sean's situation. He hadn't mentioned a partner so she assumed he was a single dad, or separated, but maybe he's happily married. Maybe his wife found a text from some woman and has given him a bollocking. She shouldn't care this much. Embarrassment makes her flush with heat and she wants to leave. Get back for Prue's lunch. The soft play only serves various forms of beige food that's either deep-fried or tastes like it needs to be and she was told off once for bringing in a red rice salad in a Tupperware.

Margot and Prue appear from the bowels of the under-3s zone and march down the foam mat together hand-in-hand. Margot tries, in vain, to make Prue step in time with her. It's so beautiful that Lara touches Naomi's arm, beaming at her. Naomi's not naturally tactile but she puts her own hand over her friend's and squeezes it hard. They hold the smile of new intimacy for a moment before Lara breaks it to reach for her phone and the exchange makes Naomi realise how profoundly sad she feels.

Lara takes pictures of the girls, trying to capture the perfect portrait of their little soldier girls. Lara's big on Instagram. She has seventeen thousand eight hundred followers. She's a jewellery designer who spent years in India when she was young and free and sexy. She's still quite sexy, which Naomi assumes is the reason for the online following as she's not sure how much jewellery Lara actually sells. In the four times they've met at this soft play, she hasn't once bought the coffees.

Lara bounds up and runs towards the girls, eliciting giggles from Margot and a bodged swerve from Prue that ends up with her lying on her front. She walk-crawls towards Naomi, who holds out her arms in encouragement. Lara swings Margot in the air, yoga-triceps straining. There's a difficult balance in a place like this between having too much fun with your children and not having enough. Prue runs over and collides with Naomi's thigh.

'Mummeeeey.' She looks up at Naomi, arms wrapped around her legs as if she's trying to save a tree from a fleet of bulldozers.

'Yes.'

'Mummeeeey.'

'Yes, darling.'

'Mummeeeeeey.'

'Yes, sweetheart, what would you like?'

'Chjrink.' Only Naomi knows this means she's thirsty. She opens her baby backpack, retrieves a green cup and offers it to her daughter. Prue pushes off Naomi's legs and sucks down the water like she's been rescued from the desert, one long draught, another, a sigh of satisfaction. Naomi looks towards the quadruple doors again. Thinks of him squeezed on to the plastic chair opposite her, a displaced titan, luminescent and awkward, eyes full of sympathy that this place might be the highlight of her week, something she's desperate to share with him as if he'd be impressed. It was ridiculous to ask him to come here.

She invited The Lumberjack – she must stop thinking of him like that – she invited Sean to the baby group to neutralise him, to turn him into a parent. Most of the parents she knew were regulars at the group and if they saw them together as acquaintances with kids the same age then that was what they would be. She wanted to put him firmly in the 'friend zone' and she wanted witnesses. But he's not here. Which is probably good because if he were here, perhaps the fact that she hasn't been able to stop thinking about him for the last twenty-four hours would be plain for everyone to see.

She looks around the huge room at bored dads looking at football news on their phones, harassed mums in sportswear attempting to martial small-scale civil wars between siblings and sugar-amped children rocketing around like derailed dodgems. She never feels further from her life in London than when she's somewhere like this. The people here have real concerns and they're heavier because of them, their faces seem weighed down and most of them look ten years older than they probably are. And yet they seem more fully in the world than the people she used to share space with in artisan bakeries. When they laugh they really laugh; when they tell their children off, their children understand they've done something wrong. There's no self-consciousness, no archness, no post-modern ironic cynicism. And very few of them are alone. There are grandmas and aunts and cousins and old friends, friends who've known each other from birth, and although they probably live in a smaller house than Naomi, although they're unlikely to go to the ballet or art galleries, with their sense of community, the village they always say it takes to raise a child, they are infinitely richer than her.

Prue's dancing on her own, squatting her bum down to the piped-in Disney music. Naomi lights on two brothers off to the left, roughly six and eight, pushing a plastic dumper-truck between them. It won't be long before Prue starts asking questions about the other kids at nursery and their brothers and sisters. Naomi can't allow her to grow up like she did, imagination straining to make up yet another game for herself, a childhood cut short by so much time in the company of adults.

'Number forty-six! Sausage and chips. Nuggets and chips.' A fishwife blast from a steaming catering window nearby crashes into her thoughts. She has a husband who she loves, they have a beautiful daughter, they will have another child,

53

whether it takes five years and ten rounds of IVF, they will have another child because she owes it to Prue, because once they have another baby, the anger she feels towards Charlie will disappear, he'll start to feel happier and things between them will go back to how they used to be. She's absolutely certain of that. Sean's not come, it's for the best.

The car park of Ladybird's Landing is in the middle of an industrial estate, the concrete surface potholed and scabrous. Naomi has just managed to wedge Prue into the car seat after her usual two or three minutes of the 'fun' standing-up-in-the-seat game. Prue waves a Duplo Peppa Pig around in front of her, making pigs fly, as Naomi slams the car door. She turns round and sees him, Sean, walking towards her, waving her down as if she was about to leave. He wears a blue water-proof jacket open and, shorn of his plaid shirt, he seems like a movie-star the paparazzi have caught dressed-down on the way to the shops, handsome still but less lustrous somehow.

'Naomi, I'm sorry,' he says, still metres from her.

'What for?' she says, smiling her most casual smile.

'I wanted to come by.' He stands in front of her, scratches his beard, pockets of shadow gliding between the muscles of his neck. 'Didn't want you to think I was rude.'

'Don't be silly.'

'My phone's on the blink, won't let me send texts or make calls sometimes.' She shakes her head to tell him not to worry. 'I couldn't have you thinking I was ignoring you.'

'It's honestly fine,' she says, winding the cord of her mac around her fist. 'How's Greg?'

He gives a bitter laugh. 'Greg's fine.' Something's troubling him and the way he leans on the word 'Greg' says that her suspicions about his situation might be right: he's separated from Greg's mum and they must have been fighting over childcare arrangements. He shifts his weight, his body seems unsure, caught between leaving and staying. She wants to ask him what's happened but she can't think how to do it without crossing a line into a circle of familiarity she knows she shouldn't enter. He looks at her, a penetrating stare into her eyes before looking away again. He shakes his head, a smile straining on to his lips.

'I shouldn't have come. Stupid. Stupid.'

'It's nice to see you.'

'My head's all over the place at the moment.' That look again, pained, like a child who's lost his most precious toy. He's close to her and she feels a wet heat radiating from his T-shirt. He turns away, hangs an arm on the top of her car and looks out towards the bleak angles of a disused petrol station, the sky, monochromatic grey behind acres of railings; he shakes his head.

Naomi flattens herself on to Prue's window to obscure her view of them. There's something coiled in Sean as he twists his body away from where she's standing, forcing himself not to look at her, that tells her exactly what he's going to say next and, she hates herself for it, but she wants to hear it.

'I shouldn't have come today, but I wanted to see you.' He glances at her for a split second before turning back to the petrol station, the railings and the middle distance. His meaning is clear. Naomi feels the blood flowing into her cheeks. She rubs her thumbnail with the pad of her other thumb. Her thoughts get lost in a thick fog. She's married. He knows she's married.

'Prue needs to nap.'

'I shouldn't have said that.'

'We need to get back.'

'Shouldn't have said it. Shit!' He shakes his head, furious with himself. He begins to wheel away from the car.

Her hand is on his arm. It's meant to be conciliatory. It's meant to be the mother calming the troubled boy, but he turns towards her and, looking up at his huge frame facing her down, she's suddenly a tiny animal stunned by headlights on a country road. She withdraws her hand and kneads the fleshy part of her palm, as if treating an ache. Prue's making a 'ba, ba, ba' noise in the car. Sean looks down at the crusts of tarmac for a moment.

'I take Greg to a swimming class at Tivoli Leisure Centre at five fifteen on Fridays.' He speaks quickly, clearly and without feeling.

'Tomorrow?'

'Tomorrow.' His quarry-green eyes are now fixed on hers. She flicks away and sees brick chimneys, long unused, standing darker than the dark sky beyond the clapped-out petrol station and all those railings. She blinks several times.

'Prue needs to nap.' Naomi turns a hundred and eighty degrees and walks away from him, the long way round the back of the car, before getting in at the driver's side. In the rear-view mirror Prue chews on Peppa's snout. Her teeth must be hurting her. The outer edge of Sean's fist presses against the passenger-side window and changes colour from pink to white before he moves away. His jaguar gait lopes back to his yellow van. Naomi pounds the button of the radio and 'The Wheels on the Bus' blasts, far too loud, out of the car speakers.

FOURTEEN

Naomi had the same night-time routine for years, involving nothing more than cold water on her face, an electric toothbrush and some toothpaste. But last Christmas, Charlie's mum, Jackie, bought her a selection of creams and lotions. Expensive brands. She knows they must be expensive because she's never heard of any of them. She rubs a dollop of clay-thick night cream into her skin. Naomi doesn't really believe in the almighty power of Jackie's toiletries, but she also has a deep-seated fear, which she knows is stupid, of waking up one morning in her forties with a face like cracked meringue, so she tries to use them when she remembers. She leans over the sink to get closer to the mirror and stretches her mouth to try to flatten out some of the creases around her eyes. When the lines remain she does it manually, fingers pulling the flesh taut.

Naomi came home after the soft play and Prue slept well, giving her a merciful hour and a half to get the house back into shape and research what taps they were going to have in the spare bathroom.

'Ah, fuck!' A sharp pain in her back makes her stand up straight.

'What's happened now?' Charlie says, wandering into the room. He moves past her and the air around him rides over her like wind-arrows on a weather map.

'My back's hurting again.' She waits for him to respond but he's in their walk-in wardrobe, his belt buckle clatters to the floor.

She thinks of Sean in the car park, the nervous energy steaming off him. He can't have known what he was saying. He said his head was all over the place and that's understandable. She can't imagine having to tussle over Prue and childcare arrangements with a partner she can't stand. That's not strictly true. She has imagined it. When they had to pull out of buying her dream house she thought about leaving Charlie. She took Prue home to her parents' house and thought rigorously about it. He had failed her, lied to her, showed the sort of cowardice that questions whether he could ever be trusted to do what's needed for his family. He'd even suggested it, telling her during a blazing row that she should leave him because he'd never be the man she wanted him to be. She made an exhaustive list of pros and cons, which, if it had been the deciding factor, leant towards her breaking up their family. But she knew she'd never do it. The life she imagined for herself was always very conventional, one husband and father of her children, one marriage she would struggle and fight with all of her considerable will to uphold. She had never given up on anything. And she still loved Charlie. She still loves him, she corrects the thought as quickly as she has it.

He reaches across her and grabs the toothpaste. The mirror covers his sink as well but he chooses not to use it, staring at the plughole as he brushes mechanically.

'My back's playing up again.'

'Ugrghm.' His mouth froths. It's the sound you'd make to a crying child if you didn't know whose it was. A dot of sympathy but not enough to encourage any more histrionics.

She swishes her navy dressing gown back on Charlie's side revealing the lower portion of her midriff, her bum and her legs. She begins to rub just above the right side of her bottom, kneading her thumb into the hollow above her pelvis. She winces with the pain and checks the mirror for his reaction. Nothing. His face still down, mouth rabid with toothpaste. Her hand eases the dressing gown further open and she reaches for the middle of her back, left hand now holding the unit for support. She sees her body in the mirror. She has good boobs still, despite fourteen months of breastfeeding. Her nipples are darker and more prominent than before but if anything that makes them look better. Her stomach is flat. Completely flat. No petty overhang of extra flesh that many new mothers have to grow used to. The curve of her hip is thicker than before but it still goes in one clean line and her skin looks vital. She's attractive. Charlie should see that. It should be enough for him to take her hand with his and rub hard and deep, with strong thumbs, into the small of her back and to take her pain away. For him to wrap his arm around her midriff and pull her into the hollow of his body and breathe her into him and hold there, one body, enclosed together.

He spits a mess of whiteness into the sink, sloshes water into his mouth from a cupped hand and puts his toothbrush back in the ceramic cup that was the one surviving product of a pottery course he'd bought her three years ago.

'I said you needed to see someone about it.' He walks over to their bed, his body flinching in a shiver, and pulls back the duck-egg duvet. She shrugs the rest of her dressing gown off and stands in front of him, naked, arms by her side, entirely open. He looks at her and blinks, before getting into bed. Something inside her crumbles.

Charlie leans over to his bedside table and grabs his phone. He reads something on it and the outer edges of his lips shift into the beginnings of a smile. It will be the WhatsApp group he has with his schoolmates. They often send him 'funny' pictures that make his face light up far more than when his own daughter does something delightful. Is that what he's smiling at? She can't tell. She thinks of his rodent shock when she walked into his study yesterday, interrupting him doing whatever he was doing that he was so ashamed of. Her head feels stuffed with wet flannels and thoughts can't get to where they're meant to be.

Something creaks. Husband and wife both look up at the ceiling. The house is full of noises, particularly at night. Charlie looks at her and registers the anxiety etched into her expression. He manages to stop his eyes from raising to heaven but she sees what he thinks of her reaction before he returns to his phone. The draught excluder downstairs whistles. She can't get used to how the hundred-year-old house murmurs when the sea-wind lashes at it. It frightens her and her husband thinks that makes her ridiculous.

She moves gingerly across the rug. The pain in her back not as bad as her walk would suggest but, as she folds into their oak bed, it twinges harshly. She sucks a sharp breath through pursed teeth, voicing her pain. Charlie sits up, puts his phone on the bedside table and turns his body towards her. He settles himself deeper into his pillow, his lukewarm breath disturbing the hair at the back of her neck. She waits, her fingernails lightly run across her hip. If he offers kindness now, he could save them.

'Why haven't you been to see someone yet? It's just not going to get better on its own, is it?'

She clutches her legs up to her and shifts herself as far away from him as the bed will allow.

'It isn't, though? If you won't do anything about it, it'll always give you trouble.' She switches off the table lamp perched on a reinforced cardboard box and the room goes dark. Charlie ruffles the duvet and settles himself into bed.

FIFTEEN

What Charlie thinks makes a good husband:

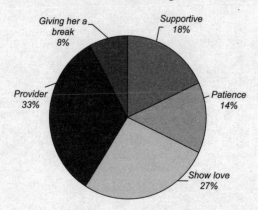

Aims	Now (0–10)	Target (0–10)
Supportive: when faced with concerns or problems don't dismiss or undermine but try to understand and support. Go the extra mile to go along with her plans etc.	2	7
Show love: show Naomi I love her with spontaneity. I.e. date nights, presents. Make her feel loved.	4	8

Aims	Now (0–10)	Target (0–10)
Patience: be patient. Sometimes just suck it up when she shouts at me.	3	6
Provider: providing for my family. Giving them the life that they deserve.	1	7
Giving her a break: taking Prue and giving her time to do things she wants to do.	5	7

SIXTEEN

Naomi sits in the converted warehouse across an old work-bench from Matilda and Victoria and bites her bottom lip. It's quarter past four and Naomi has been listening to the two ladies discuss the agenda she drew up for the last hour and a half. If she had been at her old work this meeting would have taken three minutes. Naomi has her and Prue's swimming gear in a bag-for-life on the back seat of the Nissan, just in case Prue wants to go to the class, but at this rate they'll miss it anyway.

Matilda has the Cox-apple cheeks that many ladies of a solid stature seem to possess. She's Kent born and bred and Naomi's fairly sure that she voted 'leave' in the referendum so she's always assiduously avoided talking about Brexit around the office. She's the more ineffective of the two ladies that set up the Kent Arts Biennale, but also the warmer.

Victoria is tricky. She seems the archetypal benevolent rich lady who supports the arts. Her hair is a silvery grey that she pulls back and holds up with some implement she's supposedly found lying around: a pencil, a paintbrush, sometimes a pair of chopsticks. She has the girlish comportment of a dancer and her eyes constantly swell with wonder at the little details of the world around her. But she feels threatened by Naomi and finds it hard to handle the ease with which she's solved the various issues that have cropped up over the last three months. All three women know that in the flexible twenty hours that Naomi is there, about ninety per cent of the work is done. Which creates a difficult dynamic when you are the only 'employee' in the team – Victoria and Matilda are on expenses only, of course. But if you choose to give a job setting up a local arts festival to someone who led the team that analysed and restructured the efficiency of every Sainsbury's supermarket in the country you are going to get someone who's pretty bloody effective.

Matilda is wittering on still about the artists' accommodation list. Naomi half listens, one eye on the cheap plastic clock that sits above the rudimentary kitchen area. She scratches at an ancient globule of dried paint on the workbench. The clock's minute hand creeps forward so slowly she wonders whether it needs a new battery. Victoria gives her a dimpled smile that seems to question whether she's giving Matilda her due attention.

It's four thirty-five; she has to get Prue at five. If they're going to the swimming class she'll need to pick her up a bit earlier. The after-work traffic can be very unpredictable. They're not going to make it.

'Do you want me to have a look at it for you, Matilda?' Naomi interrupts, barely hiding the impatience in her voice. Matilda wants to bite her hand off but she always waits for Victoria to speak first.

'Ahh,' the sound seems to go on for days, 'we were meant to get this out to the artists first thing Monday, Naomi.' Victoria bats her eyelids in a manner she should have grown out of.

'That's fine.'

'You'd have to do it over the weekend.'

'Honestly, not a problem.' She tosses the words away, covering up her desperation to get out of the room.

'It would be *such* a help.' Matilda's learnt to play politics and greedily seizes her opportunity to hand off the work. Naomi makes a mental note to always ask Matilda if there's anything she needs help with before they have one of their weekly staff 'get-togethers'.

'If you're sure, darling.' Victoria calls her darling.

'Not a problem.'

'Wonderful.' Victoria's interlocked fingers explode open and lower gracefully to the work surface. And with that, Naomi grabs the sheaf of papers from Matilda, stuffs them into her oversized tan leather handbag, goes around the workbench to air kiss the two ladies goodbye and heads out. It's four forty. She might still make it to the pool.

SEVENTEEN

Ipswich Town have just beaten Barcelona in the European Champions League final. Three–one. Kasper Dolberg got two and Raheem Sterling got the other. A forty-year-old Lionel Messi scored their consolation goal. Which is a bit unrealistic. Charlie stood up from his laptop at the final whistle and pumped his fist in delight.

Now he finds himself leaning on the back of his office chair looking out of the window at the sea. It's overcast as purgatory and the waves are bearded with angry white crests. No one thought it would be clear turquoise water and spotless white sand on the 'Kent Riviera' but he had never thought about how, for more than half the year, the weather would be so unremittingly furious. Charlie's just reached the zenith of football management simulations. Taking a lower league team to the dizzy heights of European domination. Masterminding his beloved Tractor Boys' ascent to a pinnacle that he would never see in real life. One of the guys he plays football with on a Wednesday night, Salinger, who plays Soccer Manager, has already messaged him and called it a 'miracle', hailed Charlie as the 'next Guardiola'. There's a half-drunk cup of tea on the desk. It stands in the shadow of a sheaf of documents and brochures and notes that are in desperate need of filing. To the right of these there's a picture in a grey frame of Prue and Naomi at their friend Alli's birthday party in an East London pub garden. Naomi and Prue are looking into each other's faces laughing, patchwork bunting hanging behind them.

Charlie's just won the Champions League. He should be delighted. He turns away from the family photo, from the computer screen that celebrates his virtual glory with virtual ticker-tape, and presses his knuckle into his temple until the pain goes from being pleasant to unpleasant and then he stops. Ever since Prue was born he does things like this all the time when he's on his own. Banging his hand on walls. Gently headbutting doorframes. Once, being unable to work out the best shape for the front panel of the headset he was working on, he went down on all fours and banged his hand on the floor like Charlton Heston at the end of *Planet of the Apes*. That time, after he stood up, he smiled at how ludicrous it was but mostly he didn't see the funny side of this behaviour, the sort of thing that as a cocksure twenty-five-year-old with the world in front of him he could never have contemplated himself doing. The pressure to provide money, to provide the life Naomi wants, to be a good father, a good friend, someone who leaves a great legacy in the world, to be famous – he always thought he would be famous, he even has a list on his phone of potential songs for *Desert Island Discs* – he finds all that pressure paralysing. Amy talks about the spiral of 'automatic negative thoughts' that drive depressive thinking.

His alternative to sinking into the quicksand of negativity is escapism. He's played eight seasons of Soccer Manager in three weeks. He calculated he'd spent fourteen seven-hour working days playing; the newest version only came out a month ago so fourteen of the last twenty working days have been wasted on fiddling with a multicoloured football database.

Once Naomi discovered they couldn't afford to buy the house they'd offered on she was distraught and took it out on him. Months filled with lightning bolts of fury over small and unconnected things that were supercharged by the over-arching knowledge that he had destroyed the happy ending that that specific house had come to represent for her. After her anger cooled she closed herself to him, distanced herself like he was toxic, an albatross she wanted slung off her neck.

It was an amazing house. Five bedrooms; panoramic sea views; huge, manicured garden; the interior done by a designer she follows on Instagram. She sent pictures of it to her friends, the friends she thought judged them for trying to leave London and disrupting their shared metropolitan utopia. She showed her parents, his parents.

Once it was all out in the open and the house was out of their reach, they made a decision. There weren't many other places for sale on the seafront and that was a deal-breaker for Naomi so he suggested they buy the only other one that was on the market at the time despite it needing a lot of work, and, with it being so much cheaper, she would pump some of the money left over from the sale of her flat into his business, Illumin8, to get things going again. He'd had some bad luck but he had two clients on the hook that wanted him to build products for major release. He needed about forty thousand to get things back on an even keel and, based upon the forecasts for the next two years, he convinced her that it was what was for the best thing for them as a family.

He grasps the back of his office chair and stares at the floor. Then he throws it on to the carpet and stamps on the fabric of the seat-back until he hears the plastic casing crack.

Three weeks ago the client who was interested in the smartphone steadicam he'd been working on said that, due to lack of progress, they were taking their investment elsewhere. In the stack of disarrayed papers that look down on him as he kneels on the floor and collects the shards of black plastic, tears pooling in the dark bags under his eyes, there are several letters from his company's bank.

EIGHTEEN

Naomi bursts through the door into the pool area that's somehow even hotter than the changing room where she's just wrestled Prue into her neoprene anti-pooing-in-the-water shorts. There was traffic and the class has already started. Red light emanates from the pool, giving the room a cloying intimacy. Six figures are silhouetted against the luminous water. And he is one of them, standing a foot higher than the others. As her eyes adjust she makes out three other dads, a mum and a female instructor.

The instructor, a gangly woman with a leisure centre T-shirt stuck to her chest, black hair pulled back tightly, paddles her hands forward to the side of the pool where Naomi stands holding Prue high in her arms, their cheeks pressing.

'You've only missed the warm-up,' she shouts, causing all the adult participants to wheel round and gawk at the latecomer. 'I'm Leonie. Who's this?' she says as she reaches them. She has the sing-song timbre of a woman who spends most of her time talking to children.

'Prue.'

'Mum, do you want to just pop Prue on the side?' Naomi tries to drag her daughter from her shoulders but she clings on and Naomi feels the warmth of embarrassment at the back of her head. She looks towards Sean for support but he's looking the other way. She still hasn't seen his face, it unsettles her. She prises Prue's fingers off her shoulder and puts her on the side of the pool. The sensation of the water on her chubby legs seems to distract her from the fact that a stranger is now holding her by the hips, making big eyes and baby noises at her. Prue doesn't like adults who try too hard. She idolises her Grandpa Ray despite him spending most of his time watching various types of car race on television.

'Now if you want to pop yourself in, Mum.' Something about the way she says mum seems intentionally belittling. Naomi slides herself into the water, feeling as graceful as an elephant seal. The pool lights are blinding, the water too hot, the harsh smell of too much chlorine.

'If you just hold on to Prue's hips and encourage her to pop herself over the side, Mum.' Feeling a glare of impatience from the other parents, Naomi yanks Prue into the water and takes her place between two dads holding pale blobs of baby much younger than Prue, whose heads seem as if they could topple off into the deep at any moment. One of the dads, ginger hair cropped close to his head with a matching chest-rug, smiles at her eagerly before his eyes dot her breasts. She looks to Sean on the far right of the circle, he has one hand on the back of his head, bicep tensed into a ball, and he's staring at her. He holds her gaze, a secret acknowledgement, before turning his attention back to Leonie as she explains the next exercise.

He's less hairy than she had imagined, less rugged. His muscles are sculpted, more of the gym than the building site, but the perfection of his form is almost comical in comparison with the other men in the pool. The other dads aren't fat but there's something slack about them. Excess flesh folds on their chests and under their arms like squeezed-out teabags.

72

Naomi realises that everyone else is singing and swishing their child backwards and forwards and she joins them, trying to copy the moves.

Naomi muddles through the rest of class, spending a lot of time staring at the tiny ginger baby. Now that Prue is such an opinionated little monkey it's impossible to think of her as being that useless, but she was once. Naomi wants it again. She wants the utter dependency of the newborn that only wants its mother, that only feels safe next to her skin and never calls for 'Daddy'.

But there are snatched glances with Sean from across the pool as well. He tips an eyebrow in her direction when Leonie demonstrates an exercise on a doll with a grotesquely large head and they challenge each other not to smile when a tiny baby is congratulated for their 'great swimming' by their dad despite having no control of their limbs. As the class progresses, the looks multiply but the humour drops out of Sean's eyes. It does something to Naomi. She's back at a school dance and the tallest and therefore most handsome boy keeps looking at her from across the room. She gets the same sensation she had then, a fluttering of excitement quickly crushed by shame. She is a mother and a wife.

'We've got time for one more activity, mums and dads. We're going to see if baby wants to go under the water!' Prue's never had her head underwater. Sean, at the front of the hastily formed queue, hands Greg over to Leonie and, after he parrots Leonie's mantra, 'Ready, Greg, Go', she dunks the boy's head under. Sean counts 'one–two–three' and lifts him calmly out of the water. Greg blinks in surprise but there are no tears.

'Well done, Greg!' Leonie bellows. 'Take a toy from the box.' The three dads and the other mum, deep bags under each eye explaining why she hasn't made any effort to engage with her classmates, all take their turns with varying success. Ginger and his very young baby are in front of Naomi and Prue in the queue and as the dad yanks baby out of the water it coughs and spits up water to which Leonie laughs and says, 'Ah, bless.'

Naomi takes Prue up into her arms and wants to flee the pool as if she's seen a dorsal fin. She doesn't want to duck her daughter under the water. She's made a risk assessment and she can't see there's anything to be gained. Leonie thrusts her hands out to receive Prue.

'She's had a bit of a cold,' Naomi tells the teacher.

'That's totally fine.'

'Maybe she can try it next time.'

'Come on, Prue.' Prue extends her hands towards Leonie. Judas, Naomi thinks.

'Ready, Mum?' Leonie squawks.

'Mm-hm.'

'You say, "Ready, Prue."'

'Ready, Prue, Go,' Naomi says too fast. Leonie thrusts Prue under the water. Naomi's on fire, the temperature of the water, the closeness of the air, shame that mingles with the sweat gathering on her top lip. Panic boils through her veins. She thrusts her hands under the water and wrenches Prue up out of it. She's coughing, spluttering and, unlike the ginger baby, she doesn't stop. Naomi's never heard a sound like it, guttural, waterlogged. Leonie turns Prue over and gives her three firm slaps on the back. Prue spits up pool-water and takes a huge breath in before wailing once and then hugging into Naomi.

'You're meant to count to three and then just ease her out of the water,' Leonie says.

'I–I'm sorry.'

'You shocked her.'

'Sorry.'

'You weren't listening when I explained the activity.' Leonie, a shadow backlit by the red pool lights, seems now just a voice, Naomi's conscience.

'She said she didn't want her to do it.' He's there, Sean, looming out of the water next to Leonie, Greg slung over his forearm.

'What?' Leonie says, trying to catch up.

'If someone doesn't feel safe with one of your activities then you should listen to them.' His voice is calm, non-combative. The water ripples aurora borealis along his blond beard.

'I didn't say she—'

'You should apologise.'

''Scuse me?'

'You upset this lady and her daughter and you should apologise.'

Leonie unsticks her T-shirt from her stomach, looking down at the water, cowed by the forcefulness of his argument.

'Prue's fine, no harm done,' Naomi offers from the surface of the pool. Sean looks as if he's about to push the matter but, glancing at Naomi, he stops himself.

'Is she OK, yeah?' Leonie comes down to Naomi's level. 'You did really well today, Prue. Really hope we'll see you next week, yeah?' She raises all her fingers out of the water like someone taking the blame and Naomi nods her accept-ance. Leonie splashes off to collect the floating toys that have been left by the other parents who leave the pool one by one.

Naomi wants to thank Sean but she doesn't. Acting like they didn't know each other seemed appropriate at first, but now, as she scoops Prue out of the water and heads over to the stairs out of the pool, this unspoken complicity begins to disturb her. She knew this class wasn't just a handy tip from one parent to another. He hadn't been able to look at her when he invited her. But nothing could happen between them. Sean wrestles a purple watering can from Greg and lifts him up the stairs and towards the changing room. The boy stares over his father's shoulder at Naomi and Prue. There's recognition in his eyes. They can't pretend to everyone.

'If you don't let me put your clothes on, we can't go home and if we don't go home you can't have any yoghurt.' Naomi tries to reason with Prue but to no avail. Running around naked and splashing in changing-room puddles, stagnant with the cells of strangers' feet, her little girl is having more fun now than she's had all week. She imagines the measured Greg has dressed himself, probably in a three-piece suit, and that he and Sean will be all ready to leave. Will he wait for her?

Naomi folds her arms and adopts a stand-off position with Prue. She's still in her swimming costume. She can't imagine ever wanting to put her tights and jumper back on, such is the ambient heat. But she shouldn't rush. If she stays in here then Sean will have no choice but to leave and that would end it. The next time they saw each other the whole thing would be diffused. He'd know. He'd understand because he's not stupid. He's sensitive. What he did in the swimming pool, what he did for her in the swimming pool, it was extraordinary. Totally unnecessary, which makes it one of the greatest shows of care she has ever witnessed, let alone been the subject of.

She picks Prue up in her arms and, holding her lower half tightly into her body so she can't squirm away, forces her vest on. Prue bats at Naomi's face with her wrist but she grabs it and holds it firm. She yanks a pair of leggings up over Prue's bottom and places her down on her towel. They both know Naomi's won so Prue accedes to having her socks and jumper put on, but the struggle has left Naomi sweating. She feels it under her eyes, pooling in her swimming costume at the base of her spine. She opens the cubicle and Prue toddles out towards some mirrors, Naomi follows and there he is, bent over a travel cot, running a comb through Greg's hair. Everyone else seems to have left. He wears a grey T-shirt and a pair of dark jeans but remains shoeless.

'You want to put Prue in here? I'll watch them while you have a shower?' he says as if he was a girl friend of hers or her brother.

'That'd be great.' She wanders over to where they are and plonks Prue down next to Greg. Sean and Naomi watch them for a moment. With Prue's wild bird's-nest hair and Greg's hair slicked back, both standing in opposite corners of the mesh cot, they look like opposing gang members in the exercise yard of some toddler prison. Naomi looks at Sean looking down on them, his face ruddy with the heat.

'Thanks for this,' she says before making her way towards the showers. In the cubicle, she presses the button on the wall and lets a weak spray of warm water hit the stem of her neck and run down her back. She closes her eyes and stands for a moment, the chlorine and sweat running off her into the mildewed drain below.

Then he's there. Her eyes remain closed but she can feel his shadow on her face. Naomi turns back towards the wall, let's the water run into her hair and over her face. If she keeps her eyes closed, keeps her back to him, he'll walk away.

She massages her wet hair, hands working into her scalp as if they can pierce her skull and rip out her brain and end all of this insanity because in this moment she wants him more than she's ever wanted anyone. More than she ever wanted Charlie. She opens her eyes and turns to see him standing in the doorframe, topless, blocking the light. She was sure she'd locked it but she couldn't be sure, perhaps she hadn't.

'Tell me to go,' he says softly.

'What?'

'Tell me to go and I'll go.' She steps forward so the water runs down around her neck, she brushes her fringe out of her eyes.

They look at each other for what seems like months before one of them moves imperceptibly towards the other, it could have been him. Then the door is closed, he lifts her up high on to his hips, his belt clangs to the floor; he's kissing her and her legs entwine slowly around his lower back. Then everything accelerates. He pushes her up against the wall of the cubicle and back into the stream of water, her hands grip his neck, fingers wrenching at muscular shoulders, hanging on for her life. Digging in to try to hold on to everything she's ever believed in as she throws it all away. And then he's pulling her swimming costume aside and he's inside her. She looks straight into his eyes and he seems so, so happy. His mouth is on her neck, he thrusts into her, her back sliding up the cold tiles, her legs tingle with the force of him as she stares at the cracked ceiling tiles halfway between ecstasy and horror. Then he shudders and it's over.

NINETEEN

Naomi parks the Nissan on the other side of the road from their house. There are spaces right by the front garden but they'd all involve a parallel park and she can't face it. Prue is babbling her own version of 'Twinkle, Twinkle, Little Star' as she has been since they left the swimming pool. Her singing's never irritated Naomi before but for the last eleven minutes she hasn't been able to stand it. As she steps out of the car the cold soaks her still-wet hair and it's like someone has put ice down her back. She feels as if several layers of skin have been removed and her nerve endings stand open on the surface and, like pores, they are filling with the world's various toxins. Exposed. She feels incredibly exposed.

She sees two dark figures standing in her front garden. One large, one small. A car flies past, inches away, and forces her back into the half-open car door. She looks at Prue who has started to paw at the car seat's restraint, before looking back to the two figures. They definitely are in her garden. She squints at them, trying to make out what the hell they're doing there, but the sea haze reflects off the halogen orange of the streetlights and she can't make anything out. One large man, one small. She gets her phone out. She feels calmer than she thinks she would have been an hour before. Is she about to call the police? It can't be Sean. Unless. Unless Sean is talking to Charlie. She should phone Charlie. Of course that's who she should phone.

The smaller man is Charlie. She sees the slight hunch he's developed, as if his shoulders are embarrassed by his chest; it's definitely him. But Charlie's not short and, next to the other man, he seems tiny. Charlie waves to her over his shoulder and, as he and the larger man turn towards her, she sees they're both carrying guns. Her throat closes. But it's Charlie. Her Charlie. Her Charlie who she has just betrayed.

She locks the car, gives Prue a tight-lipped smile and crosses the road. As she gets to the other side she sees the bigger man isn't Sean, it's one of the builders. The carpenter that's always singing. The one who has the end of a bullet as an ear stud. She hadn't mistaken the guns, both men point guns at the floor of her front garden. She tries to suck air in and calm her chest, beating like a bird trapped in too small a cage.

'What's going on?' She smiles.

'Lenny's helping me with the pigeons.'

'You're killing pigeons?' She tries to keep the incredulity out of her voice.

'Only way to get rid of them,' Lenny chips in.

'I just need to get Prue from the car.' She lasers Charlie a look that orders him to come with her. As she re-crosses the street she feels the familiar anger rise within her, the anger bred by his total inability to think about the consequences of anything he does, his inability to consider that him having to clean a bit of pigeon-crap off their front steps once a week might be preferable to murdering animals in front of their not-even-two year old, but the rage is quickly dampened by the aching guilt swimming around her solar plexus.

She leans against the front of the car, the bonnet's droplets of water soaking into the sleeves of her shirt, and she feels Sean, the memory of Sean's body against hers. She pictures the fabric of her swimming costume being wrenched aside, the black one-piece swimming costume that she bought six months after Prue was born because mothers don't wear skimpy bikinis designed to arouse a potential new mate, mothers wear something called a swimming costume because they're just meant to go swimming and go home. After he went, she rinsed the one-piece in the shower, held it under her chin and stood under the weak spray for as long as she felt she could leave Prue alone in the travel cot.

'Nay?' Charlie's voice and she's aware that he's talking to her. 'I thought we could go out?' he says. She turns to him and arches her eyebrows with fabricated warmth at his question. 'To the cinema.'

'When?'

'Tonight? Lenny says his niece could babysit.' Charlie has taken Prue out of the car and the little girl glances at her mother before nestling into her daddy's neck to shelter herself from the cold mist. Naomi pictures her black swimming costume and Prue's swim shorts, pink and decorated with yellow palm trees, entwined together, sopping in the plastic carrier bag in the footwell of the Nissan's passenger seat. The blood drains from her face, she turns her head away from her husband and daughter. A tiny bit of sick comes up into her mouth and she swallows it back.

TWENTY

Her foot slips out from under the duvet and reaches towards the floor, the edge of the bed pressing into her calf. The floorboards are warmer than the air in the bedroom. It's five fifteen. The heating comes on at six. The top part of her body longs to remain in the warmth but she can't lie there for another moment. Charlie breathes heavily next to her.

Last night he'd been nice to her and she couldn't bear it. He said that they could go out some night next week instead if she's not feeling up to it. Said he'd not do anything to the pigeons while Prue was around the house, that he'd leave it entirely if she wanted him to. He insisted on doing bedtime and told Naomi to sit and watch that Netflix thing about sex trafficking she'd been talking about. She didn't think he'd been listening when she told him about it.

Normally she loved being involved in Prue's bedtime but last night she was relieved she didn't have to. She knew her daughter couldn't really be judging her, but she has Naomi's eyes, everyone says so, and after the pool they felt more coruscating than an inquisitor's spotlight. Charlie sounding delighted as he sang songs to Prue before he put her down twisted the knife further.

Her body follows her leg out of the bed and she tiptoes out of the bedroom, across the hall and into the main bathroom, a room smeared with the browns and oranges of a seventies

82

refurbishment. The whole aberration needs to be ripped out and never seen again. She has to wash the dry tackiness of spit from her lips and her tongue. She can feel her sinuses clogged with the dust of their crumbling home.

She flicks on the tap and laps at the water like a dog and, realising how thirsty she is, puts her mouth over the opening so she has to swallow quickly to stop herself choking. She pulls away and, lips dripping water back into the milk-chocolate-coloured sink, she looks up and sees herself in the mirror. A long-lost acquaintance stares back at her through the dark spots of rust at the back of the glass. She wants to say hello to the unfamiliar face. There's vitality behind her eyes, the creases of anxiety seem to have smoothed in the dim light of the morning. It's the woman she used to be. She had a lover yesterday. The man huffing in her bed across the hall hasn't been a lover to her for nearly two years, perhaps longer. She deserves to be loved.

Deserves. What a ridiculous concept, she thinks. No one gets what they deserve; what does it even mean? She wants to smash the mirror and use one of the shards to cut the smug face off her skull.

Prue cries out. Naomi waits to hear if Charlie will stir. He doesn't. Dawn begins to show itself through the stained-glass window at the far end of the bathroom. She faces herself in the mirror and the person looking back knows that she has no choice but to pretend that what she did yesterday didn't happen. If she tells Charlie their family will fall apart. So she has to pretend to her husband but more importantly she has to pretend to herself. If she torments herself, if she destroys herself with guilt, then Prue will be damaged by it too and she cannot let that happen. Naomi sucks air through the tiny gap between her top teeth. She will wipe the slate clean. Providing a stable family for Prue is the only thing she has to absolutely ensure happens. Everything else, her, Charlie, Sean, gentrification, international terrorism, longing, desire, everything else is meaningless.

She goes down to the first-floor landing and hears Prue babbling to her cuddly toys. She's so lucky to have this resourceful, independent, beautiful little girl who, when no one comes for her, makes her own diversion with her teddy bears.

Naomi looks downstairs and sees the front door standing half-open. The morning light burgeons through the mist that still swamps the street outside. She's stunned for a moment. Charlie was still snoring as she passed the room so it can't be him. Is someone in the house?

She walks down a couple of steps and sees Charlie's huge bunch of keys still hanging from the lock on the outside of the door. As she bounds down to the hallway, she feels the familiar rush of anger at his carelessness that has become so commonplace she's started to think he must be doing it on purpose. She plucks Charlie's keys out of the lock and slams the door, shoving her back against it as if it was the mist that broke into their home rather than her husband leaving the door ajar after he put the bins out last night. She stands there, back against the hard surface, just as it was against the tiles in the shower cubicle.

Prue, having heard the sound of the door, begins to call out for her mummy. As Naomi heads back up the stairs she tells herself out loud, 'Everything else is meaningless.'

TWENTY-ONE

Thursday 05:22

Hi Sean. Prue and I are going to
Sing, Sign and Movement at
Ladybird's Landing (the soft play on
Althorpe Road) at 10 a.m.
if you and Greg fancy it?
No worries either way.

Saturday 09:19

Yesterday shouldn't have happened.
It was a mistake. I'm so sorry.

Saturday 23:14

Did you get my message?

Sunday 03:47

I understand. I won't make
things difficult. Don't worry xx

THE FIRST TRIMESTER

ONE

As her feet pound the concrete of the promenade she can't believe what the people she passes are wearing. A lady in a thin jumper. A small boy in shorts. A wide man in a check shirt with red braces. Some sort of native style choice she doesn't understand. It's four degrees and her weather app said that, with the onshore wind from the sea, there's a 'RealFeel' temperature of minus two. British people constantly bore on about the weather but seem to have absolutely no understanding of it. It's all linked to their superiority, she thinks. They believe the elements will respect them and give them an easy ride because they're the world's chosen people. In Vilnius people don't need to talk about the weather because they put the appropriate clothes on in the morning.

Uggy, born Ugne but no one here can pronounce it, can feel her heart pounding through her skin-tight thermal vest. She doesn't sweat much but she can see her high body temperature in the dense puffs of vapour in every breath. She's been running hard for fifty-five minutes. Her short, dyed-blonde hair, parted in the centre, bounces as she runs, reminding her she needs a haircut. She'd like to shave it all off but she's having enough problems at work as it is. She's worked at the Bank of Friendship Nursery School for over a year and is now convinced that whoever named it must have been making a joke. She certainly hasn't found it friendly. But nor has she found Great Britain to be all that great.

She was called into the office earlier by the manager, Lisa, the woman who gave her the job and seemed keen to nurture her ambitions to work her way up from junior nursery nurse to room supervisor and beyond. Lisa had a face like she'd eaten weeks-old sour cream when she told Uggy that one of the parents had requested their child be given a different key worker from her. When Uggy asked why, Lisa reminded her that it wasn't their policy to question the parents when requests were made. She was very sorry and said she knew it didn't reflect on Uggy's caregiving or hard work. No it did fucking not, she thinks.

She notices a smooth, white rock jutting out of the sand too late and clips the top of her right toe on it, her body nearly goes horizontal, but she manages to stay on her feet and within a few strides, arms treading water in the air, she's back to a decent rhythm.

She didn't need to ask Lisa why the request had been made but she did anyway to make a point. When she first started at the job, she knew straight away which parents didn't want her looking after their children. This wasn't the first of these requests, today's was the third she'd received.

The parents at the Bank of Friendship, like the inhabitants of the town in general, fall into two categories. The ones who've lived there all their lives, who wear pretty ugly clothes, and the ones who've moved down in the last few years, who wear pretty nice clothes and whose English was clearer. She knew it wouldn't be one of these 'trendies' who wanted their children taken away from her. They think having Uggy as their child's key worker is fantastic, that it opens up their children to different cultures. One of them, a woman with pink hair cut like a lesbian, actually said that to her a few weeks ago. Because that's how she stops the kids from screaming, by teaching them her mother's recipe for Cepelinai.

She'd like to ask Tani and little CJ if they wanted to have Jess or Sophie as their new key worker. She'd like Tani's parents to watch her hide amongst the cuddly toys in comfy corner before jumping out and making their daughter giggle for ten minutes as she did every day after morning snack time. She'd like CJ's fucking horrible granddad, faded blue tattoos on his neck and face the colour of beetroot soup, to watch how she'd taught his grandson to play the drums on the pots and pans, how she'd painstakingly taught him a sense of rhythm one deafening afternoon after another. But Granddad wants CJ to be looked after by Jess, who spends most of the time texting her mates, because she has an accent and hairstyle he can understand.

Uggy's running through the old town now, the sides of her trainers getting caught in the gaps between the cobblestones. Dirty, stone-grey facades with bright snaps of colour from window-boxes blur past as she ups her pace away from the sea towards the rougher part of town. Her quads are burning as she runs up the hill; the finish line in sight spurs her on to almost sprint.

She stops on the other side of the road from her flat. It's not her flat but it's where she stays now. She's moved out of her place, a studio on the third floor of a four-storey Victorian terraced house that's been converted into thirteen different apartments. The roof was in dire need of repair and a week of heavy rain meant that most of the ceilings were riddled with water damage and at risk of caving in. Elyssa in the flat above hers, a single mum from the Ukraine, had a part of her ceiling fall on her lower leg, fracturing her ankle. It could have been worse, her nine-month-old was in the same room.

Uggy's never seen that point made on the TV amongst all the talk of taking jobs and ruining British values. Who else would pay council tax and landlords to live in places that are totally uninhabitable apart from immigrants? Because there's a third category of person in the town and they wear whatever they can get their hands on. They take a lot of stick and don't complain because they don't feel they have the right. Uggy has never had to swallow so much shit as since she's arrived in England. Nor had it under her fingernails, nor felt its tang in her nostrils after changing thirty, forty nappies a day, and even that isn't good enough for them.

She crosses the road and lets herself into the glass-fronted hallway of the new-build block of flats. It's not perfect, the view of the supermarket car park across the road would be unlikely to be mentioned on an estate agent's profile, but it's quiet and the shower works and the owner isn't here much so she basically has it to herself. She opens the fridge and takes a plastic measuring jug of water out and gulps down about a third of it. She notices that there's some vegetable detritus at the very back of the fridge. She keeps the flat immaculate. Her mother always said that there're so many things in life you can't control you have to put all your energy into keeping on top of the things you can. She also feels obliged to keep the place spotless because she isn't paying any rent. She feels more than obligation, she wants to show her gratitude. To please him. He's the only person who's shown her kindness here.

She met him first in the baby-room. He was quite handsome but came across like a bit of a dick. He never smiled, never laughed at the funny stories that she or any of the other girls would tell him about what the children had been up to during the day. He didn't want to be there at all. He reminded her of some of the men her mother dated back home, arrogant, self-assured, cruel eyes. But then he bumped into her in a café around the corner from her old flat and insisted on buying her a coffee. They talked mainly about the nursery. He agreed that most of her colleagues were morons and that he knew she was different. He said he wanted to see her again. She politely declined. Then one day after work he was waiting for her. They drove to the out-of-town shopping centre together and had sex in the toilets of a Mexican restaurant called Chiquitos.

She gets her box of cleaning products out and starts on the back of the fridge. After Chiquitos they started meeting at this flat and, after about eight weeks, she told him about her housing situation and he said she could stay there. He'd drop in every so often, usually during the day, and they'd spend afternoons together making love. They didn't talk too much and he never stayed.

She sprays the non-toxic kitchen cleaner she bought that smells of rhubarb and thinks how much she'd like him to come into the flat at this precise moment. She's on all fours, lycra stretched across her body, endorphins pumping into her brain, he could pick her up by the waist, sit her on the work surface and do whatever he wanted to her. That was how the sex was and that, she discovered, was how she liked it. She'd done things with him that she never thought she'd do. And he, in turn, seeing how well she responded, became more and more precise in what he wanted.

She closes the fridge, taking one more sniff of the chemical sweetness, and heads towards the shower to wash the salt air out of her hair, and to wash away the shitty thought that the nursery might cut her hours again. And to think of him. Uggy knows she's in love with him. Although there's nothing romantic about the sex they have he always holds her, in silence, afterwards. When she's enveloped in his arms she feels safe, more at home than she's felt since she was a child. And she knows he feels something similar. Most of the time he seems troubled, like there's some chaos in the machinery of his mind, but in those moments, lying together on his bed with its leatherette headboard, something in him stills. He'd never tell her how much he cares for her but he does things for her that say it for him. The sort of things a man should do for a woman. When her landlord put a debt collector on to her he somehow got them to drop it and let her off paying the rent she hadn't paid since she'd moved out. He fixes things in the flat she might mention without telling her, he always makes the drinks if he stays into the late afternoon and turns up sometimes with a takeaway lunch, ordering exactly what she'd choose without having to ask. He kisses her forehead every time he leaves the flat to make sure she knows that she's more to him than a low-rent courtesan.

She strips her clinging clothes off and steeps herself in the cold shower. Always a cold shower after cardio. She knows she shouldn't be in love with him. He's one of her customers and if she loses her job at the Bank of Friendship, and she would lose her job, she'd have to go back home and she's not ready for that yet.

She turns the shower off, grabs a towel and thrusts it into her face, rubbing vigorously, the hard fibres scouring her skin.

No, she shouldn't be in love with Charles. But there are so many things in life you can't control.

TWO

He smears his thumb into the edge of the foil packet to get the last crumbs of pork scratching and pops it on to his tongue. The Albion has been refurbished to try to appeal to the London crowd but they've cut corners. Although the walls have been painted the colour of clay and adorned with ironic magazine covers in Ikea frames, the sticky tartan carpet and faux-wood bar have survived the update so the pub feels confused. The clientele reflects the disparity. A gaggle of regulars for whom drinking seems grim employment, old local couples who stare past each other and wait for their turn to go and have a cigarette and the 'down-from-London' thirty-somethings who spend most of their time telling each other how great the pub is despite only being there because the other places in town terrify them.

The occasional Wednesday night in the pub after football is the extent of Charlie's social life now. When they first moved he was glad to have a fresh start away from his core group of mates. None of them were married, none of them had kids and all of their careers seemed to continue to go from strength to strength as his faltered. His best friend Felix, who he'd known since he started senior school, and who he'd always thought of as being less intelligent, less charismatic than him, was now a barrister and by all accounts on his way to becoming a superstar in criminal law. When he and Felix met up with their wider circle in the pub, Charlie found it impossible not to resent his friend downplaying his successes. He found himself fabricating his own to try to impress whoever they were with, which made him feel both ashamed and fearful of being caught out. So Charlie began to cancel on Felix and ignore his messages, which distanced him from their wider friendship group as single, childless Felix became the fulcrum of it. When Prue was born he had an easy answer to the WhatsApp snipes about how his friends didn't see him any more. 'How are your kids, mate?' he'd always respond.

Sali returns to their table and plants three pints of Guinness on it. He bends himself round a stool, clinks glasses with Charlie and takes a large gulp of his pint. Sali is a mate from football. He thinks he can call them mates now. Sali, Charlie and Tayo always break off from the older lads in the changing room before and after the game to ask after each other's weekends. They laugh a lot, try to outdo each other by taking the piss out of Tayo's hats, Sali's mediocre first touch and Charlie always moaning about how tired he is. He hadn't realised how much he had missed the gambolling bullshit of male conversation he'd left behind with his old group of friends in London. But making friends, cementing new friendships, seems so much harder than it used to be. He's never spent time with Tayo or Sali outside the confines of the football cages or the pub afterwards and Charlie can't move past his feeling that if he were to ask them if they wanted to do something outside Wednesday nights he'd be imposing himself on them in some way. His counsellor, Amy, says this is a symptom of his low self-esteem and has encouraged him to try to overcome it.

'Do you even want another kid?' Sali asks, lip frothing with thick white foam. Before he nipped out for a cigarette, Tayo had been telling them about how young some of the girls pushing buggies along the streets near his house were and how grateful he was that he had such a conventional upbringing – he's trying to actively practise gratefulness. And that, in the way that pub conversations often do, led Charlie to talk about his and Naomi's struggles to conceive for the second time. When he laced up his astro-boots a few hours earlier he didn't anticipate mentioning it at all, but here they were.

'I do, yeah.' Charlie dips his face into his pint. He only has Guinness because that's what Tayo and Sali always drink. He couldn't help but think it tasted a bit like when you licked a cut.

'Because you don't want your little girl to be an only child?'

'We just want,' Charlie stumbles over his words, 'two kids. Feels like a proper family.'

'I don't have any brothers and sisters.' Sali looks at Charlie blankly, neither joking nor challenging.

'I didn't mean—'

'I know, I know, mate; I wish I had a sibling.' He looks at Charlie with a seriousness he's never shown him before. 'It's a good thing you're doing for your kid,' he adds, clapping a hand on Charlie's shoulder before turning to his pint and gulping about a third of it. Charlie smiles, letting his friend's sincerity linger in the air before Sali adds, 'But you'll never get pregnant if you don't want one.'

'My uncle never wanted kids and he had six,' Tayo is back, bringing with him the tarmac tang of cigarettes and a puppyish energy that lightens the mood.

'Na, those swimmers of yours won't do the work properly if the big boss,' Sali taps his index finger on his temple, 'doesn't tell them to.'

'Says the man who treats his swimmers like Kamikaze pilots. Surprised they've not gone on strike.'

'Wish they would, lad. Save me a fortune in johnnies,' Sali retorts, and the two men, both clad in their synthetic football shirts, burst into uproarious laughter, delighted with their own jokes.

In the rotating group of lads who play football, Tayo is seen as the token hipster, tolerated by some of the more conservative players because he's bloody good at football, and Sali is the anointed lothario. He never talks about it but, almost every week, their football lads' WhatsApp group is full of salacious chat about his latest conquest. Charlie's jealous of Sali and Tayo and it's that more than anything that's stopping him from trying to push their friendships further. It's their contentment, their total confidence with the choices they've made and the life they're leading, that he envies. Charlie's life is, by the standards laid down by society, much richer than theirs. A big house by the sea, a wife, a child, a great education, the safety net of family money. Yet he feels, for most of his waking hours, completely adrift. But Sali, a guy that lives from hand to mouth doing up houses for mates and 'a bit of furniture dealing, mid-century stuff', and Tayo, a man who presents three different Internet radio shows, for free, and has an 'Etsy' shop that sells West African-inspired prints he's made, 'about one a month' he'd joked once, both seem to be relentlessly happy.

It was Sali that got Charlie back in to playing Soccer Manager. In the pub Charlie hinted that it had been a tough year work-wise. Sali told him that last year he'd run himself ragged hustling for jobs and it was getting to him so he'd got back into a computer game he used to play as a kid, spent every evening playing it for a month. And during the days he was suddenly chatting away to tradesmen he was working with, he was helping a mate out with a big doer-upper in Herne Bay, and people started offering him jobs, giving him tips about places he could buy old furniture to restore. Charlie wasn't surprised to find out the computer game was Soccer Manager, he didn't know many men of his generation who weren't into it, and when Sali suggested he join an online league, it seemed like he had to say yes. Although Charlie was properly addicted as a teenager and had frequent relapses at university and beyond, often losing whole weeks, he needed something to change. When he first started doing CBT with Amy she asked him what he enjoyed doing for himself and he started crying because he couldn't think of a single thing.

Charlie looks at the two of them, nodding and smiling as they talk about some obscure album Tayo's just bought on vinyl. They erupt into laughter and the joy illuminates The Albion and its greying patrons. Amy says that Charlie's low mood is exacerbated by the guilt he feels at not being happy with what should be a perfect life. That the feeling is compounded by the external negative reinforcement he receives from Naomi. That depression is like a black hole that sucks every positive thought into it and annihilates it. That Charlie has to be active in his own therapy, that he has to seek out positivity, seek out things that make him feel good about himself and boost his self-esteem.

'Do you boys want to come for dinner at ours some time?' Charlie blurts it out, interrupting Tayo in the middle of a detailed description of a cymbal sound. Both men seem taken aback, Charlie's not the sort to derail a conversation in the way confident men do. Sali reacts first, the reassuring paw on his back and a beefy smile.

'Sounds great, lad. I eat everything.'

THREE

Naomi sits on the toilet and pulls her tights and pants down but she can't look. For the last year, these have been the most painful moments. The hours, sometimes days, of blind hope crushed by the taunting spot of scarlet on the sanitary pad that tells her that they've failed again.

She glances down quickly as if over a cliff. The pad is pure white. She takes a sharp breath through her nose, dips her hand into her bag and brings out a pregnancy test still in its box. She unwraps the white stick from its vacuum packing, holds it under her and pees on it. She puts it on a shelf above the sink with the indicator panel facing the wall. Remembering how Charlie messed up their first pregnancy test for Prue by rushing it, she decides to give it double the ninety seconds that the instructions recommend.

She gets her phone out of her handbag and logs into the 'Ovul8' app. She's already looked twice this morning but she needs to see it again. It shows a calendar with the dates of her period logged in red and, based upon that data, the predicted best days to have sex for conception in mint green. The phone tells her that her period is three days late.

She goes back a month in the app. Then another. They didn't use it for Prue but after the first unsuccessful month of trying to get pregnant this time, Naomi downloaded it and for the next six months she was obsessive about updating it. But as time went on, logging the ever-punctual arrival of her period became like torture and she asked Charlie to take responsibility for it. It syncs on to her phone but she only ever checks it to determine when the next window of opportunity will be, to make their preparations and ensure they weren't going to be away from home.

Since the swimming pool she's been looking at it five or six times a day to check that D-Day was D-Day and that what happened – D-Day+2 – had no chance of resulting in a pregnancy. As she goes back five months she sees, again, that it's fine. She has nothing to worry about. Her period has been logged and accounted for every month. This month's D-Day highlighted in green: she can only have been ovulating when she was with Charlie.

There's classical music playing in the open warehouse beyond her toilet cubicle. She realises she's been avoiding going to the toilet at work, avoiding going in a cubicle, knowing that it might remind her of him, but now she's here it's fine. The scab of detachment she's grown over her infidelity seems on the verge of healing over but it's not been easy. She's spent two weeks doing an impression of herself, her normal self. She's had to be as frustrated with Charlie, as enamoured with Prue and as manically motivated with the builders as she was before, when the reality is that she feels almost the opposite. She has no patience with Prue and her growing wilfulness, she doesn't give a shit about the house and she now sees everything about Charlie that's wonderful. But, to a certain extent, the trick's worked. Playing the role of herself, fabricating her own behaviour, has helped her bury the guilt alive, suffocating it and, with time, probably a long time, it will expire. It's given her a new perspective on the moral superiority that's been so ingrained in her by her mother. Naomi didn't know she had such resources of duplicity and if what she'd done hadn't been so abhorrent she might even have been proud of the way she's dealt with her mistake. It was a mistake.

She reaches up for the pregnancy test and pulls it down into her lap, still not looking at the indicator. She knows that it would be Charlie's but, does she want Charlie's now? Does she deserve to have a child with Charlie, with anyone? It wasn't meant to be like this. The baby should have been born by now. All this, the pregnancy test, the excitement, the tiredness and the sickness and the labour and the first few months of sleepless nights, that should all be done now. He or she should be in a sling held against Charlie's chest as they walk along the beach holding hands and Prue runs ahead collecting shells. Charlie should be here, she should be sharing this with him, a team like she'd always insisted they had to be. She hasn't told him she's late. If he looked at the app he'd know. Perhaps he does know but hasn't had the balls to mention it. She turns the stick round in her hand and sees the word 'PREGNANT'.

She pulls her tights back up, untucks her blouse from them and flushes the toilet to maintain the pretence because Victoria is the sort of woman that would somehow smell the hormones and she certainly doesn't want to reveal anything to her. She replaces the cap on the end of the pregnancy test and puts it in a pocket in her bag, which she zips up. She'll tell Charlie tonight.

She marches into the open warehouse and sees Matilda loitering by the kettle. Naomi's certain she's going to, in a roundabout way, ask her to do some of her work for her. And Naomi will do it happily and accept a large piece of the homemade ginger cake that she's baked because she's eating for two. This is what she's been dreaming of her whole life, to have a family, more than one child, a complete family. And this, this news, this wonderful news, has to draw a line under the madness that happened in the changing room. A moment of madness. Sean hasn't texted her again. She hasn't seen him. He must have changed the days he does the pickup to make things easier for her.

Over by the kettle now she nods as Matilda explains how difficult something, somewhere is and bites into a piece of the fiery cake that's been thrust into her hand. She's finally pregnant.

FOUR

23 March 2001

MSN Messenger

(*)ELIZA(*) says:
You OK K? Heard you chucking up in science block bogs?

Then you missed afternoon classes???

KARINP83 says:
Had a dodgy kebab after a gig on Tuesday.

(*)ELIZA(*) says:
You went to gig? Cool

KARINP83 says:
Eels. My dad took me. How was chemistry?!

(*)ELIZA(*) says:
People saying it might have been because of what you did
at Doug Mason's?

You told me you'd been like super tired all the time and now you're throwing up at school. In the morning ... 🙁

KARINP83 says:
Which people?

Did you tell them I said I was tired?

Which people?

Nay TWATterson?

What's that stuck-up bitch been saying????

(*)ELIZA(*) says:
Thought you should know.

Misty's been so cute recently. She keeps sneaking into my bed and I wake up and she's like staring at me. Dog-breath though! 😕

KARINP83 is offline

FIVE

4 weeks

'I thought *The Florida Project*?' Charlie says nonchalantly. He and Naomi stare at the listings above the concession stand at the small cinema that somehow keeps afloat on the high street near their house. There are two other film options: *Geostorm* and *Blade Runner 2049*. Naomi had forgotten that tonight was their postponed cinema date. It was unlike her to forget things but her mind has been elsewhere. Most of her day she's spent considering how she is going to tell Charlie. Should she tell him she's done the test and face down the questioning about why she did it on her own or should she do one with him, as if for the first time, and fake a delighted reaction? But when she arrived home to see a teenage girl – the carpenter's niece – watching *Paw Patrol* with Prue on the sofa she knew she wasn't going to tell Charlie tonight.

'You want to watch a film about transvestites?'

'I've heard it's good and it sounds right up your strasse.' Charlie does that thing where he looks at her and tries not to blink. It's his impression of sincerity. It jogs Naomi's memory as to why she suggested a trip to the cinema in the first place. The ticket she found in his pocket. The illicit solo work-day cinema trip that just happened to be left off the agenda of that evening's 'meeting'. She suggested coming here to try to catch him out in a lie. And now she has, because there is no way that Charlie wouldn't lobby hard for the *Blade Runner* sequel unless he's already seen it. If Charlie were a film, he would be *Blade Runner*. He made her sit through the director's cut when they first got together and had to pretend he wasn't annoyed that she fell asleep in the middle of it.

'Don't you want to see *Blade Runner*?' she asks.

'You'd hate it.'

'You don't know that.'

'It's meant to be even slower than the first one and—'

'And I fell asleep in the first one.' His face creases into a patronising grin. 'But you really want to see it.' She can feel herself pushing too hard and so can he.

'I'll wait for Netflix.' They're at the front of the queue now. '*Florida project*?'

'Sure,' she says.

The cinema is a third full and smells of centuries-old dust. Charlie produces a freezer bag of homemade popcorn from his rucksack and the half-bottle of white wine that's been in the fridge since the weekend. He's made a lot of effort. It would be sweet if she wasn't so angry with him. He would say he's not lying to her but what he's doing, eliding the truth, is just as bad. She's got no right to be angry about it after what she's done to him but anger doesn't work like that.

He passes her the bottle, wet with condensation. She's going to have to have a slurp of wine or he might suspect something. She's read that foetal alcohol syndrome only really affects Native American communities where prospective mothers were drinking a half-bottle of whiskey a day, but she still abstained during her pregnancy with Prue. Charlie gets settled back in his chair and puts a hand on her thigh. He hasn't touched her with such confident propriety for a long time, it feels alien but not unpleasant. Naomi puts the bottle to her lips, swills wine into her mouth and back into the bottle like mouthwash. She's desperate to swallow it but it's not just about what she wants any more.

There's an advert for a holiday company on the screen. A man and a woman are gambolling around a beach, then dancing on a rooftop and then smiling at a swimming-pool bar sipping cocktails from coconuts. They look so blissfully content. They can't be married and they definitely don't have kids. Real relationships don't look like that, she thinks. There's no anxiety behind those smiles, no memory of painful compromise, no wistful looks into the middle distance wondering whether they've made the right choice. The adverts and the social media declarations of love and the sentiments of every song that's ever done well in the charts, they don't tell a story of what it means to love, how hard it is to be loved. To feel loved. Love is just a nicer word for tolerance. She looks at him staring at the screen, his eyes sugar-glazed, too-full mouth chomping on popcorn. It's not just tolerance, she does still love him. The moment she watched Sean stalk out of the cubicle, as she let the shower-water stream down the sides of her face and collect to cascade from her chin, that was when she knew. It took betraying her husband to remind her that she still loves him. But love, like a star, burns brightest at the start and a marriage is often powered only by its afterlife.

Charlie turns to her, smiles and slides his arm over her back. His hand is about to encircle her shoulder when she leans forward and away from him.

'Have you seen *Blade Runner*?' she whispers.

'What?'

'Have you seen *Blade Runner*?'

'No.'

'You have.'

'What?'

'You didn't watch *Blade Runner* when you went to the cinema in the afternoon three weeks ago?' He looks away and shakes his head. 'Cineworld, screen 4, 1:35, three weeks ago?'

'What the fuck?' he whispers through clenched teeth.

'What the fuck. Exactly. What the fuck.' She's glaring at him now. The intensity of the darkness and being forced to whisper makes her anger swell up and clog the top of her throat. She knows she should have left it, that it wasn't worth mentioning, but she's said it now and she can't turn back. He puts both hands on her armrest and raises himself up and is about to say something but she won't let him.

'You went to the cinema in the afternoon—'

'Have you been spying on me?'

'You left the receipt in your pocket.'

'You went through my pockets?'

'You're not even good at lying.' She sees in his face she's scored a hit.

'I went to see *Blade Runner* because I wanted to see it and—'

'You were meant to be working. During the day, you are meant to be working,' she hisses. He looks at her, his eyes telling her how petty he thinks she is but she stares him out, the implication of every grievance she has with him, for his delusions of greatness, his inability to knuckle down and provide for them and for what happened with the house, her dream house, that, if it weren't for him, she would be living in now, swirls like a blizzard in the space between their faces. He turns back into his seat and slumps down, putting his head back, eyes closed, and he sighs so long it could have been his final exhalation. The cinema gets darker as the trailers begin. Naomi twitches, adrenalin pumping into her brain, but Charlie's not engaging. This isn't what he does. This isn't how it goes. He moves in halted movements like an insect in a jar and he swallows his words and he punches his knuckles but this, it's like someone has pressed the off switch. She sits still and waits for him to resurface.

'You're right,' he mumbles.

'What?'

'You're right to be angry.' His eyes are still closed and he speaks too loudly. A punter two rows in front turns and gives them a look. Naomi eyes Charlie, wary of what this uncharacteristic strategy might be. He says something but she can't hear him, she bends her head down to him.

'What?'

'I've let you down. I'm letting you down.' She can't see, but she thinks from his breathing that he might be crying. He turns to her, blinking the beginnings of tears away and then looking squarely at her.

'You, you and Prue, mean everything. You do. I'm going to be better. For you, I'm going to get better.' He's speaking in full voice now and people in the rows in front look back at them with open contempt now the trailers have begun. 'Do you believe me?' he says, eyes pleading. She feels the embarrassment of the whole cinema looking at her, the sensation a woman must have if she's subject to a proposal on live TV, so she nods and gives him an understanding smile. He grabs her head into his shoulder and kisses her hair. She feels his warm breath and is reminded of Sean, of the shower cubicle. She nuzzles further into her husband to rid herself of the thought. She should tell Charlie about the baby. Now would be the perfect time to tell him that she's pregnant with their child. She could whisper it into his neck.

'I do love you,' she says instead. She means it. He's not perfect but he's made sacrifices for her too. He's turned down opportunities to go and work at MIT in Boston to stay with her; he agreed to have Prue much earlier than he thought he'd have children to fit in with what she wanted; he moved their life out of London, away from his friends, away from the buzz of innovation at the Hackney Wick 'incubator' for start-ups he used to work at, when she decided that it was the right time. He's a good man who is struggling and she is his wife. It's her responsibility to help him through this. She moves her head from his neck on to his shoulder and watches the trailer for some period film, an adaptation of a book she read years ago about a young couple who've just wed and are filled with anxiety about consummating their marriage. Charlie puts the bag of popcorn on the armrest between them.

SIX

'You've got no shoes on, Prue,' Imogen, Prue's key worker, who has a benign moon-face, exclaims joyfully as soon as she and Naomi enter the baby-room. Naomi looks down at her daughter's feet and sees her pink and white striped socks. All the other nursery nurses peer over from the table full of troughing toddlers at the little girl who's been brought in without shoes.

'I'll go and get some from home,' Naomi says as breezily as she can.

'Don't be silly, we've got loads of spares.'

'Crazy morning,' Naomi says to the room in general as the staff turn back to their charges' breakfasts. She scans the children for Greg as she does every morning. In the days after the swimming class she was continually alert to seeing Greg, with Sean or, worse, with his mother. She'd had brief visions of an angry blonde woman, in her head she was blonde, accosting her outside the 'Badgers' room in some sort of cartoon cat-fight. But it hasn't happened and if they'd still been together, after the shower cubicle, Sean would have been contrite, he would have mentioned a wife, a girlfriend to her surely. He seemed too straightforward for that sort of duplicity. Either way there's been no sign of Greg. Not seeing Sean has been much easier for her, she knows that, but he'd still become a part of her day and she misses the routine of him.

Prue penguin-walks over to the table and gets herself a chair to sit down. She's always loved nursery and Imogen, it's been one of the unqualified successes of their time by the seaside. Imogen hasn't followed Prue to the eating area but lingers next to Naomi. She wants something but is too polite to bring it up. Naomi searches her face for the answer, which only makes Imogen smile wider and shrug hopefully.

'Nappies!' Naomi blurts out. 'Shit, they're in the car.' Imogen bites her lip and makes an 'Oops' face at Naomi's language. 'Sorry! I didn't mean to—'

'It's fine! First six months I was here I spent the whole time trying not to swear. Spent a whole afternoon once trying to make a little boy say "burger" instead of "bugger".' Imogen radiates warmth like a campfire. 'Are you OK?' she asks. Naomi is not OK. It has been two days since she found out she's pregnant and she still doesn't know how to tell her husband.

'Absolutely shattered, to be honest,' Naomi confesses.

'Not easy juggling everything, is it?' If only Imogen knew how many balls Naomi had in the air. 'Prue's always happy as Larry with a Happy Meal so you're definitely doing something right.'

Naomi thinks she might cry so she pinches her eyes together before laughing the whole exchange away. Imogen laughs with her, putting a hand on Naomi's upper arm. And if they hadn't been where they were, Naomi would have embraced her and sobbed into the inviting crook of her neck for hours. Her emotions have been all over the place in the last week. She's tried to chalk it up to what she did at the swimming pool but it's something more than that. Something primal over which she has no control. She was affected by the hormones with Prue, but not this early. She feels constantly on the edge of tears and her mind is fuzzy; the mistakes she's made this morning, forgetting her daughter's shoes, nappies, they're totally out of character. Imogen gives a deferential nod and heads towards the toddler table but then stops, a sudden look of concern on her face.

'I've been telling all the parents,' Naomi's body tenses, 'I'm actually moving up to the threes' room next week, so Prue will be getting a different key worker.'

'Oh no! That's such a shame.'

'I'm going to be the manager.'

'Who'll be looking after Prue?' The edge in Naomi's voice makes Imogen look at her shoes. The temperature of their exchange has gone into the blast-chiller.

'I'm pretty sure Uggy,' Imogen indicates a nursery nurse with a centre-parting, 'will be looking after Prue, but it's best to talk to reception about it.' Naomi's never talked to 'Uggy'. She's much skinnier than the other girls and far less smiley but whenever she's seen her with the children, they seem to like her. It could have been worse. It could have been the moronic one with the tattooed eyebrows who's always on her phone when Naomi looks into the nursery garden on her walk through the park to work.

As she walks into reception towards the beanpole figure of Lisa holding the door open, she realises that everyone, the nursery nurses, the little ones who looked up from their cereal, everyone in the baby-room was smiling at her, wishing her well for the day as she went. Everyone except Uggy.

SEVEN

5 weeks

Naomi sits at her desk in the corner of the warehouse, which, on a bright winter day, is bearably cold. It used to belong to a removals company but now resembles something from an episode of *Scooby Doo*. Almost all the old buildings in the area were allowed to fall into disrepair when low-cost flights to Spain robbed the town of its tourist trade and its purpose. Victoria was attracted to the building's history and, as sunbeams catch ancient motes of dust, Naomi can see the appeal for someone with her sensibilities. But as the smell of Matilda's Thai Curry Soup wafts over from the microwave, Naomi would happily trade it in for a nice, soulless, segregated office space.

Naomi's working on a press release that she can't get right. Words have dropped out of her head today. She's used 'wonderful' and 'amazing' three times apiece. The smell of lemongrass turns her stomach. She gets to the end of a passage about the festival's 'amazing' street-food offering that will insist on sustainable cardboard packaging, when the buzzer for the intercom jerks into the cavernous space. Naomi ignores it, assuming Matilda will rush out of her nook at the first excuse to stop working, but she doesn't appear. The buzzer keeps snapping, a robotic dying bird. It's insistent, rude almost. It's not the tentative buzzing of the delivery man who will take the parcel back to the depot, nor one of Victoria's fabulous friends just dropping by with a box of Florentine biscuits. Naomi saves the press release, closes the laptop and heads towards the door. Worry burns up her back and, as she reaches for the intercom's receiver, she gets that deep sense of dread and pictures a gang of hoodied youths standing menacingly outside the door. There are boys that sit smoking on the steps of the multi-occupancy block she walks past to get to work who look at her with the most frightening hunger. She puts the receiver to her ear.

'It's Naomi's husband Charlie.' Her skin stings with goose bumps as abstract fear becomes concrete. What's he doing here? She wants to replace the receiver, go over to a corner of the room and maybe he'll go. 'Can I … come up?' His tone's inscrutable but she can tell he's not planning on leaving.

He knows. That's the only logical explanation. He's never come to her work before. She'd offered to show him round and he had no interest. He must know.

She presses the button on the intercom quickly, as if pulling off a plaster, hears the buzz of the lock and Charlie clicking into the door downstairs. Naomi turns and heads away from the door like a duellist walking their ten paces. Just as she turned away from Sean in the shower, pretending she didn't know he was there, she wants to delay facing the consequences of what she's done to Charlie for as long as she can. She stares out of the window, glass reinforced by chicken wire, hears him open the door and then it sounds like he's running and she turns just at the moment that her husband grabs her round the waist and lifts her up in the air and he's happy. He's beaming. When he puts her down she sees he's holding a pregnancy test. Not knowing how else to respond, she hugs into him again. Then he's whispering short sentences that seem to overlap each other.

'We did it. I love you. I'm sorry. We did it. Are you OK? How you feeling?' And she mumbles and nods and now she's crying. Really crying. A flood of tears that's been dammed up ever since she saw the word pregnant on the plastic stick breaks her defences. He holds her tighter and his body tells her that he believes this is a watershed moment, but she knows that there's never any such thing and even if there were, there can't be for them, not any more. She sees Victoria glancing down at them through the glass door of her upstairs office with venomous curiosity.

'Shall we go and get a coffee?' Naomi says, pulling away from Charlie. He nods and taps the pregnancy test on the back of his hand before realising it could still be covered in pee.

'Do you want to keep this?'

'Yes please,' she says and grabs it from him too fast. She hasn't moved the pregnancy test since she put it away in a sealed pocket at the bottom of her handbag. So how does Charlie have it?

They're in the same café that she went to with Sean. Charlie suggested it. The same hipster man-children are there at the same table. One of them wears a headband over his long hair now so he looks like an eighties rocker. She steals a side-glance at them, conscious they might recognise her from before. Luckily, with their over-loud Home Counties accents competing to talk about the various house improvements they're doing, they seem entirely disinterested in anyone else in the café.

Kids run riot between the replica Eames chairs as Charlie bustles between them carrying a tray. Some people talk a good game when it comes to doing everything for their children but the parents here have come for the artisan coffee and to talk to people like them in a décor that resembles something they've seen on Instagram and sod it if their child has to fight with ten others to play with the lone Ikea kitchen. She resolves to take Prue to the soft play in the future rather than here. The soft-play is also more anonymous. Charlie puts the tray on a next-door table and from it produces a huge doughnut. She raises a dubious eyebrow.

'Zygotes like doughnuts, don't they?' He unloads the coffee and takes the seat opposite her, pleased with his joke. She wants to ask him why the fuck he's been going through her handbag but she knows she now has several vertical miles to climb to reach the moral high ground. She decides to get ahead of him, to cut any questions he might have off at the pass.

'I did the test without you, I know, but I thought, after the year we've had, if it hadn't been anything …'

'It was nice, actually.'

'What was?' She smiles wider.

'You leaving the test out for me to find.' She didn't leave the test out for him to find. She left the test hidden in the bottom of her bag. She picks up the doughnut and bites into it.

'You found it?' she garbles through dough.

'You left it in the middle of the worktop; I know I'm not the most observant but even I couldn't miss it.' He sips his macchiato and leans back in his chair. He seems so relaxed now, like he's just finished moving house. Naomi's sure she didn't leave the pregnancy test out. Her mind's been a fug and she's been making mistakes, mistakes she would never normally

119

make, but she can't have forgotten that she left her pregnancy test out on the worktop. She reaches into the handbag sitting next to her on the bench and feels around the inner lining. She knows it's irrational. Where would he have got another positive pregnancy test? But she definitely didn't leave it out for him to find. The pocket in her bag is empty.

'What've you lost?'

'Was there anything else with it?' she asks him. She took some things out of her bag in the kitchen yesterday evening and perhaps it fell out somehow.

'What do you mean?'

'Was there other stuff with the test?'

'It was on its own. Did you not want me to see it?' Charlie shifts forward in his seat. Naomi knows she can lie now, she can dismiss it and focus on their joyful news. That's what he wants to do, she can see the desperation in his eyes, pleading with her not to do or say anything that might tarnish the relief she can see radiating off him, but now she's really worried. She couldn't have left it there by accident. It's Charlie who loses Prue's sippy-cups and has his phone fall out of his pocket and leaves their front door open. She doesn't make mistakes like that.

'I did the test the morning before we went to the cinema.'

'Makes sense you were in such a funny mood now.'

'Imagine if I'd miscarried or something. It happens a lot and I wasn't sure, with, you know, you at the moment.'

'Me at the moment?'

'Your depression.'

'Right.'

'I wasn't sure how you'd handle something like that.' He looks down into the splash of foamed milk on the saucer of his espresso cup and breathes out. Then he reaches across the table, takes her hand in his and rolls her fingers in his palm, his fingertips pressing into the flesh at the top of her hand. It's a gesture straight out of a television drama.

'I meant it. What I said at the cinema. I'm going to be better now. I will be. You don't have to worry about me any more. It's just great. Isn't it? It's going to be great. Nothing's going to go wrong now,' she goes to interject but he knows she's trying to moderate his conviction, 'it can't. We deserve that. You, you deserve that.' His sincerity drills into her and the moment to tell him that she didn't leave the pregnancy test on their worktop for him to find as a delightful surprise when he made himself a cup of tea has passed.

EIGHT

https://www.pregnancyforum.co.uk/b841/forgetfulness-in-pregnancy – jjlapp43

Why am I more forgetful now that I'm pregnant?

A large proportion of women say they become forgetful during pregnancy, or get what's known as 'baby brain' or 'pregnancy brain'.

Nobody's completely sure why it happens. It could be to do with your perceptions when you're pregnant. Your memory is pretty much the same as before but you're more tired, making focusing hard, and you probably have more on your mind now you're pregnant. This is particularly the case for second or third pregnancies where there's less opportunity for mum to rest.

'Baby brain', which also affects decision-making, has been shown to start in the first trimester and stabilise in the second and third trimesters. Its effects are therefore most prominent in the first twelve weeks and symptoms can present themselves before some mothers even know they're pregnant.

It's possible that physical changes that occur in an expectant mother's brain could explain the phenomenon. During pregnancy, a mother's brain rewires to improve her sensitivity to emotion and her ability to read facial expressions. These adjustments make mums more attuned to their babies' needs once they're born. However, in order for these new superpowers to develop, certain other areas of the brain, the areas that control everyday abilities like judgement or short-term memory, are temporarily hampered.

NINE

6 weeks

A small pigeon stands on the front step of Naomi's house staring at her as Prue struggles in her arms. Naomi feels seasick. The pregnancy nausea has been relentless this time, ten times worse than with Prue.

The bird has made two attempts to fly away but there's something wrong with it. Its head bobs as if it might fall off its neck at any moment. Naomi hates birds. In corporate seminars and team-building exercises in her past life, whenever she had to reveal a 'fun fact' about herself, she would always tell everyone about a poem she wrote when she was a teenager about the pigeons on the seafront in Bournemouth and how much she hated them. It talked about their eyes being the colour of fire but without warmth. 'Cold, soulless and dripping with desperation.' The poem wasn't very good. She'd found the original in a school textbook a year ago and posted it on Instagram, it got a lot of likes.

In addition to Prue, Naomi's carrying her little girl's nursery rucksack and a full canvas shopping bag. They're half an hour late for Prue's afternoon nap because Naomi thought her baby bag had been stolen at Ladybird's Landing. It hadn't; Lara found it on the changing tables in the ladies' toilets.

She wants to scream out for Charlie but he's at the top of the house and wouldn't hear her. This is his fault. He's been shooting them during the day when she's not there, this is probably one that he only managed to maim. Prue's gone quiet. She loves animals but she can sense this one's wounded and has the potential for malignancy. She squirms higher on to her mum's shoulder and a wellington-booted foot kicks into Naomi's ribs making her grunt in pain and drop the shopping bag on to the front path.

Naomi is exhausted. The biennial's six months away so she's having to work in the evenings after Prue's bedtime and, due to the builders layering endless barrels of cement on to the walls in the basement, she's wiping away cement dust from the whole of the ground floor three or four times a day.

Tiredness has slowed her, as if her mind and muscles are steeped in molasses. When she's looking after Prue she can't find the energy to engage with her properly, the best she can manage is sitting in a circle with her cuddly toys and being the least enthusiastic guest at her tea party. In the evenings she can't face talking about logistics with Charlie so the builders are doing things they haven't been asked to, cutting corners most likely. In the last few weeks the fridge somehow never has more than some browning green beans, a bag of radishes and a jar of mango chutney that she's been giving far more attention than she should. It's just spicy jam, she's been telling herself as she spoons it on to partially thawed crumpets.

She's been thinking about Sean. Waking up between four and five every day and as the mist of sleep clears he is the first figure that slinks into her head. She gets the chemical kick she got every time she used to see him at The Bank of Friendship and then there is no hope for her sleeping. So she spends the next hour and a half, before Charlie's alarm bleats into life at six thirty, trying not to think about the man she had sex with in a swimming-pool changing room. Sean's absence has intensified her memory of him and distilled their moments together into absolute clarity. Yet her recollections of him feel distinct from other parts of her past, like they didn't really happen to her, scenes from a film she saw many years ago that have stayed with her. She has managed to both forget him and put him on a pedestal. The mind's capacity to lie to itself is extraordinary. She and Charlie visited Auschwitz together as part of a city break to Krakow. They barely talked while they walked round the museum and the gas chambers, but in their hire car on the way back to their hotel, they laughed and joked and sang along to a David Guetta song on the radio. Being there amongst that horror didn't feel real, like they had woken up from a horrible nightmare. Their subconscious did that little clean-up job without their permission and it's clear that it can do the same thing for our own behaviour, however appalling.

In those endless black-night mornings, she replays her and Sean's friendship. The thought of sex turns her stomach at the moment, so it's less an erotic reverie and more a long-form exercise in *esprit de l'escalier*. She forensically picks apart the times when she should have said something different, behaved better. She doesn't always castigate herself for encouraging his attraction to her. There are moments when she thinks that her biggest error was telling him she'd made a mistake. Naomi shouldn't be thinking like this. She's been given a get-out-of-jail-free card and she's not going to do anything stupid, but perhaps if she'd left him a sliver of doubt, a thin basement window of opportunity for The Lumberjack to climb in through … In her marital bed she's safe to luxuriate in thoughts like these and, some of the time, she doesn't even feel guilty for it because the whole episode is exactly that, an episode, finished.

The wind picks up some rain and Prue scrunches her face, lower lip trembling, readying to cry. Naomi looks up at the top-floor window and sees the glow of Charlie's lamp but there's no sign of him rescuing her from the pigeon. Every time it flaps its wings it gets inches off the ground and, on returning to earth, its body stutters frantically. Naomi edges towards it with no idea of what her plan is. A few steps away and there's another frenetic flap, the spiny rattling of feathers on their newly painted door. Naomi puts Prue down behind her, hands her her backpack to hold and picks up the shopping bag. The icy rain turns to sleet. Naomi strides forward, subconsciously swinging the bag whose bottom layer is built from cans of chickpeas, chopped tomatoes and tuna. The bird can sense the movement and begins to hop up, flapping its useless wings, straining to get off the steps. Naomi puts one foot on the bottom step and swings the bag at the bird gently, intending to steer it around her and back out into the open. She guides it past her legs and out of the porch and then it stops, exhausted by the effort, right in front of Prue. Naomi opens the front door, intending to grab Prue, lift her over the bird and into the house. Then the bird starts flapping hard and rises up towards the level of Prue's face, the little girl banshee-howls and throws her rucksack on the floor. Naomi piles her shopping bag into the side of the bird, the full force of eight tin cans smashing it into the wall of their front garden. Prue screams and runs towards the road where she's stopped by the metal gate that Naomi had Charlie install.

Charlie's there in the doorframe now. He strides out in socks, leaving footprints on the wet paving stones, and goes to get Prue from the gate. Her screams abate as he holds her into his chest. As he passes Naomi his expression asks her, *What the hell's going on?* She purses her lips tight together and gives him a murderous look.

The pigeon looks dead.

TEN

'Congratulations.'

'Thanks.'

'You must be delighted.'

'Yeah, we are.'

'You said to me that you thought it might never happen.'

'It's great.'

'Naomi's doing OK?'

'She's knackered and feels sick. Apart from that … She's … not had the energy for anything and so I've had to pick up the slack and – I know I need to just man up and— '

'That's not a helpful phrase.'

'It's been hard. Doing everything, round the house, with Prue. Anyway, it's fine. It's great.'

'Great.'

'She's really jumpy. It was different with Prue. She was like a warrior. We went walking in the Mendip Hills when she was seven months' pregnant. This time, it's early days and she's already super sensitive to everything. Last night she woke me up at three because she thought she heard something in the front garden. Said she heard a bin lid or something. I had to go down and check and, course, there was nothing there. Where we live, when wind picks up off the sea it really whistles around the house. There's always a lot of noise, floorboards creaking, that sort of thing, and she's constantly up in the night because of it.'

'Not sleeping well is very common in pregnancy.'

'That's what she says about everything. After shouting at me for eating a packet of crisps next to her the other night, she didn't apologise, she just told me it's very common to find things like that infuriating.'

'Last time you said you were finding it easier to recognise the negative thoughts as they occurred and you were feeling good about some new friends that you'd made.'

'They're just people I play football with.'

'You called them friends last time, what were their names? The ones we talked about.'

'Er, Tayo and Salinger, Sali.'

'It really seemed that spending time with them was helping you tap into your own positivity again.'

'I haven't seen any of the boys from football for a bit.'

'Why not?'

'There hasn't been time.'

'It's so important to make time for things outside work, outside your family.'

'That'd go down like a glass of warm gin.'

'You don't want to head back into that state of resentment. The scores on your measure are down.'

'Not surprising.'

'Why is it not surprising?'

'Naomi and I used to love getting drunk together and not going out. We'd arrange to meet friends and work our way through a bottle of rum and we'd keep texting them, telling them we were on our way and we'd never turn up. We found it so funny because we knew that our little gang of two was the best. We'd talk about philosophy and religion, she's got school friends who are super-Christian so she's fairly tolerant of people's beliefs where I think religion's a load of rubbish so we'd stay up all night, me trying to convince her that God definitely doesn't exist and— That sort of stuff, anyway. It was our little world and it was perfect. And, you and I have talked about this, Prue's now there and we've got a different little world and it's not perfect yet but I can see how it will be one day but this ...'

'You're not excited?'

'I'm excited that we're going to have the family that Naomi wants and I always wanted kids but I also want to talk about, I don't know, what's going on in the Middle East or the future of infrastructure in urban centres. I want to talk about those things, with Naomi, like we used to, because she's much cleverer than me and it made me think. I don't think now because it's always the same conversations. When did Prue sleep? What did she eat? Is she ill? Did you buy that thing she needs? It's necessary, I get that, but it's boring. I wash and I cook and I try to work and I feel like an automaton, a robot. But a broken one. The next baby is going to come and it'll get ten times harder because everyone says it gets ten times harder and I'm going to be back here with you, talking all this self-indulgent bloody ... Sorry.'

Charlie's eyes fill and Amy hands him the man-sized box of tissues that sits on the coffee table between them.

She looks down at her notes, at his 'measure', the met-ric that's worked out based upon a questionnaire that her patients fill in no more than twenty-four hours before they see her. It indicates that he has 'moderate to severe depres-sion'. The measure classified it 'mild' last week so he's taken a definite tumble. Amy knows the street that he lives on. She knows almost all the houses on that street are about four times the size of her flat. Amy's twenty-six and has a three-year-old who, with the help of her mum and ex-boyfriend, she juggled looking after with finishing her university course and qualifications to work as a mental health counsellor. She likes Charlie. His problems are by no means the most severe of her patients, his financial and family situation one of the most stable, but she still finds him one of her most challenging clients, in many ways one of the more upsetting. There are very few people she sees that are depressed at not being able to talk to anyone about the future of infrastructure in urban centres.

ELEVEN

8 weeks

'And what was the date of your last period?' Naomi's midwife, Lillian Babangida, asks, face inches away from the form she's filling in.

Crinkled coloured paper flutters on the wall as a result of the fan heater blasting behind her. The children's centre is one step up from a portacabin, standing in the shadow of a 1970s primary school, and they've covered every wall with children's artwork in an attempt to warm up the utilitarian interior. Splodges, handprints, smears, footprints, potato shapes of various colours, collages of metallic paper, feathers and an orgy of glitter. Charlie has to keep getting up to stop Prue pulling things off the wall before sitting back down with her on his lap, trying to be attentive to the midwife until the toddler slides down to the floor and the whole music-hall routine begins again. It's getting on Naomi's nerves. He'd insisted they all come along to support her even though she said it was unnecessary.

She fishes in her bag for her phone so she can check 'Ovul8'. She's sure her last period began on the thirtieth of August. She's seen that date marked in dark red on the app, must be nearly a hundred times since she realised she was late. But her brain's felt so addled recently she's lost all confidence in her surety of anything so she has to check.

'First of September,' Charlie declares, clutching his iPad-sized smartphone. Naomi looks at him as if he's clinically insane. 'That's what I've got.' He waves the phone in the air in front of him.

'The first of September,' Lillian says.

'Is that right?' Naomi says, stopping Lillian's pen. Charlie hands Naomi the phone and 1 September is circled in dark red; he's right. Then a green circle arrests her attention, bright green, a green that, with the brightness settings on the vast smartphone set far too high, feels vicious. The green surrounds the number fifteen: 15 September. 'This can't be right?' she says. Lillian gives Charlie a look as Naomi pulls her phone out of her bag and goes into the app. There it is: 30 August circled in dark red. Big, green ovulation day: 13 September. D-Day. The D-day that started so inauspiciously but did result in a not unpleasurable lunchtime shag with her husband. She hands the phone to Charlie. His face creases with confusion as he looks at the incongruity.

Lillian's amused by these two polite young people getting crinkled by something on their phones.

'Clap, clap, clap.' Prue has marched over to Charlie and is demanding one of their phones. 'My phone. Clap, clap, clap.' This refers to an animated video of the song 'Wind the Bobbin Up' that their daughter could watch on a loop until the end of days. Naomi stares into her handbag as if the polka-dot lining might have an answer to the question. Whose phone is right? He puts in when her period starts and stops so it must be his phone. But it's always synced before.

'It's meant to sync up,' Charlie says as if reading her mind. 'Anyway, the— It's only to work out the due date, right?' he asks Lillian who nods, smothering a smile that they could read as being cruel. 'Let's split the difference and say the thiry-first, yeah?' he defers to Naomi and she can tell that, with Prue now trying to wrench his phone out of his hand, he wants to get the form filled out and get home as soon as they can.

'OK.'

'When you have your twelve-week scan, they can give you a more accurate due date,' Lillian says.

They proceed to fill out the rest of the form together. Naomi gives one-word answers. Charlie has given in to Prue and she sits on his lap watching her video six times in a row. At the end of the appointment, Lillian asks if either Naomi or Charlie has any questions. Charlie looks at his wife, expectant. Naomi always has more questions. There's a list of them written in biro on a journalist's notepad in her bag but they're not important now. Charlie misinterprets her vacancy for tiredness and takes over with charming 'thank yous', taking Lillian's phone number and the gathering together of Prue and her detritus.

Naomi has a question, a fundamental question, but it's not one that anyone in the room will have an answer to. Because no one else in the room, not her midwife, her husband, not even her daughter, knows what she did in a shower cubicle of a public swimming bath on the fifteenth of September.

TWELVE

10 April 2001

MSN Messenger

(*)ELIZA(*) says:
Karin? Says you're online .... ☺

Where you been for THREE weeks?

Miss Sindall kept me behind to find out what was going on

No one really thinks you did it

Until you stopped coming to school!!!!!

I called your house and your parents said you weren't there

Where are you???

THIRTEEN

The sun here purifies the sky somehow. When clouds hang above the sea the whole coast seems suffocated but when they clear, the palette changes and it feels like a different country. The horizon, broken only by the optimistic pylons of offshore wind farms and ancient tanker ships that feel like they shouldn't exist in the age of drone strikes and Amazon Prime, lengthens out over the sea and it could be anywhere on the other side. The fact it's Essex is something that, when the weather's like this, everyone pretends they don't know. The wind is up and the sea bursts into pockets of whiteness that remind Naomi of clashing beer glasses from a Disney film she watched when she was a child.

She's walking on the beach near their house. It's not the most beautiful of the seven or eight bays along this part of the coastline but it's also not the ugliest. She doesn't go to the beach as much as she thought she would. The idea of something is never as good as the reality, but looking out to sea this afternoon it is glorious.

She's alone now. Alone with this secret and the sea has no answers for her. Since their appointment with Lillian she's been treading water in quicksand, trying to convince herself that what she knows to be true is not true. If the data is to be believed, if the accepted facts about the time-scale by which babies are created is correct, she is carrying the child of a man that isn't her husband. A man she barely knows.

The wind swells and almost lifts her up. She puts her left hand over her stomach as if to stop the baby inside her getting sand in its eyes. She turns around, walking backwards into the wind and stares up at a huge sky and shouts as loud as her voice will go. Her vocal cords hurt but she pushes them further until she can hear herself through the whistling that swirls in and out of her ears. She sounds like barbed wire being dragged across a rock. Then she feels sick so she puts her hands on her knees.

A liver-coloured cocker spaniel bounds up and sniffs the ankles of her jeans. She glances round and sees that its owner, an elderly lady with a scarf over her head, is a long way away and making slow progress. Naomi squats down to the dog's level and grabs its neck, ruffling the fur under its ears. She looks into its hazelnut eyes and something in them tells her that it's going to be all right and for a moment she feels like it could be. Then he darts away in an expansive loop, bounding back towards his owner.

She stands up and moves towards the stone steps up to the promenade. On the upper level, the eddies of sand blow into her face so she shelters in the doorway of a beach-side café, its flat roof bordered by crumbling wood painted a cheerful baby blue. What she wants is for nothing to have changed, for them to be able to carry on and have the family that she and Charlie have planned. Perhaps it can still be like that. She scratches at a crack in one of the beams and a clump of rotten wood comes away, her fingernail stained brown by it. She looks at the hole she's made, woodlice busy inside, exposed to the bright sunlight, they scrabble and burrow deeper into the unknowable recesses inside the sodden wood.

FOURTEEN

27 October 14:55

I need to talk to you. I'm picking
Prue up at 4:30. I'll be in the
park afterwards. X

29 October 06:44

This is Naomi. There's something
we need to discuss. I'll be in the
park from 8:15 today for one hour.

1 November 16:22

If you think you're being kind
you're not. Vital we speak.
Can meet anytime today.

FIFTEEN

10 weeks

7 November 2017 at 16:42

Phone still broken – did he get it fixed?
  not receiving texts (iCloud)
  no reception

Ignoring – making it easy for me?
  busy NO
  too painful NO
  digital detox NO
  callous arsehole
  hates me
  loves me

Naomi looks down from the higher driving position, heat blasting from the Nissan's vents, and watches the daily battles and delights of the nursery drop-off from the overflow car park next to the leisure centre. A little girl wearing far too few clothes for the cold marches forward in sparkling wellington boots followed by a dad struggling with an industrial-size bag of nappies. He's going to be fuming when nursery tell him they only have room for fifty nappies per child and he's got to take them all back to the car. Another dad, dead behind the eyes, holds his son horizontally as he clings on to his car seat like it were a cliff he was about to fall off.

Naomi has taken to spending an hour or so in the car park after she drops Prue off and then again before she picks her up. She also came both days Prue wasn't at nursery, asking Charlie if he could take their daughter for a couple of hours while she was getting a wax one day and had to go to an event with Victoria the other. Both times he bristled, she could see how much he wanted to tell her how much of a hindrance the extra childcare would be to his work day, his work does seem to have picked up, but he managed to tell her it was fine and that he'd make the time up after she's gone to bed.

Since he found out she was pregnant he's been amazing. It's agonising spending her nights too wiped out to do anything but lie on the sofa while he brings her dinner and cleans up around her. It's almost like he knows what she's done and he's punishing her with his new-found virtuousness.

There's no yellow van in the car park today and after a full week and an extra day today, she is satisfied that Greg no longer attends The Bank of Friendship. She wants to ask Imogen but Naomi hasn't seen her since she's moved up to the 'threes' room' and she's nervous about asking the manager Lisa, who takes her safeguarding responsibilities very seriously and would take exception to searching questions being asked about one of her charges, even her former charges. In addition, when Naomi once described Lisa as an officious jobsworth to Charlie, he'd laughed at her and said he always found her very friendly. This was typical Charlie, even when he professed to being in the deepest depression with her, he always managed to be charming and winning with people he barely knows. If Lisa was sweetness and light to him, perhaps, if Naomi was asking her questions about Greg, Charlie might receive the answers. She knows that paranoia is a symptom of early pregnancy but she can't risk him knowing anything. Not until she's talked to Sean.

She bites into a croissant. Naomi doesn't eat things like croissants but she hasn't been sleeping and the body craves carbohydrates when it's tired. A hormone called ghrelin continues to be produced when exposed to excessive light at night and it causes us to feel hungry. She'd read an article about it three nights ago on her phone, which, ironically, the piece warned against using at night-time. It said that during pregnancy the body produces more ghrelin to make sure that mum is consuming enough energy for her baby and it's this, in combination with the nausea, that leads to the horrible feeling of being ravenous and disgusted by food at the same time. She's read lots of other articles about hormones. About the ones that flood into the body of a pregnant woman to facilitate the miraculous process that grows a baby inside her. Progesterone, the 'PMS' hormone. Oxytocin, the love hormone. Cortisol, the stress hormone. Adrenalin, the hormone of fight or flight. She read about how the cocktail of all these in a pregnant woman's body can have a drastic effect on her and her baby, a dangerous effect even.

In the last week Naomi's made a decision. One she didn't take lightly. She drew up a table and mapped all the different options on it and used it to evaluate, objectively, what her action plan should be. She researched the psychological damage that a marriage breakdown can have on a child and she found a thirty-year study of children that didn't know their father. It didn't make for pleasant reading. So her conviction that she not tell Charlie, that she carry on as if he were the baby's father, has solidified. He would be crushed, it would destroy Prue's childhood, her sibling would be born rudderless and, looking at it pragmatically, Naomi knows that there's no need for any of that. There is no need to tell Charlie.

The only thing she can't control, the only risk, is Sean. He seems like such a nice man but she doesn't know him at all. What if they were to bump into him with the newborn? He would ask how old he or she was and he would have questions, legitimate questions. He might not make the link immediately, but what if he gets to his late forties and Greg's mother has turned their son against him for whatever reason. He's isolated and angry and he thinks back to the woman he slept with, who he had unprotected sex with, who just happened to have a child who was born nine months after they were together. It wasn't even just the possibility of bumping into him. What was she meant to do? Eliminate her and her family's life from social media and the Internet for the next forty years because what's to say that mid-life-crisis Sean won't get misty-eyed one day and search for her and find pictures of the teenager that might be his and try to connect with them? She can't take the chance. Hoping for the best isn't in her nature.

'Why is it you want to know?' Uggy's tone isn't as aggressive as her question sounds. Prue's marching around behind her new key worker attempting to hold a saucepan above her head while stirring it with a wooden spoon.

'We're having a party for Prue and wanted to invite some of her friends from nursery.' Naomi had prepared this answer in case anyone questioned why she was asking about Greg's whereabouts. She knew it might come across as odd. He was a little bit older than Prue and, although they had been in the same class, she was never told they were friends.

'Prue's birthday is soon?'

'Er, no.' Does Uggy know Prue's birthday? 'We don't know many people in the area and wanted to try to, you know, meet some other parents with children Prue's age.' Uggy crosses her arms. This is the longest conversation they've ever had. She's always been curt and to the point, 'Prue slept well', 'Prue ate well today', 'we went to the park this morning', but with little detail and nothing that would prompt a conversation. She's not unattractive but she's all hard edges, not a natural fit for a career looking after children, Naomi would have thought, but Prue loves her. At home she often intones her name, 'Oooggy' she calls her, and when she's dropped off in the morning she goes to her more willingly than she used to with the more obviously maternal Imogen. Uggy looks at Naomi with suspicion, more like a battle-hardened policeman to a suspect than a nursery nurse to a parent. Naomi's almost tempted to call out her hostile attitude but remembers that she needs her help.

'We met Greg in the park and they played for a while and got on really well.' Something flickers in Uggy's expression but before Naomi can work out what it was, Prue is between them, reaching her arms up and demanding to be carried. Naomi lifts her into her arms and, shielded by her daughter, studies the woman opposite her. She's always found it easy to read people, to read the way their bodies and their faces betray their lies, but, perhaps it's in her national character, she finds Uggy completely inscrutable. Her head went somewhere else when Naomi mentioned meeting Greg in the park but what was it, was it to do with Greg's parents? Is his mum a

145

nightmare? Is she sexy? Uggy could be that way inclined. Or is it Sean? Naomi always suspected that his attractiveness must be a talking point everywhere he goes. When he told her he worked on building sites she imagined him being called 'pretty boy' or 'dreamboat' and suffering daily because of his good looks. It's the ridiculous thing about British 'banter', she thinks, any positive attribute or talent a person possesses becomes a stick with which other people beat them and creates a deep-seated guilt about whatever it is they have or are good at. Naomi had it at school.

'Greg's parents took him out of nursery a few weeks ago.'

'Were you his key worker?' Before Uggy can answer, a blancmange of a girl covered in green paint cries out and she turns round to attend to her. Prue flips her weight towards the door and it prompts a bubble of nausea in Naomi's throat. Her daughter's impatient to get out into the real world, away from the stink of shepherd's pie that seems to linger in the room regardless of what they've had for lunch, but Naomi needs to know more.

'Did he move to a different nursery?'

'Um,' Uggy's cheeks stipple with blush, 'I can't remember. Maybe.'

'Do you know why he left?' Uggy faces Naomi now. The shiftiness from before is gone and, cradling the blancmange in her arms, she's almost defiant.

'People leave and come back or they stop for a month or two here or there all of the time. Nursery is not so cheap for some people.' She leans on the 'some' just enough to make the point to Naomi that she has her pegged as one of the 'down-from-Londoners' who assume everyone is as wealthy as they are.

Indignant rage mingles with the nausea in Naomi's stomach like lemon juice in milk and she wants to ask Uggy where she gets off being so rude to her customers. The thought shoots into her head that a British girl wouldn't dare use that tone but when Prue extends her clenched fist to Uggy for a fist-pump that makes her daughter erupt into giggles, Naomi feels ashamed of herself for thinking it.

'Well, if Greg's parents come by, or you bump into them, if you could give them my number.'

'You can talk to Lisa in reception.'

'Say bye-bye, Prue.'

'Bye, Prooodence.' Uggy's head wobbles as she over-enunciates the 'ooo' sound, making Naomi feel over-protective of her daughter's name.

'Ba-bye, Ooooogy,' Prue says, reaching an arm towards her as Naomi whisks her out of the room into reception. Lisa opens the door for them with her Aspartame fake smile and eyes so creased you can't tell if they're there.

In the park, Prue chases brown-paper leaves that swirl in gusts of wind under the huge sycamore that looms over the nursery. Naomi glances back in through the French door of the baby-room and sees Lisa asking Uggy about something with a stern look on her face. One of the others, Sophie, looks on guiltily, alternating between listening in and pretending not to. It can't be about Greg; Uggy didn't give her any information at all, didn't break any of the nursery's precious safeguarding doctrine. But Lisa's having stern words with her about something. Prue puts a clump of leaves in Naomi's jacket pocket before running away as if it were an incendiary device. Uggy looks at the floor, swaying the little blancmange-child in her arms.

SIXTEEN

He's stuck in the middle of the pitch and Ollyphant, so called because he's a big boy, is shoving a sharp forearm into his back. Their first game of November has been delayed for ten minutes by a huge hailstorm and the AstroTurf looks like someone has unpacked a huge parcel of polystyrene balls on to it. They play in an enclosed cage in the same park as Prue's nursery. With the floodlights, the high walls of steel and the clouds of breath from toiling men, it feels dystopian.

Charlie protects the ball, waiting for someone to run past. Tayo sprints round him in a wide circle offering an option to his right. The big man behind slices his foot around Charlie's shin to try to get the ball. Charlie feints round him the other way. He looks up and straightens an arm to tell the opposing team he's going to pick out Tayo's run but it's a dummy. He dinks the ball under his standing leg to take it away from two onrushing defenders. The space opens up in front of him and he spurs forward towards the goal, he can hear the panting of the unfit opposition players, straining to make up the ground to him, cigarette-phlegm hacking in their throats. The goalkeeper hurls himself forward and goes to ground, spreading his body wide and Charlie, adrenalin making him feel like a god, lifts the ball lightly over the keeper's legs and hurdles himself over his prostrate body. The goal gapes in front of him, time swells somehow and there's no one else there. He's always had this feeling playing football. He sees pictures of what to do next in every moment. It feels so logical, as your opponent tries to close down one angle, you recalibrate and pry open another. There's a truth in space, of motion in space, that his mind has always found beautiful. The body is a machine that, for him, with this level of opposition, does as it's told, so the possibilities are endless. He picks his spot in the half-height goal and is about to roll it towards the bottom left-hand corner when— Thunk. Everything goes black.

'How many fingers?' Sali holds three fingers far too close to Charlie's face. Charlie bats them away, laughing. They're in the row of portacabins next to the four football cages that serve as changing rooms.

'You seriously not gonna let me buy you a beer to say sorry?' Sali says, back at the mirror, running a hand through his hair.

'All the greats have to put up with being scythed down by absolute donkeys,' Charlie says without looking up. Sali grins and nods his agreement. Most of the other lads are changed now. There's not much of a take-up for the pub tonight. Tayo had to leave early to go and host some minidisc night above a yoga studio. He made the mistake of inviting everyone along and was laughed out of the changing room. Charlie's doing everything slower than usual, his ribcage buzzes with pain and he's got a pounding headache.

'Sure I can't tempt you?' Sali says, rolling down a fresh section of old-fashioned cloth-towel dispenser and wiping his face on it. 'Otherwise it's me stuck with the Ollyphant hearing about how they need to "hurry up with that facking Brexit" as he gets a boner over the Polish barmaid with the nose-stud.'

'Really can't tonight, mate.' Charlie sits down and pulls socks on, trying to avoid the puddles on the changing-room floor.

'Date night with the missis?' Sali asks and Charlie half-laughs, an edge of bitterness. 'Oh right. Short-term tenancy in the doghouse.'

'I said I'd get back.'

'She OK?'

'Yeah, yeah.' Charlie puts his elbows on his knees and supports his head in his hands. Looking down at his shoes and socks for so long has given him a head-rush. 'It's a big old house we've bought and it's really creaky with this weather and, I don't know, she's not sleeping so she's pretty much always fuming.'

'Time of the month?' Charlie smiles off his question. Sali sits down next to him, leans back against the coat-hooks and wrinkles his nose, aware he's been a bit crude. Charlie wants to tell him that they're expecting but they haven't had their twelve-week scan yet and it's bad luck. And Sali the stud probably isn't the best person to get pregnancy man-sympathy from. 'That why you ducked out of the SM league?' Sali asks, picking bits of mud off his trainers. SM is what dedicated players call Soccer Manager.

'Work picked up so I had to bin it off.'

'The computer's running your Ipswich team now. It sold Sterling to PSG and now you're in a relegation dogfight.'

'Fuck's sake, really?'

''Fraid so, lad.' Sali puts a hand on his shoulder in mock-consolation, which makes Charlie feel ridiculous for having a genuine pang of sadness that the team he built up from nothing to being the best in the world has slid into decline. He deleted the game from his computer the afternoon after he found the pregnancy test and so far he hasn't relapsed but it's still galling to hear they're doing badly.

'Anyway.' Charlie shrugs off Sali's paw and stands up. He's desperate to drag his moment of freedom out for as long as possible but he said he'd be back straight after football.

Charlie doesn't know if it's the pregnancy hormones, he hopes it is, but Naomi's behaviour is becoming impossible. She wakes him up almost every night because she thinks she can hear things in the house. The pigeons are still roosting, they think under the rafters, and since the thing with the lame one on the front step, every time she hears them she gets het up and makes him go and knock on their window to get them to fly away. She's been forgetting things; not been able to find stuff and then, when she does, swears she didn't put it there. She keeps borrowing his phone and when he asks her why she looks at him like a hissing cat and says she has to 'check something'. He's had to have Prue on his work days while she goes and does things out of the house, 'stuff for her' she says, and that's fine, he can't argue about it anyway because she's pregnant, but she does it at the drop of a hat, forcing him to reschedule calls and meetings and it's pissing Rinalds off.

Things at work have started to pick up. They have a new client, an entrepreneur with an interest in video equipment, who's really keen on the steadicam he was working on and might want to collaborate on making a whole range of movie industry equipment for smartphones – steadicams, tripods, focus-pulling equipment. Charlie had to do a Skype call with the client with Prue playing in the background earlier in the week and, typically, she had a poo explosion, a poonami, he had to deal with there and then to avoid ruining the new rug he's bought for his office.

He's talked to Amy about Naomi and she said that when someone's put so much pressure on conceiving, when they finally do, it's human nature for them to feel anxious about the baby's well-being. And if they're someone who already suffers from anxiety, a condition that releases too much adrenalin into the blood, their brain and body are primed for combat, so they will find danger and threat in any every-day moment. However 'natural' Naomi's behaviour may be, it hasn't stopped it being a massive pain in the arse for him.

'Anyway, I said I'd be home.' He dawdles before picking up his bag and jacket. Sali stands with him and they walk out, shoulder to shoulder, towards the leisure-centre car park.

SEVENTEEN

www.yourchildcare.gov.uk/kent/northkent/earlyyears

~~Abbey Children's Centre – 4, Poesy Avenue, St Nicholas, WT8 4HG~~

~~The Bank of Friendship Nursery – Tivoli Park, Cliffgate, WT9 7JL~~

~~Diamond Mill Nursery – 82, Wantombe Street, Burchington, WT8 5HH~~

The Grove Montessori – 18, The Grove, Cinque Ports, WT11 4KD

Helter Skelter – 128 East Gate Rise, Eastgate, WT11 6GJ

Morningside Montessori – 22, Palm Crescent, WT13 7GG

Mrs P. Vieira – 38, Welwyn Avenue, WT9 6QG

Youngs Early Years Centre – 173, Tiler Street, WT8 7AW

EIGHTEEN

11 weeks

Prue sweeps her fingers across the screen of the tablet like a skilled artist making the final touches to her masterpiece. She woke up with the pallid complexion and raw-meat eyes that accompany a storming cold and she wants the world to know how terrible it is. Her world today is her mother and she's been giving Naomi both barrels. Which is why they're now curled up on the brown velveteen armchair in the corner of the master bedroom, and she's being allowed to play on the iPad for far longer than her daily ten-minute allowance. The screen goes black and Naomi notes how drawn her face looks in the reflection before she scrabbles around the squishy orange cover for the lock-screen button that Prue's accidentally pressed. The little girl squawks like the seagulls that seem to Naomi to have tripled in both number and volume recently. She reignites the screen, silencing her daughter.

Naomi has a banging headache that pulses like a bassline, vibrations of pain widening out in her head, forcing her to close her right eye, as if, if she didn't, the pain would escape from it wrenching her frontal lobe out with it.

The sound of a circular saw grinds below her. The builders have been making progress. The walls and ceilings of all the rooms on the first floor are finished and now the carpenter is cutting pieces for the skirting boards and architraves. She's come up here with Prue to hide from him. He's a talker and something about the things he says – this morning he described himself as a pagan, for example – and the way he looks at her, she finds disquieting. He's friendly but she's convinced he hates women. He tenses the muscles in his hands if she gives him instructions and he uses phrases like 'happy wife, happy life' and she's heard him saying to Charlie 'whatever you do, make sure she thinks it's her idea'. The strain of the saw, the eternal thumping hammers, the dentistry hiss and thunk of the nail-gun, the fucking seabirds. This is the soundtrack to their life away from the stresses of the big city.

'Mummay!' Prue flips the iPad up and the corner clots into Naomi's cheekbone.

'Ow!' she says too abruptly, shocking Prue. Her little lip begins to curl so Naomi gives her her make-up bag to head off another bout of high-pitched howling. The sawing stops.

Naomi needs a moment, one moment, where she can hear nothing, do nothing and think of nothing. She closes her eyes and doesn't even flinch when her eyebrow pencil-sharpener cracks open and she feels the shavings drop into her lap. She could just go to sleep.

Crackle, pop.

Her eyes spring open at the sound. She looks on Charlie's bedside table expecting the little green light on his digital radio to be on but it's lifeless. The same sound again. A short hiss of static. She shifts Prue, who's trying to pull the cap off her eyebrow pencil now, on to the seat of the armchair and goes over to the radiator. It's cold so it can't have been the pipes or the hot-water tank. The saw starts up again and she hits her hip with frustration. Perhaps it was something outside. Maybe she mistook the sound of a car passing, the wind on the next-door neighbour's fence. The saw stops whinnying and she sits straight-backed on the edge of the bed and closes her eyes.

The sound again. She glances around the room, bird-like, trying to place it. It could be downstairs, Lenny, but— The pop happens again and she's up, walking away from the bed towards the window. She stands there for some time. It didn't come from outside. Prue hops off the chair and saunters over to Naomi. 'Mummay.'

'Shhh.' Naomi extends her arms out as if they were antenna as Prue takes hold of her pyjama bottoms. Naomi holds her breath. A wheezy old diesel van thrums past the house.

'Mummay.'

'Please, sweetheart, quiet.' The little girl does as she's told. Naomi sways her head, like someone looking for a mobile phone signal, willing the sound to show itself and there it is, a dull fuzz now, almost imperceptible and maybe it is coming from downstairs but it sounds so close, she cranes her ear down and—

'Mummay! Mummay! Mummy. Look, Mummy!'

'Shut up! Shut up! Just shut up, can't you shut up!' Naomi shouts into her little girl's face. Prue's cheeks fold in on themselves and the tears begin to pour out of her, huge globules of anguish, and it's only then that Naomi notices that she's drawn eyebrow pencil all over her forehead and she wanted her mother to see. The shame feels like a shard of glass in her throat. She enwraps her daughter in her arms and whispers 'sorries' into her ear. The noise she heard, the meaningless sound, is forgotten. Prue starts saying sorry to her now and Naomi's tears wet Prue's yellow, cotton cardigan. She stands up with her, holding her head into the crook of her neck, bouncing her up and down with her like she did when she was a few days old. The long sneer of the saw downstairs crows again.

NINETEEN

http://www.umich.edu/hgg/articles/HGG177829/

Cortisol levels and very early pregnancy loss in humans

Raman S. Chanderpaul,[*†‡§] Sally R. Leech,[¶] Francine McLaverty,[†||] Juan B. Exteberria,[‡] Artur Farnerud[†††]
Author information ▶ Article notes ▶ Copyright and License information ▶

Abstract:
Maternal stress is commonly cited as being a potential determining factor in spontaneous abortion.

Before this study there was very little physiological evidence for this proposition. The lack of evidence can be put down to a paucity of research on maternal stress during various gestational periods. We examined the link between miscarriage and levels of maternal urinary cortisol levels at week 8, week 12, week 16 and week 20.

Results:

Rate of Miscarriage

	Normal Cortisol Levels	Increased Cortisol Levels
Week 8	31%	88%
Week 12	25%	73%
Week 16	23%	69%
Week 20	16%	56%

Discussion:

The high rate of miscarriage in human reproduction has led experts to describe it as 'inefficient' and therefore entirely paradoxical in evolutionary terms. However, evolutionary scientists have put forward that the spontaneous abortion of foetuses that are unhealthy, defective, substandard or are born into potentially imperfect birth environment can be reproductively advantageous. The above results, which imply that higher cortisol levels increase the chance of spontaneous abortion, should be considered to support this hypothesis. Imperfect birth environment can be understood as conditions in which the newborn has less chance of surviving i.e. war, widespread disease, famine. Miscarriage in these types of dangerous environments ends pregnancies with diminished chances of success, freeing up the valuable resources of health, nutrition, strength and physical dexterity to be used on a woman's own survival and for their already existing offspring, which could be crucial during a period of conflict.

TWENTY

Naomi's thumbnail shoves the cuticle on her other thumb up into the flesh. A muscle in her forearm spasms. The living room is glacial and the rain in the clogged gutter on the side of the house creates a repetitive splash cymbal outside. She feels sick. Prue, face still puffy with her cold, sits on the floorboards playing with some miniature zoo animals. The mid-wife, Lillian, sits down on the marked beige sofa. Naomi never thought she'd look back on her and Charlie's aborted attempt to conceive on that sofa as a 'simpler time'. She hovers above the older woman in a way that might make someone seated tell her that she's making them nervous. But not Lillian. Lillian's unpacking things from her bag with the precision of a surgeon. A pack of tissues, a notebook, a pen. It's difficult to age her. Her skin is firm, legs toned and youthful but she has the manner of someone who has seen everything and all that the world has to show neither pleases nor disappoints her. This is a woman who has seen more tears, more pain, more joy, more anguish, more wonder than a hundred people see in their lifetimes. And more death.

'You're feeling very sick, yes?' she asks before extracting one of the tissues and dabbing at her nose.

'That's right, yeah.'

'Not much you can do about that, to be honest. You can go to the doctor and get some anti-nausea medication but—'

'I don't want to take medication.' Naomi crosses her arms. After shouting at Prue she called her midwife and said she needed to see her today. She didn't have any slots but Naomi pleaded with her and she said she'd pop in on her lunch break.

Lillian leans back in the sofa and looks up at the ceiling. She could be admiring the coving. Naomi's skin feels riddled with flies, the pricking heat puckering around her chest, but Lillian's silence tells her she needs to get on with it. She'd already told Naomi that the midwife-led unit at the Kent Hospital Trust is both understaffed and oversubscribed. 'No matter how bad the world gets, people always want to have more babies,' she had said.

Naomi spots a stream of canary-green snot running under Prue's nose so she kneels down and pinches it between thumb and forefinger, making Prue veer her head away. Lillian dips into her packet and hands Naomi a tissue for her to wipe her fingers on. Prue goes back to trying to jam a toy zebra into a small wooden cage.

'Is there any way of knowing when the baby was conceived?' Naomi asks. The midwife leans forward and puts the pen and notepad down next to her. 'An exact date. I need to know. I like to know things, details like that.' Naomi pulls at a pill of wool on her shoulder before clutching her hands together, aware of the edginess radiating from her.

'We go from the first day of your last period.'

'I know, I know that, but is there a way, a test? Is there some way of telling exactly what day, date the baby was conceived?' Lillian's brows crease together. She knows Naomi has a problem. She knows she doesn't just want 'details'.

'You and your husband, you made plans to have this baby?'

'Absolutely.'

'Were you monitoring your basal body temperature?' Lillian asks, holding her pen at each end.

'No. We used the test strips.'

'The ones that detect the surge in LH?' Naomi nods. Lillian can tell she is a woman that has done her research so doesn't mince her midwifery jargon.

'So you know when you ovulate in your cycle.'

'What if I can't be sure about when my period started?'

'You have one of those phone thingies that you write it in. You and your husband both have it, I saw.' Naomi can't explain the mix-up. She's been back through her text messages, her WhatsApps, Facebook and Instagram to try to decipher when her period started but they've revealed nothing. In the early days of their trying to conceive she would text Charlie to tell him the bad news, that her period had come, but the last three or four months she's been so upset a text hasn't been enough and she's had to call him, even leaving work once to go and tell him in person a few months ago. With her most recent period, she was so resigned to its arrival that she waited until the evening to tell him. She remembered the conversation but, having checked her diary, she hasn't been able to put an exact day on it and, even if she could ask him, the exact date is something Charlie's unlikely to be able to help her with.

'There isn't a test that can be done?' Naomi asks, biting her lower lip. 'There must be a test to find out when exactly the child was conceived, people must need to know. It can't be that hard, can it?' Naomi stares at her thumbnail, unable to face the judgement Lillian might have on her face. She looks out of the window at the cascade of water from the broken gutter on to the muddy scrub of their back garden. Lillian shifts herself on to the floor, making a slight sigh of discomfort as she comes to rest on her haunches. Prue's on her side, staring at the undercarriage of a plastic buffalo. Lillian takes one of her little wrists and tickles it tenderly. The little girl glances up but doesn't move, her body mellowing under the older woman's touch. She speaks in a low murmur to Naomi, all the while brushing Prue's wrist with her narrow fingers.

'All this phones and tests and plans. All brand new. Everyone needs to know everything about everything straight away these days. You know, people used to just make babies. And the truth is that no one knows how the miracle happens. And it is a miracle.' Naomi's about to interject but before she can Lillian has grabbed one of her hands and shows her her own ragged fingernails. 'But this? All this? This craziness you are doing to yourself. You think I don't see the bags under your eyes? I can't see the blood around every single fingernail you have and where else? All of this, this is hurting that little miracle you have inside you. So when? You asking when? It doesn't matter.' Naomi pulls her hands away from Lillian and stands up.

'Thanks for coming by,' Naomi says, brushing dust-mice off her jeans and walking towards the door. The midwife leans down to Prue and blows into her ear making the toddler 'ha' in delight. Lillian gets up using the edge of the sofa as scaffolding, collects her things together and walks past Naomi into the hallway. She opens the front door as she shifts her long arms into her black, puffa coat, the rain-soaked horizon behind her a Turner painting, purple with rage.

'I've been asked the same before. Women who are in the same situation as you.' She locks eyes with Naomi. She knows exactly why she's asking her when the baby was conceived. There's no judgement in the midwife's face but her knowing still makes Naomi feel like a fallen woman from a bygone age. There's a relief in someone else knowing, even if neither of them can say it, even though it flushes shame up the back of her throat, it makes her feel calmer. Lillian steps back down the craggy floorboards towards her.

'There is no way to know exactly what hour, what day you conceived. One day here, one day there. No way. There is a test you can do after the baby is born, to find out, but you know that.' Naomi kicks at a bit of ragged underlay on the floor. 'You have a beautiful daughter. You have a good enough husband,' Naomi gives her a dubious eyebrow, 'he came with you to see me. That is better than most. Look at this house, big enough for twenty children.' Naomi nods her head involuntarily. Lillian puts one of those magical hands on her upper arm and stills her. 'Knowing everything, maybe it's not so important?' She squeezes Naomi's elbow and then shoulders her way out of the doorframe and into the stark, grey outdoors.

TWENTY-ONE

14 May 2001

MSN Messenger – (*)ELIZA(*)

(*)ELIZA(*) says:
Cathy Davies saw you hanging around behind the station
on Thursday night.

She said you looked really drunk

Tell me you're not doing drugs

KARINP83 says:
Tell me ur not a fuxking snake-in-the-grass, disloyal bitch

(*)ELIZA(*) says:
I didn't say anything to anyone.

KARINP83 says:
EXACTLY

U didn't say N E THING

Namo Twatterson and her worshippers saying those disgusting things to me and you stand beside them, pretending to laugh

(*)ELIZA(*) says:

I DID NOT LAUGH

KARINP83 says:

You think she'll be friends with you now? You think she'll let you and your beloved little rat dog into her perfect gang with her perfect face and her perfect happy family?

She only likes anorexic control freaks like her

I KNOW YOU'RE ONLINE

(*)ELIZA(*) says:
Have you told your parents?

KARINP83 says:
'parents'

(*)ELIZA(*) says:
Are you at home now?

Karin?

I came over and your brother said you'd not been home for a week.

He's really worried about you. We all are.

Are you at home?

KARINP83:
not my home

(*)ELIZA(*) says:
Can I come round?

I think you need to talk to someone

I wanted to stand up to those girls, she's so scary.

Please can I come round?

KARINP83:
2 little 2 late

(*)ELIZA(*) says:
I didn't KNOW you were pregnant

KARINP83 says:
I'm not pregnant.

That's how an abortion works.

TWENTY-TWO

12 weeks

Eastgate is a small village six miles inland. It's surrounded on all sides by fields full of what could be cauliflower, or maybe cabbages. There is a church, a small school and an independent hardware store that Charlie raves about. The proprietor is a real tool nerd and opened up an old belt-sander for him so he could have a proper look at the mechanism. The store is behind Naomi as she leans against the Nissan watching the sun dipping to her left, giving the fields a sinister aspect. As if, as soon as the sky darkens, the monstrous cabbages will transmogrify into triffids to swarm on the village from all sides.

The Helter Skelter nursery stands on the other side of the road. It must have been built to be a bed and breakfast, probably in the sixties. Its front-yard car park is rammed and a snake of optimists behind the wheels of estates and SUVs clog up the road around, hoping a space will magically appear for them.

Naomi has three nurseries left to watch. It's inconceivable that Sean would have moved Greg somewhere that was more than a half-hour drive from his old nursery so she was confident that the list she'd drawn up was comprehensive. At the last-but-one nursery she'd bought herself a Costa coffee and a pack of doughnuts from the petrol station in homage to the stake-out cop she seems to have become. She ate all the doughnuts within the first twenty minutes. The baby loves a sweet-treat.

Getting through the list of nurseries has been slow going as she's had to spend two hours at each place to cover the full span of potential pick-up times, so she hasn't been able to go every weekday. She knows that even when she's been to every nursery it still won't be definitive. Greg went to The Bank of Friendship two and a half days a week so she has to go to every nursery, every day of the week at both teatime and lunchtime to be certain. But she's decided that once she's been to all of them once, that will be it. She will take Lillian's advice, focus on her family, forget Sean and hope her deepest fears won't be realised.

She needs to focus on her family. 'Daddy' is now the first word Prue calls when she wakes up each day. When they're all sat together in Prue's room before her bedtime she chooses to sit on Charlie's crossed legs with her bedtime story rather than on hers. Daddy is flavour of the month. Charlie tries to mollify her, telling her that it's good, that with another baby on the way it's important Prue doesn't need her as much. But Naomi finds it upsetting, bordering on wrong. She knows that in the modern world, fathers are meant to be as involved as mothers but she doesn't want that level of equality. When it comes to who Prue needs more, it has to be her. When she falls and grazes her knee, it has to be her mother who kisses it better. When she has a huge bust-up with some bitch of a friend when she's older, she knows how cruel girls can be from her time at school, it should be Naomi whose counsel she seeks. When some scumbag boy is pushing Prue to do things she's not comfortable with in the bedroom, it has to be Naomi that tells her to kick the arsehole to the kerb. She knows that her being away from home more is the reason for Prue's shift in preference so she has to draw a line under this as soon as she can.

The sun has gone. An excoriating light above the front porch of Helter Skelter pours down on parents with their little familiars, as they traipse out in an irregular but steady stream. She's noticed that the mood is more buoyant on the way home. Parents look at their children, ask questions and smile at their answers. They pick them up in their arms, bounce them, tickle them, blow raspberries into their necks. Both adult and child stride through the car park like giants as opposed to the fraught shuffle of the morning drop-off. She's seen plenty of children Greg's age but hasn't yet spotted his helmet of jet-black hair.

She looks at her phone, aware of the public feeling towards adults who hang around outside nurseries. She wants to look like a mother waiting for her husband and child. If she were a man, someone probably would have called the police by now. She looks at her emails, nothing that needs action, a compulsive check of Instagram. Pictures of perfect families with perfect lives in sunny locales are not what she wants to see so she slides them back into her coat pocket. When she looks up again she sees a little boy stepping off the nursery's porch and she breathes in, hand squeezing around her phone. His hair is obscured by a hat but she recognises this boy. He's the right age, the same slight build and there's something about the way he ambles forward, shoulders rocking like a tiny prizefighter before a bout, the same jaguar gait she'd seen in Sean, that tells her it's Greg.

Or at least it could be. At every nursery there have been one or two of these false dawns, her mind so desperate to see him that it plays tricks on her memory and creates characteristics Greg doesn't have. She looks for Sean but he's not there, or at least not yet. A gaggle of parents, two men and a woman, a member of staff maybe, in a burgundy tabard, follow behind the little boy. She looks above the group of adults expecting to see his huge torso encased in plaid, squeezing himself through the door, but he's not there.

As the boy that could be Greg heads further away from the entrance, she sees a portly man with dark hair and a beard emerging from the group of adults and walking a few steps behind him. He's in a grey hooded sweatshirt and wears a tool-belt. Almost all the local men seem to be tradesmen. She's been amazed at the numbers of vans branded with the contact details of builders, electricians, roofers, window cleaners that she's seen in the many different nursery car parks she's watched. A car swings round towards the little boy and the man skips forward to put an arm over his chest to hold him in place. They're together. It can't be Greg.

Naomi turns around and leans her head on the top of the Nissan. She can feel her pulse beating against the cold metal. She's texted him, she's asked at the nursery. If he doesn't want to be found, she won't find him. How has this happened to her? It feels so cruel.

She lifts her head and sees an old woman gazing at her as if she's lost her mind, maybe she has. Naomi opens the car door and finds sanctuary in the Nissan. What she's doing is ridiculous. She's exhausted, she feels constantly sick, she has seven or so months to enjoy with her little girl, without a newborn demanding constant breastfeeding. She should be at home with her family.

She starts the car and glances out of the window at the nursery and there they are, the boy and the heavy-set man. She thought they would have got into a car already but they come out of the gate and walk down the street. The boy turns his face towards Naomi, looking right at her car, and it is him. That boy is Greg. The same boy she first saw at nursery, that played driving with Prue in the café, that was there in the low light of the swimming pool, paddling faster than all the others. That boy is Greg.

She fumbles for the handle of the car door and clambers out into the road. She speedwalks on her side of the street, closing the gap on Greg and the man walking next to him. Who is he? A friend picking him up? An uncle? She jogs a short stretch to get ahead of them and glances over her shoulder at the boy. She's sure now. She saw the helmet of hair at the back poking out of his woolly hat and now she sees his skin, so pale that the contrast with his red mouth makes it look like he's wearing lipstick. It's him.

The man walks at the same pace as the boy. They don't converse. He pulls something from his pocket, car keys, and a black Transit van six or seven car lengths up from them blinks its orange indicators. They disappear from view, behind a line of vans. Without thinking, Naomi steps into the road to follow them, forcing a gargantuan silver Mercedes to stop sharp, a few metres away. The expression of the silver-haired man behind the steering wheel asks her why she's so stupid.

Naomi waves a coquettish apology to confirm her idiocy and he waves her over the road with a beneficent grin. By the time she gets to the other side, the heavy-set man has the passenger door of the black van open. Greg swings his little backpack into the bottom edge of the van a few times. The man takes the bag from him and shoves it into the footwell of the vehicle. Naomi wants to get closer but fears Greg may recognise her and, whoever this man is, she doesn't want him telling Sean she's here. Perhaps he already knows about her, she has no idea what Sean would have said about her to his friends, his family.

The man squats down on to his haunches, a hand on his hip indicating some pain. Greg runs into his outstretched arms and the man lifts the little boy high above his head before pulling him into his chest. He reaches into the cab, to clear the straps of the car seat, Naomi thinks, and while he does, little Greg tickles the man under the chin. The man tickles him back and Greg convulses with laughter, snapping his chin down and burying his exposed neck into the man's collarbone to escape the man's wiggling fingers. His father's fingers. Because a little boy doesn't interact like that with a friend or an uncle. She's never seen anything this intimate between Sean and the boy. This man is Greg's father.

THE SECOND TRIMESTER

ONE

I watched her whole pregnancy with Prue on the Internet. Every week a new photo of her in her gym clothes, bump getting bigger. People want to show the world they're doing life properly, living up to the conventions of their conventional upbringing, following the well-trodden path to happiness. But their version has to look better, wackier sunglasses, more joy, prettier sunsets, brighter lights. I only found them two months before they announced they were expecting a baby but that didn't stop me from scrolling through their life together before that.

In the early days she'd posted whole albums of the two of them and their smiling faces as they lived out their charmed life on Facebook. When they first got together, selfies in music venues clutching cans of Red Stripe, a bare stage with glinting drum kit in the background; her on his shoulders at a music festival, feathered headdress and covered in glitter; arms linked with several others on a lamp-posted street somewhere that must be London, dinner-plate pupils, a sheen of sweat. Then they got married. I spent weeks studying those couple of hundred photos, it was the most detailed account of a day in their life they'd given me, though I know someone's wedding day isn't exactly representative. They had it in a big tent in a field, the tag said it was in the South Downs.

She was sat on hay bales, forehead pressed to her friend Lilly Sharpells, he with a bunch of laughing lads with a full range of different facial hair. The two of them, cheek-to-cheek, sandwiched between their parents. Both fathers red-faced with champagne, mums in wide-brimmed hats.

Married life didn't seem to tarnish their picture-perfect existence one bit. Paint-spattered dungarees in their North London flat, the flat that, when I looked it up on the land registry, I was surprised to only find her name on; dinners at restaurants with friends in well-cut suits; playing outdoor games I don't know the names of in parks I've never been to, surrounded by people holding bottles of expensive-looking beer. It took me so long to find them and when I saw what sort of people they were it was so much worse than I'd expected.

I shouldn't be here still. I should have left. I did what I came to do as soon as I got here. I don't usually spend long in the house. In and out the front door that's always left on the latch by the builders. I've had a key cut, they leave a spare in a bowl on the hall table, but haven't had to use it much. He's upstairs in his study. He doesn't come down much during the day and if he does he never goes in his bedroom. He doesn't talk to the builders. Doesn't consider them to be worth his valuable time.

I've found something in their bedroom that won't let me leave. The picture that got me here, that started me down this path, the thing that sparked the idea that burrowed into my head like some sort of insect telling me what I had to do, is here, printed out, enclosed in Perspex, up on the mantelpiece. They've got a mantelpiece in their bedroom. Sometimes when I have doubts about what I'm doing, things like them having a mantelpiece in their fucking bedroom give me a little kick up the arse. They're so entitled. But what they think they're entitled to and what I do are on different sides of the map.

The picture shows Naomi in a hospital gown with newborn Prue clamped to her left breast. The husband stands to their left, the chunky hospital bed putting him a few feet behind them. They're all smiling. Not Prue obviously. She looks so tiny. Naomi's eyes are droopy, warm and lazy, like she's on drugs. She probably was. I've not heard them talk much about her labour, how long it lasted, whether she was in pain. A silver canister of some gas is on his right-hand side. The first time I saw the image, near two years ago on her Instagram, I didn't notice the scratches on the gas bottle. Or maybe I did, because it reminded me of the last scene of *Jaws*, the scuba tank in the shark's teeth. The sheriff shooting it and the animal exploding. Maybe if the gas bottle hadn't been in the picture I wouldn't be here now in their bedroom. If I hadn't thought of Sheriff Brody on the mast of the *Orca*, his relief at having overcome the monster haunting him, then the anger I felt in my chest when I saw those faces beaming at their baby, their perfect new baby, might have fizzled out as it did with all the other photos of them I'd looked at. I like *Jaws*. I've watched it at least a hundred times. The last place they put me, when I was a kid that is, only had two videos. *Jaws* and *Terminator 2*.

A car parks on the street outside the house. I pick up the Perspex box with the photo in it and plant a kiss on Naomi's neck, or as close as I can, before putting it back on the mantelpiece, about half a foot to the right of where I picked it up from, just to see if they'll notice I've been amongst their things. I look at it again and see my lip-balm's left a mark on the clear plastic. The bottom lip is clearly defined but the hair of my moustache has smudged the top lip so the shape will be misconstrued as a mark left by sticky fingers. My lips cover her chin, her neck, her chest and Prue fits into the bottom left-hand corner of my mouth. They won't notice it's moved. They never do.

At the big window at the far end of their bedroom, I watch her getting out of the Nissan wearing a fitted jacket over T-shirt and jeans. She always looks well put together, not like the other mums at nursery. She has this running joke on her Instagram she's done since Prue was born where she posts a picture of herself in one of these expensive jackets or summer dresses with baby-sick or some puréed vegetables all over it, her with a sarcastic thumbs-up for the camera. It used to piss me off, showing off her fancy clothes, but I started to look forward to these pictures more than the others. Seeing her smile even though something she loved was ruined. She squirms across the back seat to get Prue and, from the way her legs are thrashing around, you can tell she's struggling with the car seat. I could go and help her, take her leather handbag, lock the car for her, open the door and let her in.

As she knocks the gate of the front garden open with her hip, Prue jiggling in her arms, her movements are heavier than usual, like she's hurting. I should have left the house when I heard the car.

The key rattles into the front door. The swish of the rubber draught excluder on the doormat. One of the builders laughs at something. I pad across the room towards the door, the hundred-year-old floorboards creaking under my work boots – she hates it when floorboards creak, especially at night. I've stayed the night once or twice, though I've not had the balls to come into this room when they're sleeping in here, not yet. I don't know if I'd be able to control myself.

I have to stay in control or else everything I've done will be for nothing.

I grab the brass doorknob and feel the indentations with the end of my thumb. Downstairs Prue is testing sounds out in her mouth and Naomi's in the kitchen as I knew she would be. She'll be moving the washing-up from her husband's lunch from the draining rack into the cupboard on the right-hand side of the sink. I can hear the door of their pantry-cupboard, that's how she refers to it, being opened. She's making a snack for Prue.

The builders are plastering the new stud wall in the bedrooms opposite. They're not the brightest sparks but they're doing a good job. They're not as thorough as I would be but they're making good progress considering the state the house was in. I've not been able to find out what they're charging. They can't have given them a paper invoice, I've looked everywhere. I slip out of the bedroom and make my way down the stairs.

'Peanut butter or cream cheese?' Her voice stops me halfway down the stairs, metres away from the door. Even in the state that she must be in, the state her head must be in, she manages to stay so consistent. It might be a problem. She's in week thirteen so I don't have long.

'Going the shop. Anyone need any ciggies?' I shout up the stairs in the soft Kentish accent I've been perfecting since I moved down here. I skip down the rest of the stairs, two at a time, open the front door and walk out over the threshold of the dream house for the dream family. As I pull the door closed I look at them in the kitchen, almost willing her to look round. But her head's down, focused on spreading peanut butter on to a rice cake, oblivious.

TWO

The warm gel squirts on to her stomach. The sonographer has stuck tissues into the top of her folded-down jeans to stop them getting smeared in it. Naomi and Charlie are together again in a darkened room, Prue's with them, leaning over the back of a chair towards a sink on the wall. Charlie holds her hand, encouraging her to sit down, telling her in hushed tones that if she watches the TV she might be able to see the baby. Naomi looks at the screen high on the wall in front of her. A murky monochrome, grey clouds in a black sky. The sonographer, who reminds Naomi of a giraffe, small round head sitting on top of a long body, sits very upright on her swivel-stool by the controls of the ultrasound machine.

'Let's see if we can find this little munchkin,' she says as she puts the scanner into the gel and pushes it around her stomach. The three of them look up at the screen. Naomi could tell from how he was in the car, how defensive he got when he couldn't find the right car park, that Charlie thinks today's a bit of chore. There's no sign of the reverent excitement, the frisson of fear he had when they went for Prue's first scan. This time it's routine, he assumes everything will be fine. He always assumes everything will be fine.

The sonographer plunges the instrument into the flesh below Naomi's waistband. Charlie puts a hand just above her knee, raises his eyebrows at her. He's trying to give her what he thinks she needs, encouragement, affection. The thing she's spent months asking for but, although his palm is hot on her leg, she doesn't feel the warmth of reassurance spread through her body. She puts her fingers over his.

Since she saw Greg with his actual dad three days ago, the scan has loomed large in her thoughts. Her plan, her resolve to sort things out with Sean, to have the baby with Charlie and wipe the sordid ordeal from her head has been thrown into turmoil.

Who is he? Why is he picking up someone else's son from nursery, taking them to swimming classes? She's tried to rationalise it as best she can. He's Greg's uncle. A family friend. But why lie; at least, why not say that Greg isn't his son? It would be the first thing she'd say if she was looking after someone else's child. And where is he? How can someone who was a feature of her daily life disappear?

'And there's your little bundle of sunshine,' the sonographer beams at them. Naomi and Charlie scan the picture but the shifting bands of grey don't reveal anything recognisable. The sonographer points them towards a shape on the screen in front of her and both adults make an 'ah' of recognition. Charlie's hand encapsulates Naomi's fingers and squeezes them. It's the baby's back. Its neck and head now easy to make out. The sonographer makes a joke about it not wanting to face its audience yet and Charlie joins in, saying that opening night isn't for a while.

Virtual white arrows stretch out across the pale body as the sonographer clicks at buttons on her console, taking measurements. The little figure looks unreal, a living doll jiggling in cramped quarters. Its head half the size of its body, it could be a baby sperm whale until its little limbs kick out at the enclosing walls, revealing its humanity. The sonographer says something about how it's trying to escape. Charlie laughs politely and digs their daughter's ribs, inciting a little giggle out of her. When Naomi first saw what would become Prue on the screen, she was overrun by conflicting emotions. Relieved that there was nothing wrong, anxious that she wasn't experiencing enough love and pride and yet having the glow of both those things coursing through her. This time the emotions are stuck like flies in a honey trap, present but paralysed so she only feels numb.

Who is the child on the screen? It's part her, but who else? It could be her husband who's trying to involve their daughter by guessing which body part's being measured on the screen. Or it could be the offspring of a stranger.

The sonographer makes a sound, a hesitant noise that jars with her cheery disposition. Naomi's eyes flick towards her as she digs the scanner into the side of her stomach and takes another measurement. The white arrow extends again on the screen and no one speaks.

'What's wrong?' Naomi's voice comes out more frightened than it should do. She knew there'd be a problem. She didn't say anything to Charlie but she was certain there would be something wrong.

'So your munchkin is measuring quite small.' Naomi looks at Charlie, he seems unconcerned. 'Have you definitely got the right date for your last period?'

'Definitely,' Charlie takes control, 'we were trying for a while so we've been logging everything pretty carefully.' Naomi almost scoffs at him being so confident about the dates, but he's right in that sense, there's no way they've miscalculated by a week or more. She looks at Prue who's lifted her arms up above her to try to make herself narrow enough to slide out of Charlie's loose hold and on to the floor. There were no complications in her first pregnancy, Prue always measured large, which made sense. Charlie was a big baby, none of their parents are small, her dad Ray's six foot five.

'Could it be down to stress?' Naomi asks, looking straight ahead at the oversized head on the kidney-bean body, stick legs appearing and disappearing in the darkness. The sonographer changes the view, the top of the baby's head. Two lobes of brain developing in a cross-section of skull. 'Long periods of stress can produce small babies. I read it online.'

'You've got to be careful with any diagnosis from Dr Google.'

'But it can, can't it?' Naomi's tone is curt. Charlie is about to speak. She knows he's about to say that it'll be fine but he stops himself. Prue attempts to scale the hospital bed. The sonographer turns back into her screen, as if what she's doing now requires more concentration than before, gliding the scanner over Naomi's stomach, gel smearing messily up towards her chest.

'We're living in a bit of a building site,' Charlie chips in, trying to support his wife, 'could that be a reason?' The sonographer puts the scanner in its holster and turns fully on her stool to face them. She presses a button and the printer in the far side of the room clicks into action. Naomi takes the opportunity to pick Prue up and sit her next to her.

'It's something you can talk to your midwife about.' She looks at Prue, clutching into her mother, hand already sticky with the ultrasound gel. 'But if stress is ongoing, it can contribute to a small baby. Usually only following divorces and bereavements, though,' Charlie catches Naomi with a wry look, 'so I'm confident the little munchkin's going to be absolutely fine.' The sonographer turns to Prue. 'And you're going to help your mummy rest and help your little brother or sister grow big and strong, aren't you?'

'Yeah!' Prue says with vigour, no idea what it is she's agreeing to. Charlie's hand is on Naomi's shin now. He squints his eyes and nods, telling her he agrees with the professional. The sonographer comes back from the printer and presents them with a picture of the baby. Naomi glances at the tiny, too tiny, human growing inside her, an ethereal hand swims disembodied in the blackness above the curved body. Prue tries to snatch it off her, creasing one corner of the picture so Naomi passes it to Charlie. He holds it in both hands, leant forward, elbows resting on his knees and he smiles at, what he thinks is, his second child.

THREE

13 weeks

Naomi hasn't spent much time in this part of town. Up the hill, away from the sea, it feels like a different time. The Victorian terraces still stand in attendance but their fronts are black with grime and bits of timber protrude from cracked roof tiles.

Her car's parked a few roads away. She's followed Greg's real dad home from his new nursery and, when she knocks on the door, she wants it to seem like she was just passing and recognised his van from the nursery car park. She's plotted out what he might think of this stranger turning up on his doorstep. Back at her old company this is something she did with her clients, map what's called a two-by-two framework with the cause and effect of various strategies before going about implementing one of them. It wasn't something everyone did, many of her colleagues would take the client brief and simply action whatever plan they had formulated. But Naomi presented the options and let the client choose, she'd always steer them towards her preferred one, of course, but she knew that people like to feel in control and when the clients came back with new projects, they always clamoured to work with her again.

It's warmer than it should be at the end of November and the noon sun hangs high in a clear sky. She wears a pair of old jeans, a checked shirt she used to wear for breastfeeding, Charlie's parka, undone, and hardly any make-up. She has no idea who this man is to Sean, what he may or may not have said about her, so she wanted to look as neutral and non-threatening as possible. She's also aware that most of her clothes, not overly expensive but still bought when she was earning a decent London salary, would make her stand out around here. But now she's here, looking at the ground-floor flat she saw the boy and his father walk into fifteen minutes ago, her dress-down outfit makes her feel like she's going into war without her armour on.

Four houses away she has to lean on a wall, her hand sliding against the moss. She still feels so sick. She's in her second trimester now and should be feeling better. Maybe it's nerves, she thinks. Her head has been clearer since the scan, the hormones are meant to have settled down by this stage but it's not just that. Seeing her baby, knowing that it isn't growing properly inside her, has solidified her conviction that she has to be strong and calm and to deal with this situation as rationally as possible. She built a career, built a life on resolving difficult problems and there's no sense in treating this one any differently. It is a relief to feel like herself again, as if she's come out of the other side of a particularly long and arduous hangover. A couple of mornings after the scan, Charlie was surprised to find her spooning him. They kissed tenderly, lips playing over each other like they used to, re-finding each other, his hand caressing the back of her neck. Prue was up so they didn't have time for sex but it was a step towards the sort of intimacy they'd taken for granted a couple of years ago. After he went off to get their daughter, she lay in their bed, languishing in the feeling of arousal before she was ambushed by the thought of Sean and guilt swam up into her consciousness.

As she walks up to the house, she notices the lettering on Greg's father's black Transit van – 'PPS Building Renovations'. There's no phone number or email. The flat looks in much better shape than most of the other properties on the street, so perhaps that's all the marketing he needs. In the front garden there's a wooden structure, a covered sundeck, that butts on to premium-looking AstroTurf with a football goal at one end and a stack of bikes at the other. Four bikes, all of them too big for Greg. They must have older children.

She's at the door now and, unable to stall any longer, presses the rubber button of the doorbell. No answer for a half-minute. She can make out the sound of little feet padding around inside, plates clattering against each other, then the hallway is illuminated and a dark figure walks towards the misted glass and the door opens. A woman, blonde hair with pink tips, about forty but with a blotchy complexion that makes her look older, answers the door with a tea towel slung over her shoulder like a stole. She says nothing, pursed frown pushing all her features to the front of her face.

'Is your husband in?' Naomi asks, bewildered by the door being answered by someone else. The woman looks Naomi up and down and something in her face changes. There's a glint of, not recognition, but some sort of comprehension.

'Merrick,' she shouts over her shoulder, 'a woman here for you.' She colours the word 'woman' with the hint of a snarl. A little boy of around ten runs up to the door and squeezes past his mum's legs to get to Naomi.

'Who are you, then?' he asks, aping something he's heard an adult saying. Naomi laughs, tries to engage the mother with a look that says, *don't kids say the funniest things*, but the woman stares back, dead-eyed and unimpressed.

'Get in,' she says to the boy who has the same straight, dark hair as little Greg, before taking him with her back into the guts of the house, leaving Naomi alone on their doorstep. She looks at their doormat. It has some 'Keep Calm It's Only …' mantra on it that she can't read properly upside down. The hallway darkens as Merrick trudges towards her from the kitchen. He's a big guy, bigger than she remembers. About the same height as her, but wide. He's wearing three-quarter-length tracksuit bottoms and his ankles are the size of most people's thighs. He gives her the same unfriendly stare but she senses he's withholding a warmth that his wife might not possess. She's seen him giggling with his son and the mask of hostility doesn't fit his face.

'Can I help you?' he says.

'Hello, um, I'm Naomi. My daughter used to go to nursery with your son? Greg? There was someone else that used to pick Greg up.'

'Listen, love, we don't want any trouble so—'

'What do you mean?' she says. He opens his mouth but doesn't speak, closes it. 'What do you mean trouble?'

'It's best just to leave him alone now.'

'What are you talking about?' Her indignation hasn't taken long to arrive and makes the man scratch his face and look at her feet. It seems this was exactly the reaction he was trying to avoid so she tempers herself. 'What is it Sean's said to you about me?' She cranes her neck down to make eye contact with him, forcing him to look up at her. 'Please.'

'Look, Sean's – Sean's a mate, all right. He said you might come round here and I think it's best if you just nip it in the bud, you know?'

'Who do you think I am?' she asks, her forthrightness forcing the large man to take a half-step back.

'He told me that there was a mum from nursery he'd gone for a coffee with who had …'

'Who had what?' She angles her head to the side. What story has Sean been telling people about her?

'Got a bit obsessed with him. Wanted to leave her husband and that, he said.'

'That's ridiculous,' she says, the ridiculousness of the word making her cheeks flush, which the man reads as an admission of guilt.

'None of my business but he showed me some messages, says you've been trying to track him down, following him around.' His thick fingers rub at the stubble at the base of his neck.

'Following him around? How can I have been following him around? He's disappeared.' The man crinkles his face at her as if Sean's disappearance is entirely the consequence of this mad woman standing on his front step and she has to look away, eyes blinking. 'Where is he? I have a right to speak to him.'

''Fraid to say it's not just you, love. There's this other one, sent him dirty photos and that. He said he couldn't help us out any more because of it, said it wasn't right for Greg. He didn't want to show me but it came out of the blue so I wanted to see what had got him so shook up. He showed me the texts you sent him as well, all the missed calls.' Naomi scoffs out of her nose, the middle of her brow pinched in consternation.

'What do you mean, helping you out?' She talks to him as if he were an idiotic customer services advisor. 'What the hell was he doing with your son?' Merrick fingers a flagging piece of wallpaper, desperate not to get into a dialogue with one of his friend's wanton women. He sighs, a long dying breath almost before he speaks. 'Last four, five months he's been doing some pick-ups, the odd drop-off for us. Missis couldn't drive,' he looks over his shoulder and mimes a drinking motion to Naomi, a ban he must mean, 'and I have to get the boys over in Downhurst the same time we have to get Greg from nursery. Sean offered to help us out. He's a mate. We've worked together a while. He's a cast-iron bloke, Sean, do anything for anyone. He was gutted when he said he should stop doing the pick-ups, him and Greg got on well, he'd started taking him to a couple of after-school things. He seemed to like it, don't think he's got much of a family. It's a massive pain in the arse for us as well, to be honest, but he said it was getting too much for him and that he was scared for Greg.'

'Scared?' Naomi parrots the word back to him, incredulous at the person that Sean's painted her as. She's not obsessed with him. She called him a few times and sent some texts. She called him more than just a few times, in fact, but that was because she needed to see him, there was a chance she was having his baby and she needed him to know. There's nothing to be scared of in anything she's done.

'I don't know what's gone on with you and him, don't want to, to be fair, but after he showed me those pictures of that other one, me and the wife thought we'd move Greg out of that place. Don't want him around that sort of— Anyway. Best you just leave it now, no reason to carry on. You know it'd be the best for everyone.' She stares at the doormat, unable to face the man's pitying tone, and picks at the cuticle of her thumbnail.

'Do you know where he is?' she asks. He creases his face, like a mechanic who's about to tell you how much your car will cost to fix, when Greg appears out of a door behind him. That earnest little face under its dark pelmet of hair looks up at her with measured recognition. Merrick's wife emerges from the room and grabs him up into her arms hungrily and eyes Naomi as if she were a bird of prey ready to snatch her boy up in her talons. She gives her husband a face that says, *Get her and all the rest of Sean's desperate women out of our lives*, before wheeling back down the hall towards the kitchen, Greg's legs kicking into the air like they did in the swimming pool that day.

'You've got a kid, yeah?' Merrick asks, head still in the direction of his family. 'We've got four and we're up to our necks in it. I can't cope with any more drama, you know?' He looks around her, hoping she doesn't need anything else from him before he can go without feeling bad about it. He nods, a bow almost, and closes the glass door on her.

Naomi turns round and sees a seagull on the pavement outside the house burrowing its beak into a split black bin bag. She knows she was never obsessed with Sean and yet, when the bird looks up, staring directly at her, she feels like a schoolgirl who's been caught doing something she shouldn't.

FOUR

Lauren Forbes Community Acting Workshop

WORKSHEET: Stanislavski 10 Questions

NB: Your character doesn't know he/she is in a play. They haven't read it! Answer the questions from your character's perspective to get to the heart of them.

1. Who am I?	*Sean, carpenter from Leeds. 32.*
2. Where am I?	*In and around Bank of Friendship Nursery. The park. Car Park.*
3. When is it?	*Mornings and afternoons.*
4. Where have I just come from?	*Lived here for 3 years. Living in Reading before that.* *AMs – From my flat, East Cliff.* *PMs – coming from working for Merrick, 48 Terrence St.*
5. What do I want? (OBJECTIVE)	*For Naomi Fallon to sleep with me.*
6. Why do I want it? (SUPER OBJECTIVE)	*Because I'm in love with her. I need love.*
7. Why do I want it now?	*She's married and isn't the sort to cheat. But she is unhappy, sexually frustrated and needs comfort NOW.*

8. What will happen if I don't get it now?	If she has too much time to think about it, she will reassess and realise she can make things work with her husband. That sleeping with me would be a terrible mistake.
9. What am I going to do to get what I want? (ACTION)	a) Be a knight in shining armour at first opportunity. b) Try to be nothing like her husband. c) Make it obvious I'm interested (not too obvious!) d) Make the first move, but make it her choice.
10. What must I overcome? (External and internal forces)	Naomi's unwillingness to cheat. Other people noticing that something is happening between us. She is very busy. Self-doubt. Knowing it's wrong to sleep with a married woman.

I haven't been Sean for a while but I still like to look things over. Going over the old steps helps me think about the next ones. She's walking towards me. I'm in a glass-fronted café, one of the trendy ones, drinking tea from a glass cup. Feels fancy. I've watched her whole conversation with Merrick. You can't tell she's pregnant yet, not in the coat she's wearing. I haven't thought about what I'd do if she makes it to week twenty-four. Well, I have. But I hope it won't come to that.

The café has these thick magazines and most of my face is concealed by one of them as she walks right past me. She's so confused. It looked like Merrick told her what I'd said to him, that she was a married mother obsessed with Sean, that Sean was starting to worry about poor defenceless little Greg. I saw the flash of self-righteousness on her face at someone muddying her upstanding reputation. Doesn't feel good, does it, Naomi?

Does she look ashamed? Not really. Maybe she doesn't feel shame. Maybe that's what they see in each other. I never factored how she'd react, how she'd respond, into any of this. I thought it'd be enough. Seeing the app, knowing the kid wasn't Charlie's. I thought that'd be plenty. Still, it took me nearly two decades to find who I was looking for. So what's a few more weeks? She turns right and walks back towards her car.

She's so alone now. That's what I wanted; I have to keep telling myself that this is what I wanted. I keep a picture of her in my wallet as if she were someone I love or someone I once loved. It's a picture she posted when she was pregnant with Prue, she isn't wearing any make-up and she looks thoughtful. It was the only photo on her feed where she didn't look delighted with her life. I sometimes think I could have loved her. The sun's going down behind the figure of her walking away and there's long lines of pink clouds. Her hair looks black against it. She looks up at the sky. I wish I could tell her that it's not her fault. If Karin had known that it wasn't her fault, I think it would have changed everything.

FIVE

15 weeks

'Oh, that's lovely, darling. No, I can see that being wonderful,' Naomi's mum Linda says from the screen of the iPhone Naomi's waving around their newly finished, green spare room. 'Is that Apple Mist?' Linda asks. Naomi's parents redecorate a room in their house every spring, so she's always up on which colours are on-trend.

'Can't remember what it's called.' Naomi can, and she knows her mother's right, but she doesn't want to engage in a conversation about how the colours that come in to fashion reflect what's going on in the world – something her mum read in a magazine once and enjoys trotting out whenever she can. Naomi continues to show her the room for longer than necessary to avoid her seeing how tired she is. The voice makes affirmative noises and tells her how much bigger it looks now they've knocked that wall through – her suggestion, which she pointedly won't mention.

Naomi loves her parents. It's only since becoming one that she appreciates how much they compromised themselves for her but, since they've retired, she's found the things they want to talk about, the petit-bourgeois concerns they never had time to worry about before, increasingly tedious.

Prue's trying to yank a doorstop out of the wall and Naomi uses a bare foot to steer her away from it and on to her back. She tickles her belly with one of her toes and Prue makes sounds somewhere between laughter and discomfort. The builders have completed most of the upstairs and they've got decorators going from room to room finishing them up. Charlie's had an advance payment from Teddy, his new client, who he seems to have a bit of a man-crush on, so he insisted they get professionals in. Normally she would have fought him on this, tried to remind him of what happened before, that perhaps they should save money and do the work themselves, but she didn't have the energy. And she wants the house finished. She needs all of that out of her head.

Following her conversation with that man Merrick she's been going over every moment she had with Sean since they first starting talking in the nursery car park. How could he say that she was obsessed with him, that she was in some way dangerous? Straight after the swimming pool she'd thought that he'd initiated everything, and it had been him who'd invited her to the class, but had she been massaging the narrative to alleviate her guilt, her embarrassment? She asked him to go for a coffee, she invited him to come to a soft play with her, but that was as a parent. She thought he had a son and he'd done nothing to make her think otherwise. She had texted him, she had called him, but there was nothing she'd said that could be construed as obsessed.

And the other woman? The woman sending him naked pictures. What had Sean told his friend about her? Had Merrick thought to ask what Sean had been doing to elicit those sort of messages or was he somehow willing to accept that someone so handsome just has that effect on women?

Would Merrick believe that the sexter too just happened to be 'obsessed' with him? Or was everything Sean had told his friend nothing other than unadulterated and face-saving bullshit because it seems Sean failed to mention to his friend and co-worker, the man who'd trusted him with his youngest son, that he'd been using his son to ensnare women at the nursery, that he and one of these woman had had sex up against a wall in a leisure centre changing room. He had initiated that, coming into her shower. But she hadn't told him to go.

She should take Merrick's advice, Lillian's advice. Forget about Sean. He's a scumbag who's made up stories about her, who wants nothing to do with her. He was nothing more than a clichéd seducer and she'd fallen for it.

Naomi's iPhone continues to talk at her. Her mum is wittering on about the virtues of different types of blinds and seems to be pushing shutters, 'despite the initial expense'. The thought of what a pathetic fool Naomi has been makes the bile pique at the back of her throat.

What would Naomi gain from telling a man like that that she's pregnant? He'd deny any involvement, it'd make him run further away from her than he already has. She has to think of it as a blessing. She's been lucky. The Sean she thought she knew might want to do the right thing. But he's revealed his true colours and it has made life easier for her. She knows she should just put the whole thing out of her mind, but it's not in her nature to leave loose ends untied and, maybe she's going mad, maybe tiredness is causing her to make bad decisions, but she knows that this is something she has to resolve.

Prue's got her hands in Naomi's pocket now and is calling for Granny. Naomi hands the phone to her daughter and listens to her mother asking Prue how she likes the new house. Naomi normally speaks to her mum on FaceTime a couple of times a week but she's not called her for a while now. Not since the scan.

There's a rustling sound upstairs. Charlie's in London. She goes to the doorway to listen. The shrill batting of wings. Then the cooing. The fucking pigeons. Naomi's sure they're getting louder.

'What's that, Nay?' her eagle-eared mother asks.

'Pigeons, Mum,' she says, not deigning to go back towards the phone. 'Charlie's trying to get rid of them but the builders said they'll do it when they do the bit of exterior stuff they still need to do on the top floor.'

'Oh, sweetheart, that must be hard for you.' Her mother's tone is patronising; she thinks her daughter's fear of birds is irrational. But it has been hard. Horrible, in fact. They can't tell where they are but their warbles seem to penetrate every room. Naomi's started to hear them everywhere, even when she's not in the house. She gets flashbacks of that lame pigeon flying towards Prue's face and keeps having this vision of them flocking around her as she walks across the road and she's hit by a car. She puts a hand on her bump at the thought of it. It's not much of a bump yet but she knows it's there.

When she was younger Naomi used to rail against her parents for not giving her a brother or sister and Linda knows how desperate she is that Prue doesn't feel as alone growing up as she did. And Naomi's told her how long they've been trying for another baby, how hard it's been, so Linda will be over the moon when she finds out her daughter's pregnant. But Naomi still doesn't want to tell her. She doesn't want to tell anyone. She wants to wait until the twenty-week scan. After twenty weeks the baby's chance of survival is significantly higher. She's scared. She can't sleep, she feels constantly on the edge of an illness, and Prue has been more full-on than usual. All of it is contributing to the baby measuring so small. She's sure of it. But she has to tell her mum. Her bump will soon be impossible to hide and she can't have her spotting it in a picture on Facebook. She told her about Prue the minute she came out of the twelve-week scan, the conventional time to tell the world. She thinks she can get away with telling her mum a couple of weeks later without her suspecting there's something wrong, but not a couple of months.

She picks up the phone that Prue's now crouching over, showing Granny the view under her unicorn T-shirt, and tells her mother that she's expecting a baby. Linda's delighted. She machine-guns a barrage of questions: How many weeks are you? What's the due date? Where are you having it? Is Charlie excited? Does Prue understand? What room are you going to put the new one in? All of which, sitting with her back against the radiator in the furniture-less room, Naomi answers with as much enthusiasm as she can. Then her mother pauses.

'You must have had the scan weeks ago. Was it—Everything's OK?' she asks, her voice now heavy with concern.

'Yeah, no, everything's fine, Mum.' Her mother looks doubtful. 'It took us so long. I really just didn't want to jinx it. I know, stupid.' Linda scrutinises her daughter's face through the phone screen and just like when she was a child, Naomi finds herself blushing – her mum has always been able to tell when she's lying. She could tell her about Sean. Would she judge her or would she be able to help? Understand the context, perhaps make sense of how she's feeling, how confused she is.

'It's measuring small.' Her parents have been married for more than forty years. They may not have always shown each other unerring devotion but there was never any question of infidelity. No, she can't tell anyone what she's done. She has too much to lose.

'How small? Worryingly so?' her mother asks, suddenly posher for no reason.

'The doctors aren't worried.'

'That's good, then. Are you sleeping OK?' Naomi turns her head away, annoyed, as if her mother's concern for her well-being were an accusation that she doesn't know how to look after herself. She hears Prue clamber up the four stairs from her room where she's been rustling around amongst her toys and wonders whether she too will bristle at Naomi mothering her when she's older. Of course she will, she thinks. We're always trying to impress our parents with how grown up we are by letting them know how little we need them.

'I'm fine, Mum. Charlie's being great. I'm resting up on my days off.' Prue runs through the door and crashes into her mother's lap. 'And Prue's really helping.'

'Yes, I can see that, being very gentle, aren't you, little miss squidgy! And what is that you've got there, is that a dummy?' Naomi shakes her eyes into focus and looks at the small square in the bottom corner of the screen that shows Prue, large in the foreground with her own face squinting behind. Her mother's right. Prue is sucking a dummy. Prue doesn't have a dummy. Prue has never had a dummy.

Naomi tries to turn her daughter's head round and she reacts by turning as far away from her as possible and tensing her neck, desperate not to give up what she has in her mouth.

'I thought Mummy didn't let you have a dummy?' Naomi's mum crows in the background. Naomi needs to see what her daughter has in her mouth. There aren't any dummies in the house. They never bought one because they thought it would be a temptation to use it and she was adamant that her children would never need them. She asks Prue, as calmly as she can, to give her the dummy.

'No!' she screams and throws herself off Naomi's crossed legs. The phone tumbles on to the ground and Naomi's mum is left looking at the ceiling, saying that she doesn't see the harm in them as Naomi goes about trying to wrestle it off her daughter. She puts her hands on Prue's shoulders but she throws herself on to the floor and balls herself up like a hedgehog.

'If you let her have it, darling, she'll probably give it back in a—' Naomi presses the red button on her phone, vanishing her mother. Naomi stands up. She wants to scream at Prue to give her the fucking dummy now but her mother is right, anger won't work.

She walks to the window and looks out, trying to ignore her daughter for a moment. She takes a few deep breaths and looks at the dark branches of a tree in one of the neighbours' gardens swaying angrily in the December wind. She pictures a yellowing rubber teat crumbling between her daughter's teeth and a wedge of frost runs up her neck. She thumps over to Prue and picks her up by the waist, her little legs and arms beetling in the air. She clamps Prue's neck in the crook of her elbow and clutches the plastic ring of the dummy. Prue bites down harder on it in retaliation but, after staring at her daughter with unimpressed eyes for a long, long time, Prue's defiance melts and Naomi plucks the dummy out of her mouth. She lowers her little girl on to her feet. Prue hugs into her mother's thigh and utters a whispered, 'Sorry.'

'Don't worry, sweetheart.'

'Not worry.'

'No.' Naomi puts a hand on the top of her head that sweeps down to cup the back of her skull, tickling the base of her neck. She holds the dummy up in front of her. It doesn't look new but it also doesn't look like it's been used. The teat is clear rubber, no marks apart from the fresh ones left there by Prue's teeth. The front part is white plastic but it's faded. There's some text on it. It's branded. One word, lower case black letters. 'Eels.' What the hell is this doing in her house? She thinks of the sleepsuit, the infant sleepsuit she found in Prue's drawer a few months ago. How have these things got here?

She wants to throw it away, out of the window, as far away from her daughter as possible, but she slides the dummy into the back pocket of her jeans, then squats down to Prue's level and looks her in the eye.

'Where did you get this, sweetheart?' she asks. 'Don't worry.'

'Not worry.'

'Was it in your room?' Prue nods. 'Show me where?' Prue thrusts her hand forward like a coquettish girl agreeing to dance and, when Naomi takes it, drags her out of the room and towards her bedroom.

Prue walks to the middle of her room, stands on the rug and waves her arms up and down. She's forgotten why they're there. Naomi scans the room for anything that seems out of place. Some of her cuddly toys have been pulled out of the corner and sit on the floor in front of her chest of drawers.

'Was it here? The dummy? Was it with your toys?'

'Naoo.' Prue smiles. She looks at the wardrobe, the door is open and Prue's nursery bag, bright green with the face of the Very Hungry Caterpillar on it, lies open on the floor of it. Naomi grabs it and kneels down next to Prue.

'Did you find it in here? Is it from nursery?' It has to be, Naomi thinks; they never have any of Prue's friends round to the house, it's not safe enough yet. Prue falls down on the rug and begins to clamber on to Naomi's legs. 'Prudence.' She tries to keep the irritation our of her voice but she needs to get a straight answer. She picks Prue up under her armpits and stands her up to face her. Looking into her eyes she says, 'Prudence, you need to tell me where you found the dummy.' Prue starts making her eyes googly, trying to make her mother laugh. 'If you tell me we can go downstairs and have some blueberries.'

'Log-ert!'

'Tell me where the dummy came from and we can go downstairs and have some blueberries and yoghurt.' Prue takes her mother's hands out from under her arms and walks over to the bookshelf. She picks up the hot-pink potty that lives next to it and carries it over to Naomi as if she were competing in World's Strongest Man. She lifts the lid, it has a lid to ape a real toilet, and points into the bottom of the potty's bowl. 'In there?'

'Yeah.'

'It wasn't in here?' She holds the bag up to her again. Prue shakes her head emphatically, no. Naomi sits back, the rucksack settling in her lap. She needed it to have come from the nursery bag. A simple rational answer so she could put it out of her head.

'Log-ert?' Prue puts her hands on Naomi's forearm; it's the most comforting thing she's felt for weeks. 'Log-ert!' she shouts, trying to galvanise her mother.

'Log-ert,' Naomi confirms quietly. She pushes herself up off the rug with her fists and gets to her feet. She gets a head-rush and has to lean on the changing table for support. Exhaustion swamps around her like sea mist. Her daughter trots out of her room, Naomi follows her on to the landing. The sun shrieks through the glass in the front door, and, as Prue shimmies down the stairs on her bottom, Naomi watches dust motes in the hallway sashay in its rays.

SIX

'Think about it,' he says. Uggy's not seen that look in his eye outside of the bedroom. She opens her mouth to speak but he puts the pads of two fingers on her lips. He presses hard, not to hurt her but enough to make his point. 'I told you to think about it.' She turns back towards the kitchen. She was so excited when he said he was coming over to the flat. She hadn't seen him for weeks, since he'd come over to tell her that Greg's parents found the pictures of her on his phone. She thought he might ask her to move out but he didn't. He was so nice about it. Said it had been selfish of him to put her at risk by keeping them, told her that he should have protected her better. But now he's asking her to do something that seems so wrong.

'Baby,' she says from behind the kitchen counter, stirring the beef stew she started cooking for him three hours ago, 'I only don't want to involve the kids. You know?'

'I begged Merrick and Fran not to show nursery the pictures of you. Begged them. Me and Merrick fell out over it.'

'Baby—'

'I put you before Merrick; mate of mine for years and I put you first.'

'But this is—'

'Everything I've done, sorting out your landlord, giving you a roof over your head, for Christ's sake. I haven't asked for hardly nothing in return.' She goes to him. Tries to put a tender hand on his neck but he brushes her off, walks over to the window and looks out at the supermarket car park. He shakes his head. Punches a fist into his open hand. She has done everything she can to show him how grateful she is for what he's done for her. Things she never imagined doing.

'I shouldn't have bothered. Not with you, not all this.' He indicates the flat, the nicest flat she's ever lived in. 'You think there aren't other women who want to be with me? Who wouldn't do little things I ask them to help me with?' He's right. He could have picked so many other women, better women, and he's chosen her. What they have might not be something from a fairy tale but here, in this country, this town where she couldn't feel less at home, he's become everything to her. She can't have him angry with her.

'Baby, if I knew why?'

'It shouldn't matter why.'

'I don't get why we have to include in it the little ones?' He drops his head down, puts it to one side and then the other, stretching his neck muscles. She'd love to stretch now, she hasn't felt this tense for weeks.

'The little girl's mother,' he says, eyes still looking at the floor but his tone has lost its edge and he sounds exhausted. 'Fuck, I didn't want to say anything.' He flicks his head up to her, breathes in so his shoulders puff up. 'Sit down.' Uggy sits on the sofa as if he's pushed her, eyes down at her fingers twining around each other. 'I met her in the park after nursery one day and she asked me to go for a coffee. She seemed … I don't know, she seemed sad.' Uggy pulls at the skin around her nails. 'She asked for my number, I shouldn't have given it but, I don't know, she seemed nice enough.' Uggy eyes him then looks at the tight-knit carpet. 'After that she kept inviting me to things – baby groups, that sort of thing.' He sidles over and sits next to her, his right hand encapsulating both of hers. 'I didn't go, made excuses. But then she starts coming up to me in the car park at nursery asking why I was ignoring her, sending me loads of messages, calling me at all times of the day, saying how she thought we had some sort of connection. I told her where to go, said she was off her head, that we'd just had one coffee.' He shakes his head, eyes lost in the middle distance. 'I've seen her car parked near the site we're working at. She must be following me from nursery. I just— Don't know what she's going to do next.'

She puts her other hand over his and he squeezes the tips of her fingers. 'That's why you were asking me about her, about what days she was dropping off at the nursery.'

He nods. 'I should've said something but I didn't want you confronting her or anything. Promise me you won't.' She closes her eyes and smiles an agreement. 'She'll make up all sort of things about you, get you sacked. I didn't want you involved but—' He stands up, walks back towards the window and puts both hands on the rain-speckled glass. 'I just – I've tried everything. Told her to leave me alone, got Merrick and Fran to move Greg, said I'd tell the police. I just thought that maybe if she thought she'd taken her eye off the ball with her kid – I don't know.' She watches him press his forehead into the window. Uggy's never seen him this defeated. She rises from the sofa and goes to him, laces her hands around his waist and clutches her wrists, squeezing him tight. She thinks back to when the mother was asking after Greg, asking what nursery he'd moved to. She should've told him then, or someone at the nursery, perhaps Lisa could have talked to her. He won't look at her and she can't help but feel that she's failed him.

'Baby, I'm so sorry. I want to help you but—' She feels his stomach muscles tense, his body shift her hands loose from him, she can't lose him. 'Maybe we are able to come up with a better way, the police, like you said, that is much better way.' He spins around, takes her bird-like head in his hands and kisses her hard on the mouth. He pulls away but doesn't let go of her head; there's sadness in his eyes.

'We go to the police and it's he said, she said. Who you think they'll believe, you and me? Or her?' Uggy's eyes try to wander past him but he squeezes her jaw to get her attention back to him. 'She's not a bad person, she's just – I don't know, post-natal depression that never went away or something. She seems like a good mum, though, no?' Uggy blinks. He's right, she's one of the most conscientious parents at the nursery. 'If we can remind her what's important, let her know she's not paying enough attention to her kid, it might shock her out of whatever she's decided is going on between us.' Uggy looks at him for a long moment. She's never seen him look so boyish, so adrift. She loves him and he needs her to rescue him. Perhaps he could love her too. She nods her agreement, smiling with one side of her mouth. His fingers spread over the back of her skull, one of them plays around the occipital bone at the back of her cranium before his hands move down over her neck, her shoulders, over her sharp hip bones and round under her bum. He lifts her up as if she were weight-less, on to his chest and she wraps her legs around him. He kisses her roughly, his beard sandpaper against her skin. Her eyes are open and she watches blue light flashing against the wall of the dark supermarket as an ambulance zooms past.

He puts her down and puts a hand on her cheek before sweeping past her towards the kitchen. 'We can do it now,' he says, excited like a child, noisily pulling something out of a kitchen drawer.

'We cannot rush,' she tells him firmly. 'After Christmas. We'll do it after Christmas.' He passes the steel kebab skewer he's holding from one hand to the other and smiles his agreement before returning it to its place amongst the spatulas and knives.

SEVEN

Charlie emerges from the brass-gilded revolving door of the private members' bar and shelters under its awning. A graffiti mural in front of him tells him that 'Shoreditch is Dead', but based upon the throngs of people bustling along, their expensive Canada Goose coats repelling the wet snow, it seems very much alive. Every time he gets off the train in London he gets swept up with the electricity of millions of people fighting to make something of themselves, but it never lasts long. Now as he looks at the hordes raiding towards the suffocating prison of the underground train, he's desperate to be back by the sea.

He merges with the cattle on their way to the tube and checks his phone. Four missed calls from Naomi. He puts it back in his pocket, unfazed. He would have been more surprised if she hadn't called. She's calmed down a bit since the scan but she's still on edge, liable to lose her shit with him over the tiniest things. He was doing some washing-up the other day while Prue was in the hall and she bit off half a crayon. Naomi came downstairs to find her spitting out bits of blue wax and she lost it with him. Started screeching that Prue can't be left unsupervised, questioning whether he could keep them safe, telling him that she can't be responsible for her twenty-four seven. Charlie decided not to argue. He said sorry and took it even though she left Prue to play on her own all the time. Afterwards, when she'd calmed down, he pressed her as to why she reacted like that, trying to enact his communication strategy that requires them to do a post-match analysis of every argument they have. She said she had a dream the night before that they were all walking on the cliff by the sea and then Prue just wasn't there. It seemed like there was much more to it but she said she was tired and wanted to watch *MasterChef*.

Charlie whisks through the barriers and down the escalator into the bowels of the city. He texts Naomi to tell her that he's rushing to get the 15:22 from Stratford back home and will call once he gets past Ashford and all the tunnels. He needs some time to decompress after the meeting he's just had.

Teddy Whale, the entrepreneur he's working for, called him up to his club – his word – to discuss something confidential. They'd met once at Rinalds' office but they mostly communicated by phone or FaceTime so Charlie was apprehensive that he wanted to see him in person. Teddy, a sartorial presence in Harris-tweed three-piece suit and Converse trainers, sat him down in an oxblood leather booth and insisted he go through all of his security procedures where it came to communications and data storage. Once they'd gone through everything Charlie asked him why and Teddy told him something disturbing.

There was a company that hired film equipment called Forsber Movies that he was a non-executive director for, he was a hedge fund guy before he became a tech entrepreneur, and he'd received a strange call from them. Someone, a man called David Jerome, wanted to know whether they'd be interested in some products he was designing. Three products. A device that would link to a smartphone app for pulling a camera focus, a shoulder-mounted LED lighting rig and a smartphone steadicam. The exact products Charlie was designing for Teddy.

Charlie got flustered, worried about the implication that he'd been trying to tout the designs out to other companies, but Teddy never suspected he was. It wouldn't make sense for someone with a contract, a generous contract, to try to undercut the man who was processing the patents, he said. He trusted Charlie, believed in him, he said.

Teddy thinks that Charlie's files have been hacked. He told him that one of his people has set up a hyper-secure network that will be the only place they'll save all of their work and that their communications will all run through an encrypted messenger service. He gave Charlie a deadline for the patent applications and stressed the importance of getting things firmed up legally. June. Just when the baby's due. As he left he pointed out that they were very lucky that whoever had stolen their designs had tried to sell them to a company he was on the board of. Then he gave Charlie a huge bear hug, said he was delighted to be working with him and left. It was a weird meeting.

A line of Spanish schoolgirls sit opposite him on the Central Line, chewing gum and pulling each other's lanyards. As the train flips into a Wi-Fi zone a message from Naomi arrives – 'Fine.' No kiss. She's angry.

He should tell her about what Teddy's told him. Complete transparency is the only way to mend a lack of trust in a marriage, that's what Amy says. Naomi will understand that everything is fine, that it's just one of those strange things that happens in his game. An occupational hazard that's being taken care of. She might even acknowledge that he could be right about Burman VR having stolen the designs to his headset. What's more likely, however, is that she'll freak out and assume that, as with the Burman fiasco, he's not protecting his intellectual property and is on the way to squandering another year's work because of his slapdash approach to everything. He'll see how she is when he gets home and make a judgement call.

He's out of the tube now and walking towards the train, out of the sleet and into the processed heat and heaving crowds of Westfield shopping centre. He suddenly realises that, although Teddy seemed relaxed, confident that upgraded security measures will put the problem to bed, whoever David Jerome is, he might already have all his designs. They're not finished but the steadicam in particular is most of the way there and could easily be extrapolated by anyone with half a brain. There's a boy walking next to him, filming the lower floor of the shopping centre, Charlie watches the crowds on his screen. Termite shoppers flowing against each other like oil and water. People knock him as he films and the video jerks and jolts. Charlie imagines the boy using his steadicam, imagines the smooth movements in the video and looks round at the thousands of kids filming their friends and knows that it can't go wrong this time. Teddy's a major player, someone in the inner circle who has his meetings at Shoreditch House, and he believes in Charlie. He's investing a lot of money into the products and people like him don't fuck about when someone is threatening one of their investments. He's working with the sort of man he thought he would one day be and now, under the excessive white Christmas lights, that doesn't seem too distant a possibility.

He approaches a Pretzel Shack and buys one that costs three pounds. He bites into it, licking sugar and cinnamon off his lips, as he makes his way towards the railway station. He strides alongside a stupidly long queue of agitated parents waiting to take their kids into the Santa's grotto. He notices some of the dads eyeing his unencumbered stroll and pretzel with raw envy.

EIGHT

Naomi hears his key in the lock then the sound of the door clattering into the door-chain. She skip-walks from the kitchen to the hall to see Charlie's bemused face wedged in the narrow opening. They've never used the chain before. She unhooks the lock and opens the door.

'My phone—' he begins to say before she 'shhes' him into silence. Prue's just got off to sleep after fifteen minutes of crying out for 'Daddy'. Which hasn't been great for Naomi's nerves, but Prue crying never is. She nods him towards the kitchen and walks back down the hall. The dummy sits on top of the kitchen island. The black of that word, 'Eels', picking up a shine from the spotlights.

'You said you'd call,' she says as he arrives in the kitchen after taking what seems like an age hanging up his coat.

'Phone died, sorry.' He waves the blank phone around before reaching past her to plug it in to their charger. He puts his arm around her shoulders and tries to kiss her cheek but she shrugs him off. She indicates the dummy in front of him.

'Prue found this today. In her potty.'

'Can I just get in the house?'

'We don't have a dummy.'

He sucks his lips in. She knows that face. Trying to hide the fact that he thinks she's trying to involve him in something inconsequential. He picks up the dummy, examines it in the light.

'Where did it come from?' she asks.

'Where did you find it?'

'Prue found it in her potty. I just said that.' He puts the dummy back on the island and walks around her to open the fridge. He grabs a bowl of leftover roasted vegetables from last night's dinner and a can of Heineken. He plonks himself down on one of their breakfast-bar stools, cracks the can open and begins to eat.

She looks down at the tiled floor and breathes out, incredulous. There was a quote from a TV show they'd watched together. A character was telling someone how they always managed to stay so calm and they said, 'I decided to stop getting angry with people for being themselves.' When it comes to Charlie, Naomi finds this very, very difficult. But she won't allow his flippancy to get them into an argument now, she needs his help. She gets a plastic shopping bag out of one of the kitchen drawers and places it on the island in front of him.

'I didn't tell you about this at the time,' she says. He looks nervous. The mystery of the bag finally instilling a sense of gravity in him. He opens it, pulls out the *Powerpuff Girls* sleepsuit and holds it up in front of him.

'Is this Prue's?'

'Look at the label; it's for premature babies. Prue's never been that small. We had to put her in three-to-six months clothes from the start almost.'

'It is tiny.'

'It was in her chest of drawers. I thought it must have come home from nursery but they don't have children that small there.' She comes over and sits on the stool next to him. All afternoon, throughout Prue's dinner, her bath, reading her stories as enthusiastically as she could, she's been trying to think of every possible place the sleepsuit or the dummy could have come from – the builders, Lara, the previous owners of the house – but none of them made any sense. She's been trying to swab away the thought that keeps nudging her, the only other possibility of where they could have come from. She grabs a shrivelled green pepper from his bowl, wipes the oil on the edge and eats it. He slurps some of his beer. The sleepsuit is laid out flat on the island; the dummy perched next to it.

'I found this a couple of months ago. Creeped me out.'

'What do you mean?'

'Someone else's clothes being in Prue's room. It's horrible.'

'Is it?' He stands up and goes to wipe his hands on a tea towel before depositing the bowl in the sink and running water into it.

'Didn't they both come back from nursery? That's what you thought, right? They're not dirty or anything.'

'They didn't come from nursery, it doesn't make sense.' He exhales as quietly as he can. He's tolerating her and she can feel the butterflies of rising anger flutter in her stomach. 'I googled "Eels". They're a band who were big twenty years ago. It's the same logo.'

'Oh yeah, they were good. They were on one of my Spotify Suggests things a few weeks ago. Those algorithms are unbelievable.' The water gushes into the sink. He pours Fairy liquid from a great height into the sink and she watches the bubbles subsume the plates and bowls.

'A branded dummy from a band who were popular in the nineties turns up and you think that's totally normal.'

'It's a bit weird but I don't get what you're worried about; they're just kids' things.'

'I'm worried about how they got in our house?'

'Prue came back with half a picture of Archduke Franz Ferdinand in the pocket of her hoodie the other day.'

'Which she got when we went to the library; I saw her tear it out of a book.'

'Kids grab stuff and nick it. They're worse than magpies. Think how many hats and gloves we've lost at nursery.'

'You've lost.' He gives her a fake smile. The pattern, their argument pattern, is gathering pace and unless he says something decent soon she knows she's going to erupt. She bites her thumbnail, tries to measure the words she's about to say, knowing already how he will react.

'Someone could have put them in her room.' He cleans the suds off the breadknife with a long sweep of the sponge before putting it on the drying rack and turns to her, giving her his full attention.

He's about to speak but stops himself, smiles, then says, quite simply, 'Who?'

When she found the sleepsuit she couldn't explain how it had got in Prue's drawers so the thought popped into her head that someone might have planted it there, but she dismissed the idea because, as Charlie is asking her right now, who would do something like that. But now a dummy, a branded dummy, has turned up in Prue's potty. And the pregnancy test; she was sure she hadn't left it out but there was so much going on at the time, she was so frazzled, she'd thought she must have done. She's decided not to mention the test to Charlie, there's no knowing where his questions would lead. He's looking at her expectantly and seeing she hasn't got an answer, a sympathetic grin starts to spread across his face. 'Who?' he wants to know. There is someone, someone who pretended he had a son, someone she cheated on her husband with, someone who, when she said that what happened between them was a mistake, said he wouldn't make things difficult for her. She'd believed him, why wouldn't she have, but maybe that had been another of his lies.

'You're right,' she says, shrugging, 'no one would do that.' And it's true. It doesn't make sense. Why would someone put things in their house? Why would Sean do that? He wouldn't. She leans her shoulder against the wall-mounted oven, suddenly exhausted.

Charlie comes over to her. 'I'll talk to Prue in the morning. Try and explain that she can't take stuff from nursery. You're right. It is weird. Really weird. You have to try and take it easy, though.' He puts a hand on her bump. 'Both of you. Anything like this. I'll sort it out.' His hand lingers on her stomach, the protuberance around her belly button, the start of what will soon be a huge bump containing a baby he believes is his. What would he do if he knew? He never can.

She turns the tap back on and moves away from him into the hall. He sighs and clatters a plate as she goes to the door and clips the chain back across it.

NINE

'Hello?'

'Oh, hi. Um, hello. This is Uggy? Prudence's key worker.'

'Is everything OK?'

'Sorry to be calling from my mobile but I wanted to talk to you before going to my manager. I didn't want Prudence getting into trouble.'

'What's she done?'

'She's been very emotional, physical a little bit. Have you noticed some recent bad behaviour in Prudence?'

'Can you be more specific?'

'She's been quite needy of me? Yesterday, one of the children and me were in the "little world" area and she came in and pushed the other little girl and then she jumped into my lap. Pulled my head down to hers and cuddled me. I said she had to say sorry to the other girl and she did. But she did not want to let me go. She's been doing this a lot. Pulling me to her. Sometimes pinching me too.'

'Pinching?'

'A few times.'

'Oh goodness; I'm so sorry.'

'It's OK.'

'No, it's not.'

'Has she been the same at home?'

'She's been a bit boisterous, sorry, I mean a bit rough, but she's always been very active, physical as you said.'

'The nursery has a very strict policy for things like this. Safeguarding for the other children.'

'Safeguarding, yeah.'

'Prudence is normally very well behaved so it's probably just a phase.'

'She could be feeling insecure with the new baby coming. So much has been going on for us recently.'

'I have to go back inside for the children's lunch now. But over the Christmas break, if you look out for it. Her behaviour.'

'Absolutely.'

'We all love Prudence.'

'That's nice of you to say. Thank you. Thank you for the call.'

'Please don't mention this to anyone at nursery. We're not meant to call parents—'

'No. No. Course.'

'Goodbye, Mrs Fallon.'

'Bye, Uggy. Thanks.' Prudence's mother hangs up and Uggy breathes out, her head slumping forward. Charles slips the phone into her coat pocket and pulls her into his chest. He blows warm air into her ear and she squirms. They're leaning against the broad trunk of a horse chestnut tree in the park outside the nursery. It's warm for December but he still has her wrapped in his huge black parka. He can be strangely paternal with her sometimes.

'Maybe this will be enough for her to stop bothering you?' she says, lifting her eyes to his.

'I hope so.' He dapples the back of her neck with thumb and little finger before massaging his fingers towards her throat. 'I really hope so.'

TEN

It's Christmas Day but I'm not having turkey. I've spent a year eating chicken breasts and I'm off poultry now, maybe for good. I used to weigh thirteen stone and now I'm about fifteen. All muscle. All chicken breasts. It's a strange thing being stronger. I'm still not used to it. When I pull a door open it feels like I could knock it off its hinges.

We spent a lot of the time at Mrs Forbes' making plays up, it's called 'devising', and she always said to make the character like yourself to begin with, so that's what I've done. I wanted to be an actor for a job. Mrs Forbes said I was good. She got me meetings with agents and things but they were a bunch of stuck-up cunts. Phonies. One of them said I had a great look but that she was worried I wouldn't 'meet' well. I knew what she meant.

I've got frozen Pizza Express pizzas in the oven and I'm going to eat them by the Christmas tree. The front room's looking nice now. It's painted a sort of grey. Purbeck Stone it's called. Stupid name but it looks nice. Chalk-based so it's got a nice depth to it. I'm never sure how well those Farrow & Ball paints go on but they've got a good finish out of it. There's a new sofa in there. Nice big telly. I'm going to eat a pizza and watch whatever cartoon film is on BBC. When we were kids we were with a foster family who used to send us away for Christmas. Three years in a row. They said it was 'family time' and they thought we should respect that. We'd been moved around so much by then we just nodded and went back to the shared home for a couple of weeks. Three years is a pretty good stretch but they always let us know we weren't part of the family. That they were doing us a favour. We were only ever at one place that made us feel like a family. The last one we were in. Julie and Clive. They had us call them Mum and Dad.

Uggy texted me to ask if I was coming back to the flat so maybe I'll go round there later. I was planning on staying there tonight, it's more comfortable than where I've been crashing recently. But then I had to come in here to get a few things prepared for when they're back and I haven't left yet. I've never slept on a mattress like they've got. Pocket sprung, they called it. Apparently the more pockets it's got, the better. He can be fucking boring when he gets going on stuff like that. Don't know what Naomi sees in him, what she used to see in him anyway.

They've gone to Bournemouth, to have Christmas with her parents. Naomi's Instagram's been full of trips to the German market, a pile of presents so big under their tree it looks like it might topple over and videos of the new playroom Linda and Ray surprised Prue with in the basement for whenever they come to visit. It wasn't a surprise to me. Linda's Facebook page has shown the redecoration step by step. It looks nice. It seems like they're all having a relaxing time away. Naomi needs a break. Stress can be such a damaging thing, particularly to someone in her condition. If she has anything else to deal with, I'm worried something might happen to her.

The pizzas are done. Two pizzas. It's Christmas. I've cut them up and am on my way to their new sofa when I spot the scan. There's a picture from their scan in a bowl on a knackered old table in the hall. Little white splodge. She didn't post this one on social media; I wouldn't have done either. I never thought to look for it around the house. Didn't see the point. I pick it up and have a closer look. It looks like an alien off *The X-Files*. You can see its fingers. Massive.

I put the scan back in the bowl. The pizza will be cool enough to eat. I'm hungry and I think *The Incredibles* is just starting. Will they find out the sex of the baby? I hope it's a little girl.

ELEVEN

Uggy looks over to Prue in the cosy corner of the baby-room. She's surrounded by three baby dolls and a plastic dinosaur playing tea party, repositioning her guests until they're in the right place before deciding they all need to be moved again. She's so sweet, Uggy thinks as her high-pitched babbling carries over to where she's sat amongst the musical instruments. One-year-old Aidan and nine-month-old Elsa sit opposite her bashing a saucepan and tambourine respectively. It would be hard to describe the noise they're making as musical. On her way to waddling over to the T-rex Prue clocks Uggy with the two little ones and her eyebrows pinch and the hint of a pout appears. Uggy gives her a little wave and Prue lifts the dinosaur, shakes it around in front of her face in response. Uggy can't tell whether she's trying to be friendly or scary but she assumes the latter and feigns fear. Prudence smiles and goes to put the dinosaur down by the plastic teapot.

Over in the kitchen Jess puts the stereo on. 'Jingle Bells' comes on. Even though Christmas Day was more than two weeks ago, she doesn't seem to think it necessary to change the CD. Uggy looks down at the sleeve of her left arm before picking Elsa up and plonking her on one of her crossed legs.

'There we go, sweetie,' Uggy says to Elsa. Uggy looks up and sees Prue glaring at them, thunderclouds in her eyes at the baby sitting on her key worker. She grabs the baby doll up into a bear hug and stomps over to Uggy. 'Hi, Proodence,' Uggy says as she arrives. Prue points her hand sharply at Elsa, she wants to sit where she's sitting. 'Why don't you come and sit on this side?' Uggy pats her available knee. Prue puts her baby doll on the floor, steps over Aidan and shoves herself on to the empty spot on Uggy's leg. She continues to stare daggers at Elsa.

Uggy begins to rock on her sit-bones and sings 'Seesaw Margery Daw'. Elsa is unsteady with the motion and Uggy takes her hand away from Prue to put both hands on the little baby. Prue barks a nasal sound and reaches over to Elsa.

'Prudence, no. No, don't—' Prue snatches at Uggy's hands, causing her to gasp in pain. Jess, still by the stereo, looks over. Prue is wrenching at Elsa's hands now, trying to pull her off Uggy. Uggy's arms tangle with the two little girls' limbs. Prue lurches over to the side her rival's on, causing Uggy to topple over on to her back.

Jess moves over towards the melee, tapping their supervisor Siobhan on the elbow as she goes and then—

'Ow! Stop that! Stop that, Prudence!' Uggy screams, shock etched on her words, piercing the joyous atmosphere of the baby-room.

Mabel's been crying on her for twenty minutes now but Uggy can't keep her eyes off the office door on the other side of reception. Prue's mother has been talking to Lisa in there for ten minutes. She jigs Mabel and sings to her but nothing's calming her so she gives up. Sometimes Uggy wants to scream for twenty minutes too but she spends her mornings and evenings running to make sure she doesn't.

There she is. Lisa, at the door, arm raised, beckoning her in to the office. Uggy hands Mabel over to Laura, who looks about as pleased as if she'd been given a bag of dog-poo. Laura is Mabel's key worker but the other girls have decided that Uggy is the best at calming down the screamers so she spends most of her time these days cuddling tiny, incandescent babies. She doesn't like it, no one does, but she manages to stay calmer than all the others who, when children are being particularly difficult, look like they might throw them against the wall.

She edges into the office where the walls are covered in timetables instead of finger-paintings. Lisa invites her to sit down on the chair at the side of the room. Prue is sitting on her mother's lap and extends her hands out to Uggy. The mother puts her forearm out and clamps her daughter's arms down. Uggy takes in her fitted jacket, gun-metal grey and flawless, the flick of eyeliner that gives away she's wearing any make-up at all. She tries so hard to look like she isn't someone's mother and that makes her seem older than she is. She has treacle-brown eyes and a delicate nose. She's very beautiful. Uggy used to get jealous when Charles asked questions about her, but looking closer, her pupils too large, eyes too wide – maybe it's what he's said about her, perhaps it's what Uggy's done, but she feels frightened of this woman.

'Sorry to bring you in, Uggy, but Mrs Fallon wanted to see your wrist,' Lisa says, tapping the knuckle of her thumb on her desk. 'Do you mind?' The mother pulls her daughter tighter to her, territorial. Prue looks behind her, she wants to get down and play with the wooden train carriages she knows are in a tray by the door but seems to understand that she shouldn't. Uggy rolls up the left sleeve of her under-shirt, shifts forward on her seat and holds out her arm. The mother looks at a semicircular row of small red indentations on her pale wrist and takes a sharp intake of breath, shocked by how angry the marks look. Uggy turns the arm over and reveals the mirror image on her forearm. A bite-mark.

'Prue did this?' She directs the question at Uggy but quickly shifts her focus to Lisa as if Uggy can't understand the question.

'This morning. Uggy didn't want to report it initially, but it's important for the safety of our staff that we take things like this seriously so I'm glad she did.' Lisa ends her thumb-drumming with a final strum of shellac nail on the desktop. The mother cranes her head down to look at her daughter's face before looking up into the corner of the room, gathering herself.

'Can I see your arm again?' she says.

'Uggy needs to get back to the other children.'

'I'd just like to see it again if I could.' The mother stares at Uggy, making her feel like a tiny animal in front of a predator. When she'd reported it this morning Lisa hadn't even asked to see the mark, trusting her staff implicitly. The nursery manager had gone down on her haunches in front of Prue and, in a voice filled with Zen, tried to explain to her why we don't bite. Prue had bared her teeth like a tiger and chomped them together, thinking the older woman was explaining some game to her. Lisa stood up and shook her head with a gravity that made Uggy want to tell her that they shouldn't make a big deal of it but she'd stayed silent. Uggy leans over towards the mother, showing her arm. 'Did you do this, Prudence?'

she asks, voice comforting. Prue looks at Uggy for answers, then peers over at the marks her mother's pointing to, red pinpricks. Uggy doesn't breathe. Prue smirks, the pressure of three sets of adult eyes boring into her becomes too much so she turns towards her mother and buries her head in her jumper and hums indistinct sounds.

'Two of our staff were there, Mrs Fallon; they saw what happened,' Lisa tells her gently.

'I'm so sorry.' The mother's voice is flat. 'I did speak to her,' she says to Uggy, phone call unspoken between them. 'I told her that this sort of behaviour wasn't on.' Uggy smiles at her. She should say something but she can't find any words so she focuses on the pile of box files on Lisa's desk.

'Mrs Fallon, we know that pushing and hitting behaviours are a natural part of a child's development but we can't have our staff feeling the children could harm them in any way.'

'She didn't mean any harm.' The mother has cottoned on to what Lisa's getting to and a hint of desperation creeps into her voice.

'The nursery has a policy. It's not an exclusion but we just give the child a few weeks out, a few weeks at home to overcome the developmental stage until they can be brought back in.'

The mother's face drops, she opens her mouth to speak but then closes it. She looks at the nape of her daughter's neck. Her daughter sitting so nicely on her lap. Poor Prudence, Uggy thinks. She doesn't deserve any of this. She wants to appeal to Lisa to relax their rules but, when pressed earlier in the day she told her that this wasn't an isolated incident. She told her she'd caught Prue nearly biting other children a few times but managed to stop her.

'How long?'

'A month.'

'I have a job.'

'We can review it in three weeks.' Prue's mum blinks in bewilderment and Uggy thinks that perhaps she shouldn't feel as bad for her as she does. It's not just how she's behaved with Charles; this woman is a mother and she's reacting to the news that she has to look after her child for a month like a bereavement. If Uggy ever has children she wouldn't dream of letting someone else take care of them. That's why she came here – to raise a family. To meet a man like Charles and to raise a family somewhere safe, somewhere where her children would have a chance to be something more than she is. So no, she won't allow herself to feel sorry for this woman, however upset she looks. Prue looks up at her mother, who's still reeling from the news, and pokes a finger into the underside of her chin, which she shakes off as if it were an irritating fly. She slides her daughter off her lap, lifts herself off the red plastic chair and stands in front of the desk.

'Can I call in a fortnight, then?' she asks, almost childlike.

'Good idea. Pop in in three weeks or so and we can have a chat. Prue's such a lovely girl and it breaks my heart to have to do this. I know Uggy's really fond of her and they have a wonderful bond.'

'Yes,' the woman agrees and looks at Uggy who tries a smile that says, *I didn't want this to happen.* Then Prue's mother looks at the mark on her arm again, her haughtiness replaced by a resigned sadness. She takes Prue's hand and leaves the tiny office, pausing in the doorway to read the kids' menu for the week, though her little girl won't be eating any of that food. Prudence gives Uggy a wave as she goes and Uggy waves back with a huge, fake smile.

It had made sense when he told Uggy that the mother was a big deal in the London stock exchange. The material of her clothes looked more tightly woven and better cut than even the other people who'd come down from London. Uggy had been a hairdresser for a while and she'd never been able to find a flaw in the woman's colouring. She can see how she's become so besotted with Charles after he rejected her. Maybe if you're used to always getting what you want, you don't know how to cope when things don't go your way. Uggy watches her walk past the window of the office, through huge piles of dead leaves, somehow half the size of the woman who dropped Prue off this morning.

She looks down at her arm and picks a bit of dried blood off one of the dots where she had pressed the kebab skewer in a little too hard. She spent her morning break in the staff toilet making the marks. She and Charles had practised it last night on her calf.

She looks back at the window. Prue and her mum have turned the corner into the car park and only the black branches of the bare trees remain in the picture. Uggy should be pleased.

TWELVE

www.webmums.co.uk/webmumschat/pregnancy/
labour/33299401#1

valerine n(5)

Member

Join Date
Sep 2006
Posts 28

Can stress cause premature birth?

Hi Everyone

Just wondered if stress can cause premature birth? Life
has been super stressful lately. OH and I have been having
mega-big rows for no reason. I can feel myself getting so
angry and so mad sometimes and i keep telling myself to
calm down because i know it's bad and read that it could
make me go into labour prematurly. My bff had gave birth
at 24 weeks and the little boy didn't make it. Now got crazy
worried about it. Help???

katherine(33)

Member

Join Date
Mar 2001
Posts 1030

hi. stress doesn't help anyone at any time but what you're saying doesn't sound like it would cause preterm labour. This article says it's only 'chronic stress' that causes it: See below. Hope it helps. Try and take it as easy as you can.

Stress Can Cause Preterm Labor

Labor is a complex process and we don't fully know how or why it begins when it does, but studies show that mothers who experience significant stress are more likely to go into labor early. And if too early, that can be harmful to baby and mother.

A sustained period of high stress, which doctors label 'chronic stress', causes long-term changes in the body's vascular system, hormone levels, and ability to fight infection. Doctors suggest that it is these changes that influence labor to start before the baby is full term (at least 37 weeks' gestation). Dealing with a divorce, the death of a loved one, a period of sustained harassment or abuse, or extreme anxiety related to your pregnancy could all cause the kind of chronic stress that could drastically increase your risk for pre-term labor.

THIRTEEN

18 weeks

Naomi's walking back from a yoga class at one of the four studios that have opened nearby in the last year. She's never fully bought into yoga but was of the opinion that if so many people she respects spend so much time doing it, there has to be something in it, so she tries to go once a week. She'd gone up to tell Charlie about the situation at nursery and he suggested, in a moment of rare insight, that she get out of the house during Prue's afternoon nap. This was after he reacted to the news of the biting by saying that things were ramping up with Teddy so he wouldn't be able to take a day off a week to look after Prue, as Naomi had hoped. He envisioned a few more trips to London, he said, and to a factory they were talking to in Germany but that he'd help out where he could. Naomi wanted to scream at him for not being able to click his fingers and solve their newly minted childcare catastrophe but if things are going as well with this Teddy as Charlie says they are, she knows it's not in their interest for him to take time off. Victoria will let her work from home some of the time, she imagines, but will also laud her magnanimity over her in recompense.

The yoga teacher, Belinda, spotted her bump when she went into the class straight away. No one else has yet.

Naomi's trying to think about the life inside her as little as possible, knowing that the more she thinks about the fact it could be his, the less it will grow and the more chance there is of there being something wrong. She spent a lot of the class in 'child's pose' thinking about her daughter's teeth clamped into the flesh of that woman's arm. She should have fought her corner more in that pissy little office with its walls of officious spreadsheets, designed to give the impression that Lisa's running a very serious operation. She should have asked for details of the incidents where they'd 'suspected' that Prue might do something like this. Prue can be rough, a little clumsy. She's hit Naomi a number of times, grabbed toys off other children at playgroups, she rugby tackled Margot once, but biting down hard enough to make those marks. It doesn't feel like something her child could do.

She turns from a tree-lined street on to her road and the sea sparkles, vast in front of her. The sun warms the bare skin between her leggings and ankle socks. She's seven or eight houses away from hers and she notices that the Nissan isn't outside. When she left, Prue was asleep in her room and Charlie was upstairs working. Naomi grabs at her phone in the bottom of the coat pocket and expects to see a message from her husband but the screen is blank, the battery's dead. She quickens her pace, mind tripping over the various rational explanations for why their car wouldn't be in the road while her husband was watching their child in the house. Perhaps Charlie decided to take Prue for a drive, maybe it's been stolen.

She barges open their front gate and jogs up the steps, fumbling with the keys as she goes to open the door. There's something in the oven, the smell of cooking wine hitting her as soon as she's in the hallway. The house is eerily quiet. Her husband and daughter must have gone out, she thinks, she woke and Charlie thought he'd take her out to the beach to give Naomi some peace, but then Prue's cough bursts into the silence. She's had the same chest infection for most of the winter and her sleeps are often punctuated by the cough of a forty-a-day smoker. Staying frozen to the spot, she listens to her daughter settling down and then, trying not to assume the worst, that her husband has, for some insane reason that she can't even begin to imagine, left their sleeping daughter alone in the house, goes through to the kitchen to plug her phone into the charger.

She hears something upstairs, steps on the floorboards, or is it the pigeons? Where the fuck is Charlie? She looks up the stairs and sees light spewing from the open door of Prue's nursery. He must be in there. She walks on the sides of her feet up the stairs, not wanting to wake Prue. She gets halfway up and sees him, standing in the doorway. Mountainous back in plaid shirt, waves of blonde hair. It's Sean.

She launches herself up towards Prue but stumbles, losing her balance and falls forward, hands splatting loudly on to the wood of the landing. Sean turns round, he looks pleased to see her. She looks round his legs and sees Prue's little head wheeling awake and blinking at her through the bars of her cot. Naomi begins to push herself up from the floor, he walks forward and bends down to help her but she brushes off his offering hands. She rises up to face him, he's too close to her and her heel teeters over the edge of the top step. He reaches out his hand and she loses her footing, slipping back down the flight of stairs. His huge fist grabs her by the elbow and pulls her towards him to the safety of the landing. She looks up at him, breathing spiky, mouth dry with spit. He puts his hand on the small bump, showing through her lycra top. The sound of a key turning in the front door. Sean takes his hand away.

'Sorry, Sali mate,' Charlie says, 'massive queue in Tesco's.'

FOURTEEN

My mate Sali is at home.
I invited him for early dinner.
Tayo coming too. Hope OK.
Gone to get beers. Nothing in house!
Sali listening out for Prue.
You'll be back before she's up.
Love x

The men are in the garden. Prue stands in the middle of them, giggling as they kick a football around her. The sun is moving down in the sky and the next-door trees cast shadows over their ragged lawn. Prue runs over to get the ball away from Sean and he puts one of his big hands on her fine hair, holding her off. She waves her arms like something from *Looney Tunes*. The men laugh.

Earlier, when she was getting Prue up from her nap and Sean and Charlie went downstairs to get drinks, she heard him – 'Sali', as the boys call him, a shortening of his surname Salinger – explain to Charlie that he and Naomi had already met at nursery, 'actually'. He told him that he used to pick up his friend's kid from time to time. Charlie was surprised but didn't seem fazed by the information that his cool friend spent time as a pro bono nanny. There was no mention of the two of them going for a coffee or of anything else. Sean seems to have no intention of telling her husband, his friend, that he had sex with his wife. She heard the conversation so clearly. It seemed like Sean was almost shouting, like he wanted her to hear, to give them an opportunity to – like criminals in separate cells awaiting interrogation – get their stories straight. His lies, his elisions, were effortless. He said how weird it was that they'd never made the connection and Charlie made the point that 'no one talks about their kids at football, almost an unwritten rule'. Charlie talked about how the nursery pick-up can be a bit of a 'ball-ache'. Sean said he didn't mind it. Said he has good banter with some of the parents, some of the staff. There's nothing in his voice that betrays any anxiety, any concern about how fucked-up the situation is. Thankfully, Prue hasn't given anything away. She's lost her confidence with men and is very shy of any-one apart from Charlie; the blogs say that's very common. So there were no bear roars or licking imaginary honey off her hand that might reveal any more than a passing acquaintance.

She slices a kitchen knife through a little gem lettuce and shoves the pieces off the chopping board into a glass salad bowl. She cuts up half a cucumber, retrieves a small can of sweetcorn from the fridge and tips it all in to join the lettuce. The risotto Charlie's made is drying out in the residual heat of the oven. They're just awaiting Tayo, who's on his way back from London. She goes to slice a cherry tomato but the knife snags on the skin and when she pushes harder, she crushes it, its seeded innards spewing out on to the board. She wipes the knife on a tea towel, gets a long metal sharpener out and begins sharpening it. She looks out to the garden and Sean is looking straight at her. His eyes flick wider at her holding the knife as if to say, *Oooh, scary*, then they go back to absolute neutrality. He pats Charlie on the shoulder and points out his wife holding the knife and puts his hands up as if in surrender. Charlie laughs at his friend. Naomi smiles and turns back to the work surface.

She's got away with it. The man she's slept with is her husband's friend, amongst the new people they've met since their move, his best friend, and they've got away with it. She cuts cleanly through one of the tiny tomatoes.

'How many weeks are you, Naomi?' Tayo asks as she rejoins the dinner table. Since they've been sitting down Tayo has dominated the conversation. He's charming but she can't look past the fact he's still wearing his trilby indoors.

'Eighteen.'

'Charlie's told us he can't wait to have another kid,' Sean says, looking at Naomi.

'Can't wait slash terrified of death by lack of sleep.' Charlie draws sympathetic laughs from the other two men.

'Being a dad to two kids is a proper achievement, though,' Sean says, eyes twinkling. 'Beats anything I've done.' Tayo makes a joke about a table that 'Sali' made for him but Naomi can't decipher what it means. Throughout the meal she's used every excuse she can to leave the table, getting people water, helping Prue with the Duplo she's scattering over the living-room floor, checking on a wash she's put on, but every time she's sat down with them Sean has sparked into life with some comment like this about her and the baby. The others haven't noticed – why would they? – but it's like he thinks this whole situation is a game, a game of cheat he's determined to play more and more brazenly until

242

they get caught. And she has to greet everything he says with a benign smile.

Maybe it's paranoia. Neither of them could have imagined being in a scenario like this. Perhaps he's making awkward small talk to cover for his nerves. She's not been herself during dinner, almost struck dumb for fear of giving anything away to Charlie. Nothing Sean's said so far has jarred with what she knows of him, what he told her about himself. They know him as a guy that does refurbishments, makes a bit of furniture. He's talked, at length, about a project he's been doing in Cornwall on an eco-house and how he's not been around much, the men have backed it up with their banter about him being scared to come back to football after Charlie 'skinned' him for the thousandth time. Tayo even asked him if he'd got his phone fixed yet. Every question she has about him, about his disappearance, his total blackout in responding to her desperate text messages, has been answered.

'You going to find out if it's a boy or a girl?' Sean asks her, that same strange look in his eyes.

'I want to but you don't,' she says to Charlie, 'so I guess we won't.'

'You only want to know so you can go up to the loft and sort out all of Prue's clothes.'

'To make room for some more pigeons?' Sean says and the men laugh but he's looking at her again, pointed. She feels hot, her neck flushes, shame pricks at her pores like lemon juice on a cut finger. She stands up suddenly. 'I'm just going to go upstairs for a bit. I'm not feeling great.'

Charlie stands up, concern written on his face. Naomi's smile tells him it's fine as she goes to pick Prue up.

'We'll keep an eye on the little one for you if you want, give you a break,' Sean says, face filled with benevolence. Charlie begins stacking up the plates.

She looks out of the French door at the end of their bedroom. The same shabby, yellow van that she clocked with a smile in the car park of The Bank of Friendship for all those weeks sits outside their house. If she'd stayed downstairs for a moment longer she would have had a panic attack. She's sure of it. She's never doubted herself before, not really. She was never someone whose judgement went out the window when she was drunk or on drugs. She's felt out of control before but she's always been able to go away and do the research, do the work that allows her to get back on top of things. But now, is this what madness feels like, she thinks. Is that the first step? Losing all confidence in your own judgement?

She's so tired. So so tired. The pigeons have somehow got into Prue's side of the house and she's been up in the night with the sound of them cooing. 'Naughty birdies' she calls them. How does Sean know about the pigeons? Charlie told him, of course Charlie told him, but why did he look at her like that? She gets her phone out of her pocket and takes a picture of Sean's van. She doesn't know why at first but then she realises it's because she's scared. She'd read about pregnancy making the tiniest thing seem scary but it can't all be in her head.

'Could it be mine?' He's there, Sean, at the doorway. She drops the arm holding her phone to her side, concealing it from him.

'It's Charlie's,' she says.

'You certain?'

'Absolutely.' He moves slowly over to the window, the loping jaguar gait she remembers.

'I didn't know he was your husband. Obviously. I got some of your texts. Thought it was better to do the media blackout. Long term, I mean. When you said it was a mistake, I was gutted to be honest. But you two have got a kid,' he pauses, looks down at the floor, 'and you've got to respect that.'

'What the hell are you doing?' Her voice is angrier than she expected. 'Greg? You're not Greg's dad? What the hell are you doing here?' He nods to himself before wrenching down the handle of the French door and opening it. Naomi looks at him, shocked.

'This door doesn't lock.' He looks at the hinges, the doorframe, examining it. 'The frame's misaligned so it barely closes. Charlie asked me to have a look at it for you. Didn't he tell you? It's not been locked since you moved in.' A cold wind blows in and disturbs Naomi's hair. He slams the door shut again. 'I'm sorry about Greg. I kept meaning to say something but after I didn't first time, in the park, it got harder and harder to tell you the truth.' She interrogates his face, he's earnest again, none of the knowing looks from the dinner table. His open face and dopey eyes are there again and she remembers how fixated she'd been on him. She thinks of what Merrick said when she went to his house, how Sean had told his friend that she was some sort of obsessive bunny-boiler.

'Is this all a game to you?' she asks.

'What?'

'Looking at me like that at the table. He's my husband.'

'I didn't know that.'

'You think this is a joke? I'm pregnant.'

245

'I know you are.' He opens the door again, steps out on to the Juliet balcony and turns back to her. With the sun setting into the sea behind him, it could be a holiday photo. 'I was trying to act normal when we were having tea. Thought I was doing OK with it, but maybe you're right.'

'What do you mean, right?'

'You think we should tell him.'

'What? No.'

'You just said it, said I was acting weird. I probably was, though, cos I feel fucking weird.'

'That's not what I said at all.'

'We're trying to pretend but we're not actors, this—'

'You can't tell him.' She stops him dead. 'He can't know.' She puts her hand on her bump.

'You'd been trying for a while, the baby.'

'Promise me,' she says, head craning through the balcony, hands gripped on to the frames of the door.

'Rubber's perished, look.' He fingers the seal on the door millimetres from her hand. Some of it comes away. 'Whole thing will need replacing.'

'He can't know. He can't. He's not well. He goes to therapy.' She feels instantly guilty for throwing her husband's mental health under the bus but she has to get through to Sean. Why would he tell Charlie? It makes no sense. Earlier it didn't seem like he felt guilty about it at all.

'He talks to me after football, when everyone else has gone. I knew he wasn't doing well but I didn't know it was that bad. Whatever you think's best. You know him. You're his wife. Jesus. You're his wife.' He turns away from her and leans over the balcony. The whole thing needs replacing, the wood's rotten with seawater. He's huge, must weigh fifteen, sixteen stone, it might not support his weight. She wants to get him back inside but he's still talking. 'I won't cause any trouble for you, for your family. I can find a different bunch of lads for football.'

'You're making the house cold.' She goes back to sit on the bed and he follows her in.

'This is pretty fucked-up,' he laughs and she becomes aware that Charlie will be wondering where his friend has gone and why he's talking to his under-the-weather pregnant wife for so long.

'You should go downstairs.' He nods his head slowly down until he's looking at the floorboards and pauses, on the verge of saying something, then flicks hang-dog eyes up to her.

'I liked you, Naomi. I really liked you.' She swallows. It's agonising to be sitting on her bed in front of this beautiful man, the man that, at one time, she couldn't stop thinking about.

'Go back down,' she says.

'I'm working a lot in Cornwall and my flat's being bought so, I could just go. That's what I'll do, I'll go.' She flicks her fingers out as if to say, *Only if you want to*. 'Nothing keeping me here. It's better.' Naomi doesn't want to agree too vehemently but him leaving would solve all her problems. And he should leave town. He had sex with a married woman, a mother, vulnerable, and he's a liar. He lied to her about Greg. 'I hope everything's all right with the pregnancy,' he says, looking at her bump. He nods respectfully, like a sad cowboy, and leaves the room.

She puts her hands beside her to lift herself up off the bed but can't find the strength to stand up.

FIFTEEN

Charlie stands in front of the large window, brushing his teeth and looking out at the sea in the dark. The whole thing went well. On reflection, leaving Prue was probably a bit careless. If she'd woken up and poor Sali had to deal with her screaming for ten minutes, he might not have been that keen to come over again. But conversation flowed well. Tayo can talk for England and that was good because Naomi was a bit quiet, she can be like that with groups of lads. And she's pregnant, so fair enough. He had hoped that having people over would distract her from the biting thing and it seems to have worked. She's hardly mentioned it.

He feels something on his bare foot. There are fragments of something black. He kneels down to examine them and sees that they've come away from the rubber seal around the French door. He opens it.

'What're you doing?' Naomi says from the sink where she's applying one of her creams.

'Did you unlock this?' he asks. Naomi turns to face him, face slathered in pale green cream.

'It doesn't lock,' she says.

'What do you mean it doesn't lock?' He turns back to the door and starts moving it up and down in its frame, trying to turn the key to make it lock. But she's right, the lock's broken. 'Has this been like this since we moved in?' She turns away from the mirror.

'I thought you knew.'

'If I knew I would have got someone round; if this doesn't lock, the house is totally open. How long have you known? Aren't you freaked out by this?'

'Erm—' She turns back to the mirror, takes a muslin cloth and scrapes the cream off her face in neat lines. 'Your friend, Sali, he said you'd asked him to look at it.' His face pinches in confusion.

'I told him there were a few things that needed looking at, I wanted him to check the builders' work, but I didn't know about the lock.'

'You didn't ask him to look at it for you?'

'How could I if I didn't know about it?' Frustration piles into his voice.

'He said you knew.' Charlie thought that Sali had been upstairs for a long time and when he heard him talking to Naomi he did think it was a bit weird, but this explains it. Why didn't she mention it, though? She's been on edge about every tiny thing since she's been pregnant; the fact that their house has been unlocked for the whole time they've lived there seems like it would have been the first thing she said once the boys had left after dinner. He glances over at Naomi who's now flossing, face pushed close to the mirror.

They hadn't actually talked since the lads left. He was clearing up and she was putting Prue to bed. Perhaps Sali put her mind at ease about it; she's always been in awe of tradesmen or IT professionals, people confident in things she has no understanding of. Used to piss him off when something would go wrong in their old flat, a broken switch or low pressure in the boiler, and she'd automatically doubt his diagnosis and insist on getting in a professional.

'Good of him to have a look round everything for us anyway,' Charlie says, leaning across her to spit into the sink. He rattles his toothbrush into its ceramic home before putting an arm around Naomi and looking at their two faces in the mirror. 'He's a good lad, isn't he, Sali?'

'Mmm,' Naomi agrees, nodding slowly, two strings of floss hanging out of her closed mouth.

SIXTEEN

www.keepurselfsafe.com/doyouhaveastalker/5788839

Do you have a stalker?

The police define stalking as a sustained pattern of inappropriate behaviour that leads to its victim feeling threatened or scared for their own well-being.

It's thought that the vast majority of victims know or have had some sort of relationship with their stalker but, even in such cases, it's entirely possible to have no idea that someone's stalking you.

What to do about it?

Stalking is a tough crime to prove, which makes it very difficult for the victims, their families and the police to deal with as it's virtually impossible to collect concrete evidence against the perpetrator who can often be devious and manipulative. And without such evidence, it's the victim's word against the accused, and in such cases it can be very intimidating for them to come forward.

BUT if you think there's even the smallest possibility that you are being stalked or harassed, it's vital that you share your fears without delay. Tell people close to you, talk to your friends about the situation. Stalking can begin innocuously, but almost always escalates and you need your loved ones to be watching out for you.

It might seem scary but the best thing you can do is talk to your stalker. Tell them to leave you alone and stop whatever behaviour it is that's making you feel threatened. They may want to be drawn into some sort of dialogue so make your message clear and leave it at that. If you choose to phone them, follow it up in writing. A text or an email.

DO NOT agree to meet with them. Once a stalker is made aware that their attention is unwanted it may provoke them and there's a good chance you won't be dealing with a rational person.

If the unwanted behaviour persists, it's time to go to the police.

SEVENTEEN

We did a lot of improvisation in Mrs Forbes' classes. They were free, out of the goodness of her heart, but it meant she didn't have any funding for textbooks or scripts or anything. Didn't seem to bother her too much.

There was one improvisation game, more of a principle I suppose, called 'Yes and ...' The idea was that whoever you're playing with, your scene partner, would accept whatever you said, whatever scenario or action in the scene, and then add something to it.

Let's say I start with, 'I don't know how we're ever going to get to that island.' The person I'm up on stage with would say, 'Yes, and we've only got an hour before the sun goes down.' If they said something like, 'Excuse me, sir, do you know the way to the steam fair,' that'd be wrong. It stops the scene from flowing organically and creates 'blockages', as Mrs Forbes called them. I got it straight away. Since I'd chipped off from the last home they had me in, I'd been living life like that. Getting work by saying I could do things I couldn't, finding places to crash by convincing desperate divorcees I was older than I was, telling social workers what they wanted to hear, that sort of thing. So I liked it. I was good at it. You always like what you're good at.

There was this short-arse bloke. Late twenties, older than most of the other people in the class. Small-man syndrome.

He came along for about six months, there weren't many that stayed on as long as that. He was a pretty good actor, convincing. Whenever Mrs Forbes would have us play this game, if I'd get up, he'd always jump up on the stage to do it with me. He had a problem with me. Maybe because I was good or because I was tall. I never knew. I'd say something and he'd say 'Yes, and …' and do the scene within the rules of it but he'd always move it away from where I'd started. Slowly, so Mrs Forbes never really twigged, but he'd always do the same. So we'd be building this scene and I'd take it down a serious route, a family drama sort of thing, and then he would slowly take it away from me and my dad would end up being a tranny or my mum a dolphin. And then everyone would be laughing, laughing with him, at me. I'd try and bring it back but I never could and the game would end and he'd be loving it. Loving that I was standing there embarrassed, ashamed and that he'd done it to me.

It feels the same way now, like I'm losing it. She's not like that little short-arse, she doesn't know what she's doing but she's not saying 'Yes, and …' she's saying no. Flatly refusing to go with it.

I found out Mr Small-man-syndrome was a teacher. One day the school he worked at happened to find pictures in his desk that showed some of the boys in the communal shower. He was sacked and put on the register. He didn't have any funny 'yes and …' for me after that.

This scene, with Naomi, hasn't ended where I want yet, but it will.

EIGHTEEN

20 weeks

Lara takes the girls into the front garden of Naomi's house while she gets the shopping out of the back of the car. Charlie's parents are on their annual winter-sun trip in Sri Lanka and her mum can't get the time off work so Naomi's had no help. Charlie has tried to make himself available, but for the first time in years he's genuinely busy. Naomi's watched him nodding his head in earnest excitement when he's on the phone to Teddy and companies she's heard of, Leica and Nikon, have expressed an interest in their line of products. He's shown her the emails.

Prue, bored of spending so much time with her mother, is pushing the envelope to a worrying degree. There hasn't been any more biting, but every quotidian moment has become a battleground. Naomi's been using a breathing exercise Lara learnt from a hypnobirthing class to try to stay patient with Prue's tantrums and it's actually working. She never would have gone in for anything New Age before but she can't stop thinking about the little kidney bean in her stomach. Her bump's much smaller than it was with Prue at five months. The baby's still not growing.

Prue, of course, has realised she can penetrate her mother's Zen-calm very easily by doing dangerous things, like trying to climb through the railings on the clifftop when they go for walks or not holding her hand when they're next to a busy road. She kept a large pebble in her mouth for twenty minutes a few days ago and was laughing and taunting her mother, closing her mouth and pretending to swallow it until Naomi was forced to turn her upside down and pry it out. A loss of composure she instantly felt guilty for.

Prue's been waking in the night as well. Almost every night. Crying until Naomi or Charlie go in to soothe her. They've racked their brains as to what it could be but all the normal problems – teeth, a cold, being scared of the dark – don't make sense. Children begin to have nightmares at around two years old so that could be it. Or it could be the noises in the house.

Naomi's tried not to think about Sean, about how he knew that the French door in their bedroom didn't lock. There is a rational explanation. He came from upstairs when she first came in because he was checking the builders' work like Charlie had asked him to. But why check the door? The builders haven't been near it. But if he has been going into their house, planting strange kids' things in her daughter's room, why tell her exactly how he's been getting in? When you spell it all out, it doesn't make any sense.

Sean has been true to his word about not seeing Charlie. He's stopped going to football. She asks after him and Tayo after Charlie gets back on a Wednesday night and each time he says 'Sali' wasn't there. He sounds so disappointed, as if he's a long-lost brother rather than someone he's just met. Charlie thinks he might be working in Cornwall but Naomi knows he isn't. Or at least his van isn't. Naomi's seen it three times. Once on a street two down from the warehouse where she works and twice while walking Prue around in the buggy near their house. So she texted him, asked him whether he would consider going through with his suggestion to move somewhere else. She spent more than an hour drafting the text. Trying to get the tone right, to make it clear how difficult it would be for her and Charlie, for their unborn child, if he still lived nearby. He hasn't responded.

'Oh, Prue, no, no put that down, sweetheart,' Lara says. Naomi looks over to see Prue dancing on the steps to their house holding something in her hand. Naomi pulls the bags out of the car and slams the boot shut. Lara tries to trap Prue in the porch but she ducks under her outstretched arm and towards Naomi, squealing with excitement at her new game. It looks as if she'll try to escape her mother as well so Naomi drops the shopping on the crazy paving and picks her daughter up by the hips. Prue immediately puts whatever she's holding behind her back and grins, face flushed by the exertion. Naomi holds Prue into her and looks over her shoulder, sees what it is and lets out a disgusted screech. Her daughter is holding the dismembered wings of a pigeon.

She bends Prue's wrists towards her, grabs the wings and drops them on to the floor. Lara appears with a wet wipe and Naomi holds Prue's hands out to her so she can scrub them.

'She found it on the front step,' Lara says. 'I tried to get it off her.' Naomi nods back, smiles it off. She looks down at the thing on the ground. Both wings are intact, two full sets of feathers joined in the middle by strands of spiny bone. 'Must be foxes,' Lara says. Naomi can't take her eyes off the bird's remnants. 'You're all right, my little baked potato.' Lara grabs Prue's chin and waves it around erasing the growing concern on the little girl's face. 'Can we go in? I'm bursting for a pee.' Naomi smiles wide and goes up to unlock the door. She puts Prue down on the doormat and encourages her to toddle in and take her wellies off.

She goes back down the path to get her shopping bags but on the way to them she kneels down to look at the carcass. Something about the bones that remain, the ones that link the two wings doesn't seem right. She doesn't know much about foxes but to eat every morsel of head, body and tail feathers and to leave the wings, attached, completely untouched like this, as if someone had managed to isolate just the arms and shoulders of a human but left nothing else behind, would an animal do that? Even by accident, could an animal do that? She edges her hand towards it, she knows she should pick it up and look closer, see if there's any sign of it being cut, but she can't touch it.

'Mummay, water, Mummay. My water,' Prue shouts from the doorstep, waving her arms, irate. In the gloom of the hallway she sees Margot drinking out of Prue's cup. She picks up the bags and heads back towards the house. She pauses on the threshold and looks up and down the street at the row of cars on the esplanade. She doesn't see the yellow van.

NINETEEN

21 weeks

'How far are you along?' DC Crawford is in her fifties, straight brown hair with a long fringe that she has a habit of blowing up at to get it out of her eyes.

'Five months,' Naomi says.

'In the manageable bit.'

'Yeah.' She's in an office off the main console of desks that make up the police station. It's a small operation and the duty officer at the desk was unwilling to get someone for Naomi to talk to, but she played the pregnant card and DC Crawford came up to the door to invite her in for a chat.

'Best thing about giving birth to my third kid, knowing I'd never have to be pregnant again. Any woman that tells you they loved pregnancy is a liar or a nutcase. With my last one, I was on crutches for the last trimester. Crutches. They literally crippled me those kids.' Naomi smiles, wondering why some women feel the need to share their pregnancy horror stories with expectant mothers. 'And my mind! All over the place. My husband, God bless him, I would have divorced me! I was an absolute bloody nightmare. Everything he did, I thought he was trying to wind me up. He'd set the table for dinner and I'd say he was clattering the cutlery loudly on purpose to antagonise me. He'd take the kids out to give me some space and I accused him of trying to turn them against me. I thought he was having an affair. Him. An affair. I love him but I tell you what, Mrs Fallon, my Morgan is no oil painting. It's a crazy old time.'

'You think I'm overreacting?' Naomi says, pushing the blank incident report form slowly back across the table.

'You did the right thing coming to talk to me today.'

'But …'

'Mrs Fallon, this Sean, he's your husband's friend.' Naomi nods. 'And he's a carpenter, he refurbishes houses. So him having a look round your house for problems with it, which you say your husband asked him to do, that's a nice thing, isn't it?'

'He told me he had a son and he doesn't.'

'Yeah.' She packs some papers into a paper file, has a slurp from a mug that advertises an electrical parts supplier. 'I've done the school run for fourteen years. Nursery run for a couple of years before that. This town has changed a lot since then. The demographic, know what I mean? Now I hope you won't think I'm out of line saying this, but in all those years, there weren't many mums looked like you.' She smiles apologetically as Naomi's cheeks flush. 'Your husband said his mate was a bit of a ladies' man and, who knows, getting you in the sack would probably be like winning the FA Cup for a ladies' man round here. Sorry.'

'It's fine.' Naomi laughs, embarrassed.

'I'm just saying, you went for a coffee with the guy, he probably knew his mate's kid was moving nurseries, didn't expect to meet you again after that so from his point of view, why ruin his chances by telling you he hadn't been totally honest to start with. Let me let you in on one of the trade secrets here: most men are cowards.' Through the window Naomi sees two uniformed policemen come through double doors and head for the closed door of another office. DC Crawford's attention shifts outside the room.

'You honestly think it's a coincidence?' Naomi says, trying to rein her back in.

'Sorry?'

'A man propositions me, I turn him down and then he turns up later, at my house, as my husband's friend?'

'There's fifty-five thousand people in this town. Thirty per cent are over the age of sixty. Everyone's connected to everyone else round here.' The detective is barely looking at Naomi now, keen to end their meeting but wary of upsetting her. 'The thing you said, with the pigeon. That sounds like it would be very traumatic, especially for someone in your condition—'

'I'm pregnant, I'm not mentally ill,' Naomi snaps.

'Finding your little one holding a dead something sounds horrible, but without the carcass for me to look at, it's hard to know if there's anything suspicious about it.' Naomi told Charlie about the pigeon wings, about how she thought someone might have put it there, but when he went out to find them, they were no longer in their front garden. She brought up the dummy and the sleepsuit again, asked him to explain how they'd got into the house. He looked at her like she'd lost her mind, suggested she get an early night and she hit the roof. He and this detective think that pregnant women are irrational beings who should be coddled and doubted at every turn. She was fucking angry with him. She's angry now.

'Have you got any biscuits?' Naomi asks. DC Crawford snaps her head back to Naomi and seems happy to be able to do something concrete for her. She goes to the back of the room and opens the top drawer of a filing cabinet and pulls out a long Tupperware box. Inside there are homemade flapjacks. Naomi takes two. She eats them in silence, not wanting to leave but unwilling to say anything else for fear of being dismissed again.

DC Crawford sighs. 'If anything else more specific comes to you, any reason he might want to "stalk" you, please do give the station a call. Because as it stands it's really hard for us to make a case to even go and talk to Sean. He told you he was interested in you, you said you were married and that was the end of it. You said you've texted. Is there anything he sent that supports the idea that he means you harm? That his interest in you is threatening in some way? I'm not saying you're wrong, Naomi, and as I said, it's really good you've come in to mention this to us. If anything does escalate then it'll help your case that you've come in. But him giving you funny looks, acting weird, a dead pigeon in the garden—'

'I've seen his van three times since,' she says quietly through a mouthful of flapjack.

'He's a tradesman, you said.' DC Crawford looks out of the door, her body leaning out of the office already. Naomi sees an older man in uniform come out of his office and gesture to her. She fishes on her desk for a card and hands it to Naomi. 'Look, this will get you through to me without having to bother with the switchboard. If anything else happens, let us know and we can look into it.' She holds her hand out towards the open door to nudge Naomi out of her seat and escorts her through the office towards the double doors that lead to the station's entrance. 'What does your husband think?' she asks. Naomi feels hot, caught out, as if she were the suspect being interrogated and the detective has found the hole in her otherwise watertight story.

'I ... We don't have many friends down here.'

'You've not told him?'

'I didn't want to cause a stink if there's no substance to any of it.' The detective makes the expression of someone who's smelt something noxious.

'But you thought you'd come to the police with it?' Naomi doesn't respond. 'Maybe talk it over with him, yeah? If you genuinely think the guy might be dangerous, that's not the sort of friend you want around your family, is it?' Naomi clenches her teeth, musters a bitter smile, a sheepish nod and leaves the detective to her vital work.

TWENTY

Tuesday 17:55
Are you going to leave town?

Thursday 04:22
I can't keep lying to him?

Thursday 11:51
I'm going to tell Charlie.

Saturday 12:59
You were right.

If you tell him he'd be
destroyed X

Unless you leave, I have to.

He wouldn't survive it.

What?

What do you mean??

I've got to know his therapist, Amy. She's school friends with one of the boys from football. He told her I was Charlie's mate. She says he's fragile. Having suicidal thoughts so he needed his friends. Sure he's putting on a brave face, for the baby. Please don't tell him I said. XX

TWENTY-ONE

23 weeks

'Are you OK?' Naomi asks, sitting on the bed pretending to read a book.

'Can I take your spare phone charger?' She nods in response.

'You're feeling OK?' He walks over to her side of the bed and fishes her charger out of the bedside table and turns his head quickly to surprise her with a peck on the forehead.

'Never better.' She smiles at such uncharacteristic sweetness. 'Do you want a hand?' she asks as he heads back towards his holdall.

'I want you to lie on the bed and do absolutely nothing.' He's packing for a trip to Gävle in Sweden to talk to a company that makes carbon fibre frames for bikes that he wants to make the parts for his video equipment. He doesn't seem suicidal. In bed at night, he's loving and affectionate. He makes jokes about Prue's tantrums, which Naomi finds annoying as he's not the one dealing with ten of them a day. He seems more like the man she married than the person he became six months or so after Prue was born, when he would tell her, in almost every conversation, how low, how worthless he felt.

She found him once lying in the foetal position in the room that's now their dining room. It was ten months or so ago.

They'd just bought the house and the builders were saying that, due to problems with the drainage, the refurbishment would cost one and a half times their original quote. She bent down to him and he said that it'd be better if he wasn't in their lives. That Prue would grow up a better person if she had nothing to do with him. Naomi can believe that at one time, when he was talking to his therapist, he might have said he was having suicidal thoughts. But not now. And what did Sean mean? He's 'got to know' Charlie's therapist? Is he making it up? After Greg, she doesn't trust a word he says. But how would he know Charlie's therapist's name? When she mentioned Charlie's CBT to Sean before, he didn't seem to have a clue about it, and there's no way Charlie would have told him. Even if he does know her, what sort of therapist talks about their patients? The one golden rule in therapy is patient confidentiality. It's in every TV show featuring a therapist.

It's also flouted in every TV show featuring a therapist. Naomi's never met Amy but she knows she's young and there's a shiftiness in Charlie's eyes when Naomi asks about her that tells her that she's not unattractive. And Sean is not Sean the sensitive dad, he's 'Sali' the lothario who the football lads idolise and who keeps dirty pictures of all his women on his phone, which he probably shows to everyone in the pub. It's not inconceivable that he's sleeping with Amy. As DC Crawford delighted in telling her, it's not a big town. Who knows how strict this Amy's ethics are when she's wrapped up in his arms?

Naomi's not jealous. She doesn't think about Sean like that any more. She's managed to eradicate her guilt for cheating on Charlie, for the good of her family, and any embarrassment for falling for Sean's charms has gone as well. She was using him as much as he was her, more even. And it might sound ridiculous, but it's helped her marriage. Her transgression has allowed her to forgive Charlie for all the casual thoughtlessness that's threatened to derail the life she's worked so hard to construct. And that life is coming together. They still need to finish off some of the carpentry in the basement, but that aside the house is pretty much done. Charlie's work is taking off. The biennale will be fine and Victoria is warming to her. Prue's a nightmare, but that's pretty normal for children of her age, and Naomi's pregnant with their second child. Everything is close to perfect.

If you genuinely think the guy might be dangerous ... The detective's words come back to her. Charlie's mental health, her feelings, their life being back on an even keel, if she truly thinks Sean means them harm, none of that's important. Prue's safety and the safety of the baby inside her are all that matters. So she has to tell Charlie. She could tell him the PG version she told DC Crawford, the 'I'm not a cheating wife' version where Sean made a pass at her and she politely declined. But how long before that unravels. And what would it achieve? Even if she tells him everything, would he believe that his friend's any more than a back-stabbing arsehole who can't help trying to get every woman he meets into bed? Is everyone right? Is she just a hysterical pregnant woman?

The sound. The flapping of wings, like someone has put paper in a fan, starts up again. Her shoulders hunch and she bites her bottom lip. Charlie stops packing for a moment and looks up at the ceiling.

'It's coming from above us. We're going to have to pay for scaffolding to get Lenny to have a look. He said health and safety won't let anyone go up that high on a ladder.'

'I know,' she says.

'I should have sorted it.'

'Not your fault.'

'I know how much you hate it.' The noise stops. He still looks skinny. The bumps of vertebrae on his back sticking out like humps on the Loch Ness Monster as he bends over to rifle through his holdall. She's going to tell him. She has to tell him the truth.

Then she feels it. 'Oh,' she says out loud and he looks up, worried. 'I felt it move.' Charlie stands up straight, drops some shirts on to his bag and bounds over to the bed. He pulls up her top and places his hand on her bump. She's twenty-three weeks, almost everyone feels the baby before that. She'd read online that second-time mums usually notice it much earlier because they're more aware of what it feels like. Every day when she couldn't feel anything she became more and more anxious but here it is, that fluttering feeling.

'I know I won't be able to feel it,' Charlie says, their faces close. 'I'm fine. Everything is perfect.' He kisses her. It's clumsy at first, their noses clashing, but then they fall into an old rhythm and Naomi feels turned on by her husband.

Within a minute they're having sex and after a couple more Charlie's lying on her, telling her how amazing it was. In truth it wasn't amazing, but, with the weight of her husband on top of her, on top of their baby, she feels a sensation she'd almost forgotten. Calm.

TWENTY-TWO

Naomi sits on the toilet, puts her forehead in her hands and tries to breathe.

'Mummeeee. Mummeeee. Mummeeeeee.' Her daughter sounds more manic with every drawn-out word. She's been screaming at the bottom of the stairs for fifteen minutes. It's nearly an hour past her normal bedtime. Naomi needs her to go to sleep soon or she's worried about what she might do. It's been three days without Charlie and she's been edging towards breaking point from almost the moment he left. Prue has never been this bad before. It's like she's doing it on purpose. Naomi has sent Charlie messages calling their daughter names she wouldn't call her worst enemy. Better that than scream them in the little girl's face, she tells herself.

Naomi hears a bump, probably Prue's little head on the floorboards. The floorboards that are still covered in staples and nails. She jumps up off the toilet and runs down the stairs to her daughter. Apart from the mania in her eyes, Prue is fine. Naomi tries to pick her up but she bats her mother off so she goes to the fridge and, as if she were a cartoon mouse, lures her daughter up the stairs with little cubes of cheese.

It's only when she stops running the bath and Prue's angry sobs smoulder to nothing that Naomi hears it. A loud noise, almost like a fan being turned on and off, punctuated by the sound of scratching and scrabbling. The muscles in her cheek begin to spasm, she clenches her teeth to stop them. Prue's singing 'Baa, Baa, Black Sheep' to herself. The sound flurries again, twice as loud as before.

She gets Prue out of the bath, wraps her in a towel and heads out of the bathroom towards the sound. It's coming from upstairs. As they pass the spare room, the room they're planning to turn into a nursery for baby number two, Prue screeches and grabs on to the doorframe. Charlie puts all the toys that cause Prue to get the most angry when they're taken away from her into that room, but he hasn't hidden them behind the door so her toy pram stands in plain view at the end of the room.

'My have it,' she calls out. Naomi can't face more histrionics so she grabs it and heads up to the top floor, holding the pram in one hand and her damp two-year-old in the other. Further up the stairs the sound gets much louder and Prue cowers from it, nuzzling into Naomi's neck. She struggles up to the top of the stairs and opens the door to Charlie's study. The room is still. The noise comes from above. The attic. It sounds like something blowing wildly in the wind followed by what could be thousands of tiny fingernails scratching at the ceiling.

She leaves the pram at the top of the stairs and puts Prue down on Charlie's swivel chair in the middle of his room. Her daughter holds her hands up to her, not wanting to be left alone, so Naomi gets her a pen and a stack of Post-its from Charlie's desk to placate her. Naomi grabs the metal pole and opens the attic hatch with it. The small space into the attic is pitch black but the noise becomes deafening.

'Mummay,' Prue moans, but Naomi has to find out what's up there. The ladder shifts around on the landing as she climbs up it. She gets to the top. There's a flurry of noise, of wings flapping. Pigeons. Standing on the floor of their attic is what seems to be hundreds of pigeons. She makes a sharp screech of disgust and it's like they all notice her at once. They lift into the air and they're suddenly flying round her head, wings flapping past her ears, dank air fanned into her eyes. One hand comes off the ladder as she races to climb back down, struggling to hold on. Then there's a creaking sound, a sharp snap, the ladder comes away from its fixtures and the foot of it slides towards the gaping staircase. She doesn't let go of the ladder, instinct won't allow her to grab on to thin air. Its top end clatters against a wall, the bottom end jolts further towards the staircase but then crunches to a stop, wedged into the toy pram that's caught on the top of the banister. Naomi rolls off on to the floor. The top of the ladder slides down the wall and takes the pram with it as it crashes down the stairs.

She looks into Charlie's office and Prue's face is in the moment of shock before it creases up into a terrified wail. Naomi pushes herself up, runs to her daughter and grabs her up into her arms. Some of the pigeons are out of the hatch, flapping in the high space of the landing, her bare foot kicks at Charlie's door to shut themselves in. She notices acute pain in her back for the first time.

The thought hits her, the baby. She feels her bump for movement, tapping it as if trying to get a message through to her growing child by Morse code. She pushes her thumb into the bump, winces with the pain, trying to wake her baby up. There it is, the fluttering. Not a kick or a punch but its body moving towards its mother's touch. Naomi pulls her daughter's head away from her chest, sees the wells of tears in her eyes and kisses them roughly before planting kiss after kiss on the fine hair on the crown of her head. Prue finds a giggle at her mother's crazy behaviour.

It was the pram that stopped her going down the stairs. This little girl, her little girl, might have just saved her unborn sibling's life. Naomi catches herself in the mirror on the back of Charlie's door. She watches Prue, naked of her towel now, grabbing at Naomi's hair, trying to put it in her mouth. The curve of her daughter's wet cheeks catches the light through the Velux window. There are more days of sunshine in this part of the country than anywhere else. She grips Prue's chubby legs and pulls them in close to her, squeezing her flesh into her body until it's almost too hard.

Everything else is meaningless she mouths at her reflection as Prue throws her hair back into its shape with a flourish.

TWENTY-THREE

'I'm looking at flights now.'

'Don't be stupid; we're fine. Lenny's dealing with it.' She's in the living room talking to Charlie on FaceTime. Prue is in bed. She was still quite amped after her bath so Naomi had sat reading with her for an hour while the carpenter made his way over.

'Can you offer him a beer or something, it's late to be coming round.'

'I've already given him one.' Typical Charlie to be worried about Lenny. The carpenter has grown on Naomi, though, and was the first person she contacted, before Charlie even. There's something grandparental about him and despite all the talk of guns and death she can tell, the way his eyes smile when he looks at Prue, that he's deeply kind. To humans at least. When she texted him to say what had happened he said he would come over immediately and deal with it, no charge. When he arrived he presented her with a bag full of wood-pigeon breasts from his freezer that he's been promising Charlie for weeks. He's kind but not tactful.

'Do you know how many have got up there?' Charlie asks.

'I just sent him up there as soon as he got here. I've not been past the first floor.'

'I'm sorry, Nay, it's horrible. I can come back tomorrow, it's honestly not a big deal.'

'Prue's fine. The baby's fine.'

'Please go and get yourself checked. You fell off the bottom of the ladder.'

'I feel fine.' She ducks out of the screen's sight to take a gulp from a glass of red wine. It's the first drink she's had since she did the pregnancy test and it tastes fantastic. She's downplayed the incident to Charlie, told him she was only a couple of rungs up when it broke. She hears heavy footsteps on the stairs and Lenny ambles into the living room. She waves the screen towards him and, seeing Charlie's face, he raises a big paw and waves.

'Thanks so much, mate,' Charlie shouts through the phone. 'Right, I'll leave you two to it then. Thanks so much again.' Naomi says goodbye and ends the call, embarrassed to be caught on the phone to her husband, embarrassed to be so happy talking to him, as if Lenny's caught them kissing.

'All dealt with,' the big man says.

'Really?' He swings a black bin bag up from behind the doorframe to show her.

'There were quite a few up there. Somewhere between fifteen and twenty.'

'And they're all dead?' she asks, kneeling up on the sofa to look at the full bin bag he's holding as far away from her as he can.

'Yep. I've had a quick scoop of all the, the—'

'Shit?' she suggests, smiling at his thinking her too delicate for the word.

'Yeah, I've scooped up all that. Got this chemical I can bring tomorrow. It'll get rid of all of it properly.'

'I can go and clean it; you've done more than enough already.'

'Bacteria and diseases in that stuff to a pregnant woman? No way.'

'Well, thanks. Thank you so much. Do you want a bottle of wine?' She gets up from the sofa and moves past him.

'There wasn't that much. Surprising really.' She stops and turns back towards the big man standing in her doorframe.

'What do you mean?'

'Well, there were near twenty birds up there and not that much shit.'

'Why is that surprising?'

'Well, they can't have been there long. Usually one or two will get into a part of the house and then more and more will join them if it's a good place, warm, safe. But it's like they've all come in at the same time. And I've had a look around the attic and I can't see where they've got in. If it were a big gaping hole, it'd make sense.' Naomi pinches her eyes together, trying to understand what he's saying, trying to work out how to ask the question that's on her mind without seeming like she's paranoid.

'How would they all have got in then, do you think?'

He smiles, scratches the back of his cropped grey hair with both hands and gives a big sigh. 'Pigeons,' he says. Her face flinches in annoyance. 'They can get in anywhere. Past brick walls, bird-proofing nets, bloody reinforced concrete probably. Excuse my French, but they're just fucking pigeons.'

She looks down at the black bag, imagines the dead birds and their shit inside. She gets a flashback to that moment where they flew up en masse, flapping their forty, fifty wings in unison.

'No, but you said,' she tries to keep the frustration out of her voice, 'you couldn't see how they'd got in. So, so … How did they get in?' He shrugs. The awkwardness he used to have when talking to her, a man not used to having to converse with 'the wife', starts to reappear. His free hand tugs his beard. 'Let me get you a bottle of wine to take home. To say thanks.' He nods acceptance and she goes to get him a bottle of red from the booze cupboard. She thinks about giving him back the bag of pigeon breasts that sits on the kitchen island but thinks better of it.

When she comes back into the hall, he's thrown the bin bag out of the open door and the cold has flooded into the house. He nestles the wine bottle in his toolkit amongst screwdrivers and spanners. The sound of glass scraping metal makes her shudder.

'Do we need to replace the ladder to get up there?'

'No. I fixed it,' he says, slamming the lid of the toolbox. He grimaces and puts out a hand towards the stairs, remembering the sleeping child. She waves away his concern.

'Once she's down, she's down. Do you know what was wrong with it?'

'The ladder? Nothing wrong with the ladder.'

'So why did it come off.'

'The screws that hold the fixtures in place were loose.'

'How had they come loose?' she asks, putting a hand on their new mangowood console table to steady herself.

'No idea; use, I guess. You been up there much?'

'No.'

'Charlie, then?'

'Don't think so.'

'The ladder's not that old. Could be whoever fitted it didn't screw everything in properly. Or if the ladder's been used a lot by the previous owners, carrying heavy things up and down,

277

it's possible the fittings could come loose.' Her face must ashen because he comes closer and bends down to get her to look up into his eyes. 'Don't be hard on Charlie boy, eh? Easy to forget things like that when you've got such a big project. It's looking great the house. You two have done a fantastic job.' She musters a smile but she knows he's wrong. The previous owners had fitted the loft ladder. Along with the plumbing and rewiring that was as far as they'd got. It's barely been used. And they didn't do anything themselves. They made a point of telling them they'd got registered professionals to do all the work. Naomi made sure they were given the receipts. There's no way someone who fits loft ladders professionally wouldn't manage to screw the fixtures in properly.

Lenny opens the latch and begins to head out the door.

'How did you kill them?' she says. He stops on the porch, turns back to her.

'What?'

'The pigeons, how did you kill them?' His eyes twinkle like a naughty schoolboy and from his waistband he pulls what looks like a handgun with a large telescopic sight on the top. Naomi feels her mouth flood with saliva.

'Umarex Beretta M-92 Xxtreme. Fully licensed replica Beretta air pistol. Sound compensator,' he points out what she thought was a silencer, 'why the little girl didn't hear anything. Point-177 lead pellets. Decent weight.' He waves the gun towards the ground. 'Want to feel?' She shakes her head. 'Normally I'd use a rifle but in cramped conditions with this bit of kit? Like shooting pigeons in a loft.'

'Thanks again,' she says, holding the edge of the door. Lenny puts the gun back behind his back, a little sheepish at having flashed it at her.

'Sorry I couldn't work out where they'd come from. When I go round the house blocking everything off we'll probably suss it.' He bows like a gentleman and makes his way down the path. She watches the man who told her he was a pagan leave. He has no idea how the pigeons got up there but Naomi does. More than an idea, she knows how they got there. She's sure of it. He looked right at her, sat around the dinner table with Charlie and Tayo, and made a joke about making room for pigeons in their loft. For the first time, she's sure.

TWENTY-FOUR

25 weeks

She carries Prue down the stairs and her daughter's sobs subside.

'I'm going to take her in the car,' she calls over her shoulder to Charlie who's in the kitchen.

'We said we were going to try to have her sleep in the cot, she's only been up there for a few minutes.'

'Can't listen to her screaming, hormones. It's like Chinese water torture. You don't get it.' And with that Naomi's out the door and bundling Prue into the car. After driving for ten minutes her little girl's asleep. She has two hours to look for him. She's spent the last week, ever since Charlie got back from Sweden, looking for the yellow van. She's explored every inch of the town and all the other seaside resorts around it. There's a coastal road that loops them together. It's not exactly the Big Sur, more bungalows and bowls clubs, but there are a few stretches that are stunning. White cliff-faces, stacks of rock with grass haircuts and long stretches of sandy beach. The sea has been calm and glassy and makes her think that when the summer comes they should buy one of those stand-up paddleboards she always sees celebrities on. It's perverse but she's started to enjoy the drives. Enjoy looking for him even. Something about the certainty of knowing he's out there, knowing that she wasn't wrong about him, is strangely empowering.

She toyed with the idea of calling DC Crawford and telling her about what happened in the attic but she knows she still has nothing concrete and she can't sit in that room in the police station and be written off as paranoid again. She told Charlie a version of what Lenny said, the mystery of how the pigeons got there in the first place, but not enough for him to suspect that it had been set up.

The drive becomes less scenic as the Nissan heads away from Belleview, the most well-to-do village in the locale, with its white lighthouse, carpet-green golf course and wide arcing bay, into the area known by most people as 'up the hill', the deprived part of town where she went to see Merrick. This is where she's been concentrating her efforts. It's the only place she can link Sean to but there's been no sign of the yellow van.

On these drives, there are moments when she thinks she's lost her mind, that she's going too far. There are rational explanations for everything. For the pigeons, the ladder. For Sean acting as Greg's surrogate dad, being Charlie's mate from football and knowing about the unlockable French door because he was 'checking the builders' work'. People always choose to believe the rational answers because they make them feel in control, so their brains can go back to living-every-normal-day mode. It makes them feel safe. But just because something's rational, Naomi thinks as she slowly overtakes a line of horses on the side of the road, it doesn't mean that it's right.

She angles the rear-view mirror to look at Prue, her big cheeks squashed into her chin making her look a bit like Winston Churchill, so grumpy to be asleep. She's been a horror at times in the last month while she's had her full time, but, when she's taken her to baby groups, she always seems much more fun than all the other kids her age. She's brighter, quicker to laugh, quicker to play and imagine and to wring every ounce of life out of every waking minute. Which is why her sleeping face is a grumpy face. She hates missing out. She could be Prime Minister, a CEO, a world-leading engineer, a great artist, an athlete. She could change the world. She could be an amazing mum to some children. Naomi has so much to lose.

Then she sees it at the bottom left-hand corner of the mirror. The nose of the yellow van, just visible down a side street. She turns in the next available road and loops round to pass the side street again and there it is, definitely his van. It has to be. She parks in a supermarket car park between two other nondescript family cars and switches off the engine. Prue stirs slightly as they've come to a stop but she nuzzles herself back into her car seat and falls back into a deep sleep.

The one piece of advice common to all the articles she'd read about stalking and harassment was that you should never attempt to confront your pursuer. But then what's the point of this manhunt? She has to confront him, has to ask him why, she has to show him that she's not scared.

There he is. Walking out of a corner shop about a hundred feet to the left of the alley where his van's parked. He's wearing the same blue waterproof he wore when he intercepted her outside Ladybird's Landing. She can't help but find him attractive still. Amongst the urchin-looking kids in sportswear roaming the streets, he looks like he's from another planet. He has a plastic bag in each hand, one white, the other black. He's moving fast, unselfconscious. She opens the car door and steps out but as she tries to move between her Nissan and the people-carrier in the adjacent parking space, her bump catches on her wing-mirror. She looks back at Prue through the windscreen, sleeping soundly. Naomi has no idea what she's going to say. He's almost right in front of her now on the other side of the road. She needs to confront him, she needs answers. He stops and presses a button next to the glass door of a newly built block of flats. She spots a flurry of activity above him, a figure moving away from one of the upstairs windows. He looks round, Naomi squats down behind her car door. Through the window she watches him reach into his pocket and grab a fist-full of keys, but before he has to use them he pushes the glass door and walks into the building.

She stands up and slams the car door, furious with herself. More than a week looking for him and she let him walk right past. It was perfect. A busy street, broad daylight, and she watched him slip out of her grasp like a scared little woman. She looks at her daughter, shame mixes into her anger before she clocks what's on the seat next to her. Three dresses she picked up from the dry cleaner's this morning. She glances down the side street, down at the yellow nose of his van. She has an idea that, weeks ago, she would never have dreamt of putting into action, but since then everything has changed.

She gets back into the Nissan and drives towards his van. The only place to park with a direct line of sight to his van is up near the high street, near the building Sean's in. It's not ideal but she can't wake Prue up. She pulls the sunblind up to hide her and locks the car. Naomi's never left Prue in the car on her own before but she's safer there than with her. As she walks towards the van she watches a YouTube tutorial on her phone in one hand and clutches a wire coat hanger in the other.

She peers in the cab and it's more of a mess than she'd expected. Sandwich packets, newspapers, a protein-shake bottle wedged into one of the cup-holders. She has no idea what she's looking for but she can't have finally found him and go home knowing as little as she does. There's a tiny gap in the top of the window so she ignores the tutorial she's just watched, bends the coat hanger into a straight line and jams it into the window attempting to pull the lock up from the inside. The streets are empty, but she's fairly confident that if anyone came past and saw a pregnant women tampering with a car, they would just think she'd locked herself out by mistake.

She tries a few times but she can't get the end of the coat hanger to grip the lock. She feels pricks of heat under her chin, the embarrassment at her ineptitude and the fear of getting caught. She gets the coat hanger out and makes the hook she's fashioned smaller. An image comes into her head of him coming round the back of the van and grabbing her by the throat, his big hand gripping her bump and squeezing. And she feels sick. Hot, sick, her ankles screaming in pain as she stands on tiptoes trying to get the stupid fucking coat hanger to pull the lock up but it's not happening. She pushes the coat hanger in further, trying to catch the wire under the top of the door-lock knob. She leans too far in and it tumbles on to the bench seat of the van.

'Fuck,' she shouts. She turns around, her head feels like there's a sandstorm in it. She sees a terracotta plant pot outside the warehouse. Without thinking she picks it up and throws it at the window from point-blank range. Glass smashes all over the road. She glances up at the Nissan, still solitary on the double yellow line, before reaching over the broken glass and unlocking the van door.

She leans into the cab and sifts through the litter and broken glass. KFC boxes, packets of sweets, a Happy Meal box. With the way his body looks, she assumed he would eat healthily. She rifles through papers, sketches of bits of furniture, receipts from building supplies warehouses. Nothing revealing. She clicks open the glove compartment. Some tools. Screwdrivers, a plastic tub of screws, a Stanley knife. She pulls out the manual in its plastic folder and opens it up. Documents fall out. She looks at the first one she opens, the V5C registration document.

The car isn't registered to Sean Salinger. It's registered to Alexander Palmstrom. She looks at the other papers, the warranty, the insurance, all of them are in the name of Alexander Palmstrom. She folds them up and puts them back in the folder. He stole the van, she thinks to herself. She looks up the road. The Nissan stands unmoved. Everything Naomi discovers about this man makes her more frightened of him.

She backs out of the van's cab and closes the door behind her. She's disappointed. The man's a criminal, a car thief. But that doesn't tell her anything, not why he's doing what he's doing, no indication as to why he's targeting her and no clue as to what he might do next. She could report the stolen car to the police. That's something. If anything else happens he could say that she knows where Alexander Palmstrom's van is. She looks at the empty frame where the window was and smiles. She's never done anything like that before. Then she realises she hasn't taken anything.

She opens the door again, desperate to get back to her daughter, and looks around the cab. There's nothing that looks valuable, nothing that would attract the attention of a thief. It's unlikely he'd think it was her, but if nothing's been taken he might work it out. She sees the straps of a black rucksack hung over the driver's headrest. She grabs it and makes her way back to the Nissan.

Then she sees him, shoulders stretching the waterproof material, standing at the end of the road. His hands are gesticulating, as if he's talking to himself, he must be on a Bluetooth headset, she thinks. The Nissan's ten feet behind him. If he turns round he'll see it. Prue is closer to him than her. She locked the car. She's sure she locked the car. She clicks the button on her keys to make sure, but the indicators don't flash. She's too far away. He begins to turn to his right, towards her car, towards her daughter, but then he steps the other way and walks across the road and towards the supermarket. She realises she's been holding her breath and lets out a fractured, juddering breath. She runs back to the car and slinks into the front seat. Prue is still sleeping soundly. Naomi begins hitting herself on the thigh, harder and harder until she gives herself one last punch just above her knee.

'Stupid, selfish arsehole,' she whispers to herself, still unable to believe she'd leave her daughter in the car alone. She looks out the windscreen to see if she can see Sean but he's gone.

When she pulls the car to a stop on the esplanade outside her house, she closes her eyes and leans her head forward on to the steering wheel. Large raindrops start falling on the windscreen, spreading like ripples on a pond. She looks through them at her house. The rain blurs her view, every clear, definite line of the building being constantly shifted by each new smear of rain. She pulls the rucksack on to her lap, opens it up and looks in. The main body of it's mostly empty, a book, a few pens. The book is one she's heard of but never read, *The Catcher in the Rye* by J. D. Salinger.

Then it hits her. The van isn't stolen, she thinks. It's his. He's not Sean Salinger. He's Alexander Palmstrom.

TWENTY-FIVE

2 March 2018 at 02:47

Identity theft
Fantasist/schizophrenic
Corporate espionage. For C's camera equipment?!
C's parents' money
Something about the house X
Paedophile X
Obsessed with me
WHY ME? WHAT HAVE I DONE?

Action:
Confront him – NO
Tell C – NO
Police –

'What are you doing?' Charlie's looking over her shoulder. She stuffs the phone down into the sheets and their bedroom goes black.

'Baby's pressing down on my bladder, feel like I'm going to wet myself. Just googling.'

He shifts himself up into a more upright position. 'You need to sleep.'

'I'm googling how to get comfortable.' The duvet glows with the yellow light from the 'Notes' app on her phone and she can feel him looking down at it. He knows smartphones. He knows she's lying. He scratches his stubble and is about to say something but then stops himself. He moves down the bed towards where she's put the phone, she closes her grip, but he doesn't reach for it. He rests his face on the side of her bump.

'Get off my wife's bladder, you cheeky bastard,' he says in a sleepy drawl. He gives the bump an affectionate rub and moves back up to his pillow. 'Try to sleep, darling.' He paws a hand into her hair and tickles the crown of her skull, the word darling somehow never sounds right when he says it, insincere, like he's heard other people saying it and is testing it out. He turns over on to his side. She fumbles in the sheet for the phone and kills the screen's light.

TWENTY-SIX

26 weeks

'You are not eating.'

'I am.'

'You look like a model and not in a good way. Pregnant woman don't look like models.'

'I'm trying to eat healthily, for the baby.'

'You need more bread and before you say you're gluten-free or any other of that made-up rubbish most probably you are not. You're not drinking enough water, your urine is like treacle.' Lillian's not looking at her, she must wear the wrong prescription glasses because her face is laughably close to her folder of notes.

'I've had to look after Prue full time for the last three weeks,' Naomi says.

'I don't care, Mother. You get that husband of yours to take her and you go to a hotel and you sleep and you eat and you drink lots and lots of water.' Lillian has the results of all the tests they do near the end of the second trimester. The heater wheezing behind the midwife must be ready to be put out to pasture because the portacabin's freezing. It's been near constant rain in the last week and the temperature has dropped dramatically. Big snowstorms have been forecast. Naomi's blood pressure is too high, her iron levels too low, she's dehydrated. The baby has grown, but not enough. Lillian suspects she may develop pre-eclampsia, a condition that affects five per cent of pregnant women and usually doesn't cause problems but can lead to the baby not growing enough and the need for an early birth. Naomi's read all about it. They'll have to monitor her more closely.

'I'm not worried about you because you're a woman and women are incredible. But I am ordering you now to get some peace. You are a vessel holding something that is worth more than millions of pounds of gold. If you had millions of pounds of gold you would do everything in your power to make sure that the vessel that has to carry the gold back to your house is up to the job. Wouldn't you?' The ageless lady arches her eyebrows, enjoying her metaphor. 'This is not a rhetorical question.'

'Yes.' Naomi says, laughing, 'I would. I absolutely would.'

'All right then.' The midwife gets a pad out and begins scribbling something on it.

She still hasn't done anything about Sean, about Alexander. She was expecting some response from him, as if he must know that it was she who broke into his van, but there's been nothing. She nearly phoned DC Crawford a couple of days afterwards but then realised that what she'd done – smashing the window of his van, stealing his property – was significantly more criminal or at least more provable than anything she thinks he's done.

Lillian finishes writing and hands her a note as if it's the last page of her paper revealing the cure for cancer.

'For your husband,' she says. Naomi looks down at the scrawl of blue biro.

'Wow, thank you,' Naomi says, swallowing a laugh.

'Now get out of this ice-box shed and go and eat some chips.'

Naomi begins to gather her things together. The tests haven't revealed any serious problems and, despite Lillian's concerns, as it stands she hasn't got pre-eclampsia. If she does develop it, she's got friends who've had it and it hasn't caused any problems. It would just involve a few more trips to the hospital. And if she has to be in hospital until she gives birth? There aren't many places safer for her and her baby. It'd be much safer than at home.

Because that's the thought she can't escape no matter how much she tries. He wanted someone to get hurt on that ladder. He wanted her to get hurt on that ladder. If Charlie fell downstairs he'd be fine. But what if she did? Everyone knows what happens if a pregnant woman falls down the stairs, it's practically a trope. Last week she had the lock on the front door changed. Charlie was in London until late and she called in the morning to say she'd got herself locked out with Prue in the house and couldn't get hold of the builders so she had to get a locksmith in, if nothing else this whole affair has made her a much better liar. She also got a window fitter to come round and fix their French door, so now it'll be much harder for him to get in the house.

She stands up to go but stops when she sees a collection of pictures above Lillian's head. Some beautiful children smiling in a paddling pool, another of a cricket team photo, another of a striking woman holding a baby.

'Are they your children?'

Lillian puts her glasses up on her head. 'My grandchildren mostly. That one, the one that got my looks, that's my youngest daughter.' The woman looks thirty at least, which makes Naomi think she must have been way off in thinking Lillian in her fifties. She points at the different pictures. 'Tani, Lou-Lou, James, Peter, Jimmy, my daughter is Andi and,' she points out a beaming boy, about ten years old holding a drum in the air and a big drumstick ready to thrash down on it, 'that's the baby boy, Lexi.'

'He looks like trouble.'

'He is.' Naomi is even more delighted that she's been given such an amazing, formidable midwife. She looks at the little boy again.

'Did you say his name's Lexi?'

'That's right.' She puts her glasses back down, as if the name's being judged. 'Short for Alex, it's not a girl's name, if that's what you're thinking.'

'No, I like it, just not heard it before.'

'Well, sure he'll be calling himself something else in a few years.'

She thanks the midwife again, grabs her stuff and hurries out to her car. It's freezing inside but she doesn't stop to turn on the heaters. She grabs the iPad out of her bag and goes on to Google.

LEXI PALMSTROM she types in. Nothing comes up. She scrolls to the next page, then the next and all the way to the fifteenth page of the Google search. There's nothing, no one of that name. She's already looked online for Alex Palmstrom, Alexander Palmstrom, Al Palmstrom even Xander Palmstrom. Lots of names had come up but nothing that helped her in any way. She'd thought, maybe it was Lillian making her laugh, she somehow thought that Lexi might yield something. She thinks, scratching her nose.

She types something else. LEX PALMSTROM. There's an American soccer player, Axel Palmstrom, and that seems to give the most results. Some scholarly articles about something to do with L.E.X., whatever that means, written by various people called Palmstrom. She flicks through pages, then she finds it. An old Facebook account under the name 'Lex Palmstrom'. She clicks on to it and it takes her to a private profile. She can't access any of the content that's on there.

But there is a profile picture and it's unmistakably him. He's skinny in the picture, he's bulked up a lot since, but it's him. The long, straight nose, those stony eyes, his solid jaw. His hair's terrible, short back and sides with the front gelled down. She feels a buzz of excitement at having found him, the real him, and of knowing, knowing for certain, that she is right.

She scans the page for any other information but there's hardly anything there. Just his name and the name of a school. The Limes College. No contact details, no date of birth. She wonders why his school is on there but then remembers the old days of Facebook when you had to sign up through your university or school. She tries to click on a few links to friends and photos but she knows she won't be able to access them on a private account. She's never heard of the school so she cuts and pastes the name into the Internet browser. As the page loads, the sound of hail on the bonnet snaps her back into the real world and she looks at the field outside her window blanketed in white. 'The Limes College' comes up at the top of the page, a Suffolk council website. She clicks on Google Maps; the school's in Ipswich. She clicks on the pin, there's no website listed. The map shows a large patch of green next to the school, Naomi blinks, the hail still hammering down. She looks at the green, sees some blue at the bottom of the map, a circular pond and then a larger one above it, 'Wilderness Pond' the screen calls it. She recognises the name. She zooms into Street View and sees a pond surrounded by autumnal leaves. She's been there. She skips to the next point on the small inset map, a pale grey plinth, a war memorial. She's definitely been to this park before. Then she sees a name on the map she's heard many many times, she clicks on the pin next to it. A grand red-brick building, wide and imposing, dominating the street. Students in smart navy blazers over pale blue shirts. Ipswich School, one of the oldest private schools in the country. She's been there as well. Four years ago. A weekend away to Aldeburgh and they stopped in on the way through to have a look round. Charlie wanted to show her where he went to school.

TWENTY-SEVEN

27 weeks

'No Prue?' Felix calls from across the City gastropub.'Mummy mini-break. Love it. I'll get us some Virgin Marys.' He gets to the table where she's been waiting for fifteen minutes and takes off his coat to reveal a full three-piece black suit and collarless shirt, faintly clerical, the uniform of the off-duty barrister. He dusts rain out of his brush of ginger hair. Felix, Charlie's best and oldest friend, looks like a caricature of an early-ageing public school boy. Shortish, beginning to get round and with a permanent expression of delighted surprise. A bachelor, though not by design, he dotes on Charlie like a god and has always been Naomi's favourite of her husband's friends. She texted him to say that she had a meeting near his chambers and would he be free for a little chat. As he settles himself into a chair opposite her, she can see his joviality is tempered with mild concern. She and Felix have never met up before without Charlie.

A waitress comes over to their table and he orders them Virgin Marys before correcting his to a Bloody one. A silence descends and he bats it off with a sound, something like a satisfied sigh, and smiles, sharp incisors trying to find each other in his mouth.

'So, two kids. Bloody hell! Whereabouts are we now?'

'About two-thirds of the way.'

'Shit me. You look absolutely fantastic TBH,' he says, shifting in his seat. He empties his pockets, the apparent source of his discomfort, out on to the table. His phone, a clunky leather wallet and a packet of cigarettes. Naomi eyes them, she hasn't thought much about smoking this pregnancy, despite what's been going on, but she could murder a cigarette now.

'This is my last pack, Scout's honour. I've got this personal trainer and she said if I smell of cigarettes at my next session she'll kick me in the balls. And speaking of strong women, how's my little Prudence? Living up to her name?'

'If it's prudent to turn your parents into angry zombies by waking them every night then very much so.'

'Fuck. Really?'

Naomi nods, a wan smile. The murky drinks arrive on their table. Felix clinks the top of her glass with his and slurps from the straw before wincing slightly from the strength of the booze. Naomi takes out her straw and drinks her Virgin Mary. The horseradish stings behind her nose but sitting here, with a friend and a drink in her hand, feels more indulgent than a spa day. She and Prue have been staying with her mum and dad in Bournemouth. Prue needed a change of scenery and Naomi an extra pair of hands to help with her little girl for a few days. But, with Prue crying out for Naomi every time she's tried to leave her with her granny for a few hours, it's not quite been the break from her family that Lillian insisted she take. So although her reasons for being here are anything but fun, she couldn't help but enjoy the child-free train journey and now being in a bar, being part of the mass of people at their lunchtime carousing. It makes her nostalgic for the big boozy City lunches she used to have every couple of weeks at her old work. At the time she thought they were gross. She was there to work, not to get drunk and overstuffed with rich food while batting off the flirtations of sleazy middle-aged men but, when most of your meals consist of a toddler's leftovers, lukewarm beans and oversteeped Weetabix, it's hard not to miss how adult, how successful, drinking good wine and eating good food made her feel.

'I'd take Prue off your hands for a bit, give you a break,' Felix says, index finger tapping on the cigarette packet, 'but unless she likes train journeys and eating fry-ups in bumfuck regional towns, no offence, then I'm not sure I'm your man.' Naomi laughs but she can tell that Felix is waiting for her to tell him why she wanted to see him.

'Charlie's fine,' she says. 'That's not why I wanted to catch up.'

'That's a relief. Thought you'd had another catastrophe.' He uses the French pronunciation, without the final 'ee' sound. 'He's been dodging me, don't know if he told you. For a long while, really. We've not caught up for months. He told me he'd got bloody busy, things taking off with whatever gizmos he's working on, so I didn't throw my toys out of the proverbial. But I did think that that could've been a bit of a … a fabrication as it were, so when you texted, I was a tad concerned.'

'No, no. Things are really taking off, he's got this steadicam he's made. Big companies are fighting over it.'

Felix's face lights up with relief that his best friend hasn't got some unacknowledged beef with him. 'Well, chin chin,' he says, thrusting his drink into an air-cheers before taking

another slurp. Naomi smiles then turns her attention to fold-
ing the corner of a beer mat until it breaks.

'I got a "friend request" from someone, Felix,' she says.
'They also started following me on Instagram and, I don't
really use it, but on Twitter as well.'

'Right.' He draws the word out, his features overlayed with
earnestness. She's reminded of how grave the consequences
of his job are, how every time he's in court he's working to
keep people out of prison. Charlie told her that he'd texted
to say he's been trusted with a big embezzlement case at the
Old Bailey involving some sort of organised crime. 'Batting
way above his average' was the phrase Charlie said Felix had
used about the sorts of cases he was being handed. They had
a little laugh at his expense, at his good-old-boy bonhomie.
Charlie never felt at home with the nepotistic private school
backslapping. Naomi always thought that was what sent him
so far in the other direction in his career, wanting to make
something new rather than support all the old structures that
he thought ridiculous. The irony is that he still feels the need
to be seen as a 'great' man, exactly the sort of out-dated concept his school spent so much time instilling in their students.

'The person's name is Lex Palmstrom. I did some googling and someone with that name went to school in Ipswich,
close to your old school.' Felix's brow furrows. 'You always
remember stories from your schooldays. So I was wondering if the name rang any bells?' She shrugs slightly, nervous.
Naomi knew it was a risk coming to see Felix, he's fiercely
loyal to Charlie and has strange views about the brother-
hood of men. She remembers a story about how Charlie
had split up with his long-term university girlfriend, Annika,
and Felix had drawn the troops of men from their shared

friendship group together and told them that it was their responsibility to be there for him and that they shouldn't talk to her again. It's not surprising that a four-hundred-year-old all-boys private school would produce someone with such a deep-seated fear of women's power.

'Charles doesn't remember this person?'

'I haven't told him.' Felix makes some sounds, the sort politicians make in parliament when they're not happy about something. He undoes the button of his collarless shirt, revealing a tuft of orange chest hair. He's literally got hot under the collar over being thrust into a conspiracy with his best friend's wife. 'He's been struggling with the business for so long and I probably shouldn't tell you this but it's been getting him really low. It's become pretty bad.'

Felix nods sagely as if he knows more about his friend's precarious mental health than she would have thought.

'But things are finally going well and he's starting to get back to himself again so this, this person following me online, it's probably nothing.' Felix taps the cigarette packet on the table. 'I'm probably just pregnant and paranoid.'

'If you're worried, you should still tell him.'

'I'm not worried, just curious. I thought this bloke might be someone you used to knock around with. Maybe he's trying to get in touch with Charlie, or you. Neither of you do the social media thing.'

Felix looks more uncomfortable than she's ever seen him before. It was a mistake coming here, but she didn't know what else to do. She had thought about showing Charlie the old Facebook profile picture of his best mate 'Sali', show him that he wasn't who he said he was. But what if Charlie had confronted him about it? At the very least he would want to know why his wife had taken such great pains to unmask someone who, as far as he was aware, she barely knew. The fact that she had slept with Sean, with 'Lex', was bound to come out.

Felix prods the ice cubes in his drink with the stick of celery. She should have emailed him, or come up with a better reason to speak to him in person. She'd thought of others. She'd drawn out a few different options with a list of pros and cons. Asking on Charlie's mum's behalf was one. Or pretending she'd had a job offer from someone whose LinkedIn profile said they went to school near them, and she wondered if Felix had any background on him because Charlie couldn't remember. But she needed something that he wouldn't then talk to her husband about and Felix is a barrister, he ties people's lies into knots for a living. She knows she has to try to stay as close to the truth as she can without revealing anything too alarming.

'Lex, you said?'

She nods.

'What was the surname?' he asks, still seeming unsure he should help her without Charlie knowing.

'Palmstrom.' He squints his eyes remembering, then they flick open and roll around his eyes. He goes for his Bloody Mary again, the drink's almost finished. He's about to speak before he's distracted by a large group of suited men cramming into the bar. The noise level doubles. Felix leans forward.

'There was a Swedish girl. Well, she wasn't actually from Sweden but everyone said she was Swedish because of her name. I can't remember what it was exactly, but Palmstrom rings a bell.'

'What was her first name?'

He shakes his head. 'We just referred to her as "Swedish". She wasn't at our school, obviously because she didn't have a dick.' He holds up an apologetic hand for being puerile. 'She was at Colchester Grammar, maybe? Some people from school used to hang around with the girls from there. Charles and I didn't really know the Colchester lot.'

'Who did?'

'The "cool" gang, the ones that were good at sport, got into drinking before everyone else. They used to knock around with the girls from Colly Grammar, the good-looking chicks. Guess the lads from our school had more cashish than anyone at their school. Don't know why the girls would hang out with those wankers for any other reason.'

'Everyone's an idiot when they're at school.'

'I wasn't, obviously.' He laughs, glad to lighten the mood for a moment. 'Anyway. Lex Palmstrom. I've never heard the name. He's not someone I knew, so not sure I can help really.' He has helped but Naomi can't tell him how.

'Do you know what she's doing now? The Swedish girl?'

'Not the foggiest, TBH.'

'You can't remember her first name?'

'Nay, just ignore the friend requests if you're worried. Get rid of your Twitter if you don't use it. These online platforms aren't safe anyway. The companies are selling your data to whomsoever they like and the whole world can see the pictures of Prue you're probably posting. Lock it all down.' Naomi smiles, nods. She sips on her Virgin Mary. The waitress comes past and she orders a shot of vodka.

'It's going in here,' she explains to Felix's raised eyebrows. 'Otherwise it's just like having soup.'

'Hear, hear!' He relaxes, happy that he seems to have got through to her. 'So, any other news in the Fallon peninsula?'

'Prue bit someone at nursery.'

'Shit.'

'They won't have her back for another week so I've been looking after her full time.' Felix makes the right sympathetic noises. 'It's funny being a mum. All the things you used to do, everything you used to do for fun, the things that make you who you are, are suddenly taken away. I've only had one proper night out since Prue was born and I was back by nine o'clock.' Felix chuckles, gives her a wan look that says that he wouldn't mind going out a bit less. 'And even staying in, people keep telling me about box-sets and Charlie and I will start watching something and Prue will scream out, or we'll be too tired. I found myself actually asking to watch *Britain's Got Talent* the other day. You're braindead. You honestly are. Charlie's had to work all the time so it's literally been me chatting to a two-year-old for a month. Imagine Charlie when he's had too much to drink and you have to get him home?' Felix guffaws, eyes to heaven.

'Like herding a particularly sweary cat.'

'Well, Prue's twice as hard to deal with as that, so when this name suddenly appeared on my phone, "Lex Palmstrom", it was a distraction, a bit of excitement. It took me ages to find him on the Internet but it was something to do. I know it sounds stupid.'

'No.'

'When I saw he went to school so close to Charlie and you I thought …' She thought she finally had something to go on, the tiniest hint as to why this might be happening to her. She'd traced back through her whole life trying to work out who this man was, why he would target her, but it was only when she saw the image on the iPad of the grandiose school entrance hall she'd walked through with her husband just a few years ago that she realised she's been scouring the wrong past. 'I don't know. You're right. I should leave it alone. But, with what you're saying about this Swedish girl … Argh! I want to know who he is,' she says, laughing at her own fabricated folly.

'You could ask him,' Felix replies, holding the shot of vodka above Naomi's glass. 'This is OK, right?' he says, glancing at her bump. She nods and he pours it in.

'I could ask him. Yeah. Not much fun, but yeah, I can.'

'Cheers,' he says, clinking her now proper drink. 'I honestly didn't know the girl. Don't even know that is her surname. It could have been anything, Svenson, Bjornson, Lingonberries; don't think I ever knew it.' He looks round at the gaggle of suits buying champagne for a group of young women, laughing at the much older men. When Felix turns back to her, he has a little glint in his eye.

'What?' she says, readying herself for the inappropriate joke about them it seems like he's about to tell.

'Swedish had a mate,' he says, tickled by the memory. 'The woman at the bar talking to the tall fella reminded me of her.' Naomi looks over his shoulder at a petite woman with long dark hair nodding seriously at a lanky, balding man. 'You know, I haven't thought about her for years, more's the pity.' He shakes his head, eyes brimming with nostalgia. 'Now she was a filly and a half. Well-endowed in the, er, chest department—'

'God,' Naomi says, grimacing with embarrassment.

'She *was*. Wavy hair, Italian-looking. Very much my type. I remember I tagged along with your husband to a party at the house of a guy called Douglas Mason. He was the big swinging dick at the "swich". The year above. Charles got friendly with those lot for a little while when we were fifteen. He was in the football team two years early, star player and all that, so he dabbled with those tossers for a bit. Anyway, this girl, Swedish's mate, I asked her if she wanted to come out for a smoke and she only bloody did. We were having a chat, having a good time, I thought, and these girls come out, her pals, and they just start, well, they were being pretty harsh, to her, but about me. You know, my hair and, I had a few of the old zits as well. They were awful, sort of bitchy girls who tear people down because they can. That was the end of my involvement in the "cool gang". That was the only time at school that Charles and I weren't thick as thieves. He carried on hanging out with them for a bit but they always come back to old Feline; it was a matter of weeks if I remember rightly. He never liked them, thick as pigshit, bunch of bastards, TBH. Not his scene at all.'

'Charlie's never told me about any of that,' Naomi says. She still hasn't sipped her souped-up drink, the bravado of ordering it having worn off.

'He won't remember it. He's never looked back. Always into the future. Even when we were eleven. Never liked dinosaurs. Always rocket-ships.' Naomi stares at the cigarette packet that Felix flips over in his hand. She notices the health warning picture on the pack, she tries to make it out as it keeps turning over. She puts her hand out to stop it, surprising Felix. It's what she thought it was, a foetus surrounded by bloody membrane, the words saying 'Smoking can cause early miscarriage'. She pushes the drink over to Felix.

'Do you want the rest of this?' He looks at the picture, apologises and puts them back in his coat pocket. 'Do you remember what she was called?' she asks.

'Swedish is all we ever—'

'No, the one you would have bedded if it wasn't for those pesky girls.'

'Eliza she was called.' He laughs to himself. 'I remember confusing Dr Dolittle and Eliza Doolittle from *My Fair Lady* when I was trying to flirt with her.'

'I'm amazed she didn't sleep with you there and then.' He raises an eyebrow and waggles his glass at her as if to chastise her for ribbing him before finding a space beside the celery to drink from.

Swedish. She always thought Sean could have been a Viking. His height, blond hair, chiselled features. She's going to call Charlie as soon as she gets out of the pub. She's going to ask him about the girl known as 'Swedish'.

TWENTY-EIGHT

> **Thursday 11:51**
>
> I'm going to tell Charlie.

> **Saturday 12:59**
>
> You were right.
>
> If you tell him he'd be destroyed X

> Unless you leave, I have to.

> He wouldn't survive it.

She didn't call Charlie. She bustled for the tube and despite being obviously pregnant no one gave up their seat so, hot, uncomfortable and feeling faint, she had to run for her train and only just caught it. By the time she was in her seat, on the way back to Bournemouth, she decided to contact Sean, the man who was Sean, before she called her husband. But she didn't get that far. She looked at her previous messages to him and saw that one line, *I don't think he'd survive it*, and saw it as the threat it was intended to be. He'd gone on to talk about Charlie's depression but it seems so unlikely that he actually knew Charlie's therapist or that, if he did, she'd tell him about her patient. That was designed to give him what lawyers call deniability, she'd been reading that that was something that stalkers and their like were very adept at doing. The wording of that sentence, after what happened to her on the loft-ladder, after finding out there's some link between that man and her husband, seems crystal clear to her now.

But maybe she's so desperate to make sense of what's been happening that she's reaching for an answer that isn't there. Felix didn't recognise the name Palmstrom. All the stuff about some Swedish girl seems tenuous to her now. Ipswich isn't a small town, Wikipedia says its population is one hundred and eighty thousand. It could be nothing more than a coincidence that he and Charlie went to school so close together.

She got back to her mum and dad's house after eight so Prue was in bed. She ate some leftovers, feigned tiredness and went up to her old bedroom. All of her teenage posters and trinkets have been replaced and the room is now beautifully decorated and furnished from the upper tier of Ikea products. Her iPad sits on her old desk, the Facebook app open on the screen. There are seven messenger windows. All to different people called Eliza.

As soon as she came up to her room she started looking for Colchester Grammar Groups from the early 2000s. It was a few years before Facebook became ubiquitous so there weren't as many groups or events as she'd hoped. There was a photo album entitled 'Leaving Dance 2003', three different groups for reunions for those that left in 2002, 2003 and 2004, and there was also a Friends-Reunited-style 'Where are they now?' group for people who left school around the same time. She didn't find the name Palmstrom anywhere and couldn't even find anyone who looked Swedish, not Swedish enough for it to be the basis of their nickname anyway.

So then she started on the 'Elizas'. There were five of them. There was also an 'Elisa' and one 'Elize'. She managed to track all of them down on Facebook, even the married ones who'd changed their names. Naomi sent them all the same message:

> Hello, I'm a family friend of the Palmstroms from Sweden.
> One of their relatives has passed away and I need to get in contact with them about a bequest.
> Thanks in advance.

Naomi stares at the screen. There are three responses so far.

> Eliza Klein
> Don't know who you're talking about, sorry.

> Elize Phipps-Jones
> Don't know the Palmstroms.

> Eliza Belbin
> Good luck with that.

Two of the others have gone offline having seen the message. She doesn't read into it; Naomi never checks new messages these days. She knew it was a long shot.

Sat at the desk now, she closes the windows and goes to the settings page. Thinking about what Felix had said, she clicks on the privacy section and sees that her profile is nowhere near as secure as it could be. She thinks of her Instagram, she shares every day of Prue's life on there and Felix is right, there's no telling who is looking at that. She goes to the 'Delete Facebook' tab and has a look at what's involved. As she's reading about how hard it is to leave, a message window pops up on the bottom right of the screen:

Eliza Orsdall
STOP IT. I'm showing this one to the police.

Eliza Orsdall has blocked you.

TWENTY-NINE

Five minutes from Reading station, flakes of pastry from a sausage roll tumble on to the Burberry mac barely covering her bump. Naomi looks out at the river, standing in a court-yard in the centre of an almost circular, new office building. The national headquarters of Thames Water. The Associate Director of Internal Communications at Thames Water is Miss Eliza Orsdall. She'd got this information from LinkedIn as she has been blocked from Facebook. A complaint of har-assment has been made against her and she has to make her case to them. The Facebook customer services person she spoke to couldn't reveal anything about why the complaint had been made. So here she is.

With the biennale just over a week away she has to be back at work tomorrow so she didn't have much time to think about what she was doing. Eliza was her only avenue to explore and it was today or never.

Her reaction on Facebook gave Naomi hope. She knew that Eliza Orsdall couldn't have any sort of problem with her so it must have been the name Palmstrom.

She's starving, her diet has gone to shit in the last few weeks. All the advice says that this is the period of her pregnancy she should be eating better. Leafy greens, oily fish and red meat. She bites into a Danish pastry. Tomorrow will have to be the day for mackerel on a bed of kale. It's one thirty-eight and there's been a steady stream of office workers coming out of the building and heading round the corner to the high street for their lunches. There's a train at two forty that would get her back to her parents' house in time for Prue's bathtime.

There she is. Eliza Orsdall. Naomi can see what Felix saw in her. Very petite, five three at most, curvy figure and she still has beautiful wavy dark hair. The sort of woman that Naomi always assumed all men would prefer to her. Someone pocket-sized, soft and overtly feminine. She looks down at her phone as she walks. For someone who has problems with Facebook, she's absolutely loving whatever it is that she's looking at, smiling broadly. She gets closer, her skirt suit a little stretched over her legs, and passes Naomi without noticing she's being stared at. She walks down the steps towards the river.

'Eliza?' Naomi calls out. The woman turns around and looks up at Naomi who, with her designer coat, sleek hair and make-up, suddenly feels that she should have worn something less corporate to have a casual chat with a stranger who's threatened her with going to the police if she contacts her. Naomi trots down the stairs to meet her. 'My name's Naomi Fallon. Is there any chance we could have a chat?'

'What about?' The woman is suspicious. Up close, she's not as striking as Naomi had first thought, her features a little small for her face.

'I wanted to ask you if you knew Lex Palmstrom.'

Eliza's face blanches. She shakes her head and walks away from the railings that overlook the river, past Naomi and up the pavement in the direction of the town, almost shifting into a jog. 'Wait, Eliza!' Naomi follows her, going as fast as she can with her bump. The distance between the two women widens. 'Eliza, please slow down, I'm pregnant.' The woman doesn't slow. Naomi's scared. In all of this she still hoped that everything she'd thought about Sean was exactly what everyone kept dismissing it as: paranoia. But this is the reaction of someone who is scared, very, very scared. There's a busy four-lane road between them and the high street and Naomi sees that Eliza has nowhere to go. She begins to walk up to the right and away from Naomi when she realises it's a dead end. When she returns to the junction, Naomi stands there waiting for her.

'Look at the size of me. I really can't be running around Reading town centre. I've come a long way to speak to you.' The green man flashes up on the opposite side of the road. 'Let me buy you a coffee, or lunch if you've got time.'

'Who are you? Police?'

'He's been trying to contact me. Persistently. Lex Palmstrom. If you've got ten minutes …' Naomi puts her hand on her bump. The crossing beeps at them. Eliza closes her eyes for a moment then nods her head in the direction of the high street, turns and walks across the road.

Eliza sits in a high-sided chair in a chain coffee shop, legs wrapped around each other. 'I'm sorry about the Facebook thing,' she says, gnawing at her thumbnail, not looking at Naomi. 'That was you, wasn't it?'

'It was.'

'He set up fake profiles, for years. He'd pretend he was an old friend and then would send me these pictures.'

'Pictures of what? Do you mind me asking?'

Eliza picks up her coffee, eyes restless as if she's already had too much caffeine. Naomi bought a doughnut. It stands on the table between them. If Eliza doesn't touch it within the next minute, Naomi's having all of it.

'How did you find me?'

'A friend of mine, Felix Brandt?'

Eliza shakes her head, telling Naomi she has no idea who Felix is.

'He said you were friends with a girl that people knew as "Swedish"?' Naomi continues. Eliza looks down at her lap. 'He thought her surname might have been Palmstrom. I just—'

'Her name was Karin.' Eliza pulls a column of hair down over her face, as though she's trying to draw the curtains and block Naomi out.

'And was— Did Felix remember right? Was she Palmstrom?'

'She was Lex's sister.'

'Was. She's dead?' Naomi asks, but it's more of a statement than a question. Eliza nods, eyes raw with the memory. She picks up her coffee and drinks. It's too hot. She swears and puts the cup back down, so some of the coffee splashes on to the table.

'How did she—'

'Suicide.'

'When?'

'2001. She was my best friend at school. Well, I liked her. I'm not sure she ever liked me as much. She was tall, beautiful, like a supermodel. She didn't follow all the stupid shit everyone at school was into. She went to gigs, into bands no one else had heard of, she liked Manga cartoons.'

'Do you know why she, um, took her life?' Naomi can tell that the woman is on a knife-edge but she needs to know more.

'Do you know what it's like having your best friend top themselves?' Naomi shakes her head. She tears the doughnut in two, jam spurting on her fingers, and offers one half to Eliza who can't help smiling. 'I'm doing Body Coach, I can't.'

'Extenuating circumstances,' Naomi says. Eliza accepts the proffered half and takes a bite of it before putting it back down on the plate.

'Karin and her brother were in foster care. I never knew what happened to their parents. She never talked about it. By the time I'd got to know her in year nine, they had been with the same foster family for a while, but I got the impression they'd moved around a lot in the past. Anyway, she went off the rails when we were in year eleven.' Eliza dips a finger into her coffee to test if it's cold enough to drink.

'Was there some reason?' Naomi asks, knowing there's more Eliza wants to say.

'Something happened at this party.'

'Whose party was it, someone from your school?'

'No, someone from Ipswich School, it's the expensive private school in the area.' Naomi decides not to tell Eliza that she's already heard a thousand stories about the escapades of Charlie and Felix in their days at the 'swich'. 'Karin got really drunk. She disappeared for a while and then she turned up passed out on a sofa. I got us a cab and we stayed at my house. A few weeks later, at school, a rumour got out that she'd slept with some Ipswich guy and everyone was asking her why she'd kept it quiet. The whole school became obsessed with it. It got really out of hand.'

'You were in year eleven; weren't there quite a few people having sex at parties? How did it become such a big deal?'

'These girls, Lilly Sherman and Namah Patterson, the queen bees in our year, they hated Karin because all the boys liked her. They turned it into a major scandal at school. Karin didn't go to parties. People thought it was because she thought she was too cool to do what everyone else did at weekends, but that wasn't really true. She was really good at netball and just didn't get drinking. She didn't like losing control. But everyone thought it was like some aloof persona she was putting on. So getting drunk at a party and sleeping with some random guy from the posh school was like catnip for those girls.' Naomi's breathing deepens. Some random guy from the posh school, a boy from the 'swich'. Felix and her husband went to parties with the woman sitting opposite her, with Karin. Her husband's a boy from the 'swich'. 'Also, she kept it a secret, that was probably the worst thing. You know what girls are like at that age, they feed on people's insecurities.'

'Their shame.'

'Then everyone started saying that she'd got pregnant. People at school were calling her mummy. Someone put a baby sleepsuit in her locker. It sounds bad but no one actually thought it was true.'

'But it was,' Naomi says, seeing where this story is going. She scratches the cuticle of her thumbnail.

'No one knew. I didn't know. It was only when she stopped coming to school that I got worried about her. Course, that, her not coming in, that got the rumour mill going again and the word went round, who knows who started it, but people started saying she'd got an abortion. When her foster parents made her go back to school it was all anyone was talking about. People shouting at her in the corridor, calling

315

her names, "the abortionist", "babykiller". It was awful. She stopped coming to school entirely. Left home. People would see her around town in a state. Must have been drink, drugs too maybe. Once it was clear she was in trouble, our whole year closed ranks and no one would talk about the bullying. That's what she hated me for the most. She thought I should have been on her side. But standing up to girls like that, I would've been dragged into it and they would have destroyed me. I should have told someone, her social worker or one of the teachers. Anyway, then she, she …' She tails off, wipes the beginnings of tears out of her eyes and looks down at the ground for almost a minute. When she looks up Naomi offers the doughnut again, Eliza laughs and waves her refusal.

'Girls were the same at my school,' Naomi says; 'there's no way I would have put my head above the parapet like that.'

'Sorry,' Eliza says, trying to regain her composure.

'It's a long time ago,' Naomi says, half to Eliza and half to herself. Her hand rests on the top of her bump and slides down to cradle around her belly button. Eliza looks at Naomi's hand stroking her pregnant belly.

'What's he doing? Lex? What's he done to you?' Her voice is panicked.

'Oh, nothing, nothing really, just some weird messages.'

'He's sick,' Eliza says.

Naomi bites her bottom lip, smiles, awkward. 'What do you mean, sick?'

'When everything was going on with Karin he kept asking me what had happened. He had no idea. I should have told him but I was her only close friend so if he started going round talking to people about it everyone would have known it was me who told him. After she died, he would find me in town. He said he needed me to help him make sense of it. He said it was driving him mad, trying to work out what had happened, why it had happened. He was in awe of Karin.'

'Was he younger?'

'About two years younger, yeah. It was sad. Really sad. He was obsessed with finding out what happened. "The not knowing," he said, he said it was like God was torturing him, but he wasn't religious, I don't think. He was in a lot of pain. He started acting up to his foster parents; I think he blamed them for her death, thought they should have protected her. They sent him back into care. He actually crashed on the sofa at my parents' house for a couple of nights. It was a horrible time. He disappeared for a while after that.'

'So he never found out why, what happened at the party?' Eliza looks away at the door, turns her phone over in her hand and shakes her head. Her body couldn't be more folded in on itself in the chair and Naomi spots fear in the slices of light reflected in her eyes.

'I've got a meeting in ten minutes.' She stands up and picks up her bag.

'What were the pictures he sent you?'

'Don't let him into your life. Don't let him know anything about you.'

'Did he do something to you?'

Eliza looks down determinedly, her hand grips at her skirt. 'I have to go.'

'I'll walk with you.' Naomi stands up to go.

'No,' she says, loud enough that people on other tables look up at them, this tall pregnant woman harassing her petite counterpart.

'I can't get involved, I can't. I'm sorry but I can't.' She makes to go, Naomi grabs her arm and she turns round, fury in her eyes.

'Take this.' Naomi hands her a card. 'It's got my number and email, please. I was scared before but now, with what you've told me, I'm terrified, OK?'

'I have to go,' Eliza says through gritted teeth.

'Who was he?'

'What?'

'The boy she slept with.'

'I don't know.'

'Please,' Naomi says, still holding on to the sleeve of Eliza's coat.

'No one knew who it was.'

'What was the rumour?'

'Let me go.' Naomi releases Eliza and she almost falls away towards the door. She storms out of the café. Naomi's mind is on fire and saliva collects at the back of her throat as if she could throw up at any moment.

'Shit,' she says to herself. A mother on another table, feeding biscotti to a little girl the same age as Prue, looks up at her, full of righteous disdain. Naomi wants to tell her to fuck off but instead she bolts out of the café and begins jogging back towards the offices of Thames Water. She sees Eliza ahead, her little legs striding towards the crossing. Naomi tries to turn her jog into a sprint, but she can't. The bump, the extra weight, slows her down, her back and ankles burning. A mass of office workers begin crossing the road towards the river and Naomi sees Eliza run to catch up and join them. Naomi speed-walks down but as she gets to the crossing it's too late. The cars zoom past, blocking her way.

'Eliza,' she calls across the traffic. She tries again, louder this time, 'Eliza, wait, please.' Eliza stops dead in her tracks on the other side of the road and, shaking her head like she's furious with herself, turns round to face Naomi.

'It was my husband,' Naomi calls across the road. Eliza shakes her head, she can't hear. There's a gap in the cars and Naomi begins to cross when a sports car flies round the corner, forcing her back on to the pavement. 'The boy Karin slept with at the party,' Naomi shouts. Eliza's chin rises up, she can hear. 'I think it was my husband.'

Eliza's face falls and she looks so sad. Naomi tries to find a way to cross the road but the passing cars are unrelenting. Eliza mouths something, it could be 'I'm sorry', then she turns and runs back to her office, as fast as her tight-fitting skirt will allow.

THIRTY

22 February 2001

MSN Messenger – Chazinho

KARINP83 says:
Hey

How's u?

I wz so WASTED @ Doug's party!!!!

25 February 2001

KARINP83 says:
How's ur week been?

Ur playing us at football next week? I might come watch

What u think?

1 March 2001

KARINP83 says:

U blanked me at the football. Not OK.

What we did at the party. Iv never done that b4. I'm not that type of gurl.

You cnt just ignore me.

Don't panic I dont want to be your gf

12 March 2001

KARINP83 says:

did u tell people? every1 at school is saying I had sex with someone at Dougy Mason's house

You PROMISED you wouldn't. I dont remember much but I remember that!

Thought u liked me. If u just took advantage because I was drunk, at least tell me to my face.

21 March 2001

KARINP83 says:

I have to talk to u. In person. I don't have a mobile phone. I can get to Ipswich this afternoon.

U CANNOT IGNORE THIS

26 March 2001

KARINP83 says:

I am pregnant.

27 March 2001

KARINP83 says:

U can't keep ignoring me! I could get thrown out of my house if my foster parents find out. Please talk to me. Everyone at school is calling me a slut.

I have to talk to you. I have to talk to someone. I don't know what to do.

I feel so alone.

6 April 2001

KARINP83 says:

I took care of our child. It was the worst day of my life. I want you to know that.

17 April 2001

KARINP83 says:

everyone knows i had an abortion

I wish you knew what this feels like

23 May 2001

KARINP83 says:
u said u liked Eels. maybe you were lying

iv been listening to this song on repeat

life is hard

and so am i

you better give me something

so I don't die

THIRD TRIMESTER

ONE

'What do you want?'

'How are you going to get what you want?'

'What will happen if you don't get what you want?'

Sean Salinger's dead. He doesn't go to football. He doesn't hang around nurseries looking after other people's children. He doesn't even work any more. 'Charles', the character I am for Uggy – couldn't help myself using his name, something about the idea of Lord Charles Fallon screwing a nursery nurse just tickled me – he's still going, but barely. I never put much work into him. Didn't need to.

Who is Alexander Palmstrom? He's someone who let his sister murder herself because of what that spineless piece of shit did to her, what they all did to her.

'She was too good for this world.' That's what I said at her funeral. There weren't many there. Clive and Julie, that bitch Eliza. Karin was too good, too special. Sometimes those sort of people get through, reach their potential and they're the ones with all the success, all the money they could ever want. But some are like dolphins in a net of tuna. If she'd not been so smart she wouldn't have got into the grammar school in the next town over, would have gone to the joke school I went to instead. The one on the other side of the park from the mighty Ipswich School. They never mixed with us. 'Chavs' they called us. If Karin hadn't been so clever, so perfect, she would have never met him.

After she was killed, no one would tell me what happened. People knew. It felt like *everyone* knew but me. I looked through her room, turned Clive and Julie's house upside down looking, but I couldn't find her computer. It was Clive's old laptop from work. She spent a lot of time on it, chat rooms, following bands on Myspace, we didn't have mobile phones so it was her only way of talking to people once she stopped going to school. I knew it would have the answers. Took me two years to track it down. She'd given it to a drug dealer called Alan Chung, whose house she crashed at for a few weeks before she was killed. Amazingly it still worked, I had to try over four hundred different passwords to get into her MSN Messenger chats but that's how I found out what happened to her. After that, I visited that snake Eliza.

I still couldn't find out who 'Chazinho' was. I guessed it was a Charles or Charlie but there were four in Karin's year, seven in the year above, nineteen at Ipswich School in total. I dismissed Charles Fallon early on. Everyone I spoke to said he was a bit of a geek who didn't go to parties. I spent years trying to work out who it was, spent a long time watching the ten or twelve Charleses I thought it could be, made friends with a couple of the ones I suspected most to try to find out for certain, but nothing I did led anywhere.

After another two and a half years I realised I couldn't do it on my own. I worked two, sometimes three, jobs for eighteen months until I had enough money to employ an investigator to track the email address linked to Chazinho's profile. After a few more years, when I had saved more money to hire what was basically a hacker, I found out it was him. The man I'd dismissed at the start, Charles Fallon.

Naomi Fallon knows that Sean is a fictional character now. He always was for her in a way. If she'd known any more about Sean Salinger than that he was everything that her husband wasn't, she would never have slept with him. I couldn't believe it was her who had broken into my van but then, a week or so later when I found the registration papers jammed into the side pocket of the manual's casing, I could see she'd surprised me again. She knows my name. Maybe she knows more. She's changed the locks. The builders have been chucked out. The French window has been fixed. But it's too late for all that, Naomi. On Christmas Day, when I slept in the sheets she sleeps in every night and relived that afternoon in the swimming-pool shower, I thought about us. We're both broken. Perhaps the two parts of us could fit together like shards of a smashed mirror. She could be the mother of my child. It could be that we have created a life.

She said it was his, but I changed the app on his phone at football so there's no way she can be certain. Perhaps she feels it is his. There was a draft of an email to Eliza that Karin must never have sent where she said that she felt that the baby was a girl, even so early. A little girl.

'What will happen if I don't get what I want?' A perfect soul will never be redeemed.

'How am I going to get what I want?' By doing something I didn't want to do. Nothing else has worked.

'What do I want?' For him to experience exactly what it feels like to have no idea why you've lost your whole family.

TWO

28 weeks

She walks back through the long, wood-panelled porch of the Bank of Friendship Nursery. Prue walks ahead of her, seemingly oblivious to the fact that she hasn't been here for over a month. Naomi presses the doorbell and she's buzzed in. There's an external deadlock that has to be operated internally. They know all the parents by face and the receptionists ask anyone they don't recognise for a password the parents have to set up for their child in order to access any of the rooms where the children are. She's seen it happen when a grandmother who was doing the pick-up for the first time couldn't remember the password and had to call their daughter. Naomi gives Lisa a knowing smile and, for the first time, notices a CCTV camera in the corner of the room behind her. She's never really thought about the security of the place but she can see that it's stringent.

Lisa talks to Prue, telling her how much she's grown, how pleased they are for her to be back. Naomi's been in for a meeting, explained how there haven't been any other instances of Prue biting or misbehaving and that it must have been a one-off. She flattered Lisa, telling her that, having had a chance to spend more time with Prue, she's seen how far

330

she's come since she started at The Bank of Friendship. She went on to say that, on reflection, she totally agreed with their policy and that it was good to know Prue was safe from being bitten or hurt by the other children herself. She'd had to say all this through her best fake smile because really Naomi thinks their policy is draconian, but she needed to get Prue back into nursery. The biennale is in a few days and Charlie has been going to London more frequently as his prototypes get close to being completed.

But her need to get Prue back into nursery is about more than their busy work schedules. Prue is no longer safe with her, she's not safe with Charlie. That man did something to Eliza, and though Naomi has no idea what it was, the woman is terrified of him. And now he is in Naomi's life, in Charlie's life. And she knows that he has a motive.

He wants revenge. Naomi's husband impregnated his sister. She got an abortion and then, unable to deal with the guilt, she killed herself. When put like that it sounds awful but, as Charlie has got into bed with her every night since she visited Eliza, as he's rubbed tummy butter into the bump that seems to have grown exponentially in the last week, a fragment of good news, she's told herself the other story, the real story. Charlie had sex with a girl at a party when he was fifteen. That was all. He wasn't the one who bullied Karin and she can't believe he was the one spreading rumours about her. He's frustratingly private and hates gossip; she can't see how he was responsible for that poor girl's death.

She rings the door for the baby-room and Uggy opens it to let Prue in.

'Oooogy!' Prue screeches and runs into the nursery worker's leg. Naomi fakes a smile. The baby kicks her hard, she puts a hand out on the doorframe for support. Uggy reaches her hand forward, involuntary concern.

'I'm fine. He's just having a bit of a workout.'

'When are you going to have the baby?' Prue wanders off towards the breakfast table, leaving Naomi feeling awkward, exposed.

'Three months.' The two blonde curtains of Uggy's hair fall forward as she looks down at Naomi's bump, studying it almost. The baby kicks again and Naomi winces, then laughs the pain away. Uggy's face wrinkles into a grin that seems devoid of sympathy.

'Bye, Mummay,' Prue says and both women turn round to look at her. The little girl is sat down on her tiny seat, fist full of two quarters of toast, waving wildly.

'She seems to be at home again,' Uggy says.

'I wanted to say, Prue's had a nasty cough for such a long time now and I'm just wondering if there's any way you could keep her in this week, with it being so cold out.'

She looks at Naomi sternly for a moment but then brightens. 'Of course.'

'And maybe for next week as well. If someone can just stay inside with her. That's OK, isn't it?' Naomi has no idea whether anyone else makes such requests but she needs Prue to stay indoors. It's freezing outside and here, behind two deadlocked doors, with staff trained to the teeth in safeguarding, Naomi knows Prue is protected. Prue won't like it, she hates being cooped up, but the alternative is unthinkable.

Naomi waves her daughter goodbye and heads out to the park. The frosted grass crunches under her shoes as she heads towards the Nissan.

THREE

'He's got a grudge against us, Detective.'

'Call me Angie.' The crunch of a crisp punctuates her words. It might be the distortion of Naomi having her on speaker phone, but she sounds far more Kentish than when they first met. 'I agree that there is cause for concern. Sorry, just grabbing some lunch,' DC Crawford says over the sound of chewing spit. Naomi's sat on an inflatable gym ball, arms out straight on their dining-room table. Her back's hurting and the Internet says this is the best way to stretch it out. 'I'm really glad you got in touch again.' The detective is a terrible liar.

Throughout their conversation there's been the rustling of papers, the sound of footsteps and snatched conversations with her colleagues. The woman is overworked and under-caring about phone calls from melodramatic women. 'It's weird, Mrs Fallon; it's definitely an odd one and once again, really important that you've reported it in case there's any escalation in this man's behaviour.'

'I'm six months' pregnant, I have a toddler. You can't wait for things to escalate before you take what I'm saying ser-iously. He's lied about who he is, wormed his way into our lives. He wants to hurt us.'

'You don't know that—'

'His sister killed herself and he thinks it's my husband's fault.' The woman at the other end of the phone sighs. Naomi stands up, indignant, letting the ball roll off into the kitchen.

'Mrs Fallon, I agree, this man's behaviour is very odd but he hasn't given any indication that he intends to do anything to harm your family.'

'He's left baby things in my house, threatening my daughter—'

'These items you mentioned, I'm really not sure why someone would—'

'He's been going into my house!' Naomi slams her palm down on the table to make her point to the empty room. 'He's made friends with my husband and we— For God's sake, we actually—' but Naomi can't say it. She can't tell the detective that they had sex; that it could be his child that she's carrying inside her.

'What does your husband say? Have you confirmed that he had relations with Mr Palmstrom's sister?' Naomi leaves the line silent for a moment too long. 'You have told your husband, haven't you, Mrs Fallon?' Naomi looks at the piece of A3 paper spread across the table. She's plotted her conversation with the detective like she used to for presentations at work and has written dummy responses to over forty questions that she might be asked. She finds the corresponding answer – *He's working on a very important business deal at the moment* – but it now seems redundant; the detective's right. How can she involve the police if she can't tell her husband?

'Of course I've told him.'

'And he's confirmed it was him, with Miss Palmstrom.'

'He thinks so.' Naomi's scrabbling, she doesn't want to implicate her husband in some cold case but she knows that her story is unravelling as she tells it.

'Thinks so?'

'He's pretty sure, but couldn't remember if they'd actually …'

'Had sex?'

'That's right.' With every lie she knows she's making their situation more untenable, but she needs the police to do something to stop Sean, not Sean, to stop him.

'And what does he think about your theory?'

'What do you think he thinks? For Christ's sake! He wants the police to do something because we've both paid a hell of a lot of tax to this country and our family is in danger and we want some bloody protection.' There's a pause at the end of the line. The sound of another crisp being eaten, a slurp of a drink.

'Mrs Fallon, I believe I explained to you when you came in, the issue for us is one of evidence.'

'Harassment,' she reads off the article she's printed from the online solicitors' forum, 'is defined as any repeated behaviour that is causing alarm or distress.'

'Mrs Fallon—'

'It's a crime. What he's doing is a crime and your job is to catch criminals and protect the public from the actions of criminals. It's in your annual "Roles and Responsibilities" report. 2016.' The detective takes her turn to leave the line silent. Naomi looks outside to see the frost still not thawed on their muddy lawn. There's a Siberian cold snap forecast.

'Come in and make an official statement. Anything you can tell us about this man's whereabouts would be especially useful. Then we can go and have a chat with him. How did you find out his real name, by the way?'

'Facebook,' Naomi reads off her cheat-sheet. 'A friend of a friend still had an old picture with him.'

'Can you get your friend to try and save the picture?' Naomi knows she can't because it doesn't exist but she can't come clean about breaking into his car; she still can't believe that, in the eyes of the law, her actions are more criminal than his. 'And we'll need to go through all of your text messages. Written evidence is by far the best if we're going to go to the CPS with this. We can discuss everything when you come in. Would you and your husband be available this afternoon?'

'Charlie's in London today.'

'Perhaps you can come in this afternoon and I could pop round to talk to Charlie tomorrow?' Naomi feels the child rotate in her belly, or is it the feeling of something being crushed inside her. She can't go and see the detective. She can't have the detective 'pop' in to talk to Charlie because Charlie doesn't know anything and because she's told her lie after lie. She tells herself it was to protect her husband, to protect her family. But she's only ever been trying to protect herself. Protect the life she's always dreamt of. Protect herself from the pity and judgement of her friends and family if they were to find out how weak she is, how pathetic and juvenile she is to believe that she deserves excitement, to be desired, affection and attention, as well as having a happy family and a beautiful home.

'I can't do this afternoon,' she says, both fists pressed into the table, back stretching towards the wall again but this time in rampant frustration at how stuck she is in this mess that's all of her own making. 'Can I make an appointment when I've sorted out childcare?'

'Er,' the detective sounds unsure, confused as to why this woman who was so insistent is now being evasive, 'of course. Just keep a record of everything and bring it all in. We'll have a look to see if we can get this chap to leave you alone. Better doing things outside the courts as that process, restraining order, et cetera, can take for ever. We find most people will bow out of situations when a few panda cars turn up on their drive.' And with that they say their goodbyes and Naomi ends the call. She rubs her eye until it's sore. She looks down at her stapled sheaves of Internet research, her large annotated list of questions and answers, and feels like a fraud. Both hands sweep the papers up and crush them into a ball.

The truth. Perhaps the truth is the only way out.

FOUR

Naomi stands a few feet away from their bathroom unit and stares at herself in the mirror. She wears no bra and skin-coloured pants so she looks naked. Her breasts are engorged, plum-coloured veins showing through skin that seems translucent. The same tracks of blueish-purple run around her bump. It's insane that in this thing, this beach ball protruding from her normally flat midriff, there grows another human being. A human being who will be perfect and yet possess the same potential failings as every other person on the planet. It could be his. She knows it could be his. She can't tell her husband so she has to hope that the man is a coward. Everything about him so far tells her he is. If he wanted to hurt them he could have done it months, even years ago. He hasn't got the balls.

She throws a jumper over the top half of her body but it only gets halfway down her belly so she takes it off. The snow still hasn't come yet but they're promising an Arctic storm and the news is getting suitably histrionic about travel chaos, even at the end of March, so Naomi needs to decide what she's going to wear for the biennale.

She had hoped she wouldn't have to be on-site but it seems clear that Matilda would have an aneurism if she has to deal with everything on her own. Naomi will be there at the opening, which the forecast says is going to be zero

338

degrees but bright and sunny, and then is planning to pop in every day for an hour or two and have an 'office hour' to deal with various issues as they crop up. Charlie's bringing Prue to the opening. Naomi's looking forward to it. Looking forward to seeing people enjoying the fruits of her labour in a way that she never could in her old job where she only saw numbers, projections and old men slapping each other on the back. She was always adamant that Prue see her working, it's a chance for her to understand what her mummy has been doing and, hopefully, she'll be impressed.

She goes to the wardrobe and pulls a long cardigan down when she hears beeping. Three beeps. She wraps the yellow cardigan over her bare body and goes to look out of the French window. She thought it might be the sound of a car being unlocked but there's no movement in the street outside. She looks up and down the road for the yellow van. She's found herself doing this four or five times a day since she discovered who he is.

She wants to text Lex Palmstrom, to tell him that she knows, but she has no idea how he'd react. In a bizarre way she feels claustrophobic with the secret of him. The detective is a dead end for now. She hasn't called back to chase up their meeting and Naomi imagines she's written her off as a bored housewife.

Three beeps again. It's coming from behind her. It sounded like it was coming from the floor. Naomi bends down and listens.

Three beeps. From under the floorboards. She gets her phone from her bedside table and turns on the torch. She shines it down between the cracks in the floorboards, which are still black though most of the debris has been removed. She sees clumps of hair under the floor, big bushes of dust, half pencils and old hairbands. Then she sees white plastic reflecting the torchlight back to her. She makes out a red light. Three beeps again, the light blinks with each beep.

'Lenny,' she shouts. She heaves herself up from the floor and goes down the two flights of stairs to where the carpenter is building some shelves in the basement. 'Have you got a crowbar?' The big man glances up from the piece of wood he was sanding with a look of puzzlement.

'What is it you want crowing open?' he asks, a big smile spreading across his face.

'There's something under the floorboards in our bedroom.'

He goes over to a large stand-up toolbox and rummages around until he pulls out a long iron bar. He moves over to her, she holds her hand out and he laughs and gives her bump a pointed look. 'You better show me whereabouts.'

She lets him go first up the stairs, aware that the view under her jumper might be a little racy for a man of his age, and follows him up to the bedroom.

'This one here.' She points out the floorboard.

'These boards are a hundred years old, I might not be able to keep it in tact using this.'

'I can do it if you want?' she says, reaching again for the tool but he sweeps it away from her grasp. He kneels down and is about to insert the blade of the crowbar into the floor when he stops and runs his hands over the staples that secure the floorboards.

He looks up at her. 'These are new.' He ushers her down to look. 'Colour matches all the older ones pretty well but you can just see where splinters of wood have come up around them. Very professional job.'

'Can we just look underneath?' The big man notes her impatience and goes back to his crowbar, still sticking up out of the floor. A very professional job, Naomi thinks, at least there's no doubt as to who's responsible for putting whatever it is under the floor of their bedroom. Lenny levers gently, wincing as he hears the wood coming away from the staples. Naomi comes closer, trying to peer around the big man into the hole. Lenny holds up the piece of wood to show her he's managed to get it off in one piece but she waves it away, looking past his arm at the object nestled under her floorboards.

It's a baby monitor. Large, rounded white plastic. A large 'On' button but nothing else on it. The receiver, the part you leave in the baby's room. She picks it up and turns away from Lenny, not wanting him to see. The thing beeps its three beeps and Naomi presses the button to turn it off. She blinks her eyes, sees herself staring back in the mirror above the sink, each thought parrying into her eyelids like flashes of a strobe light. The buzzing, the static she heard that day, was the device she's holding now. He's been listening to them since at least then and probably a long time before. He knows everything. Where's the receiver, she thinks. The range on monitors is very limited, their old one is in the loft because it wouldn't even reach from Prue's room to the kitchen. Is that why she's seen his van close to the house? But no, that doesn't make sense. He'd only get snippets of their conversation on the rare occasions his van's been parked nearby. The receiver has to be somewhere in the house but for what purpose if there's no one to hear it? Unless, her breath catches at the thought, he's been listening to it the whole time. Hidden somewhere in the house when they've been there, spying on their conversations, listening to them sleep, catching Prue's every screech and giggle as she jumps up and down on their bed.

'You want me to put this board back in?' Lenny asks, still on his hands and knees.

'Er, yeah,' Naomi says, although she doesn't sound remotely certain.

FIVE

The Whitstable Golf Club clubhouse is a large fifties pre-fab, on paper a pretty grim venue to use as the headquarters of the arts festival, but the set-designer/artist couple that Naomi commissioned to decorate the inside of the building and the marquee attached to the back have done an incredible job.

The theme for this year's festival is 'Van Gogh's Seaside Hideaway', Victoria's idea. The artist spent a couple of years in his youth on the Kent coast in Ramsgate, so in his honour the walls have been daubed with impressionistic dots, blues and greens and whites. The weather is still wintry, but inside the festival it feels like spring. The large grassy area just beyond the eighteenth tee has been co-opted for the event and there are various stands and stalls with artists selling their wares. A gourmet hot-dog stand billows the caramel smell of cooking onions, which makes Naomi's mouth water for the umpteenth time. She's already had two of their jumbo hot-dogs since she got here at eight o'clock this morning. There was a problem with an author of historical fiction not turning up to a reading of their new book at the independent bookstore in town – Naomi found a local young spoken-word artist who stepped in much to the bemusement of the old dears who'd come to hear a talk about a Huguenot detective – but that aside, everything is going smoothly.

Naomi walks out on to the terrace and listens to the buzz of well-spoken satisfaction. She cranes her head over the throng to try to find Prue and Charlie. Prue's loving the crowds and keeps grabbing artisanal knick-knacks from stalls and trying to walk off with them. The artists and regular patrons who she's dealt with are all a bit in awe of the hotshot from London who's running their little festival, so she moves amongst them like royalty; it's silly but feels nice, nonetheless. She looks round a stall selling hand-painted pottery at the vast blanket of green beyond their small encampment. There's no sign of them.

Charlie's bought her candyfloss, she thinks. That's the only reason they'd be hiding from her. Matilda insisted on a candyfloss stall and he's caved and bought Prue one in full knowledge that Naomi wouldn't have allowed it. The number of times that she's talked to him about presenting a united front on sugary treats.

'There you are.' Matilda grabs her shoulders, giving her a shock. She looks concerned, but then she always does.

'All OK?' Naomi tries to keep the weariness out of her voice.

'Charlie's looking for you.'

'What's wrong?'

'He's inside.' Matilda won't tell her any more so Naomi pushes past her and slices through the crowd towards the clubhouse. She sees Charlie on the decking, he's looking frantically over the crowd and as he lights on her, she knows what's wrong.

'Where's Prue?' she asks, four pensioners shifting out of her way, and she breaks into a jog.

'Shit, I thought she might be with you.'

'She was with you. She's been with you since you got here; why would she be with me?' Naomi marches away from him and round the side of the building. Her first and only thought is that that man has taken her daughter. She looks at the golf club car park. There's no sign of the yellow van, but that doesn't mean she's wrong. She couldn't find him hiding anywhere in the house. She looked in the attic, the basement, everywhere someone of his size could have been, but there was no sign. She almost wishes she'd found him there now. She runs as fast as her bump will allow back towards Charlie. He looks shell-shocked, blinking, stunned into inactivity as he always is in stressful situations. She grabs him by both shoulders and looks into his eyes; if he knew what she knew perhaps he'd be able to shake himself out of it and find Prue.

'Where did you last see her?'

'We were, er, we were in the gents' toilet. I was at the urinal, I was trying to keep her next to me, but she ran out. I chased after her, thought she'd be waiting by the door, but when I came out I couldn't see her. It's rammed in there. I was hoping she'd run off and found you.'

'Well she hasn't.'

'She's probably just hiding under one of the stalls.'

Naomi looks at the floor and shakes her head; if she looks at him she'll get angry and she hasn't got time for that. She walks to the edge of the decking and scans the crowd for Prue's pink puffa coat. There are so many people. She could be anywhere. She sends Charlie one way round the stalls and she goes the other. As she goes she asks all of the traders if they've seen Prue until most of them have joined the search.

★

Fifteen minutes later, there's still no sign of her. Matilda brings Naomi a cup of tea and ushers her into one of the stallholders' camping chairs. She's already sent a crew of people to go and look over the rest of the golf course.

'She might have gone into the woods. I remember when my Liddy went missing in a garden centre. I was this close to calling the police and then I found her, sitting behind a display fountain, throwing stones into it.' Naomi wants to ask Matilda if she can shut the fuck up and go and find her child but she lets her drone on so she can think. Has this been it all along? Is this what he always planned to do? Eliza said he was obsessed with his sister, she was all he had, all the family he had in the world, and she was taken from him. So that's what he's doing to Charlie, to her. He's ripping the heart out of their family. If he has Prue, if he does anything to her little girl, it will be Naomi's fault because she could have stopped him. She could have told Charlie, told the police, she could have kept them safe. Perhaps this is what Karin felt: unfiltered despair. If something has happened to Prue, Naomi won't be able to carry on. When she was conceived something changed in Naomi, something in her biology changed. She wasn't just herself any more, thoughts of Prue's well-being now occupied almost all of her brain. Prue became the shining figure in her consciousness. If he took her away, Naomi wouldn't be able to heal. Naomi has never focused on her mortality before. She has always worked towards crafting the best life that she can. But if Prue lost her life, like this, when she could have stopped it, she would have to end her own.

Naomi hears shouting coming from beyond the tents. She stands up, trying to decipher what the voices are saying.

'Found her.' Charlie's bellow rings out around the golf course. The arms of the camping chair squeeze her as she slumps back into it. She wandered off. It wasn't him. Matilda puts a hand on Naomi's shoulder.

'They always turn up all right,' she says. Naomi gives her a half-shrug that tells Matilda that she's right, that she was silly to get so worried. Charlie saunters into the main corridor between the various stalls, he hugs their daughter tightly to his chest.

Naomi's so delighted to see Prue's round cheeks, rosy from the cold, bouncing towards her, that she barely registers the huge hot-pink candyfloss she's clutching. As they get closer, Prue almost jumps into her mother's arms. Naomi clutches her tightly, her little feet padding against the top of her baby bump. The cooked sugar smell of the candyfloss is over-whelming but her chest flutters and Naomi feels her eyes moisten with relief. She nuzzles into her daughter's neck, breathing in her warmth.

'Please, darling, please, don't scare Mummy. Please don't run off like that,' she whispers to her.

'Daddy friend. Not worry.' Naomi pulls her head away sharply and eyes her daughter, what does she mean?

'Yes, Daddy's your friend,' Charlie says, flicking his eye-brows at Naomi, blowing his lips out in relief.

'Mummy friend.'

'Yes, Mummy's your friend too, chiclet.' Charlie pinches his daughter's nose and pretends to have stolen it. Why is she saying that? She's never called them her friend. Charlie's got it wrong. She's trying to tell them where she's been.

'Where did she get the candyfloss?' she asks Charlie, direct, angry.

'Not from me. She must have found it.'

'Oh God.'

'She's fine.' Charlie puts an arm around her waist. 'She's all right.' Prue sees the fear etched on her mother's face and Naomi see her little girl have an idea. She licks her hand, like she's a bear licking honey off it.

'Oh, I think we need to return this. Our little kleptomaniac was holding it when we found her. Thought you'd recognise which stall it was from.' Charlie hands her a beer mat. It's one of the ones from the bookshop's stall. Naomi turns it over and reads the text. She walks quickly out of the market and looks at the car park again, no sign of the van, then she scans the road away from the golf club, nothing. But she has no doubt it was him. It's a warning. He's letting her know that no matter what she's discovered about him, he is still in control. She reads the words on the beer mat again, a quote attributed to Alexander Pope.

A little knowledge is a dangerous thing

SIX

elizaorsdall@outlook.com   23 March 2018 at 08:21

To: naomijanefallon@hotmail.com

Re: LEX PALMSTROM

Dear Naomi,

Snakes. He sent me pictures of cut-open snakes. Pictures of their stomachs and the half-digested animals inside.

He turned up at my house four years after Karin's death. I was still living at my parents' house. He must have only been seventeen, eighteen, but he was a man, tall, broad shoulders, nothing like the little boy who'd stayed on my parents' sofa.

I invited him in for a cup of tea. It was nice to see him at first. I still thought about Karin all the time. He was very interested in everything I'd been doing. I'd been to uni and dropped out. I asked him how he was and he said he had been trying to move on from Karin's death. I asked him where he'd been living, what he was up to, and he was evasive, but very friendly, smiley. I should have known something was going on, it was like he was too pleased to see me. We ended up sitting together on the living-room sofa having a cup of tea when he gets up, says he has to go to the toilet and leaves the room.

Then I hear the sound of a door locking. He's locked the big double glass doors that lead into the kitchen. Then he leaves the house through the back door. Our dog, Misty, she was a little Yorkshire Terrier. She was in the kitchen. She walks up to the double doors and looks at me, trapped in our front room. Then the back door to the kitchen opens and this thing slides into the room and I can see it's a snake. A huge snake. I'd never seen a snake in real life before. I know now it was a reticulated python. One of the white and yellow ones.

I probably don't need to tell you what happened after that. But I want you to know that he made me watch the whole thing. He'd pocketed my phone so I couldn't call anyone and he cut the power so I couldn't turn the TV up to drown out the sound. It took two hours from the moment the snake bit Misty and squeezed the life out of her until I saw the shape of her moving along the inside its body. Then he came back in the kitchen and took the snake away. I assume it was him. He was in full protective clothing, face covered.

I reported it to the police but they couldn't find him. They managed to get a restraining order but he never came back.

I had a couple of years of counselling after, to make sense of it, to try and work out why he did it to me. We worked out that perhaps it was because he had to watch someone he loved die slowly in front of him and he thought I deserved to have the same happen to me. He wanted me to feel as helpless as he did. Or maybe it was because I sat by and did nothing. I'll never know why, which I'm sure was all part of it.

Anyway, all that, what he did to my dog, wasn't enough for him. Whenever I put on Facebook about something good happening to me, when I finally got my degree, holiday pictures, he'd send me one of those snake pictures.

I've tried to tell you what happened as best I can. I hope it doesn't scare you. Writing it hasn't been easy.

I never knew who it was she slept with at that party. If it is your husband, you need to go to the police now. That man is sick.

Eliza Orsdall

PS: If the police need to contact him, the only person who might have his number is his foster mother, Julie Trent-Smith. Her email is julie_t_smith@btinternet.com

SEVEN

29 weeks

'You must be fucking joking me,' Naomi says into cupped hands, index fingers pressing into the corners of her eyes. It's quarter past six in the morning and Prue is packing clothes from a pile into Charlie's leather holdall. He's going to Manchester. He stands above his bag, a silhouette against the grey sky that hangs above the sea in the French window behind him.

'It's been in the diary. I put it in your calendar,' he says, unable to look at her. She walks over to the bag, eyeballing him as if trying to speak to a rebellious child while Prue continues her work below them.

'There has been a snowstorm forecast for weeks. The news says there will be chaos on the roads,' he tries to interject but she closes him down, 'and on the trains and planes and any other way that you can get anywhere. We have a child. I am really bloody pregnant.' He turns away towards the window and sighs. Prue looks up.

'This is so predictable,' he says.

'What?' Prue watches them as if she were at a tennis match. Naomi always swore they'd never argue in front of her. It's like he's done this on purpose. Telling her about some work trip weeks before and doing his due diligence with all of their shared online calendars, but then not mentioning it again until he's packing his bags for an eight o'clock train.

'Why do we have to go through this fudging rigmarole every single time? I'm back tomorrow night. She's at nursery today and tomorrow. You'll be fine.' She walks over to him at the window and pretends to look at the sea. 'Maybe I don't want you to go because I'm scared.'

'There's two months to go. The chances of you going into labour now are so slim and then what, when the baby comes? You want me having to make this sort of trip then? Leica and JBL are competing to buy the products. Teddy can drive the prices up but I have to be there at the negotiations. This is my work.'

'Your work is more important than your family?'

'It's for our family. Everything I do is for our family. To make money so our kids can have as good a life as we do, better even.'

'You're so full of shit.'

'The family that you wanted, at the exact time that you wanted it, because the whole world would implode if Naomi doesn't get exactly what she wants exactly when she wants it, regardless of how much it's fucked up my career.'

Naomi feels the neurons vibrating behind her eyes. She tries to focus on the sea, tries not to get angry as he wheels out the greatest hits from their back catalogue of arguments. She has to make it clear to him that he absolutely cannot leave them, that they won't be safe. But how can she do that without telling him the truth?

'What if I fell and I had to go into hospital. What am I meant to do with Prue then?'

'Jesus Christ.' He turns away from her and goes over to his bag. Prue's now taken everything out of it. 'Will you help me put this all back, Prudy? Then we can have a quick juice.' Bribing arsehole, Naomi thinks. 'And then Daddy can get off to the station to go to his important work meeting that he's doing for you and Mummy and the baby.' He glances up at Naomi and she shakes her head, disgusted. He shoves things back into the bag, pants, shirts, a pair of New Balance trainers, picks it up and checks his travelling outfit in the mirror. Prue swings on the handle of the holdall, giggling, like packing Daddy's bag is the most incredible thrill-ride. Naomi glances down at the mat on the floor that covers the loose floorboard where she found the baby monitor.

'You'll get stuck. You won't be back for days. I won't be able to cope.' Charlie's seething, Naomi's anxiety, particularly when it interferes with his plans, can more or less be guaranteed to make him furious. Prue yanks the bag out of his hand now and Naomi can see a hint of venom as he grabs their daughter's hand and throws it off. The little girl looks upset so Charlie seems to reset himself and picks her up, making faces in the mirror, holding her cheek to his.

'Daddy's got an app on his phone, sweetheart. It's the weather app that film crews use. Film crews who, if they get the weather wrong, lose millions of pounds, and the app says that the storm's not coming for three days, when I'll be safely back home with you and Mummy.' His eyes shift to look at Naomi in the mirror. She can't look at him so she turns away and goes into the wardrobe. She rakes at a few of her dresses, dresses that she hasn't got a chance of getting into for a year at least, and plunges her head into them, drinking in the smell of dust and washing powder. She has to do something.

Should she tell him? Could she tell him? Is that the only way to stop him going?

'If you go, something terrible is going to happen,' she says, voice full of anguish as she walks back into the bedroom, but he's gone. She hears the fridge door slam shut downstairs, Charlie's shoes padding heavily on the wooden floor followed by the patter of Prue's bare feet. The door opens.

'Bye,' he calls up the stairs to Naomi, sarcastically cheery.

'Bye, Daddy,' Prue shouts after him. The door slams. Naomi watches him walk out on to the street and along towards the train station, the clouds more and more ominous with every moment.

They're alone now.

EIGHT

Charlie's app was wrong. Naomi knew it would be. The snow came in the evening after he left and has only just stopped, thirty-six hours later. It's all over the country and, as always happens in England, the travel infrastructure has decided it's the beginning of the next ice age. Charlie was meant to be back last night but instead he's holed up in a boutique hotel in Manchester with Teddy. They're trying to find someone to give them a lift back. He's very confident that that will happen. He was very confident about the fucking app, she thinks.

They're on the beach, Prue strapped to her back in the baby carrier. She breathes through a snotty nose into her mother's ear and names things as she sees them, 'birdie', 'helicopter', 'man running'. It's minus two degrees and the beach is covered in a thick layer of snow. She's never seen snow on a beach before. It looks like a lunar landscape, the salt flats she saw in Bolivia or the aftermath of the apocalypse, the snow grey like ash against the sand. There's no give to the ground under her and her wellingtons slide around on the frozen sand.

Prue woke at four thirty this morning and wouldn't go back to sleep. Naomi couldn't be bothered to Google why this could be the case. Knowing why something's happening doesn't help you stop it, she's learnt. Nursery was closed yesterday and trying to keep an obstreperous toddler entertained for a whole day inside was torture for both of them, so this morning, as soon as Naomi thought it was warm enough, she wrapped Prue up in so many layers she could barely move her limbs and dragged her out into the cold. Thankfully nursery's open today, so she won't have to do another twenty-four hours on her own.

If Lex Palmstrom wanted to come for them, now would be perfect. Barely a soul on the beach, no one to hear her if she called for help. She's so tired of trying to work out why he's toying with them like this, she almost wants whatever it is to happen.

Eliza's email was shocking, frightening, but by now Naomi wasn't surprised to hear he'd gone to such lengths. She loses her footing on an icy rock and stumbles forward, catching herself on the edge of the concrete launch.

'Not worry,' Prue says.

'Not worry, darling.' She hears a sound over her shoulder and spins round to see a bike coming fast along the promenade. The rider, an elderly man, waves at them as he goes past. Prue says 'Morning' to him, far too quietly for him to hear. He's brave, Naomi thinks. There are no buses on the roads, barely any cars. The whole town has come to a standstill. Perhaps she and Prue are safe then. If no one else can travel then maybe he'll be stuck as well. She looks at the road above the beach, no yellow van. But after speaking to his foster mother on the phone she has no doubt that if he wanted to get to her, he would find a way. 'Dogged,' was the word she used.

She has a scan at the hospital this afternoon. They wanted her to have another one around thirty weeks because of the baby's growth rate. She's not as worried about it as the other scans; now she can feel the baby kicking wildly and doing cartwheels inside her, far more active than Prue ever was, she somehow feels confident that the baby, despite being on the small side, is going to be fine. Perhaps she'll get a cab to the hospital if there's a company that have four-by-fours to get through the snow. It's walking distance, but today she doesn't want to take any chances.

Prue begins to beat her mother's shoulders and chant, 'Out, out, out.' She doesn't like to be constrained for too long. Naomi walks up the concrete launch and up the road that leads away from the beach.

'Clouds,' Prue says, pointing at the banks of snow piled on garden walls as Naomi carries her children towards nursery.

NINE

A skinny man in a long grey coat shovels snow out of the entrance to the Bank of Friendship. The paths around the park have been cleared and gritted but the thick snowfall seems more virginal than in the rest of town. Uggy ran ten kilometres this morning and now her right foot hurts. The beach was harder than the pavement. She stands in the door-way blocking a gaggle of eager toddlers in like a flood defence about to be overwhelmed. It's just after lunch and the tem-perature's gone up to three degrees so they've decided to take the kids out to build some snowmen.

Uggy escorts them, one by one, past a patch of ice that the skinny man's still working on. Jess and Sophie bring up the rear of the group, chatting to each other about their weekend as if the children aren't even there. She's sick of them, sick of all of the people she works with. She needs to get away from here.

The boys and girls run and stumble on to the snow-covered grass, clad in their huge coats, hats, scarves and the nursery-issue yellow high-visibility vests. Two of the littler ones, Ian and Rocky, bend down on to the floor and appear to be listening to the sound of the grass cracking as other children walk on it. Jess hauls them up to their feet, trampling their blue-eyed curiosity. Elsie, such a pretty little girl, one of the trendies' children, brushes snow off the shoulders of her embroidered coat. And Prue runs circles round a snowman that someone's already built singing, 'Circle, circle, circle.'

'Didn't her mum want her kept in?' Jess asks Uggy, chewing gum.

'She can't be in the room all of the day when the other children are playing in the snow.'

'Not what the mum said, though.' Jess hates Uggy because she's not overweight.

'I asked Lisa.' She knows that will shut Jess up and it does. She goes back over to her best friend Sophie to gossip about their foreign co-worker.

Uggy looks over to see Prue about to bite into a stone she's taken off the front of the snowman. Uggy runs over, almost slipping on the way, and grabs Prue's wrist to stop her. Prue goes for another bite, so Uggy takes the stone from her and puts it in her coat pocket. Prue stamps her feet in indignation and Jess and Sophie laugh at her. The little girl smiles wide and toothy at how hilarious she must be. Uggy's expression remains frozen.

Holding Prue's wrist in her narrow hand, she looks up at a copse of leafless trees about fifty metres ahead of them. They seem long-dead against a desert of snow. A man stands amongst them. A big man in a plaid shirt.

TEN

Edmund, as his nametag proclaims him, flings some paper towels on to Naomi's stomach. The dark room smells musty. Naomi tries not to assume it's the sonographer's body odour but, looking at him again, it's hard to come to any other conclusion. She still can't believe it's a man doing the scan today. There are some jobs where there shouldn't be equality, she thinks, however sexist that might be. He barely said hello to her when she walked in, just pointed at the hospital chair for her to sit in and asked her to pull her shirt up.

Naomi pulls the waistband of her maternity jeans down and tucks the paper towels in. The sonographer turns round and, without any preamble, squirts ice-cold gel on to her bump and uses the scanner to move it around her belly. At least they didn't cancel the scan because of the snow, she thinks, trying to make herself feel less uncomfortable in the dark room with this stinking, rude man.

On the screen in front of her she sees her baby. It's more clearly human now, squashed up against the walls of its little cave. Button nose, spherical belly, stick-thin limbs. The scanner moves around as he makes his measurements, the perspective changing so she doesn't get a clear view again for some time. She feels on edge, fingers running along the underside of the chair until she feels some ancient chewing

gum and pulls her hand away. She wants to ask him how the
baby is but he seems incapable of looking at her, subsumed
by manic clicking on his machine. The screen shows a view
as if she were looking under the baby's legs. Naomi can't
make out a penis. She thought she might ask the sonographer to tell her the baby's sex, thought it might make
her feel more in control, but she doesn't want to remember
finding out something so monumental from such a horrible
man.

The screen shows a close-up of the baby's head. A side-
profile of its brain, large in its skull. Its personality, its
prejudices, its intelligence, its abilities, so much of what will
shape its whole life wrapped into this tiny blob of organic
matter. Half of it comes from her.

'Very small baby,' he says.

'How small?'

'You're twenty-nine weeks and six days and you're measuring at about twenty-six weeks.'

'And what's that in an actual weight?' Naomi asks, trying
to temper her disdain for the man's disinterested tone.

'Two and a quarter pounds. At full term, thirty-seven
weeks, the baby will be at best six pounds.'

'But there's still lots of time to grow.' He takes the scanner
away from her belly and retreats further into his screen.

'I'm going to make a note of all this and we can refer
it to your midwife. There's information on the NHS
website.'

'Sorry.' Naomi wipes the gel off her belly and pulls herself
up on the chair. 'You know how it works. I'm asking you,
now, while I am actually in a room with a human being who
works at the hospital. What does this mean?' The man takes

her anger in his stride. He doesn't turn to her but she can see how heavy his eyelids are, he looks like he hasn't slept for years.

'If it's under six pounds at full term the doctors will induce you because it's possible the—' Naomi's phone buzzes loudly, stopping the man momentarily. 'It's possible the placenta is not functioning properly and that could be a risk for the baby.' He stands up and goes to the back of the room where the printer has just clunked into life.

Naomi pulls her top over her bump and fishes into her pocket for her phone. When she sees the screen she sits bolt upright.

A message from 'Sean'. She gets down off the seat and walks out of the dark room into the strip-lit corridor. She clicks on to the message. It's a video. The sound of wind. Prue picking up piles of snow and moving them into a big mound to make a snowman. His voice from behind the camera. His Yorkshire accent, fake of course, she now realises.

'Wave to Mummy, Prue,' it says, void of feeling. Prue looks round, face red with the cold, but smiling, before she pats snow in her attempt to make a snowman. Then the video ends. Naomi stumbles over to the far side of the waiting room and collapses down into a plastic chair. The sonographer comes out into the corridor and thrusts her pregnancy notes at her. She must have turned white because even he seems concerned.

'Do you need me to get you a midwife?' She smiles at him, eyes manic.

'No, no thanks.' The man disappears back into his darkened room. She gets another text:

Charlie asked me to pick
Prue up.
He's got low battery. He said
if you call his phone, if you
contact him, it will die.

Naomi stares at a poster that lists all the benefits of holding your newborn baby against your bare skin and sends a reply.

Bring her home.
I'll give you what you want.

ELEVEN

Charlie looks over the dashboard of the Land Rover at the motorway, a mass of hazard lights and dirty snow. Teddy's asleep in the palatial back seat leaving Charlie in the passenger seat next to 'Big Phil', the foreman of the factory that's signed on to start building their products, who's giving them a lift back to London. Phil is a huge Manchester United fan and since Teddy offered up Charlie as a football guy, he's spent the whole journey telling Charlie his views on Jose Mourinho and how he's destroying the history of his club. When he'd exhausted and re-exhausted that topic, he insisted on them working out their greatest combined Manchester United teams for each decade together. Big Phil contributed a lot more than Charlie to this particular car-game. The roads aren't half as precarious as the news reports said they'd be, but the journey to the outskirts of London has still taken them the best part of seven hours.

Charlie texted Naomi when they left, early this morning, to tell her that they were getting a lift, but was non-committal as to whether he'd be back this evening. Teddy has offered the spare room in his Clerkenwell penthouse if the trains to Kent are all suspended. Charlie feels terrible for missing the scan today and she hasn't texted him about it so his assumption is that whenever he gets home, despite having busted a gut to make the journey, she's going to be furious with him. He desperately wants to see her, and Prue. He's missed them. Far more than he usually does when he's had to go away.

He knows why, but he's ashamed of himself for it. The trip to Manchester has been a huge success. Teddy managed to play off JBL and Leica and made up some interest from China so they ended up getting nearly double what they'd been aiming for. JBL came in with far more money but Teddy wanted Leica because of the 'cool-factor' and they eventually offered them thirty-eight per cent of all sales, on the basis that they were pre-ordering a provisional five thousand units of all three products. He hasn't been able to do the personal figures, and of course there'll be overheads, but as a lump sum it's in six figures and if the product goes well, which everyone seems to think it will, there'll be more. In addition, Teddy's given him sole profits from the patents, so there'll be money from that in the long term.

He misses his family more, he maybe even loves his family more, now that he can look them in the eye and know that he's successful. He's not someone who values money that highly but it gives him the status that his father always had, the breadwinner. The unassailable, undisputed breadwinner. He knows that makes him egocentric and materialistic but Amy always used to talk about accepting the reality of who you are, accepting the ways in which the qualities about yourself that you perceive of as 'bad' are often the ones that make you as a person.

He can't wait to see Naomi and tell her how good the news is. No amount of Big Phil carping on about fat-cat football owners, or him not knowing whether there will be a train working to get him home, or even Naomi ignoring his texts, can dampen his excitement.

TWELVE

www.mumsnet.com/health/cravingacigarette-mp.34235

Best Answer

Everyone says smoking is very harmful for your baby while pregnant. In most cases it is. I know numbers of people who have smoked during pregnancy and their babies have came out fine, and they smoked the entire time they were pregnant. I dont want to say having 1 cigarette is OK, because that sounds bad. But I'm sure having one wouldnt hurt the baby. A friend of mine said her doctor told her smoking is just like drinking caffeine, and has almost the same effect.

Naomi stubs the cigarette out in the pile of waterlogged mint leaves at the bottom of her mug. She only managed two drags. The guilt kicked in the moment she felt the harsh taste at the back of her tongue. She wrinkles her toes in her tights, feeling the roughness of the floor with her feet. It's more than two hours since she got his message. It took her forty minutes to walk home in the ice. He's not here and there's been no other communication.

She waits at the bottom of the stairs. The carpet-runners still haven't been fitted so she sits on the dusty strips of underlay that were kept on to stop Prue from cutting her hands on the leftover carpet-grips. She's gathered some things together in the hall, prepared herself to see him. She's done her make-up and has put a braid in the side of her hair in an attempt to make her seem younger, more innocent perhaps. The *Powerpuff Girls* sleepsuit and the Eels dummy lie on the hall table. The door is on the latch.

She hears him before she can see him. With the weather, the esplanade outside has been silent but now there's the rattling sound of an old diesel engine. Naomi goes to look through the bay window and sees the van chugging along the icy road, coming to a stop just down from the house. He gets out of the driver's side. His hair is pulled back into a bun and he's cropped his beard. He wears his plaid over-shirt, even though it can't be warm enough. He looks handsome. Naomi stands on the sofa, trying to see Prue. He leans into the passenger side and hoists her up on to his shoulder. Naomi can see her sleeping face resting against his neck. It seems ridiculous now but Naomi was worried about her daughter missing a nap. He spots her, standing in the window, and extends a hand in the air as if he were greeting a friend.

She goes back to the hall.

'It's open,' she calls to the shadow in the door's frosted glass. He comes through the door to see Naomi holding a handgun out in front of her, pointing straight at him. He puts a finger to his lips and makes a face that says, *Isn't she sweet*, before walking past her into the living room where he puts Prue down on the sofa. Naomi lowers the gun and sleep-walks into the room after him. She remembers Eliza's email,

368

how he had been so genial and friendly even though he had a dog-murdering python waiting in his car. He takes off his plaid shirt and drapes it over Prue. Naomi looks at her little girl wearing his colours. She wants to rip the shirt off and set fire to it but she has to stay calm. He wants her to lose control.

'That the carpenter's?' he says, nodding towards the gun. She looks into the hallway, confused. 'You want to put it down?' Naomi keeps it out in front of her, her hand shaking. He smiles, nods his head towards the mantelpiece and begins emptying his pockets. A large bunch of keys, his phone, a leather wallet. Then he moves quickly towards Prue.

'Don't touch her,' Naomi says and Sean puts his arms up in surrender. But then the hand nearer Prue creeps towards her. 'I mean it.' She thrusts the gun forward in the air but his hand doesn't stop. He's getting something out of his shirt, carefully, so as not to disturb the sleeping girl. He wanders back towards the middle of the room and places it on the mantelpiece next to his things. It's a Stanley knife.

'"I'll give you what you want," your message said. Put it down and we can have a conversation about that.' Naomi edges towards the mantelpiece, closer than he is to it. She thinks about grabbing the knife but she wouldn't even know how to get the blade out. She puts the gun down, defeated. She knew it wouldn't work. A man who's put the time, effort and pure hatred into this elaborate plan to get his revenge, a man who has absolutely nothing to lose, isn't going to be put off by a real gun, let alone a glorified peashooter. 'Shall we sit down? Looking great in here, by the way.'

'Not been in for a while?' she asks, still standing. His smile broadens and he sits on the sofa in the bay window. As she looks at him, wide arm-span settled on the back of their vibrant teal sofa that picks out the green in his stony eyes, the snow-covered grass and sea view behind him, she wonders whether he has planned this moment as meticulously as all the other exchanges they've had since he 'turned up' to help her in the nursery car park. She sits down in an armchair opposite him.

'You have got my curiosity going, Naomi—'

'Speak in your real voice.' He balks at being interrupted, but then smiles again, telling her how unruffled he is. 'I want to hear the voice of a boy that grew up in Ipswich.' He looks impressed. 'In care,' she adds, as deadpan as she can muster.

'I saw –' he says in his real accent now. It's unremarkable, a twang of Essex, but more neutral than she'd imagined ' – you put some things on the hall table.'

'They were your sister's.' He points a finger at her like a game-show host. 'I met Eliza Orsdall.'

'They weren't my sister's. I bought them. Had the dummy made, in fact.'

'Why?'

He shrugs, eyes mischievous. 'Wanted to see if it'd jog someone's memory. I've been amazed by what you two have missed around the house in the last few months. You've both had a lot to think about. What did Eliza have to say for herself?' He draws out the woman's name until it's almost comical, crosses and uncrosses his long legs. Naomi didn't know how much he knew about what she'd discovered about him, he's been recording them, watching them, who knows what else, but it's obviously more than he thought.

'She told me what you did to her dog.' He nods. She's expecting some quip but there's something in his expression she didn't expect, regret. 'Why did you do it?' He shakes his head, the smile lingers but she sees a chink of anger.

'No. No one gets to ask why.'

'Because you never knew why? Your sister killed herself and you never knew why?' She can see the mandible muscles in his cheek swell as he clenches his jaw, halfway between impressed and concerned. 'How did she do it?'

'You're such a beautiful woman, Naomi. So smart. So, so strong. I really didn't think it would come to this.'

'You thought I'd get rid of the baby because it wasn't Charlie's?' He tries to remain enigmatic but she can see in his eyes that she's right. 'That I'd be so wrapped up with grief that I'd do the same as she did.' His smile has gone. 'Did you change the app? On my phone? Or on Charlie's?'

'I got a thigh strain one Wednesday evening so I offered to take some photos of the match. Didn't have a camera, though. For someone who works with technology, your husband's pretty slack with handing out his passcode to people.'

Naomi wrinkles her nose, angry with herself. She has the same passcode as him. He set her phone up for her and she never got round to changing it.

'And when it was clear I was going to keep the baby, what? You were trying to kill me? The scare tactics, the pigeons, the ladder, all of that?'

He shakes his head. 'I never wanted to hurt you. You've got to believe that.' The Yorkshire accent is back. Can he not help it? Is he doing it on purpose? Trying to gull her into thinking he cares about her in some way? She has to try to keep the upper hand.

'You wanted to kill the baby. That's what the sleepsuit and the dummy and the fucking dismembered pigeon were really for. To scare me shitless, make me go mad with stress so I'd mis-carry and lose the baby and when that didn't work you went for the old classic, push the pregnant woman down the stairs, but with your own little twist to make sure nothing could be traced back to you.' He looks down at the bare floorboards. The toe of his boot butts against a protruding nail. 'You were trying to end the life of the child inside me.' She tries to see his face but she can only see the sides of his jaw pulsing, his head looking right down. She needs him to say it. A jeep edges along the road behind him. The first car that's passed all day and probably the last. Even if she called the police or DC Crawford direct, they wouldn't be able to get to her fast enough. 'My husband slept with your sister, she got pregnant. Then she had an abortion. She killed herself and you didn't know why. You want him to feel what you felt. That's it, isn't it? An eye for an eye, just like what you did to Eliza. You want Charlie to lose everything, all his family, like you did, and you want him to know how much it hurts to never understand why.'

'He took everything from my sister and acted like it didn't mean anything, that her happiness, that her life, didn't mean a thing because he's a fucking parasite.'

'That's a long word for someone with your upbringing,' she says. He looks up at her and his face has transformed. The character of the genial friend of the family is gone. Hatred drips off him like battery acid. He stands up, goes to the man-telpiece and picks up the Stanley knife. He clicks the blade out and looks at it in the mirror.

'You used to be so open with what you posted on the Internet. I thought I knew you. Seemed like you were just like him. But you're not. You can try and provoke me but I know you're better than him. When I looked at your life

372

behind that not very closed door out there,' he gestures towards the hall, 'I saw you were totally different. I can't believe you've never been able to see through him. You see, I've read all the stuff from his "CBT" sessions. He,' he pauses for dramatic effect, 'hates you. He really hates you. But he can't leave because he's got nothing without you. He is a parasite and he's sucking you dry, Naomi.' His words sting but she reminds herself that this man is mentally ill, he has been playing elaborate games with her for months and this is just another one of his tricks. He balances the pad of his thumb on the point of the blade. 'I found her messages to him after he did it. He took advantage of her when she was drunk,' Naomi flicks her eyes up to his, Eliza never alluded to anything like that, 'and when she reached out to him, for him to help her when she was scared and alone, he did nothing. Your husband could have saved her by saying something to her, anything. If he'd been there to help her, she'd never have done that to herself.' Naomi knows he could be right. She knows that her husband, if faced with such a difficult situation, might well have buried his head in the sand and hoped the problem would go away. 'Your husband killed her,' he whispers through clenched jaw, 'his actions killed her.'

He retracts the blade back into the body of the knife. He spots her looking at the airgun on the mantelpiece. 'You can have it if you want?' She shakes her head. Prue shimmies her shoulders and his shirt shrugs down on to her chest.

Naomi has to do something. She doesn't know what he's planning to do but reasoning with him is pointless, he's decided what he needs to happen. He might have decided years ago. A draught of cold air gushes out of the fireplace. Prue looks so vulnerable, her tiny chest in her little jumper.

'Why did she go to the party?'

'What?'

'Eliza said she never went to parties, but Karin went to that one and got drunk, hammered. Why did she go to the party that night?'

'I don't know.'

'I think you do. I think you know exactly why she went that night?' He moves towards Prue. Naomi stands up to go to her but stops herself. She's angry. Furious that this man, insane, sociopathic, suffering from PTSD, however you'd diagnose him, is doing this to her family, but she has to keep her head, for Prue. Prue is all that matters. 'I spoke to Julie, your foster mother. You blamed them for Karin's death too. You tried to ruin them as well, accusing Clive of touching you up but it didn't stick. Clearly not as sophisticated in your methods then.' He stands high above Prue, eyes lifeless but fixed still on Naomi. 'Julie told me something interesting. She told me that she caught you kissing lipstick-marks on to your foster father's shirt, spraying perfume on his clothes. How old were you, thirteen? You were trying to make it look like he was having an affair. Julie thought it's because you wanted her to yourself.' He pushes the button on the knife and the snub-nosed blade rises slowly out.

'That was nothing to do with Karin.'

'Your foster parents, the only ones that ever made you feel at home, because I presume it was always you and not Karin that made the ones before Julie and Clive send you away, well they spoke to your sister a few hours before the party and told her what they'd caught you doing and that they were going to have to send you both back into care.'

'Bullshit,' he says loudly. Prue stirs at the noise.

'If it's bullshit,' she whispers, 'then why are you getting so upset, Alexander.' That was the name Julie had said she used whenever he had played up. She told Naomi about how Alexander had been constantly trying to ruin their marriage and that they only kept them for so long because Karin was such a sweet girl. 'That was the reason she went to the party, you were the reason she got pregnant and went off the rails and you were the reason she died.' He turns behind him and slices the lurid sofa cushion all the way along. Then he turns and kneels down next to Prue, holding the Stanley knife next to her neck. 'Get the knife away from her. She's two year's old. Get that knife away from my baby's throat. I'll do it. I'll do it. What you want, I'll do it.' He looks up at her strangely, the knife catching the glint of the chandelier above them.

'What will you do?' he asks.

'You want the baby dead? You want me dead? OK.' He looks taken aback. He blinks his eyes. 'That's what you want, that's what you need, to find peace or whatever insane— Whatever you need to happen. How did she do it? Your sister?'

'Shut up.'

'She cut herself, didn't she? That's what Julie said. She stuck a kitchen knife in her stomach. Fine. If you'll leave Prue, if you'll leave Charlie alone, then you can do it. Bring the knife. I'll let you do exactly what you want and all of this will be over. Come on. Come over here. Come on!' He stands up, knife stuttering in the air and he looks at her challenging him, baby bump front and centre, mocking him, and seems paralysed.

'I want this over. I'm done.' She beckons him towards her and he follows as if in a tractor beam, face etched with pain.

She can see that he's never thought of the reality of killing a human being and what he said, about how different she is to Charlie. Does he have feelings for her?

He gets closer, the Stanley knife extended in front of him like a torch in a dark corridor.

'Do it,' she says. The knifepoint inches from her belly, the big, beautiful man towering above her now. She grabs his neck and pulls his head down to hers. Her face moves towards his as if she might kiss him before she goes up to his ear and whispers into it, 'I had a scan today, at the hospital. The baby's yours.'

'No,' he says weakly.

'You can kill me, you can kill it, but you'll be killing your child. Your daughter.' He looks at her, searching her face for the truth. She holds his gaze, nerveless. Prue's stirring again on the sofa. She grabs his hand and puts it on her bump, the blade grazes the cotton of Naomi's top.

'You told me it's his.'

'I was scared. I knew she was yours. I always knew she was yours. Can you feel her?' He shakes his head. He looks like a lost little boy. 'She must be sleeping, but she can feel you.'

'You're— You're lying. You can't know.'

'I do, though,' she whispers softly. 'They dated the scan back to that day at the swimming pool. It's your daughter. Listen, see if you can hear her heartbeat.' She sees thoughts click around behind his eyes; his mind trying to make sense of it, anger gone. She nods her head, encouraging, places a hand on his shoulder and lightly pushes him down towards her bump. Her left hand ruffles his hair as he puts his ear to her belly. 'Can you hear her?' He moves his head around slightly, trying to listen.

'Can't hear,' he says.

She takes the airgun off the mantelpiece as gently as she can.

'Perhaps we can call her Karin,' she says. He closes his eyes, nods his head slowly, she thinks he must be able to hear something, a dull thud of blood pulsing around her unborn child. She looks over at Prue, balled fist waving in the air though sleeping still, looks at her chest rising and falling, the violent slash across the sofa cushions and then back to her daughter, her flawless throat, the image of the knife held against it. Without taking her eyes off her little girl, she moves the gun down towards the leonine head resting on her belly, breathes out slowly and pulls the trigger.

Lex Palmstrom cries out in pain, hand to his face, for no more than a second before he collapses off her and on to the rug. The sound wakes Prue and she starts crying. Naomi runs to her and picks her up in her arms, wrapping the shirt around her head and sshing her back to sleep, a flat hand beating a metronome on her back.

A black people-carrier pulls up outside their house. Naomi watches Charlie climbing out of the back seat. Prue nuzzles deeper into the crook of her mother's neck. Her husband sees her on the sofa and waves, a wary smile. She glances at the huge figure lying prostrate across her living room. Blood trickles out of his ear on to the floorboards. They're getting them sanded next week, she thinks and closes her eyes.

THIRTEEN

'You did some work for the Fallons?'

'I did, yeah. Been working on the house off and on for six, seven months.

'And in what capacity?'

'Carpenter.'

'Not pest control?'

'A bit. Not much. I took care of a pigeon infestation for them.'

'Are you licensed to carry out pest control work, Mr Frost?'

'You don't need a license to carry out pest control in the UK, Detective.'

'Are you insured?'

'There was a stabbing up at the Fountain Estate, perhaps you lot should be spending your time on that, what you reckon?'

'Mr Frost, a gun you supplied resulted in someone's death.'

'I didn't supply—'

'You didn't provide the Fallons with a gun?'

'They had a pigeon problem. A pigeon problem that, it's pretty obvious, was being caused by the psycho that copped it. I lent them an air-pistol. I'd lent Mr Fallon a rifle before. After Mrs Fallon had the incident on the ladder, I lent them the pistol for clearing the attic in case the bastards came back.'

'You gave the gun to Mrs Fallon.'

'I left it with my tools in the basement—'

'You left a gun in a household with a two-year-old—'

'Locked. The toolbox is always kept locked.'

'How did Mrs Fallon get the gun, then?'

'I left a key for Charlie in their kitchen drawer. I lent them the gun. No one's saying I didn't.'

'Did you teach Mrs Fallon how to use it?'

'No.'

'You didn't tell her how to take the safety off.'

'No.'

'You know a lot about guns, though, don't you, Mr Frost?'

'Fair bit, I suppose.'

'Did you tell Mrs Fallon or Mr Fallon that you can kill someone with an airgun?'

'No.'

'But you knew that you could, if a gun at the maximum legal velocity is fired point-blank into someone's temple or, more certainly, into their eye, the pellet can cause a massive brain haemorrhage?'

'Anyone who's got any sort of pellet gun knows you don't mess around with eyes.'

'Did you pass this information on to Mrs Fallon? Mr Frost, a man's dead.'

'I didn't tell her that if you fire a gun into someone's eye it might hurt them. Just like I didn't tell her, when I was hammering a nail into one of their skirting boards, that if you do that into someone's eye, it might not do them much good.'

'You were in a sexual relationship with Mr Palmstrom? For the tape, Miss Kaminskas is nodding. And you're living in his flat?'

'I was.'

'Was?'

'Charles— That man, he used a false name and bank account to rent the flat. He never paid for it. So I was eventually evicted.'

'And his relationship to Greg, the little boy he picked up from nursery, did you think it was his child?'

'He told me he was looking after him for a friend, someone he worked with. I knew Greg's mother and father.'

'And they moved Greg from your workplace because of your relationship with Mr Palmstrom?'

'They saw photos of me that I sent him.'

'What sort of photos?'

'Photos of me. With not all my clothes on.'

'And he held these photos over you?'

'No, he asked them not to say anything, he helped me keep the job at the nursery.'

'Which is why you agreed to be his accomplice?'

'I had no idea what he was doing. Nothing.'

'You faked an injury, a bite mark on your arm; you told us you did this, in order to get Mrs Fallon's daughter excluded. Why?'

'He said she was obsessed with him and it might make her leave him alone. I wanted that.'

'Because you were in love with him? Miss Kaminskas?

'I don't know.'

'But you believed him? About Mrs Fallon?'

'After Greg went to the different nursery, she came to ask me questions about why he'd left, where he'd gone.'

'And you thought that was proof that she was obsessed with Mr Palmstrom?'

'He … Mr Palmstrom was very charming.'

'Good-looking too? Miss Kaminskas is nodding. Greg's father, Merrick Clayton, he told us the same story. Told us that Mrs Fallon was stalking Mr Palmstrom. Do you still believe this to be true?'

'I— He told me many things that were not true. I know that now.'

'Let's talk about the day of Mr Palmstrom's death. Your colleague, Jess Fenton, told us that Mrs Fallon had requested her daughter be kept inside until further notice. You ignored her request on the day in question. Was this under his instruction? Miss Kaminskas?'

'I couldn't keep her inside.'

'And yet Mr Palmstrom was there waiting for her in the park. Are you telling me that you didn't aid him in kidnapping Prudence Fallon? That you didn't tip him off that you'd be in the park at that time? That you passed on to him what Mrs Fallon had said about her husband being stuck away with the inclement weather?'

'I have a glass of water?'

'Of course.'

'If I knew what he was doing I never, I never— I would have moved out of his flat and come to see you, the police. I love the children I look after. Ask my boss at the nursery, I love the children.'

'How do you know what he was doing? Have you spoken to Mrs Fallon about this investigation?'

'No.'

'Because she has appealed for us not to press charges against you for the involvement in Prudence Fallon's kidnap. Any idea why that would be? Miss Kaminskas?

'No idea.'

'It's not for me to say whether her opinion will have any bearing on the decision of the Crown Prosecution Service. You aided and abetted the actions of a very dangerous man and it's unlikely that the CPS will be able to ignore that.'

'Do you remember Miss Palmstrom, the victim's sister?'

'The victim?'

'The deceased I should say, my apologies.'

'I remember her, yes.'

'In the yellow Transit van belonging to the deceased, there were reams of paper. Certain conversation chains from online forums, pages from the Internet, printouts of his sister's conversations on MSN Messenger. There's one to Chazinho? Is that you, Mr Fallon? Mr Fallon is nodding. The messages become increasingly pleading, for your attention, in light of the fact that Miss Palmstrom fell pregnant. You ignored all of these messages.'

'I suppose I did.'

'You suppose?'

'I ignored them. I did.'

'Why?'

'I was fifteen. I slept with a girl at a party. It was my first time.'

'Hers too reputedly, according to Mr Palmstrom's notes.'

'I wanted the whole thing to go away.'

'Nothing to do with the fact that it could be construed, from her messages, that she wasn't in her right mind to consent to have sex with you.'

'It was consensual. We were both really drunk but she came up to the room with me and it was definitely consensual. I liked her and I think she liked me.'

'We can't ask her, though, can we?'

'Sorry, can I just ask, what has this got to do with anything? It was nearly twenty years ago. I didn't do anything wrong.'

'You don't feel any remorse?'

'It's irrelevant. This man befriended me. He came into our house. He flirted with my wife. He tried to kill her. He kidnapped my child, twice. Then he ends up in my living room with a Stanley knife, threatening to kill my pregnant wife, and you're asking me about something that happened twenty years ago. Excuse my language, but what the fuck?'

'I understand you're upset, Mr Fallon, but I won't excuse your language and I advise you not to use it again.'

'Fine. Fine. Sorry. But why am I here? My wife suffered a horrific trauma, this man was torturing her and she couldn't tell me, and—'

'And why was that?'

'What?'

'Why was it that she never told you?'

'What do you mean?'

'If she knew these things were happening, knew enough to report that someone was harassing her to the police, twice, why couldn't she tell her husband? Mr Fallon? Have you asked her why that was? Have you ever considered that there might be more to her version of events than she's letting on?'

'My wife is the most honest woman I've ever met. My cowardice brought this man into our lives, me, me, me. I brought it on her. And she still protected me.'

'Really?'

'That's what he wanted. You've got it on the tape, the tape recording from the baby monitor that he set up in my living room to spy on me and my wife, for Christ's sake. He sent her messages threatening to hurt me, hurt Prue if she said anything to me.'

'We've not been able to find Mr Palmstrom's phone, so we haven't been able to corroborate the messages your wife has shown us.'

'We just want the chance to try and move on. Christ, you have no idea. No idea. I came home to find her catatonic.'

'Because she'd just killed someone.'

'I can't believe this.'

'The baby monitor. Your carpenter, Mr Frost? He said that your wife found it in the bedroom.'

'Can I go? What's the point of this? I want to go.'

'If the threat involves deadly force, the person defending themselves can use deadly force to counteract the threat. That's the definition of self-defence. Someone has been killed, shot point-blank in their right eye, and we have a responsibility to meticulously assess that the threat from Mr Palmstrom can be said to have been deadly, otherwise we're looking at a charge of manslaughter or murder.'

FOURTEEN

CROWBOROUGH LIBRARY INTERNET

This network is not secure for payments.

Search history:

recipe for marrow

how to change address on my driving licence

zoopla

what will happen to dog transport across borders after brexit

how to make murder look like self-defence

FIFTEEN

32 weeks

'Good to see you.' Naomi sits back down at the table in the hipster café. Uggy bends herself into the chair by the wall. She looks uncomfortable here. 'Do you want a coffee?' Uggy shakes her head. She begins to fiddle with a flyer on the table for a vegetable-box scheme. Naomi thinks it unlikely that Uggy is going to order a weekly delivery of organic vegetables. 'How are you doing?'

'Fine, thank you.' She's not fine. She looks pale; she was always thin but now the skin's pulled taut on her sharp cheekbones and she looks almost alien. Naomi reaches across the table and grabs her hand up from the flyer.

'He's gone.'

'I know he's gone,' Uggy says, a flash of anger as if Naomi were talking down to her. Her delicate hand rests in Naomi's but doesn't grip it back.

'He went for my daughter with a knife, I had no choice.' She takes her hand out of Naomi's and brushes her hair back behind her ears. 'We had no choice. He wouldn't have stopped until I'd lost everything. He wouldn't. And you; he would have pushed you further and further until you said no to him and then he would have hurt you too.'

'Yes,' she says but she doesn't mean it. There's part of her that's still in love with him.

Naomi had been to see Uggy in his flat. She remembered seeing someone dash from the window to go and meet him the day she broke into his van and decided she needed to talk with them. When she saw it was Uggy she knew she'd be able to get her on her side. She could see from the way Uggy was with the kids at nursery that she was someone who felt more kinship with children than adults. Naomi told her everything that Lex Palmstrom had done to her. At first Uggy refused to believe her and it became clear that she too had been told that Naomi was obsessed with him, but when she showed her the faked documents she'd got from the estate agent and told her that by living in the flat Uggy was unknowingly breaking the law and could be sent to prison, her conviction began to waver. Naomi neglected to mention that she was the one who had tipped off the estate agent that a well-known con man was staying in one of their flats and that they should go check his tenancy paperwork.

When Naomi revealed to Uggy that Sean planned on killing her baby before it was born and told her the whole story about Karin Palmstrom, Uggy agreed to help in any way she could.

But Uggy had no idea how Naomi intended to stop Lex Palmstrom. She couldn't know. Naomi had to ensure that there was absolutely no indication of premeditation. The main point she had taken from the articles she'd read about obtaining a verdict of self-defence was that there could be absolutely no evidence of intention or premeditation.

Naomi pulls a giant bag of almonds and dried cranberries out of her pocket and plonks it on the table, inviting Uggy to help herself. She doesn't. Naomi plucks nuts from the bag like a child with sweeties. She's gone back to being starving all the time.

'He didn't love anyone, Uggy. He couldn't. I'm so sorry that you were dragged into all of this.' Uggy closes her eyes and takes four deep breaths. 'How's it working out with Victoria?' Uggy lost her job at the nursery, of course, so Naomi suggested she go and work for Victoria as a part-time cleaner-cum-personal assistant. Victoria showed a surprisingly maternal side following the events of a couple of weeks ago and, although a little shocked that this was how Naomi was choosing to use her offer of help, took Uggy on without any quibbles and found her both diligent and very capable.

'The work is fine. I miss the little ones. I suppose, perhaps I won't be working with children again.'

'No.' Nor should you, Naomi thinks. As she looks at the severe features of the woman across from her she wishes she'd chosen a different venue, the park, somewhere Uggy wouldn't feel so out of place. Naomi needs to ask her about her police interview. She's heard nothing for a week. She spent hours being interviewed, formally telling them everything she'd already told DC Crawford, but also her meeting with Eliza, her conversation with the foster mother and how she worked out what he wanted from them. She handed over the email from Eliza and her mobile phone, though with one or two of her messages to 'Sean' deleted. She pocketed Palmstrom's phone before Charlie saw his body sprawled on their living-room floor and dropped it in a crusher at the tip at the first opportunity. She told the police that he must have had a recording device somewhere in the house because that was the only way he knew so much about them. They found the baby monitor where she put it, under a loose floorboard beneath the sofa in the living room and the receiver with its recording device in the attic, where she'd discovered it the day she searched the house for him and where she'd decided to leave it. The forensics also found a large man-sized indentation in a big pile of loft insulation right in the rafters that Naomi hadn't spotted. They think he might have been sleeping up there from time to time though there was no way of knowing how often.

Naomi tried to save the righteous indignation about how she'd reported his threatening behaviour and been ignored by the police for the few occasions that the detectives edged towards a sticky area that she might struggle to explain and it mostly seemed to distract them into a different line of questioning. She's confident that the investigation will die away, the PR fall-out if they were to charge a pregnant mother should be enough to put them off even if they didn't have so much evidence against him. But DC Crawford seems keen to explore every detail of the case, which Naomi hadn't expected. Charlie said that when he talked to her she implied that she thought it might not be a straightforward case of self-defence.

She needs to hear what Uggy said to the detective, however difficult a conversation it may be. Naomi had to make sure Lex Palmstrom couldn't hurt her children and there was only one way to guarantee that. But she had to ensure that there was absolutely no way they could send her to prison for it so she did what she has always done when faced with a problem: she did her research and planned everything as practically and thoroughly as possible. Acting scared and making a scene with Charlie about him going away in the same room as Lex's recording device to set up that she was in fear for her life, enlisting Uggy to stage-manage Lex on a day when, due to the bad weather, a call to the police wouldn't be an option, moving the monitor into the living room to record him threatening them with the knife. All of it satisfied what she'd read at the library, which was a two-hour drive from her house – if the aggressor has a weapon, if there's a written threat, concrete evidence to avoid it being your word against the dead person's, all of that stuff is really important for getting a verdict of self-defence.

It was after the second time she met DC Crawford, when it became clear the police weren't going to help her, that the seeds of the idea were planted and then, after she met Eliza, she became more and more certain that killing him was the only way to end it. She thought the hardest part would be pulling the trigger. She'd only been able to practise, firing into a watermelon, twenty or so times because she had no way of refilling the gas in the airgun. She'd pictured his face on the melon. The firearms forums she read said that with an airgun, to make certain, it would have to be in the eye so she tried to harden herself to the idea of doing something so brutal, to ensure that at the key moment she wouldn't lose her nerve. But when it came to it, it was easy. He'd just held a Stanley knife up to her daughter's throat. He deserved it, for that and for everything he'd done to them. Perhaps, deep down, it was what he truly wanted.

'Did the police say anything about your involvement?' Naomi asks.

'They said you asked them not to charge me,' Uggy says, a hint of a challenge in her eyes. She reaches down into her bag and gets out an enormous plastic canister of water that she sucks out of. 'They asked if we'd met outside of the nursery. To talk about the investigation. I told them that we did not.' Naomi feels a fluttering of relief in her chest.

'Thank you.'

'You say you had no choice.' She looks Naomi straight in the eyes, devoid of emotion. Naomi nods and smiles back at her. The baby moves inside her, barrelling across her belly from left to right, liberated by the news that it could be finally over.

BIRTH

ONE

They decided to keep the sofa they inherited with the house. Charlie had it recovered by a mate of Tayo's, he did them a deal for reupholstering the cushions of their new teal one after they were slashed, so now it's transformed from a dirty cream colour to a sleek gun-metal grey – dark colours bear up much better under children's grubby little hands, Naomi had read online. The floorboards have been sanded and lacquered and are now the colour of golden syrup. The house was finished just in time.

Naomi looks down at her baby daughter, clamped to her breast, all snuffles and lip-smacking. Prue's next to them, on the edge of the sofa, eyes glued to *Moana* for the umpteenth time. Naomi's strict ten-minutes-per-day television allocation has been radically revised since the baby was born.

Today would have been her due date but Isla came four weeks early. It wasn't as Naomi planned, the doctors decided the baby was measuring too small so they attempted to induce her to go into labour. They induced her twice and, when the baby still hadn't come, they booked her in for a caesarean. Naomi was furious. After everything she'd been through, giving birth would have been a walk in the park. The C-section was peculiar, watching her little baby be lifted out of her and held aloft like the opening of *The Lion King* before being plonked on to her chest. But most importantly she was born healthy. They had to stay in hospital for a week as a precaution because she wasn't full term, which was difficult because Prue was playing up at home for Naomi's mum, who had come to help out.

Prue, still fixed on the screen, puts a hand on her mother's thigh and Naomi's chest swells with love. She glances outside. She wants Charlie to take a photo of this perfect moment but he's in the back garden, struggling to put together the playhouse that they've told Prue that Isla brought her as a present.

He catches her eye and she ushers him in. The baby detaches from her right breast so she flips her over on to her other one. Her tiny lips search around for the nipple, Naomi pinches it towards her mouth and she latches on. Isla's a good eater and breastfeeding hasn't been quite as painful as it was with Prue. The baby's only feeding twice a night now and Charlie's shifted his work day around so he's been around almost all the time during the day. Naomi feels better rested now than she did throughout her whole pregnancy.

Charlie rumbles in and settles himself on the floor in front of the sofa. He goes to nibble Prue's ankle and she bats him off without taking her eyes off the film. He glances up at Naomi and mouths *OK?* and she smiles, sleepy and content. She loves the way breastfeeding makes her feel, drunk almost, a-large-glass-of-red-wine drunk with happiness. Charlie settles himself down into their Berber-style rug and an image splashes into her head. Lex Palmstrom sprawled on the floor, skin blanching as blood drips out of his head like a broken tap. She doesn't feel a fleck of remorse.

The CPS confirmed that she acted in self-defence. DC Crawford has even been over to meet the baby and offered her telephone numbers for victim support counselling. Naomi was being paranoid that she was ever suspected. The detective was merely doing her due diligence. No charges were brought against Uggy either as it was seen that she was under the influence of a coercive relationship. The council offered her temporary accommodation but Naomi's arranged for her to live in the annexe in Matilda's garden. Matilda seems to like having her around so perhaps that will become more permanent.

Charlie's deal has gone through, although it emerged, in the investigation into Lex Palmstrom's activities, that he'd been stealing printouts of designs from Charlie's office and trying to sell them to various competitors. Charlie's convinced that it must have been him that ruined everything back when Prue was first born, he always suspected foul play, although there was nothing in Palmstrom's 'notes', as the police have referred to them, about what happened with Burman VR. The police haven't given them many details. DC Crawford showed her a few pictures of what they'd found. A screenshot they found pinned to the back of his van taken from Naomi's friend Alli's Facebook wall of a man-mountain Norwegian model with a blond beard with Naomi tagged in a comment saying, 'Found your perfect man.' A printout of the anti-pigeon poem she wrote at school and had posted on her Instagram. It seems he was following their lives online for more than a year before he moved down to Kent to follow them 'in real life'. Naomi's taken the whole family off social media.

There was also a picture of his sister Karin. She was wearing an Eels T-shirt and holding a *Powerpuff Girls* rucksack. She was as beautiful as everyone had said.

Charlie's hair tickles Naomi's bare foot. She's not sure how he feels about what happened. He keeps apologising and seems to think it's vital she knows that what happened between him and that girl was consensual. When the police asked Naomi about the ambiguity in Karin's messages to Charlie she'd never been in any doubt. Charlie can get angry, like anyone, but he would never do something like that. There've been moments in the last few weeks where she thought about what Lex Palmstrom said, about her husband being responsible for Karin's death, but having betrayed him in the way she has she finds it impossible to sit in any kind of moral judgement of him. She's a grown woman, a mother, and she made the most heinous mistake, driven entirely by her own selfish desires. He was only fifteen, just a boy, a stupid, thoughtless boy.

He believed her story about Sean, that he'd insisted on buying her a coffee, that he'd brazenly flirted with her and would have propositioned her if she hadn't closed him down. It fit with the 'Sali' that he'd known. He wasn't even angry, the events seeming to have robbed him of the ability to know which emotion to feel. If Isla were to grow up half a foot taller than her, or with white-blonde hair that people wanted to know the provenance of, she's sure he wouldn't suspect anything. It's always been him that lied to her and he'd never think her capable of that sort of deception. She never would have thought it of herself either.

She gave him one opportunity, told him, as their daughter lay sleeping in an incubator a few hours after she was born, that she would answer any questions he had about everything that happened with the person they knew as Sean Salinger then and there, but that after that, they had to move on as a family. He didn't want to ask her anything. He said he was sorry for the hundredth time and that he too wanted to treat Isla's birth as a chance for them to start afresh. Naomi knew how cynical it was, he was never going to ruin that moment for them so she was robbing him of any sense of closure, but she did it for him. It's not right to tell someone the truth if it will destroy them.

She looks at the straight line of his shoulders that have lost their hang-dog roundness and now sit proudly on top of his body, puffed up by lots of business voices telling him how wonderful he is. Even if he did know, if they somehow knew for definite that Charlie wasn't Isla's father, would he leave them? She couldn't blame him but she wonders. There's talk of investors wanting him to set up a larger, more far-reaching design operation. Charlie chuckles at something the God character in *Moana* says. He had a plan for his life as well and it's finally coming together.

Prue tumbles into her mother and squidges her still wobbly tummy, giggling. Charlie looks round at Naomi again and they smile at each other like the happiest two people in the world. The perfect family, the one she's always dreamt of.

Isla stares up at Naomi, still snuffling away as she drains the last of the milk. She's got Charlie's eyes. That's what everyone says, anyway.

TWO

www.questioning.com.au/mental-health-222830

Q: Is Psychopathy Genetic?

A: Dr Gina Felutti

Yes and no. Certain genes predispose the condition and when a number of them occur in the same person they can lead to psychopathy. However, it's not like a hereditary disease where an abnormality in one distinct gene can be passed from parent to child (e.g. cystic fibrosis).

But this genetic predisposition for psychopathy that some may inherit, particularly if both parents carry this selection of genes, may indeed, when pushed to the edge by environmental factors such as trauma, neglect or abuse, particularly in key developmental stages in childhood or adolescence, cause a psychopathic personality to emerge and to elicit severe antisocial behaviour problems such as theft, manipulation or murder.

However, it's important to note that people can have many aspects of psychopathy without being full-fledged psychopaths. Like all mental abnormalities, psychopathy functions on a spectrum.

'That's bright,' Charlie says, pulling the pillow over his face.

'Sorry, my love.' Naomi clicks her phone into blackness. She puts a finger into the sleeping Isla's palm. Her tiny fingers close around it.

THREE

The kitchen looks post-apocalyptic. Naomi and the children have gone to the playgroup at Ladybird's Landing and Charlie's been left alone in the house for the first time in what seems like decades. He was hoping to get some emails done, Teddy called twice yesterday and he needs to follow-up, but he can't leave the house like this. It's fair to say he hadn't been at all prepared for quite how little time he'd have with a toddler and a newborn.

Naomi's up and about now after having been sofa-bound while recovering from the C-section but Charlie is still dealing with the capricious Prue almost full time while Naomi focuses on Isla. It's made him realise how much Naomi did for Prue that he never really noticed, washing, sorting her clothes, buying whichever food she's decided she'll eat each week. There are times when Charlie thinks about what would have happened if he'd lost them, Naomi and Isla. He doesn't know how Prue and he would have struggled on. There are moments, when he looks at his wife staring into his infant daughter's eyes, where he can understand how that man, his friend Sali, Lex Palmstrom, could become so twisted by losing everything he loved in the world. Charlie doesn't feel as much rage towards him as he should.

He starts washing up the stack of crusty plastic bowls that have built up in and around the sink. He thinks about Karin. He liked her, all the boys at his school did. He should have been nicer to her after they were together but there were older boys that would have resented him for sleeping with her so he kept his head down. When she told him she was pregnant, of course he should have helped her, but the lads he hung around with would have ripped him to shreds over it. And he was right, when the rumour got out about her getting pregnant, the hunt for the baby's father consumed the whole school. Charlie could see how disastrous for him it would be if people found out the truth so when the spotlight threatened to land on him he did something he shouldn't have done. He told someone in another year, a boy whose social status meant they were bound to claim it as their own hot gossip, that Karin had had an abortion. The scandal spread like a pandemic and no one cared about who the father was any more.

When he heard she'd killed herself it all felt too big, too grown-up, to come to terms with, he was taking GCSEs early and going to football trials at professional clubs, he didn't have the capacity to deal with something so tragic. In truth, until Lex came into their lives, he'd never even considered that he might have been in some way responsible for her death.

He scrubs grains of dried-on Weetabix as hard as he can with a scourer but they refuse to budge. He reaches for wire wool and begins scraping the plastic. He should start designing kids' products, it's a huge market, very lucrative. There's no use looking back. You can't change the past.

There's a knock at the door. Naomi must have ordered another baby-gizmo that they don't need. He opens the door and there's a well-dressed, middle-aged man standing there. He holds a cardboard parcel out in front of him but he doesn't look like a deliveryman.

'Charles Fallon?' he says. Charlie nods and the man thrusts the box towards him. Charlie takes it and looks at the street to see if there's a delivery van, a brand name he might recognise. An old Jag purrs on the pavement, the sea angry with foam behind it.

'Thanks,' he says to the man, who does a little nod, turns and heads back towards his car. Charlie closes the door and walks back towards the kitchen. He shifts a chopping board, strewn with the empty husks of an avocado, into the sink and puts the box down on the kitchen island. He studies the postmark:

Wilberforce & Kay Solicitors
11 Upper Brook Street
Ipswich
IP1 3GT

Charlie takes up a buttery knife, cuts the tape and opens the parcel. A note on the same firm's headed paper:

To Mr Charles T. Fallon,

Enclosed is a bequest from the estate of Mr Alexander Palmstrom.

Yours sincerely,

R. G. Wilberforce

Charlie holds the note up against the light and realises his hands are shaking. He looks into the parcel and pulls out a smaller box, wrapped in expensive-looking black tissue paper and sealed with a gold sticker. He puts it back in the parcel. The man was a psychopath who wanted to ruin his life. Whatever is in that box is going to damage his family irreparably. Charlie takes the parcel out to the front garden, opens the wheelie bin and drops it in inside.

Back in the house he returns to the washing-up. He scrubs at the pink bowl, still ingrained with fragments of cereal, scrubs it until the metal starts to take divots out of the bottom before putting it on the drying rack. A pigeon lands on top of the playhouse in the garden and looks straight at him.

He flicks the bubbles off his hand and almost runs back out to the front garden. He flips open the lid of the bin, retrieves the parcel, goes back inside and puts it on the kitchen island. He rips the tissue paper off the small package and stares at the label.

Home DNA Paternity Test Kit
99% accurate.

The key turns in the front door. The sound of Prue busying into the hall, Isla whimpering.

'I forgot the baby-bag,' Naomi calls down the hallway. He hears her grabbing together various things, calling Prue to follow her and leaving the house, the lock clicking behind her.

Charlie places the DNA test back in the parcel and closes the lid.

ACKNOWLEDGEMENTS

There are many friends who have, in their own way, helped me to write this book but I can't mention them all, so to everyone close to me, you know who you are, thank you.

To my agent, the incomparable Juliet Mushens. You never asked me to make my book more or less than what it was because I knew you got it from the first conversation we had. Your admiration for authors, particularly your authors, shines through and I feel very lucky to have you in my corner. A word too to Robert Caskie for backing my book so vehemently and also to Liza DeBlock and Gemma Osei.

To Sara Adams and Jade Chandler, my editors. Jade, thank you for believing in the book from the very beginning and Sara, your insight, ideas and kindness have made the editorial process a dream. Thanks also to Liz Foley, Mia Quibell-Smith, Sophie Painter and all the superstars at Harvill Secker.

Thanks to my group at Faber Academy for their considerate criticism and encouragement. And particularly to my tutor, the novelist Sarah May, who taught me so much and demanded that I never let my standards slip.

A mention to screenwriter and dear friend Sam H. Freeman for his storytelling super-brain. He's always there to discuss sticky plot problems with and, most importantly, when I've doubted myself, he's told me that I'm a good writer. Which is priceless.

To my mum, dad and brother. When I said I was trying to crack another creative industry that's notoriously difficult to make a living from, you must have felt like throwing in the towel. But you didn't. Many heartfelt thanks for your enduring, unobtrusive support.

To Sadie. I based the character of Prue on you and I hope she lights up the story for readers like you have lit up our family. Otis, you inspired so much in this book without knowing it. And to my wife Joanna, you have always believed in me. You stopped me taking jobs, went back to work full-time before you wanted to and carved out time for me, amidst the chaos of parenting, so I could write. Without all of your brilliant thoughts and passionate opinions, this book wouldn't exist. Thank you.

A blast of gratitude for all those working in childcare. Nursery nurses, childminders, nannies and au pairs work long hours at minimum wage and have to smile through having to deal with someone else's child's tantrums, snottiness and explosive poos. It's vital work and they deserve far more recognition for it. To midwives, health visitors, women's physios and all those that support families with young children, you do remarkable work on extremely limited resources. Thank you.

penguin.co.uk/vintage